D1579494

T

book s   ranch of the
·hire   of before the date

READING GROUP
COLLECTION

Mari Hannah   child. Sponsored   Teesside Universit,   career cut short when she was injured   after, she spent several years working as a film/television scriptwriter. During that time she created and developed a number of projects, most notably a feature length film and the pilot episode of a crime series for television based on the characters in her book, the latter as part of a BBC drama development scheme. She lives in Northumberland with her partner, an ex-murder detective. In 2010, she won the Northern Writers' Award.

www.marihannah.com
@mariwriter

By Mari Hannah

The Murder Wall
Settled Blood
Deadly Deceit
Monument to Murder

MARI HANNAH

THE MURDER WALL

PAN BOOKS

First published 2012 by Pan Books
an imprint of Pan Macmillan, a division of Macmillan Publishers Limited
Pan Macmillan, 20 New Wharf Road, London N1 9RR
Basingstoke and Oxford
Associated companies throughout the world
www.panmacmillan.com

ISBN 978-0-330-53993-7

Copyright © Mari Hannah 2012

The right of Mari Hannah to be identified as the
author of this work has been asserted by her in accordance
with the Copyright, Designs and Patents Act 1988.

All rights reserved. No part of this publication may be
reproduced, stored in or introduced into a retrieval system, or
transmitted, in any form, or by any means (electronic, mechanical,
photocopying, recording or otherwise) without the prior written
permission of the publisher. Any person who does any unauthorized
act in relation to this publication may be liable to criminal
prosecution and civil claims for damages.

The Macmillan Group has no responsibility for the information provided by
any author websites whose address you obtain from this book ('Author Websites').
The inclusion of Author Website addresses in this book does not constitute
an endorsement by or association with us of such sites or the content,
products, advertising or other materials presented on such sites.

3 5 7 9 8 6 4 2

A CIP catalogue record for this book is available from
the British Library.

Typeset by CPI Typesetting
Printed and bound by CPI Group (UK) Ltd, Croydon CR0 4YY

This book is sold subject to the condition that it shall not,
by way of trade or otherwise, be lent, re-sold, hired out,
or otherwise circulated without the publisher's prior consent
in any form of binding or cover other than that in which
it is published and without a similar condition including this
condition being imposed on the subsequent purchaser.

Visit **www.panmacmillan.com** to read more about all our books
and to buy them. You will also find features, author interviews and
news of any author events, and you can sign up for e-newsletters
so that you're always first to hear about our new releases.

For Max & Frances
Live your dreams

LANCASHIRE COUNTY LIBRARY	
3011812989684 5	
Askews & Holts	15-Aug-2014
AF THRILLER	£7.99
ZBSR	

PROLOGUE

His hand on her shoulder made her go rigid. Her scalp tightened as each individual hair stood to attention and goose pimples covered her skin. He forced her down, his eyes slate grey and empty, his voice no more than a chilling whisper . . .

'Lie still and shut the fuck up.'

Sarah lashed out, her fist freezing in mid-air when he placed the point of a blade at her neck. A sob escaped from her mouth and urine seeped from her body as he fingered the buckle of his belt, using his knee to force her legs apart. She blocked him out with thoughts of her father waiting at home. Sitting in their cosy front room, a fresh pot of tea on the wood-burning stove, two mugs warming beside it – her mother already tucked up safe in bed.

Her attacker's rage grew as he sensed she'd gone to another place. He punched her full in the face. Warm blood began pooling in her mouth from loose teeth.

Hands.

His hands; rough between her legs.

Hands; groping, hurting, touching where no hands had been before.

A droplet of sweat fell from his chin on to her lip as he forced his way into her.

Sarah felt ashamed. She'd received her First Holy

Communion in this church in front of proud parents. She turned her head away, praying for deliverance. She could just make out an open door . . .

Where was Father Simon?

Why didn't he come?

The man stopped what he was doing and stood up. For a fleeting second, Sarah thought her ordeal was over. It wasn't. He stamped on her chest with the heel of his boot. Rib bones collapsed and breathing became difficult. Sarah felt cold and limp, but surprisingly little pain. She floated outside herself, her body jerking with every blow.

Would her father still be waiting with tea and a hug?

In an act of self-preservation, Sarah curled up into a foetus-like ball and counted the remaining seconds of her short life.

An incident room, frozen in time, littered with the remnants of an impromptu party. Streamers hung untidily from the harsh tube lighting above Detective Chief Inspector Kate Daniels' head, and a blow-up Santa lay slumped, as if drunk, across the statement reader's desk. Someone had left a pair of flashing reindeer antlers on a medical skeleton that sat upright in the Super's chair, its fixed jaw mocking her from across the room. She poked out her tongue and it collapsed in a heap, making her jump.

Feeling a little foolish, Daniels relaxed back in her chair wondering how many lives would be lost in the so-called season of goodwill. Try as she might to push away that sombre thought, it stuck with her, drawing her back to the jumbled pile of bones on the floor – a grim reminder of the task she'd been dreading all day. She took in a clock on the wall. Nine thirty. If she left now, she'd still make it to St Camillus to light that candle.

Outside, winter had finally arrived. A snow shower looked set to turn worse as Daniels ran to her car, got in and turned on the radio. A traffic report warned of chaos on the roads – worse inland than at the coast – which wasn't what she wanted to hear. She took a short cut along the river road, heading west, and cut up on to the A69 from the Scotswood Bridge.

But for necessity, she would have driven straight home. The normally busy dual carriageway was almost at a standstill, a steady stream of tail lights stretching for miles along the Tyne Valley with only one lane passable. Drivers up ahead were using too much acceleration for the road conditions, their vehicles fishtailing along in protest. Daniels knew it was madness to continue but ploughed on regardless, grateful for the Toyota's four-wheel drive. The rest of her journey was a blur, the level-headed detective in her drowned out by the dutiful daughter and thoughts of a mother taken long before her time – before either of them was ready to say goodbye.

An hour or so later, she made it to St Camillus, got out and locked the car, taking a moment to admire the village tree – a huge Norwegian Spruce decorated and paid for by the Corbridge Village Trust. Across the marketplace, a couple she knew were leaving the pub, their breath clearly visible in the cold night air. She watched them walk off arm in arm along a terrace of stone and slate cottages, past a row of pretty, festive trees. Their carol singing and laughter echoed in her head long after they were gone . . .

It was like an icebox inside the church. Daniels shut out the blizzard with the heavy oak door, conscious of an impossible journey home. She slid a gloved hand into her coat pocket, removed the candle from its cellophane wrapper and lit it. Taking a deep breath, she set off down the southern aisle, determined not to pray. It was then that she saw the girl's body, lying across the altar like a macabre sacrifice, her huge eyes staring intently at the high, vaulted ceiling.

Daniels took a step backwards. The lit candle fell from her hand and rolled across the stone-flagged floor. Sickened by images of blood and mangled flesh, for the first time in her entire life she felt very afraid. She stood perfectly still, taking stock, waiting for her professional training to kick in. It took every effort to stay focused, but she knew how crucial a witness she would be to a subsequent investigation. *At the point of discovery, subconsciously or otherwise, witnesses take in an abundance of detail . . . temperature, atmosphere, sight and sound.*

The flickering candle sent shadows across the walls. Daniels kept her nerve, resisting a growing temptation to run for her life. Her eyes scanned every dark corner, observing and fixing impressions in her mind. Inclining her head, she listened with her best ear. Nothing. All she heard were words of advice from years back, tips on self-defence she'd hoped never to put into practice.

Then she saw him . . .

Father Simon lay where he had fallen, a pool of blood seeping from his chest, a prayer card and crucifix held tightly in his hand. There was something accusing about the dead priest that made Daniels feel guilty. Being a murder detective was her dream job – what else could deliver that adrenalin rush? – but now she saw murder for what it was: cruel, brutal, nauseating, the more so when it was personal.

If only she'd got there sooner.

Eleven Months Later

1

Daniels managed to drag herself from sleep, turn on the light and find the phone. On the other end of the line, Pete Brooks had a bad case of verbal diarrhoea. He was talking faster than she could scribble down notes on a pad.

'Slow down, Pete . . .' she said, 'you're way ahead of me.'

'Give over. This is Britain's party capital, remember? I've got a queue of calls a mile long. The whole world wants to talk to me tonight. Except the poor bastard you're off to see. He's past caring.'

As Brooks filled her in on what he knew, Daniels put him on speakerphone and leapt out of bed in a room ready for call-out at a moment's notice: a suit of clean clothes hung from the wardrobe, matching shoes and briefcase beneath, next to a fully charged mobile phone and car keys. Her watch read one twenty-eight. She'd been asleep less than two hours, having spent a long day on her regular duties, then three hours teaching cognitive interviewing to rookie detectives on the CID training course. It was a skill well worth cultivating – a technique proven to enhance eyewitness recall by up to forty-five per cent – a subject so well received she'd been invited to eat with the group afterwards to carry on discussions down at the pub. Despite her best efforts to avoid it, she'd been late getting home.

'You got an address?' she asked.

'Number 24 Court Mews. Drop down to the Quayside on Dean Street, go east along the river for about half a mile. You can't miss it.'

'Who's the SIO?' Daniels hoped for someone decent; not a detective with less experience than she had – someone recently promoted because his face happened to fit.

'You are. This isn't Night Owls calling.'

'Very funny. Where's Bright?'

'Busy with another victim in the west end . . .' Brooks raised his voice above others in the control room. 'Nasty one too, by all accounts, so it looks like you're on your own.'

'You're kidding?'

'No, I'm deadly serious.'

Daniels punched the air. Some would say it was her lucky day, though in reality luck had little to do with it. Her first crack at Senior Investigating Officer had been a long time coming but finally it was here. Just thinking about it put a smile on her face.

'Who do you want out?' Brooks said, interrupting her private celebration.

'DS Gormley.'

'Ask a stupid question. You want to be careful, ma'am – people will talk.'

'You don't say?' Daniels had a wry smile to herself. 'And you've been nicknamed *The Font* by accident, I suppose?'

'Ouch! You really know how to hurt people.'

'Speak to you later, Pete. I've got to go.'

She hung up. Eight minutes later, she was on her way . . .

The road was unusually busy as she headed across town

hoping Brooks had made the call. He had. As she turned the corner, she saw her DS sitting on his garden wall. Hank Gormley stood up as he heard her car approaching. He binned his cigarette, grinding it out on the pavement with his foot. Daniels stopped at the kerb just long enough for him to dive into the passenger seat, then did a quick U-turn and put her foot down heading for Newcastle city centre.

Gormley settled back in his seat. 'What's the mutter from the gutter?'

Negotiating a right-hand bend, Daniels told him what little she knew. Details were sketchy. The key-holder from Salieri's, a popular Italian restaurant, had reported the shooting. He'd been about to lock up for the night when a woman ran in screaming blue murder. Gormley listened to every word and didn't interrupt. It was his patience and good nature she appreciated most about him.

As they neared the city, she engaged the blue flashing light on her unmarked police car and took a short cut, driving the wrong way up a one-way street. The strategy backfired as traffic ground to halt in a haphazard line in front of St Mary's Cathedral. Drumming her fingers on the steering wheel, Daniels stared blankly through the window at the building. Its impressive architecture was lost on her. She was somewhere else entirely, suffocating in thoughts of death, priests, and one church in particular.

Gormley followed her gaze. 'You've probably got time for three Hail Marys . . .' His joke went down like a lead balloon. 'What's up? You're a good Catholic girl, aren't you?'

'*Was*, Hank . . . not any more,' Daniels said, jabbing her horn at the driver in front, who refused to shift out of her way.

Realizing he'd said the wrong thing, Gormley tried to make amends. 'Listen, what happened at St Camillus would shake anybody's faith.'

'Don't even go there, Hank; it has *nothing* to do with that!'

'If you say so.'

'I know so . . .' She edged forward, nudging the bumper of the car in front. 'Let's just say, I haven't been to church since my mother died and leave it at that, shall we?'

'But you *did* go back . . . after that.'

'To St Camillus?' An image of two dead bodies flashed across Daniels' mind. Their discovery had affected her deeply, occupying every working day since, keeping her awake at night. 'Yeah, and look where it got me.'

Gormley said nothing as she moved forward in the line, troubled, but in no mood to elaborate. She blasted her horn again, keeping it depressed until the car in front mounted the pavement. She was angry . . . though not necessarily with the driver. That didn't stop her glowering in his direction as she drove by.

The Quayside was buzzing with energy. On the south side of the river, the Sage music centre sat like a giant silver bubble gleaming in the moonlight. To the left of it, the Gateshead Millennium Bridge offered the best view of the celebrations. On the north quay, there were scores of people milling about, more than usual for the time of night: a few drunks, the odd worker off the late shift making their way home, but mostly just people having a good time.

'They got no homes to go to?' Gormley asked.

'Stragglers from Guy Fawkes, I suppose,' Daniels offered vaguely.

'Well, I wish they'd move. We've a gunpowder plot of our own to attend to.'

Daniels inched forward, frustrated with the lack of progress she was making. Tail lights up ahead were another reminder of the previous Christmas Eve — though on that night it was winter weather, not crowds, obstructing her journey.

Five minutes later, she glanced sideways. Gormley was hanging like a bat from his seat belt, catching up on lost sleep. She could see the steady rise and fall of his chest, hear his breathing changing gear as he sank deeper and deeper into unconsciousness. He snorted loudly. Sensing her interest, he opened his eyes, then shut them again when he realized they were stationary with still a way to go.

Daniels tried in vain to drag her thoughts away from St Camillus. But the memory was so vivid she brushed the side of her face expecting to feel wet tears streaming silently down her cheeks, hot and salty as they crept into her mouth. She flinched as a firework exploded on the bonnet of the car. It ricocheted off into the night, transporting her back to the church, to a lit candle on a stone-flagged floor.

'I'll make the bastard pay.'

'What did you just say?'

She didn't know he'd woken, was too busy trying to shake off the image of Sarah Short's funeral. The poor girl had been buried at St Camillus less than three weeks from taking her last agonizing breath. The church was packed. Hundreds of mourners had come to pay their respects, outraged and saddened by the senseless act of violence that had brought about her death. The case had touched the nation from the outset, was reported widely in the press, repeated on every news bulletin, discussed by young and old, in every home, work-place, school and university. The worst of it was, the killer was still out there. And Daniels found that impossible to live with.

'Nothing,' she said finally. 'Just thinking out loud.'

They were approaching a block of executive apartments in a renovated seventeenth-century warehouse. A young officer in the street saw her coming and sprang into action, lifting cones, directing her into a parking space. He seemed to be having difficulty controlling a group of drunken females at the main entrance, a well-dressed crowd wearing little but smiles and goose pimples – including a much older woman trying her best to keep up appearances.

Daniels got out of the car, telling him to get rid of rent-a-crowd.

He flushed up. 'Yes. Ma'am.'

The older woman grinned. 'Who does she think she is, fucking Juliet Bravo?'

One of her mates pulled a face. 'Juliet who?'

Daniels and Gormley stifled a laugh as the young officer tried to prevent the older woman from giving him something, finally managing to penetrate his trouser pocket.

'My mobile number,' she said. 'Call me when your *marm's* not around.'

The foyer of Court Mews was a little pretentious for Daniels' liking. She took a cursory look around, finding nothing out of the ordinary. As the lift doors slid open, she moved forward with Gormley hot on her heels. She turned, lifted her hand to his chest and pointed to the stairwell door. Gormley headed off . . .

Moments later, Daniels left the lift on the fourth floor. A female officer standing guard outside number 24 greeted her. The scene was secured with thick tape: *Police Crime Scene Do Not Enter*. Before Daniels had a chance to introduce herself, Gormley arrived through a set of double doors. He bent double with his hands on his knees, taking a moment to get his breath back.

'I've got to get back in the gym,' he said.

Daniels smiled at the policewoman. 'He's being ironic. It makes our grim task a bit more bearable. He hasn't seen the inside of a gymnasium since leaving junior school.' Then, to Gormley: 'Find anything?'

'Negative . . . but it *was* different, I'll give you that.'

'In what way?'

'No hypodermics, no used condoms . . . no stink of piss. Hardly our usual murder scene, is it?' He looked at his watch and then at the WPC. 'Time our visit please. This is DCI Daniels and I'm DS Gormley. Where's the body?'

'Second door on the right as you go in, Sarge.'

'Who found him?' Daniels asked.

'His wife, Monica Stephens.'

'Where is she now?'

'Hospital, ma'am.'

Daniels thanked her and led Gormley by the arm into the apartment, checking the door frame for signs of a forced entry. It was clean. They walked on along a wide hallway, peering into the rooms on either side. Each one appeared to be immaculate; a place for everything and everything in its place, as far as they could tell – until they reached the lounge.

The room was cold and uninviting. Daniels didn't care

much for the decor: barring the blood on the walls, everything in the room was white. Surreal was the word that sprang to mind. It was more like a chilling art exhibit than someone's private living space. It was as if an artist had deliberately splashed red paint across a white canvas for others to appreciate, placing the corpse of a white male carefully at its centre for effect.

In a London gallery it would probably win a prize.

'I think we can safely assume he's dead,' Daniels said. 'Call out the troops and contact Area Command. Tell them to start the house-to-house immediately. I want a mobile incident caravan too. The whole nine yards, if you can get it.'

Gormley made the call, then crouched down beside the body to get a closer look. The dead man was dressed in a dinner suit; his clothing intact, apart from a missing bow tie. A bullet wound had caused enormous trauma to one side of his skull.

'Bet that smarted a bit . . .' he said. 'He must really have upset someone, given that it's not a robbery.'

'What makes you say that?'

Gormley looked up. 'His wallet's on the table by the door.'

Daniels knelt down beside him. But she didn't stay there long. Although she'd seen death in all its grisly forms, for the second time in under a year she suddenly recoiled from a body. It was like this with Sarah Short and now – almost twelve months later – it was happening all over again.

Her actions telegraphed alarm to Gormley, who couldn't fathom what he'd missed. His eyes shifted to a photograph she was staring at. He gave her a moment to compose herself, curiosity getting the better of him.

With her DS breathing down her neck, Daniels moved to the table near the door. She took out a pen and used it to open up the wallet. Inside was a driver's licence and money – lots of it.

Gormley read over her shoulder. 'Alan James Stephens. D'you know him?'

'Trick of the light.' She held up her glasses. 'If I wore these more often, maybe I'd see a whole lot better.'

Gormley eyed her warily and chose to leave it alone.

2

Jo Soulsby looked down at her feet, hoping the two young women hurrying towards the northern exit of Exhibition Park hadn't noticed her. Her tearful eyes lifted as they continued on their way, whispering conspiratorially as young women do. Then suddenly, their pace slowed. One of the women glanced back over her shoulder. Jo turned her back, hoping they'd take the hint. The sound of footsteps approaching made her realize they hadn't. She felt a hand touching her arm gently.

'Do you need help?'

Jo shook her head. The comment had come from the taller of the two women who then looked at her friend for inspiration. The shorter woman shrugged, nodding towards the exit gate, a heavy hint that she wanted to leave. Jo wished they would do just that.

The tall woman persisted. 'Shall I call the police?'

'No!'

'A doctor then?'

Jo didn't answer.

'Well, you can't stay here. It's not safe!'

Jo felt a twinge of guilt. Both women were now searching the darkness apprehensively, peering at shadows that didn't exist. She could see from their eyes that they were terrified.

'Look, it's not your problem . . .' she said. 'Just go!'

'We're not leaving you,' one of them said bravely.

Jo had been sitting in the park, alone and exhausted, for the best part of an hour. Numb. Unable to think, let alone make a decision. Now she had these two to worry about as well. As bad as she undoubtedly felt, she couldn't justify putting them at risk. Hauling herself from the bench, she moved unsteadily toward the perimeter fence, followed by her knights in shining armour.

Almost immediately, a taxi pulled to the kerb.

'You first . . .' Jo opened the cab door. It was an order, not a request. 'And thanks.'

The women hesitated before getting in. Jo then slammed the door shut before they could change their minds. As she waved them off, two pairs of eyes stared back at her through the rear window.

As the cab vanished into the night, a second taxi pulled up. Jo gave her address and got in. It sped off too, merging with other traffic, taking a slip road on to the motorway. She relaxed back in her seat and shut her eyes, relieved to be going home. Her attempt to snatch a little peace and quiet was short-lived, as the driver – reacting too slowly to a changing traffic light – accelerated sharply, then hit the brakes.

'Sorry!' he said. 'You OK in the back?'

Jo ignored his apology and his question. Her attention was on two marked police cars, travelling at high speed in the opposite direction with sirens blaring. As she watched them disappear, the driver studied her through his rear-view mirror. She shifted her position to avoid his prying eyes.

Five minutes later, the cab turned left into a smart Victorian terrace and stopped. The driver remained in his cab as Jo got out and slammed the door. She opened the gate to number 45 and was halfway up the path when a voice suddenly boomed out from behind her.

'Oiy!'

When Jo looked back, the driver was on the pavement advancing towards her – his engine still ticking. As he reached out his hand, she stepped away from him.

'That'll be a tenner,' he said, rubbing together forefinger and thumb.

Jo fumbled in her coat pocket for the fare as the driver looked her up and down. His smug expression disappeared when he didn't receive a tip. He grabbed her ten-pound note, shoving it deep into his pocket as he walked away.

'You're welcome,' he mumbled sarcastically, got in his cab and drove off.

The house was cold and still inside. Jo stood a moment with her back to the door before setting off down the hall, stopping dead in her tracks on seeing her reflection in a full-length mirror at the far end. She looked a sorry state: her tights badly ripped and splashed with mud, her eyes bloodshot and puffy, her cheeks stained where her mascara had run.

She walked on into her drawing room, slipped off her coat and threw it over the back of a sofa. If anyone cared to look, they couldn't fail to notice her keen eye for detail and for colour in this room: each piece of furniture hand-picked to complement the rest. In another life, she'd often thought, she might have been an artist.

Another life? If only that were possible . . .

Jo picked up a treasured photograph from the mantelpiece, longing to hear the voice of either of her sons. Glancing at her watch, she buried that thought and put the photograph back. Instead of reaching for the telephone, she reached for the next best thing. It wasn't the first time she'd sought comfort from a bottle; she doubted it would be the last. She poured herself a whisky, downed the shot in one and thought of the girls in the park with their offers to call the authorities. The last thing she needed was the police poking their noses in.

They were next to useless last time . . .

3

The sun was low in the sky, the morning rush hour in full flow. Traffic was backed up in all directions on the busy street below. Kate Daniels was preoccupied with her thoughts, gazing down through a grubby window. It had been one of those nights. She had a feeling that the coming day could be worse . . . *a lot worse.*

On their journey back from the crime scene, Gormley had given her space to think. He'd asked no questions, though she suspected he had many on his mind. By the time they reached the station, she'd decided to declare a conflict of interest and withdraw from the case. Then, at four in the morning, Detective Superintendent Bright had called her and put paid to that.

'You'll be acting Senior Investigating Officer throughout this enquiry Kate. It's your chance to shine. There's not another DCI on the force deserves it more. I know you'll do a good job.'

His words and his endorsement should have been music to her ears, had it not been for one small matter: Daniels had prior knowledge of the victim, and that was against the rules. It wasn't that she was too gutless to tell him the truth, more a case of shielding someone with a grudge against Stephens. *Question was: was it a big enough grudge to push a reasonable person over the edge?*

If Bright had been taken back by her hesitation, he didn't let on. He ended the call abruptly, as though he had far more important things to do. Daniels wondered if perhaps he'd agree to swap cases. She immediately called Brooks in the control room for some background information. What he told her had made her sick to the stomach . . .

In the early hours, a missing boy had been found strangled to death, dumped in a council skip like a piece of garbage. Bright had vowed to find those responsible. There was no way he would trade. It wasn't just a matter of continuity, it was the human angle too. Every detective she'd ever known took it personally where children were involved. The Super would want to nail the bastard himself – *and rightly so.*

The decision facing Daniels was simple: come clean with her boss or put an exemplary career at risk. It was a tough call; she'd always taken great care to keep her personal and professional life separate, gone to great lengths to further her ambition in the force. She was about to encounter what Gormley would call 'the buggeration factor'. Why now, when things had been going so well for her, was it all going horribly wrong?

People hurried about their business in the street below, unaware they were being watched. At a bus stop, strangers queued, hands in pockets. A couple of women sheltered in a nearby doorway. In the next one down a vagrant held out a bowl to a female passer-by. She threw in loose change and walked on. The young man ahead of her lost his baseball cap. It whipped high into the air, eventually coming to rest in the middle of a busy junction. He dashed into the road after it, taking his life in his hands, expertly avoiding a passing bus.

On its side, a political advertisement spelt out the words: THE CHOICE IS YOURS.

That was an understatement if ever she saw one.

Daniels pulled the cord on the vertical blinds, deflecting the sun's glare. Turning from the window, she lifted her briefcase off the floor where she'd dumped it during the night, preferring to work in the incident room when no one else was around, rather than the tiny office she'd been allocated by some faceless civilian who clearly didn't understand, much less care, about her needs. She took out her mobile and punched numbers into the keypad. When no one answered she flipped its cover closed and threw it back in her bag.

The makeshift incident room was old-fashioned and untidy, with peeling paint, tatty office furniture and little room to swing a cat. Not only was it too small, but it was located in a part of City Central police station already earmarked for renovation. Officers from the Murder Investigation Team (MIT) were hooking computer screens together with miles of wires, enough to send the Health and Safety manager into a rage. Screens came to life with the force logo as staff arrived in dribs and drabs. Gormley was writing the name ALAN STEPHENS on the dry white marker board, an ancient piece of kit not remotely like the electronic murder wall in the Major Incident Suite situated on the floor above. He looked old standing next to fresh-faced DC Lisa Carmichael who was new to MIT and eager to make a good impression.

'You've no idea how long I've waited for this, Sarge . . .' Carmichael said. 'I'm so excited.'

Gormley bristled. 'Murder victims are people, Lisa. Flesh and blood, like you and me. It's not a game. See how you feel after your first post-mortem. I could arrange one today, if you like? The Super has an interesting case on. Would that be exciting enough for you?'

Shamefaced, Carmichael clammed up and wandered aimlessly away. The DCI patted her on the arm as she walked by. It wasn't like Gormley to be so grouchy.

'That was a bit harsh, wasn't it?' Daniels said. 'What the hell is eating you?'

Gormley just looked at her like butter wouldn't melt.

'You know perfectly well what I'm talking about, Hank. Lisa's young and keen. She could go all the way. I asked you to take on her supervision because you're the best and you know how to have fun at the same time. At least, you used to. She doesn't deserve to have her enthusiasm dampened just because you have marital problems, so don't take the piss. You owe her an apology.'

Gormley stopped pretending. 'I know, I'll sort it.'

'See you do.'

Daniels pulled a packet of Benson & Hedges from his top pocket without asking. Under a NO SMOKING sign, she lit up. *Another thing for Health and Safety to complain about!* She hadn't tasted nicotine for months and felt instantly dizzy. She coughed, bent down and immediately stubbed the cigarette out on the side of a bin. As she handed the packet back, DS Paul Robson's frustration caught her attention. He tapped his watch and rolled his eyes as DC Neil Maxwell wandered in off sick leave: large as life and late, as usual. For the third time in as many weeks, his malingering had left MIT short. He was the weak link in the chain and it was no secret that she wanted him out.

Maxwell plonked his lazy arse down at an empty desk just as Detective Superintendent Phillip Bright appeared in the doorway looking every bit the impressive officer he was. His clothes were immaculate as always: a crisp dark grey suit, white shirt and silver tie matching a spotted handkerchief in his breast pocket. A hint of aftershave reminded Daniels of one her father used to wear.

Bright's appointment as head of MIT eight years before had come as no surprise. He was highly respected throughout the force and had a proven track record in murder detection. He'd also been instrumental in guiding Daniels to make the right career choices. Her path mirrored his own; so much so that she almost felt like his shadow. Wherever he had gone, she had gone too. One day he would become force Crime Manager, which effectively meant he would take charge of the CID. When he did, she was hoping to step into his formidable shoes.

'Morning, sir. Can I help?' Maxwell was back on his feet, sucking up as usual.

Aware of the problems his sickness had created for a squad already understaffed and under pressure, Bright wafted him away as if he were an irritating fly, concentrating instead on Daniels.

'Got a minute, Kate?' He pointed at the bundle of crime-scene photographs in her hand. 'You may as well bring those with you.'

Gormley raised a quizzical eyebrow as Daniels followed Bright from the room almost breaking into a trot to keep up with him. They didn't speak as they moved along a noisy corridor and up a flight of stairs to the building's west wing, eventually arriving at a brand-new facility and a door marked: MAJOR INCIDENT SUITE – No Unauthorized Entry.

The room was a stark contrast to the one they had just left, pleasantly air-conditioned, an open-plan layout designed to make best use of natural light and equipped with all the latest technology. Bright's squad were hard at work as they passed through to his private office, which still reeked of fresh paint.

He sat down at an imposing desk that wouldn't look out of place at the Kennedy Space Centre. Daniels imagined herself sitting behind it. *Houston, we have a problem.* She remained standing, her eyes scanning his new desk with its fancy videophone, state-of-the-art computer, a pile of crime-scene photographs that were even more distressing than her own. The subject bore no physical injuries. He looked like any child does when they are sleeping peacefully, except she knew that not to be the case. Her eyes shifted a foot to the left to a happy snap of her boss's wife taken at a police fund-raiser weeks before Stella Bright was confined to a wheelchair. She was posing in the foyer of the city's Malmaison Hotel in a party dress and high-heeled shoes, her shapely dancer's legs on show for all to see.

If Bright saw Daniels looking, he didn't let on. He reached out to take the bundle of photographs she was holding. 'Mind if I take a look?'

Tell him.

Daniels held his eyes for a moment and then handed them over. 'This one's not going to be straight, guv. We've identified the victim, but there's very little to go on.'

He took a cursory look at the photos, sifting them through

his hands until he'd seen them all. She thought he looked troubled and waited for him to tell her what was on his mind . . . but he sat for a moment considering. He was taking a special interest in her case and she was desperate to know why given that he was in the crucial first few hours of an enquiry of his own.

'Forensics at the scene yet?' he asked.

'Yeah, but I wouldn't hold your breath.' Daniels chanced her arm. 'Don't you even want to know his name, guv?'

She'd hit a nerve. Bright bristled, avoiding eye contact. It was obvious he hadn't been ready for her direct approach. God knows why, he'd known her long enough.

He sidestepped the question with one of his own. 'Any press sniffing around?'

''Fraid so. Chasing you too, I imagine.' She nodded towards his own crime-scene photographs. 'Unfortunately, my scene is less than a block away from last night's celebrations.' She stressed the word *my*, hoping he'd back off a bit. 'The press were on it like a dog on heat. There was nothing I could do. But I think you'll find in the cold light of day that most of the media interest will be coming your way, not mine.'

Bright didn't bite. He just sighed – that same worried look.

'You don't need to hold my hand, guv . . .' Daniels pointed through the glass partitioning to the outer office. 'From where I'm standing, you've got enough on your plate.'

'You're right, I have,' he said. 'But this is your first case in overall charge, so let's just take it gently, shall we?'

Daniels didn't quite know how to respond. She'd worked her socks off for this opportunity and he was treating her like a rookie on a first assignment. Her hackles were up and it probably showed.

He looked at her like a concerned father would. 'Don't take it personally, Kate. I don't doubt your ability, I just want you to know my door's always open.'

Bollocks! 'Is that all, guv?'

Daniels regretted her tone as soon as the words had left her lips. Despite the fact that they were on first-name terms – though never in front of the squad – there was a fine line which she had just crossed. Bright may have encouraged her to speak her mind on any subject, but he was still her senior officer and deserved her respect.

'For now, yes . . .' He smiled, an attempt to make amends. 'Just keep me posted on this one, OK?'

It was a dismissal.

Daniels nodded. She wondered whether an apology was required, decided it wasn't and headed for the door. With her back turned, he spoke again.

'You OK, Kate? If you don't mind me saying so, you don't look it.'

She turned to face him. 'I'm fine . . .' she said, her eyes drawn back to the photograph on his desk. 'And I apologize, I should have asked after Stella.'

Bright cleared his throat. Behind his tired eyes, she could see that her concern had been unwelcome, even though she'd supported him through some very dark days following the accident – a crash that had left Stella in a critical condition, fighting for her life. Daniels wondered if he was still waking up in a cold sweat having nightmares at the wheel. Not that he was in any way to blame. An articulated lorry had jackknifed on the M25, wiping out one side of his car. She felt sure he was suffering some kind of survivor guilt. She was equally sure he'd never admit it, for fear of appearing weak.

'No change . . .' he said. 'I hate to say it, but I hope to God it's quick.'

Walking back down the corridor, Daniels was too slow to avoid Gormley coming the other way. Like any good detective, he didn't miss a trick. He saw the troubled look on her face before she had time to conceal it.

'Everything OK with you and the guv'nor?' he asked.

'Yeah, why shouldn't it be?'

'I'm a detective and you're no poker player. It's obvious he's pissing you off.'

'He's got a lot on his mind, Hank.'

Gormley grinned – *he knew something she didn't.*

'What?' she asked.

'Any idea why the ACC wants you on the case?'

Daniels bristled. 'Does he?'

'That's what he told Bright.'

'You sure?'

'Absolutely.'

Daniels looked past him to the door of the incident suite. *She wasn't the only one holding back.*

4

A shaft of early morning light peeped through a chink in the bedroom curtains, crossing the delicate contours of Jo Soulsby's face. Her eyes flickered uncertainly and slowly blinked open. She lay on her back for several minutes, staring at the ceiling, feeling the effects of an extreme hangover and dreading the day ahead.

Jo showered quickly. But no matter how much she tried, she couldn't wash away the nightmare of the previous night. Her flight from the Quayside was classic behaviour, given the circumstances. *Hadn't she explained it in very simple terms to a number of patients over the years?* Words like 'emotional' and 'trigger' sprang to mind. She was in trouble and knew it. Trouble brought on by scars of the past, unresolved issues that had festered deep within her psyche, waiting to explode like a loaded gun. She had everything she'd ever wanted: a successful career, a wonderful life, a family she adored. Right now, she wished her sons were around to help her put her own problems first for once instead of helping others understand theirs.

Walking past her rumpled bed, she resisted the temptation to climb back under the covers. She still had a job to do, couldn't afford to bury her head in the sand. She sat down and stared at her reflection in the mirror. The image didn't please her. Her eyelids were red, a bruise just visible on the left side of her jaw. She applied make-up to mask it and put on smart clothes: a crisp white blouse, pinstriped pencil skirt, thick grey tights and a black boxy jacket. Lastly, she added a black leather belt around her waist, attached to which was a key pouch with a thick silver chain dangling from it.

Jo checked her appearance in the mirror, then padded barefoot down a wide staircase, across an Afghan carpet of muted shades of green and rust she'd bought on holiday years back. She circled the drawing room, turning off lamps left burning from the previous night. She opened the curtains, replaced an abandoned decanter on the sideboard and lifted a half-full tumbler of whisky from the floor beside the sofa.

By the time she re-entered the hall it was empty.

In the kitchen, Jo put on the kettle and sat down waiting for it to boil. It was a good-sized room with a four-oven Aga, a table large enough to seat eight, and all manner of paraphernalia she'd accumulated over time. If she was honest with herself, the house was far too big for her needs since her sons had left home. She'd seriously considered downsizing but somehow never managed to gather enough enthusiasm to pack up her stuff and move on. *What would be the point?* She didn't need the money and could do without the hassle. Besides, the neighbours were nice. She felt safe here. It was a proper home, providing a haven from the outside world at the end of a shitty day at the office. Once that solid front door was locked, nothing could touch her.

Jo skipped breakfast altogether. In the hallway, she slipped her feet into sensible court shoes, then instinctively reached up for her brown woollen overcoat. Finding it missing brought her nightmare flooding back. She found it on the back of the sofa where she'd dumped it the night before and carried it to the cupboard under the stairs. Reaching inside, she drew out a roll of black plastic bags, tore one off and placed the coat carefully inside. Then she gulped down a last mouthful of coffee, drew the telephone towards her and keyed a number.

It had to be done . . .

'This is Criminal Profiler, Jo Soulsby. Please put me through to DCI Daniels.'

5

There was frantic activity in the incident room. Telephones rang, computer screens danced, and there was a constant hum of voices as Gormley wandered in from Daniels' office. He found her standing beside a table resembling a paper mountain, supervising the arrival of several important documents: action forms, forensic submission forms, house-to-house questionnaires, various maps of the area. What wouldn't fit neatly on the table was being unceremoniously dumped on the floor.

Gormley put his hand to his ear as if holding a telephone. 'Jo, line one,' he said.

Daniels sighed. 'Later, I'm about to start the briefing.'

'Finally!' Bright was getting impatient.

Daniels had almost forgotten he was sitting there waiting for proceedings to get underway. She was keen to move on too, hoping he'd go back to his own enquiry and leave her be. As she called for order in the room, her squad paid attention. DC Carmichael was the last to put her own phone down, a worried look on her face.

'Boss?' she said. 'There's something you need to know.'

'Yes, Lisa.' Daniels pointed at the TV. 'After we've watched the DVD.'

Carmichael leapt from her seat, switching the TV on and

the lights off before handing Daniels the remote. As the screen came to life, the mood in the room changed. Excited anticipation gave way to calm professionalism as the murder investigation team watched the short transmission. Daniels studied their faces while they took in the crime scene for the first time: not just the blood and gore, but the classy flat, Stephens' expensive clothes and valuable jewellery, his untouched wallet.

The television screen went blank. Carmichael switched it off again and turned the lights back on. Daniels thanked her and pointed to the victim's photograph on the murder wall.

'Nominal One is Alan Stephens,' Daniels said. 'What else do we know?'

'You're not going to like it,' Carmichael said uncomfortably.

'Something bothering you, Lisa?' Bright said.

'Stephens' ex and the mother of his children is someone we all know personally.'

'Does she have a name?' Bright pushed.

'It's Jo . . . Soulsby.'

Bright laughed. 'Yeah, now pull the other one.'

'I'm serious, guv.'

All eyes were on Gormley.

'I'll call her back!' he said.

6

Jo Soulsby left her house via the back door, opened the boot of her BMW and threw in the black plastic bag. She got in the car, checking her appearance once more in the vanity mirror and didn't like what she saw. She reached into the glove compartment, took out a pair of Gucci sunglasses and put them on.

So what if the sun wasn't shining?

Starting the car, she got the fright of her life when a Dixie Chicks track at full volume began bouncing around the interior. She turned off the CD player, in no mood for 'Voice Inside My Head'. There were too many voices there already telling her to get a grip, drive straight to the nearest police station, just *tell* someone.

Anyone!

Jo sat for a while considering her options. As far as she was concerned there were umpteen good reasons to delay the inevitable, not least of which was her professional involvement with Northumbria Police. Her colleagues there were experts in dealing with the most serious offences and Kate Daniels would be offended, if not furious, not to be the first point of call. But Jo hadn't been able to raise her. Maybe she *should* call someone else. No. Waiting a bit longer made sense. It would give her time to calm down and get her head together.

She drove away, unaware that the phone inside her house was ringing off the hook.

Traffic was light for a weekday. She drove out of her road, along a tree-lined avenue, thinking of all the things she had to do today – and all the reasons why she didn't want to do them. At the T-junction she turned left heading for a parade of shops on Acorn Road, past a few swanky clothes shops, a couple of bakeries, a mini-market she used regularly.

Parking was usually a nightmare on the busy street. But Jo was in luck: there was one space available. It was tight but she reversed into it expertly, got out of the car and opened the boot. Taking out the black plastic bag, she ignored an early-bird *Big Issue* seller setting up outside the newsagent. It was a good choice for a pitch. Any moment now locals would be arriving in their droves for their papers. He stood to make a packet.

Crossing the road, she approached a dry cleaner's shop. A light was on inside, but a sign on the door said CLOSED. Peering anxiously through the glass, she knocked, trying to attract the attention of the female assistant inside. The girl pointed to a clock on the wall behind the counter, the dial of which read eight fifty-six. Her expression yelled: Fuck-off-we're-closed. Jo checked her own watch – it was gone nine – and rapped even harder.

7

Gormley put the phone down and shook his head. 'She's still not picking up,' he said.

'Try her mobile, her office . . .' Daniels looked worried. 'Just get hold of her before the press do.'

'Poor Jo . . .' Carmichael was genuinely concerned. 'That's going to make things a little tricky round here, isn't it?'

Her comment was met with an uncomfortable silence.

Daniels glanced at Bright. It was hardly a secret that he had no rapport with Jo Soulsby despite her excellent reputation as a criminal profiler. His attitude to psychological profiling was disparaging at best. As far as he was concerned, it was a load of bollocks, an incomplete science – an absolute waste of time. He tolerated her input only because the Home Office insisted that he should. But she was a fellow professional who deserved their respect and – for now at least – he had the good sense to keep his personal feelings to himself.

Daniels appreciated that and turned her attention back to the squad.

'Let's concentrate on what we know. Alan Stephens was shot at close range and there was no forced entry at his home. He'd been out to a charity dinner at the Weston Hotel, so maybe he took someone home with him. We're still looking for a weapon, so when you are out and about keep your eyes and ears open. Given the proximity of the river, chances are it's in the drink. That doesn't mean we don't look.'

'According to his wife, Alan Stephens travelled to the Weston by taxi,' Gormley said. 'Assuming for now he got home the same way we need to do a sweep of local firms, see if we can nail the timing a bit.'

Daniels nodded her approval. 'Lisa's already been in touch with the Weston for a guest list and will follow that up. Area Command are gathering CCTV footage and doing the usual with dry-cleaning establishments, rubbish tips, skips, anywhere that clothing or the gun might have been dumped. I've asked Hank to hold the fort here while I cover the PM. Those who worked through the night go home and get some shut-eye. The rest of you know what's required. For now, we concentrate on the victim's family, past and present. Monica Stephens maintains they were happily married. Maybe they were, maybe not. She was first at the scene, so unless her alibi checks out she's still a suspect. She'd also have us believe her husband was a nice guy. Well, obviously *someone* doesn't think so. Dig up as much background as you can, but bear in mind that Jo Soulsby is a colleague . . .' Daniels exchanged a look with Bright. 'So please tread carefully—'

'Whatever the story behind this shooting we've got to move quickly,' Bright said, getting to his feet. 'And there'll be no leaks to the media if you know what's good for you. So if any of you are shagging the press, keep your flies open and your mouths shut! Let's see how quickly we can put this one to bed.'

He promptly left the room leaving Daniels to dismiss the squad. As officers began to disperse, she pondered her decision to take the case. There was no doubt she'd screwed up.

But now she had to work out what was she going to do about it. Seeing her worried expression, Gormley leaned in close to have a quiet word.

He never got the chance.

'Sarah Short's parents are here,' Robson said, interrupting. 'They've been waiting a while. I said I'd let you know.'

Daniels sighed. If there was one thing she didn't need right now, it was another heart-wrenching session with parents still waiting for justice for their daughter. She nodded to Robson and immediately left the room, heading downstairs. On the floor below, she hesitated before entering reception. Through a glass panel in the door, she could see David and Elsie Short huddled together on a hard bench, holding hands as always. Both bore the scars of the past: they were pale, drawn, emotionally spent.

Assistant Chief Constable Martin walked up behind her.

'Sarah Short's parents again?' he said.

There was a distinct lack of compassion in his voice, as if their frequent visits to the station were an inconvenience to him. Daniels nodded. She couldn't imagine the ACC ever having held the hands of any families of murder or manslaughter victims. Understanding was not on his radar. The man was a complete wanker, a hate figure with a formidable reputation. Not one member of MIT had a good word to say about him – most wouldn't spit on him if he was on fire.

'How long's it been?'

'Too long,' Daniels said. 'It's painful to watch.'

'Painful for you too, I imagine. It isn't every day you come across two bodies. Doubly difficult when they're known to your family.'

'They're not . . . well, only in as much as they attend St Camillus church.'

'Still, you feel the loss deeply. I can see that.' Martin chose his words carefully so as to cause her the maximum grief and embarrassment. 'There's no shame in seeing the force psychologist if you ever feel the need to talk, DCI Daniels.'

Daniels turned, her eyes burning into him.

'Not that I'm suggesting—'

She cut him dead. 'I don't need therapy, sir. Just space to do my job.'

She opened the door to reception and walked through it. Taking a deep breath, she tried to smile as she entered the room. David and Elsie looked up with hope in their eyes; a hope that was dashed immediately they saw the guilty look on her face.

'What is it, Kate?' David Short asked.

Daniels glanced through the glass at the ACC, who was still hovering outside. She swallowed hard, a lump forming in her throat. She could hardly meet David's eyes.

'Temporarily, I'm off the case.'

'No! They can't!' Elsie cried.

The door from the street opened and Wayne Hood – a well-known local thug, aptly named – walked through it. He acknowledged Daniels with a smug grin and carried on to the front desk, pressing the buzzer for assistance. Receiving a stern look from the DCI, the civilian desk clerk ushered the offender into an anteroom to wait. As the door shut behind him, Daniels took Elsie's hand.

'I won't rest until he's behind bars, Elsie. I promise you.'

David held on to his anger. He could see Daniels was hurting too. 'Come on, dear,' he said. 'Kate has a job to do.'

Daniels looked at him. 'David, please—'

'You don't need to explain.'

'I do . . .' She hated disappointing them, yet again, but they deserved to know the truth. 'It's just that we've exhausted every possible avenue and the evidence just isn't there. I have to be honest with you: we've run up against a brick wall.'

David put his arm round his wife, as if doing so would protect her from Daniels' harsh words. 'You're dropping the investigation?'

Elsie was appalled. 'You can't!'

'No. You have my word,' Daniels said softly. 'But whoever murdered Sarah is still not in the system. Eventually he'll make a mistake and when he does—'

'He'll have killed someone else!' Elsie wept.

8

It was never this easy before he went inside, but one look at the colour of his money and the kid took off, thinking he'd scored big time. Until he brought back the goods, expecting his bit in return. Silly boy. It was like taking candy from a baby. He could hardly go running to the filth now, could he?

Besides, the dead can't talk.

They'd agreed to meet at Big Waters, a remote nature reserve on the outskirts of Brunswick where the exchange would take place without fear of detection, or so he'd told the little scrote. But as the kid stood there, his sweaty palm outstretched waiting for the dosh, it was clear he hadn't quite thought through the implications of handing a gun and ammo to a killer – someone on a mission with serious work to do.

Until *that* moment – the one that made his heart sing.

That awesome moment when the smile left the kid's face and fear heightened his senses, causing a brief but unmistakable flicker of understanding in his eyes as he found himself staring down the barrel of his own destiny. Struck dumb, he backed away into the swamp, tripping in the weeds that fringed the open water, more terrified of the gun than the fact that he hadn't learned to swim.

He fell backwards and came up gasping for breath, panic taking over.

Watching from the water's edge as the kid slipped beneath the surface, once . . . twice . . . three times . . . he felt pure joy when the bubbles erupted, proof that liquid had entered the kid's lungs, pushing out his last excruciating breath. Contentment washed over him as he sat down, clasped his hands together and pulled his knees up to his chest, gazing out over the shimmering surface of the lake, his face warmed by the sun, birdsong all around him. It was almost poetic; just another tragic accident – a daft sod messing around and coming to grief, unable to summon help in such a remote location.

Life sucks.

Reaching into his pocket, he unfolded Jenny's picture and laid it on the grass beside him. And still she smiled up at him as she had done for all those years. But was she ready to pay for his mother's brutality, he wondered? Were any of them ready? Pity if they weren't. If he had to, he'd spend the rest of his life hunting them down.

And then he'd find her too and get better acquainted.

He fondled the gun in his hand. Its provenance didn't concern him. The kid had chosen well. *Shame he couldn't stick around.* The balance and weight felt good as he lifted his right arm, lining Jenny up in the sights.

Fingering the trigger, he squeezed gently.

CLICK.

He replaced the empty cartridge with a full one.

It glided effortlessly into the magazine.

Yes . . . it'd do nicely for her.

*

Jennifer Tait entered her house laden with shopping bags, a worried look on her face. She activated the deadlock, put down her parcels, took out her tissue and wiped her sweaty brow. Heart pounding, she stood on her tiptoes and peered back through the spyhole of her front door. The image was distorted; apart from children riding round and round in circles on their bicycles the lane outside was deserted. She watched the youngsters for a moment or two, comforted by their laughter, and then sank back on to her heels, relieved.

Lifting her shopping from the floor, Jenny went through to her back kitchen where she set it down on the bench and put on the kettle. But still she couldn't help dwelling on the past few uneasy weeks. She'd had the distinct impression she was being watched: walking to and from the local shops, on the bus, even while travelling in her friend's car. At all times of the day and night in fact, though she'd not yet told anyone for fear of being labelled paranoid.

But wasn't that in itself paranoid?

Jenny had to admit it. She'd been of a nervous disposition for most of her life, since being followed home from an NHS placement at Hartlepool General when she was a student nurse. She sighed. That was over thirty years ago!

Wasn't it time to stop all that nonsense?

As she had done many times before, Jenny dismissed her feelings as an overactive imagination and vowed to stop being suspicious of folks. She made herself a promise: from now on she would stop looking over her shoulder and enjoy her old age. Today was going to be the first day of the rest of her life.

Pouring water on to a teabag, Jenny cheered herself up with

a chocolate digestive. She was clearing away crumbs when the phone rang. Dorothy was an old friend, a former neighbour, a woman she'd kept in touch with for fifteen years since they had both decided to move home and spend their retirement near their kids.

'It's about time you came to see me . . .' Dorothy repeated her invitation as she did almost every time she rang. 'You really must come, Jen – if only for a few days. The Lake District is wonderful and it's been too long.'

'I will,' Jenny lied, not wanting to tell her friend that times were hard, finances harder. 'Or you could come here! We could visit all our old haunts. You wouldn't recognize New-castle these days. It's absolutely stunning on the Quayside.'

'We could go to a show at the Sage,' Dorothy suggested. 'I hear it's marvellous.'

Jenny began to get worried. How would she possibly finance such a treat? She changed the subject quickly, began chatting about the old days, failing to notice the hooded fig-ure dart quickly past her window.

Lucky for her, he wasn't ready to kill her . . . yet.

9

Jo Soulsby approached the Regional Psychology Service, already late for her first appointment. The building was on a sink estate. Many properties were boarded up, awaiting demolition. Hers was heavily protected by electronic security alarms linked to the local nick, iron bars at the windows and closed-circuit television. In the central panel of the front door, someone had carved WANKER. Jo was so used to it being there, it hardly even registered.

She took a deep breath and let herself in.

A number of clients in the waiting area glowered at her as she passed through. First in the queue was Gary Henderson. He didn't look best pleased. Almost as wide as he was tall, he was an ugly man with a scar down his right cheek and a nose partially disintegrated from chasing the dragon.

Feeling his eyes on her back, Jo made her way to the general office and quickly checked her appointments diary. How bad could things possibly get? The worst two clients back to back when she least felt able to cope with them. In no fit state to interview anyone, she walked back to the reception area and spread her hands in apology.

'I'm so sorry, but I'm going to have to reschedule.'

The first client in the queue, Jonathan Forster, stood up. He straightened his baseball cap, rolled up his magazine and stuffed it in the back pocket of his jeans. He moved off without saying a word, followed by everyone else, bar one. Henderson wasn't going anywhere. He barged right past her, heading for her office. By the time she caught up with him he'd thrown himself down in a chair and was chewing the skin round his nails, projecting the pieces he'd bitten off across the room with ease. For a normal person, such objectionable behaviour would have been shocking. From Henderson and many clients like him, sadly it was the norm. Jo knew she was in for some stick.

'I've told you I won't accept that behaviour in my office.' She held out a tissue. 'I thought we had an agreement.'

'We did . . .' Henderson smirked, ignoring her outstretched hand. 'I turned up on time. You were late.'

'Yes, it was unavoidable.'

She lied so as not to give him an excuse to kick off. He had a tendency to do that from time to time, not for any particular reason, just because he could. Henderson cleared phlegm from the back of his throat and made a meal of swallowing it. If that was his way of winding her up, it had the desired effect. Feeling physically sick, Jo left her seat and crossed the room to get a drink. The cooler was running low; the water took forever to dribble into a plastic beaker, adding to her client's restlessness. She hoped he'd just walk out. But when she turned around and made her way back to her desk he was making himself comfortable.

'Just because I have to see you as part of my licence doesn't mean you can treat me like shit,' he grinned. 'I want my pound of flesh, miss.'

Jo took in the clock on the wall.

Ten o'clock.

As if sensing her antipathy, Henderson pulled his chair a little closer, placed his elbows on her desk and cracked his knuckles. Close up, his physique appeared much larger and more powerful than it was in reality. He cracked his knuckles again in a show of intimidation. She could see from his dilated pupils that he was high on something. With no energy to argue, she sat down and wrote his name at the top of a fresh page in her notebook.

The interview started badly. *Why didn't that surprise her?* Henderson had been difficult all his life; his impertinence and bad behaviour witnessed in every dole office, doctors' surgery and police station within a radius of thirty miles. She'd supervised him since his release on life licence four years earlier. He'd spent the majority of his adult life inside for the rape and murder of a university student. He'd put his hands up to having had sex with her, his defence team arguing that it was consensual and that some other person had assaulted her afterwards. Jo thought it more likely that the student had spurned his advances, that he'd flown into a violent rage, killing her with unimaginable brutality. The jury obviously agreed with her. It took them less than an hour to reach a guilty verdict.

Henderson might have been an accomplished liar, but his denial of the killing didn't wash with the parole board. It was only in the latter stages of his sentence that he realized he wouldn't get out unless and until he admitted culpability. Now here he was, sitting in her office with about as much remorse as if he'd stolen a pint of milk from a neighbour's doorstep.

At that very moment, Jo hated her job, hated everything connected with criminal law. But most of all, she hated manipulative clients like Henderson who managed to dupe the authorities into releasing them when they deserved to spend the rest of their depraved life behind bars. He came from a long list of offenders she didn't like, didn't want to supervise – most certainly didn't empathize with. His lips were moving but she didn't hear him. On and on he went, with plenty to say for himself. But Jo had shut down and didn't come to until he made a sudden movement with his hand.

Jo's eyes automatically shifted to the alarm button located on the inside of her desk drawer. If she hit it now, her colleagues would come running. But Henderson was close enough to grab her, to do her real harm. Everything she knew about him leapt to the forefront of her mind. She flinched as he repeated the action, relaxing his clenched fist as it reached his brow, combing his right hand through his hair, grinning all the while, making out she'd misinterpreted the movement and was spooked over nothing.

Was he trying to intimidate her?

Jo wasn't sure.

Maybe she was seeing things that just weren't there.

It was crazy seeing him in the state she was in.

Glancing surreptitiously at her watch, she was relieved to see that their half-hour session was nearly over. Somehow, she'd managed to get through it.

She looked down at the notebook on her desk.

Apart from Henderson's name, the page was empty.

10

Daniels was about to go home and freshen up when Maxwell approached, seemingly in a panic. She didn't try hiding her irritation. He was thick-skinned. Any attempt on her part to spare his feelings would've been a total waste of time.

'Not now, Neil, I'm busy.'

'Super wants to see you in his office right away.'

'Again?' She sighed. 'He say why?'

Maxwell shook his head.

Daniels vaulted the stairs two at a time. Beneath her, Maxwell took the opportunity to get an eyeful. She didn't need eyes in the back of her head to know what he was up to.

'By the way,' he shouted up after her, 'the pathologist's on his way.'

Daniels turned. 'Who've we got?'

'Stanton.'

She smiled. Of all the Home Office Forensic Pathologists available, Tim Stanton would've been her personal choice. 'Neil, do me a favour. Call and tell him I'll meet him at the crime scene. And while you're at it, contact Monica Stephens. She's expecting me shortly. Give her my apologies and let her know I'll be along to see her later in the day. But don't be pinned down to a specific time if you can help it. I don't know how long I'll be.'

Entering the murder suite on the floor above, Daniels headed straight for 'Mission Control' on the far side of the room. Reaching the door, she noticed a shiny new sign that hadn't been there two hours earlier: DETECTIVE SUPERIN-TENDENT PHILLIP REGINALD BRIGHT.

Reginald, eh?

Daniels smiled, reminded of her paternal grandfather. She could hear Bright's muffled voice through the door as he talked on the phone. His angry tone made her thank her lucky stars she was not on the other end of the line.

She knocked gently . . .

For a full ten minutes, Daniels waited patiently for Bright to finish his conversation. Eventually she got bored and stuck her head round the door, only to be waved away. Irritated, she'd gone back to work, returning half an hour later. During that time, she'd had a change of heart. She knew she had to level with him. To do anything else would be professional suicide.

She knocked on his door for a second time.

'Come!'

Daniels braced herself, wondering how she would tell him. More importantly, how would he react? She expected to get her head in her hands and bloody well deserved to. She'd been stupid and resolved to take whatever punishment was coming her way. Slowly she turned the handle.

Bright was sitting at his desk, reading a murder investiga-tion manual. Daniels noticed that beside Stella's photograph there were now four expensive fountain pens lined up in perfect symmetry.

'Maxwell said you wanted to see me, guv.'

Bright pointed to a chair and waited for her to sit. He

leaned across his desk and handed over the manual. 'New edition, hot off the press. It'll come in handy for reference if you're stuck and I'm not around.'

He meant no offence and none was taken. Daniels knew how detailed the procedural manual was. An SIO's bible: a thick strategic document, several hundred pages long, covering every aspect of murder investigation.

'Thanks.' She took it from him. 'Guv, I need a word . . .'

'Maybe later, Kate. I'm a little pushed for time.'

'I need to speak to you now.'

He waited, a curious look on his face.

'Thing is . . .' She stalled; she just couldn't tell him. 'I'm still bogged down with the Corbridge enquiry. I can't just—'

'Kate, I thought we had an agreement. That case is well and truly dead in the water. This incident takes priority now. I know it must be hard for you to accept, given your personal interest, but that's just the way it is.'

'Move on, is that what you're saying?'

'I'm afraid so. I know it sounds harsh—'

'But, guv—'

'No!' Bright took a breath. When he spoke again, his tone was more sympathetic. 'Look, headquarters want this shooting resolved ASAP. Use your loaf, you could make Super out of it – and not before time in my opinion.'

It wasn't like him to patronize her. He was her mentor, always had been. He'd been pushing for her promotion for a number of years. It was down to him she'd come this far. Problem was, any decision on her future wasn't just his to make. She watched him line up his blotter with the edge of his desk and thought of all the tossers promoted ahead of her even though she had proved her worth repeatedly. She was sick of being passed over.

Maybe this was her big chance.

'And David and Elsie Short?' She still wasn't happy. 'I gave them my word.'

'Then more fool you for making promises you can't keep. I'm sorry, Kate. We've got no evidence and no prospect of any either. That's just the way it is and it's high time you accepted that.'

Daniels stood there, knowing deep down that he was right. In spite of her best intentions she'd allowed herself to get personally involved with David and Elsie Short and was in grave danger of losing her perspective on the case. But it remained in her mind constantly and she just couldn't let it go.

Bright was staring intently at her now. 'What's up, Kate?'

'You want the truth?'

'C'mon, don't play games.'

'OK . . . firstly, Sarah Short and Father Simon deserve justice, however long it takes. And secondly, your inducement is making me nervous.'

'I thought you were desperate for the next rank.'

'I was . . . am!'

'Then don't balls it up . . .' He was trying to encourage her but was going the wrong way about it. A worried look spread across his face all of a sudden. 'Your reluctance has nothing to do with Jo Soulsby, by any chance?'

'Why should it? You surely can't think she had something to do with this?'

He didn't answer and she seized the opportunity to change the subject.

'Guv, what is Stephens' connection with headquarters exactly?' There was no point holding back. Bright had taught her always to question authority, including his own. 'Someone been caught with their pants down again?'

He sat back, crossing his arms defensively over his chest. 'Let it go, Kate.'

She could tell she'd hit the nail right on the head. The question was: whose pants? Moreover, what did that have to do with Alan Stephens? When Bright got to his feet, she knew their conversation was over. Whoever was calling the tune must be pretty high up. But that didn't explain why he was keeping her in the dark. If someone was leaning on him, why didn't he just say so?

He always had before.

She felt guilty as she rushed back down the stairs. Withholding the truth from Gormley earlier had been a spur-of-the-moment decision. It wasn't that she didn't trust him. On the contrary, she just didn't want to implicate him in her deception. But there had been nothing impetuous about not telling Bright she had prior knowledge of a murder victim. That was bordering on stupidity, and now there was definitely no going back . . .

11

Five miles from the windswept Northumbrian coast, a grey and forbidding building rose like a giant blot on an otherwise beautiful landscape, surrounded by barbed wire to prevent escape. Like most of Her Majesty's prisons, Acklington had been sited well away from the nearest residential area – and for good reason.

It was beginning to rain as Jo Soulsby drove her BMW into the staff car park, trying hard to focus her mind on her job. She was exhausted, would have been back at home in bed had she not promised the Home Office an urgent assessment on a disruptive lifer – but she'd managed somehow to struggle through. At least this was to be her last professional visit of the day.

Jo checked her briefcase. Her mobile showed several missed calls and the battery icon had turned red, indicating a critically low charge. She switched the damn thing off and threw it on the seat in frustration. She got out of the car and locked it. The wind howling through the perimeter fence was loud enough to wake the dead, the rain almost horizontal now. Pulling her coat close, she ran towards the gatehouse. Senior Officer Young was waiting there to greet her.

'Rough night?' he asked.

Embarrassed by the comment, Jo averted her eyes. 'I could think of better ways of spending my time than being locked up in here,' she said. 'Especially with him.'

Young checked the professional visitor log. He grimaced when he saw who she'd come to see. 'Think yourself lucky,' he said. 'Some of us are stuck with him twenty-four-seven.'

Pushing a button underneath his desk, he activated the electronically controlled reinforced-steel door. It clunked loudly and slowly began to slide open. Jo moved forward into position and the outer door closed behind her. Despite many years of working in prisons with some of Britain's most disturbed criminals, she still hated the feeling of being trapped between the two sets of doors.

The inner door clunked, faltered, and at last she was inside. Only then did she remove a numbered tally from the end of the chain hanging from her belt. She placed the tally in a security chute. Young took charge of it and, in return, handed her a large bunch of keys allowing her unrestricted access to the prison. As she attached the keys to the empty chain, he smiled at her through the thick security glass, his fake American accent sounding muffled through the barrier:

'Y'all have a good day, now. Y'hear?'

Managing a thin smile, Jo moved on into the grim building and hurried along a secure corridor to the vulnerable prisoner unit. She was dreading her interview with Prisoner 7634 Woodgate, serving life for his part in the gang rape of a woman half his age. Although she was duty-bound to go through the motions of a life sentence review, the very idea that he might get out any time soon was abhorrent. In the interests of public protection, she would not recommend his release to the Secretary of State and intended to make that quite clear.

But first she needed to find a phone.

12

Daniels was stationary at the traffic lights at the north end of the Tyne Bridge, waiting to gain access to the Swan House roundabout. In the centre of the island, looming high above the city, was a former government block converted to apartments and renamed 55° North. She stared up at it, wondering why on earth anyone would want to live above a traffic nightmare. Like the engine of her Toyota, her mind idled until she realized that the lights were stuck on red. She rang the control room asking what was going on. Nobody seemed to know. She thanked them for nothing and rang off. There was only one way she was getting out of here – though technically it was against the rules.

Sod that, she thought. I'm on police business.

Engaging her blue light, she felt like a bully pushing to the front of the queue, but, like magic, her actions had the desired effect. Traffic parted and at last she was on her way home . . .

The leafy suburb of Jesmond was a cosmopolitan area with good shops, hotels, restaurants and trendy bars. Although it was very different from the rural area where Daniels had spent her childhood, she liked the fact that it still retained a villagey feel. No mean feat, considering the massive change in population in the past fifteen to twenty years. During that time, professionals had been squeezed out by landlords buying up larger properties to let to students from local universities. The more they could cram in, the better they liked it. Some houses, including hers, were still in private hands, but it had to be said they were few and far between – and not everyone was happy.

Turning into Holly Avenue, Daniels glanced at her watch cursing the time it had taken her to get there. Fortuitously, there was a parking space just yards from her front door. She managed to squeeze – but only just – between two abandoned cars belonging to college lecturers who lived next door. By the time she'd reached her own front door, the neighbour's cat had caught up with her and crouched down waiting to run in too.

Shooing it away, Daniels opened the door. Stepping over mail lying on the hall floor she had to squeeze past her motorcycle just to get in. The post would have to wait. She needed to get a move on if she was to meet Stanton on time. Quickly she made her way to the back of the house, entering a modern kitchen with clean lines and no clutter. It was decked out with all the latest labour-saving gadgetry in keeping with her busy lifestyle. Shards of light filtered through natural wooden blinds.

It was her favourite space in the whole house.

There was some milk in the refrigerator. She checked it was in date and drank straight from the carton. It bothered her that Jo Soulsby might hear from the press that the father of her children was dead. Picking one of two mobiles from the front pocket of her bag, she checked the display.

No joy.

Discarding the first, Daniels picked out the second. She

dialled Jo's number and was met with the same voice message she'd heard ten times already that morning:

'The mobile you are calling may be switched off. Please try again later.'

Putting the mobiles back in her bag, she grabbed fruit from a bowl and stuffed that in too. A flashing LED on her BT answerphone caught her eye. She pushed the playback button and listened to the automated message: *To listen to your messages, press one, to save . . .'* Daniels hit one, cutting off the voice. She heard a beep but the caller had rung off without speaking. She stared at the phone as if it would somehow reveal the identity of the caller. The automated voice again: *You have no more messages . . .* She hung up. The calls button didn't enlighten her: it showed three calls in quick succession. On each occasion the number was withheld. Then suddenly one of the mobiles rang loudly in her bag.

She pulled it out. 'Hello?'

The line was open but no one spoke.

A weak mobile signal? A payphone perhaps? Bugger! Only one person had access to that particular line. Either someone had the wrong number or the caller was desperate for help . . .

Within half an hour, Daniels was showered and on her way again. Driving back to the city, she made a mental list of all the things she needed to do to get the enquiry underway. In the foyer of Court Mews, she shook hands with Tim Stanton. A tall, good-looking fifty-year-old, he had worked for the northern region for only seven years, during which time he'd built up an excellent reputation in his field of expertise. His impressive qualifications included Bachelor of Medicine,

Fellow of the Royal College of Pathologists and Honorary Lecturer in Pathology at the University of Edinburgh. He was held in high regard by the police and well liked by Daniels herself.

Though they shared the ability to function with very little sleep, quite how he managed to look so fresh remained a mystery to her. Despite a shower and change of clothes, she still felt jaded from being up all night.

Outside Stephens' fourth-floor apartment a male officer was on sentry duty.

Daniels held up her warrant card. 'This is Mr Stanton, Home Office Pathologist, and I am DCI Daniels.' She checked her watch. 'I make it five past one. Time our entry and don't let anyone else in here while the body is being examined. Understood?'

'Yes, ma'am.' The officer stood aside to let them through.

At the door to the victim's apartment, Daniels bent down and opened up a large box containing forensic clothing. Reaching inside it, she withdrew two packets and handed one over to Stanton just as the lift arrived on their floor. Waiting for the door to open, she was rattled when Bright emerged from the lift and fought hard not to let it show – Super or no Super, she'd have given him a piece of her mind if Stanton hadn't been there. What the hell did he think he was playing at?

Bright exchanged pleasantries with Stanton as they all got kitted up. Zipping up her forensic suit, Daniels slipped blue plastic overshoes over her own, reminded of a house-hunting expedition she'd undertaken with her mother years before. It had been a gloomy Sunday afternoon. Following their usual visit to church and a pub lunch, she'd driven her mother to a new housing development. Her father declined to join them with the usual lame excuse that he was too busy.

Fingering the plastic material in her hands, Daniels could almost hear her mother's laughter, see her moving around the show home looking the picture of health in a new red dress – unaware of the cancer eating its way into her lung. They'd clomped around with blue plastic feet in a house they could ill afford, giggling like a couple of teenagers.

The powerful nostalgic image made Daniels smile. Then suddenly her smile disappeared and was replaced by a dark sadness she found hard to bear and even harder to hide. Looking up, she was relieved to see that neither Stanton nor Bright had been paying her any attention. They had moved along the hallway and were having a discussion at the living-room door.

Stanton was making a small sketch of the apartment with his gold Cross pen that rolled effortlessly across the paper like water over a weir. Daniels didn't need to see the sketch to know that it would be meticulous in every detail. It was the way he did things and she was delighted that he was going to be working with her on her first case as Senior Investigating Officer.

In the living room, she walked carefully round the corpse and drew back the window blinds, allowing them some natural light. When she turned around, Stanton was already gloved up and on his knees inspecting the body, careful not to handle or move it as he began his initial observations with Bright looking on.

'The victim's wife formally identified the body in situ,'

Bright loosened his tie, his well-trained eyes scanning the room. 'Said she found him like this when she returned to the flat at approximately twelve forty-five this morning.' His comment floated in the air as he wandered off into the hallway, opening and closing doors on either side. A brief check and he was back. 'I'm sorry I can't stay. I have another appointment at two.'

'I'm surprised you have any time at all to spare guv,' Daniels said pointedly. 'With your latest case at such a critical stage, I mean.'

Stanton didn't look up. His tone was sombre. 'Awful business, I heard it on the news.'

Bright agreed and carried on, ignoring Daniels' snide remark. 'Mind if Kate fills you in, Tim? She's SIO on this one.'

Stanton sat back on his heels, looking genuinely pleased. 'Is that right? Well, congratulations, it's about time too!'

Forcing an uncomfortable smile, Bright gave Daniels a friendly tap her on the shoulder. There was something not right about his demeanour, a definite unease she'd never seen before. He couldn't look her in the eye and there could be only one explanation for him being there.

He wanted into her crime scene.

He knew that until the body was moved all visits were logged in and out.

He could hardly just breeze in there unnoticed, could he?

By now the two men were arranging to play golf, settling on a date the following week with an agreement to cancel if the exigencies of the job prevented either of them turning up. Not being part of the conversation, she turned her back on them and tried focusing on the chain of events that might have led to Alan Stephens' death, but found she couldn't concentrate with her guv'nor hanging around.

His presence still baffled her.

He could so easily have spoken with Stanton at the door. And yet he'd chosen to go through the palaver of getting kitted up in case of forensic contamination – one murder scene to another – but why in hell's name had he bothered to attend at all? In the normal course of events, his case would take precedence over a shooting. *Any bloody shooting.* Daniels knew only too well how busy he'd be. Did he think she'd miss some vital clue? Cock it up, whatever *it* was? What exactly was he expecting to find?

She was sure of one thing: her guv'nor definitely knew something she didn't.

'You go ahead,' Stanton said. 'We can manage here, can't we, Kate?'

Daniels wasn't paying attention. She was staring out of the window at the familiar arch of the Tyne Bridge. It was jammed with traffic as usual. The sun glinting off waiting vehicles looked like a long string of diamonds suspended in mid-air. Beneath the bridge, seagulls bobbed on the surface of a cold grey river flowing gently eastward to the North Sea beyond. She turned round just in time to see Bright disappearing from the room.

'Kate?'

'Sorry, did you say something?' Daniels was miles away.

'Only that we should get on with it,' Stanton replied.

He smiled self-consciously, most probably embarrassed by the frosty atmosphere he'd witnessed between the two detectives. Momentarily, Daniels thought he was about to question her about it, but then he chose not to interfere. Instead, he took a small dictating device from his breast pocket, ready to start work. He began by describing the apartment, referring to the sketches he'd drawn on the way in. He spoke softly and clearly into the digital recorder, emphasizing the fact that there were no obvious signs of blood outside of the room in which the body had been found. So deep was his concentration he was oblivious to her presence.

Daniels' eyes travelled over Stephens' body as Stanton spoke, his voice coming and going as he continued his running commentary – occasionally stopping to peer more closely at specific areas. Stephens lay face up, several feet to the right of a white marble fireplace that was heavily splashed with blood, his torso at a slight angle and jammed against the legs of a coffee table, his head nearest to the door that adjoined the dining room. His left arm was by his side, touching the ground, palm down. His right arm lay across his body, his hand resting on his chest.

'He was shot through the front of the head,' Stanton said. 'The entry wound being smaller than the exit wound at the back . . .'

Daniels had a wry smile to herself. She bore Stanton no resentment. He was not the type to teach his granny how to suck eggs, just a meticulous scientist who took nothing whatsoever for granted.

'The deceased wouldn't have been able to move very much at all after being shot.' Stanton continued taking careful measurements as he spoke. 'There are no drag marks indicating an attempt to pull himself along, no marks I can see on surrounding furniture.'

Daniels nodded. 'No indication of a scuffle at all, do you agree?'

The pathologist glanced around, considering. 'I would think it highly unlikely that the killer met any resistance or attempt at self-protection by the victim. I think this poor chap was completely taken by surprise. Mercifully it would have been over in a flash.' Moving round the corpse, he looked curiously at the bow tie that was spotted with blood and lying on a glass coffee table. Carefully lifting it up with a pair of small tweezers, he pointed at the table top. 'See here . . . I'd get your photographer to take a shot of this.'

'I will . . .' Daniels came closer. There was a perfect image of a bow tie on the blood-splashed glass. 'If he'd had time and been relaxed enough to take off his tie before the killer struck, that would suggest he wasn't followed into the apartment and shot immediately, d'you agree?'

Stanton nodded. He was about done. Dictating the last details of environmental temperature and discoloration present in the body, he ended his recording and began to remove his rubber gloves.

'Someone from the forensic science laboratory will be along soon,' he concluded. 'Then we can bag him up and get him to the mortuary.'

13

On reaching the VPU, Jo Soulsby was escorted to an interview room by a prison officer named Adams. She knew that Woodgate would be waiting and had made up her mind that the interview would be brief. With any luck, the Governor would transfer the prisoner away from Acklington and she'd never have to set eyes on the despicable individual again.

Adams grasped the door handle. 'Ready?' he asked.

Jo took a deep breath and nodded.

Adams opened the door. Jo was shocked by the physical deterioration in Woodgate since she'd last seen him. Under the harsh tube lighting there was no hiding the fact that he'd been in a fight. More likely he'd been bullied. He looked washed out, had a split lip, a scuff mark on his forehead and an enormous black eye. Now she understood why he was in 'the block'. Prisoners were only put here for one of two reasons: either they were being disciplined, or else they had requested solitary confinement for their own protection under Rule 43 of the prison regulations.

Woodgate kept his head down, refusing to look her in the eye. It wasn't the first time she'd seen him like this. Most sex offenders she'd ever worked with were in denial. This one was practically squirming in his seat; obviously not ready to talk about his offence – not to a woman, and certainly not to her.

He'd already told his personal officer that only a bloke would understand. He didn't want to see Soulsby because she made him feel uncomfortable.

Damn right too! Why should he be allowed to forget? His victim never would.

Jo pulled up a chair and sat down opposite the prisoner at the only table in the room. She wasn't ready for what happened next. Without warning, Woodgate overturned the table and everything on it, sending her crashing to the floor.

He began yelling like a man possessed.

Fearing a hostage situation, Jo was quick to act. She slammed her fist against a red button on the wall. Suddenly, all hell broke loose. The alarm bell was deafening. Several prison officers charged into the room as if World War Three had broken out. Two held Woodgate down, using their knees in the small of his back as leverage. Adams positioned his forearm across the back of Woodgate's neck, jamming his face hard against the tiled floor so they could get the cuffs on him.

Jo scrambled across the floor to the far wall, shaken by the suddenness and ferocity of Woodgate's temper. Even though she'd read reports of it, experiencing it first-hand was something else entirely. He was hauled out into the corridor, kicking and screaming obscenities, his voice remaining in the room long after he'd disappeared from sight.

'Want the Medical Officer?' Adams offered.

'I'm fine, thanks.' Jo was anything but.

For a moment or two she scrabbled around on all fours trying to retrieve her notes. But her hands were trembling so much that her case papers point-blank refused to go back in their file so she stopped trying to make them. Sitting back on her heels, she looked on as Adams righted the table and over-turned chair so she could sit down.

'You sure you don't want the MO?' he said. 'Cup of tea, slug of brandy?'

'Probably the latter . . .' Jo stood up. 'But I want to get out of here more.'

What she really wanted was to talk to Daniels and sort out her life. But that would have to wait until she reached the privacy of her own home. Using a payphone in a prison only drew the attention of passers-by. One aborted attempt to speak to the DCI was one too many.

Adams' voice pulled her back into the room. 'He might just have done you a favour.'

'Oh yeah, how do you work that out?'

Adams grinned. 'Well, there's no need for an assessment now, is there?'

'Good point.' Jo appreciated his attempt to cheer her up, could feel her heart rate returning to normal, the adrenalin rushing through her body slowly beginning to ebb away.

'I've always thought Woody too dangerous for release,' Adams said.

Jo nodded. 'Well, he just proved you right. As far as I'm concerned, you can ship him back to Dartmoor. I'll have a word with the Governor on my way out.'

14

Daniels had been a police officer for the best part of fifteen years. She'd seen the effects of violent crime on a daily basis but prided herself on the fact that she never allowed the job to affect her sensitivity to the bereaved. There was no right or wrong way for families of homicide victims to behave. Every individual coped differently: some became overwhelmed, some were too shocked to take it in, others went into denial and some – the most severe cases – went into total meltdown.

Still raw from her own experience of losing a parent prematurely, Daniels could easily identify with the emotional side of loss. The numbness, the anger, the guilt. The awful depression she'd always thought of as a modern disease, like stress. The image of a small sign hanging on her office wall suddenly popped into her mind. *Stress: the confusion created when one's mind overrides the body's basic desire to kick the living shit out of some arsehole that desperately needs it!*

Daniels wondered if the woman in front of her now felt the need to kick the living shit out of anyone. For a woman whose husband had just been brutally murdered, Monica Stephens was showing little emotion. And yet, she'd been taken to hospital in shock less than twenty-four hours before. The hand holding the cup and saucer was steady, the make-up immaculate, not a hair out of place or hint of recent tears.

'I'm very sorry for your loss . . .' Daniels said, gently.

'Thank you. You're very kind.'

Monica spoke in a marked foreign accent, but with an excellent command of the English language. Her voice was unbroken, her conversation relaxed and coherent. And a copy of *The Lady* was lying open on the table between them. Daniels found that very curious. It was this week's issue, had only come on sale that morning. *No depression there then.* Here was a woman who'd not only declined the offer of a family liaison officer, but she'd also found time to read her favourite magazine while half the force were out looking for the thug with a firearm who'd blown her husband away.

It was weird.

'Take it,' Monica said, picking up on Daniels' interest in the magazine. 'I didn't sleep well and I've read it, how do you say, back to front?'

Daniels studied the woman until she felt compelled to fill the silence.

'I can't believe this has happened, Detective. My husband was a good man. Everyone liked him. Why would anyone do such a thing?'

Why indeed?

'Did Mr Stephens have any problems recently, at work or at home?'

'No!' Monica's tone was scathing, as if the question had been ridiculous. 'We were very comfortable with money, Alan and I. Our business is hugely successful. He was an entrepreneur, a good one. He built his operation up from nothing, as you can see. He hated this house. Said growing up here was a nightmare. It is what motivated him, I think.'

Glancing around the room, Daniels saw no trappings of wealth. In fact, quite the opposite was true. They were sitting in a small living room in a house belonging to Alan Stephens' mother, a former council property that hadn't been updated in years. The furniture was frayed and unfashionable, the carpets worn and in need of replacement. Stephens may have been successful but he certainly didn't spread his money around, at least not in his poor mother's direction.

A meeting with Mrs Stephens senior a little earlier hadn't been an interview as such, more a welfare visit to the mother of a homicide victim. She was eighty-one years old, a fit, straight-talking lady with steely blue eyes. Her reaction to the tragedy had been painful to watch. When Daniels found out why, her heart sank. To survive one son was bad luck; to survive two was more than a mother could possibly bear. But Daniels had no such feelings of sympathy or warmth for the woman sitting in front of her now.

She moved on. 'He was well liked?'

Monica raised her teacup to her lips. 'As much as any successful businessman is.'

Exchanging a brief look with Gormley, Daniels wondered if the act of covering her mouth was significant. Was the woman hiding something, or merely taking a drink? Had Daniels been a gambler, she'd have opted for the former, but for now at least she was prepared to give the widow the benefit of the doubt.

'Can you tell me when you last saw your husband?' she asked.

'Around seven o'clock.' Monica replaced her cup in its saucer. 'No, shortly after – his taxi was late. He commented on it. Alan was an Englishman through and through, a little eccentric even. Punctuality was important to him. He believed it was a measure of a man, like manners. He hated sloppiness in any form.'

'Was he going straight to the Weston Hotel?'

Monica nodded. 'That's what he said.'

Daniels registered the doubt. 'And you left home when?'

'Very soon after.'

'To go where?' Gormley asked casually.

'To have dinner with a friend, then I drove her to Newcastle airport, returning here around midnight—'

Daniels wanted more. 'Which flight?'

'Does it matter?'

The detectives just looked at her.

Monica spread her hands, acknowledging her mistake. 'Sorry, of course it matters. I suppose I must account for my movements like everyone else. She was catching a flight to London, she has family down there.'

'Do you remember the check-in desk, which airline she was using?'

Monica shrugged. 'I have no idea. I didn't really take much notice. We had a drink in the bar and she left me, I don't know . . . at around eleven thirty, I guess.'

Daniels felt a ripple of excitement building. To her knowledge, there was no flight out of Newcastle to any London airport that late at night. 'Do you have any idea where she might be staying in London?'

Monica sighed, bored with the questioning. 'Do you always tell people where you are going, Detective? Surely the whole point of taking a break is that you *can't* be found?'

'Did you buy anything while you were at the airport?'

'Only drinks.'

Gormley looked at her. 'Don't suppose you have any receipts?'

'Who keeps receipts? I paid cash. It was a few pounds only.'

'Of course,' Daniels nodded. 'And your friend's name?'

'Teresa.'

'Surname?'

'Branson, Teresa Branson.'

'Thank you, Mrs Stephens . . .' Daniels smiled and got to her feet. 'I think that's all for now. Be sure to get in touch if you think of anything else. And if you change your mind, feel free to ring me at any time. And do speak with your family liaison officer if there's anything you need, anything at all. That's what they're there for.'

They said their goodbyes at the front door and made their way to the Toyota. Daniels waited until they were inside the car and Monica had gone back inside before speaking.

'If she's grieving for her husband, she's doing a bloody good job of hiding it . . .' She fastened her seat belt, turned on the engine and drove away. 'Give Lisa a bell, Hank. Tell her to get hold of a copy of the airport CCTV footage. And while you're at it, get her to check last night's passenger lists for Teresa Branson.'

15

A storm was brewing as Jo walked back through the gates of Acklington Prison. This close to the Northumberland coast, there was little protection from the biting chill on a gloomy November afternoon. She hunched her shoulders, pulled up her collar and rushed to her waiting car, checking underneath and inside the vehicle before getting in. It was a routine she followed no matter what security level was operational at the time. Turning on the ignition, she sat for a while, dwelling on the incident in the VPU. The Governor's attitude to the incident had bordered on the bizarre; he'd questioned whether she'd done anything to precipitate such a violent reaction, today or in the past. Whose side was he on? Men like Woodgate were scum. A bullet was too good for them.

Engaging first gear, she moved off . . .

The narrow country lane wound its way across country, passing an occasional farmhouse along the way, smoke drifting from chimney pots as people stoked their fires in readiness for the inevitable drop in temperature that nightfall would bring. It was a road she could have driven blindfold, but water was streaming down the windscreen and her headlights weren't picking out much more than the white line in the centre of the road, making things more difficult.

The car was buffeted from side to side as the wind reached

gale force. As hedgerows flashed by, the rain became tor-rential. Jo had to concentrate hard just to keep the car on the road. Her only crumb of comfort was that she was now on her way home. She imagined putting on some music and sinking her body into a steaming hot bath, shutting out the world and putting an awful day behind her.

And after that?

After that she would speak with Kate Daniels – someone she had every faith in – someone who'd know *exactly* what to do. But, unfortunately for her, that wasn't quite what fate had in mind for her . . .

Her world stopped turning as the tree fell, caught in the BMW's headlights. She reacted immediately but it was still too late. The car swerved violently from side to side – rolled over once, twice, and then – in what seemed like slow motion – flew through the air before coming to a sudden halt on its roof in a ditch.

Within seconds Jo had lost consciousness.

16

There is no worse place on earth than a mortuary at dusk. The examination room stank of chemicals. Stephens' naked body was laid out on a slab surrounded by people dressed in forensic suits. Tim Stanton was in green scrubs, a face mask hooked to either ear and hanging loose around his neck. A coroner's officer was taking notes as samples of tissue and blood-soaked hair were removed from the surface of the body, labelled and dated. A Scenes of Crime Officer was taking photographs.

On a nearby bench, a forensic scientist was searching through Stephens' formal dress trousers. Daniels watched him remove a pair of solid-gold cufflinks from the pocket on the left, and in the right he found thirty-five pence in change and a gold cigarette lighter. He bagged the items ready to be sent off for forensic examination then entered them in his log.

Turning her attention back to the body, Daniels' eyes homed in on the gold Rolex watch Stanton was removing from Stephens' left wrist, the receipt for which she had held in her hand not three months ago while sifting through an old box of papers. The image was so strong, she was barely aware of the pathologist's voice as he dictated his findings into an overhead microphone.

'There are massive cranial injuries caused by the gunshot wound,' he said. 'The facial features are distorted due to extensive fracturing of the facial skeleton on bullet impact. There appears to be no other external evidence visible other than slight fresh bruising attributed to the victim having fallen . . .'

Daniels' eyes shifted to the plain gold wedding band on the ring finger of Stephens' left hand, her mind contemplating the sequence of events that might have led to his death.

'What is left of the brain shows no evidence of natural disease on dissection,' Stanton continued to elaborate, the tone of his voice completely detached from the subject matter. 'Left bony orbit is disrupted, nasal bone dislodged and there is extensive haemorrhaging to the left side of the skull.'

Picking up his scalpel, Stanton began to make the Y incision. Daniels didn't flinch as he cut into the flesh. Difficult though it had been to stomach in the early years of her career, she'd learned to remain detached when observing post-mortems. In fact she found the process of body dissection fascinating, something other people didn't seem to understand. Autopsies could tell her things she could never find out by any other means, providing precise evidence that often proved crucial in a court of law.

She wondered if anyone back at the station had heard from Jo Soulsby yet. Before the post-mortem, she'd asked DC Andy Brown to visit Jo's home and left instructions for him to let her know the outcome. She took out her mobile and saw that he'd sent a text. *Still no joy. Jo hasn't yet been in touch.* Slipping the phone back into her pocket, Daniels thought about the last investigation they had worked on together. Jo's support had proved invaluable to the case, although Bright had insisted he'd have found the perpetrator without it.

Daniels sighed.

She'd walk over hot coals for her boss, but he was an argumentative prick when he wanted to be. Did he not think that she'd seen him sneaking into the observation gallery above her head? His presence irritated her, but she knew he wouldn't undermine her authority in front of everyone there.

At least, she hoped he wouldn't.

'I can tell you conclusively that the victim was a healthy man with no evidence of any natural disease to accelerate his death or cause him to collapse . . .' Stanton was about to sum up. He took off his bloody gloves, went to a stainless-steel sink, turned on a tap and scrubbed up before helping himself to a glass of water. On his way back, he winked at her, letting her know she was still in charge but also that he was aware Bright was listening via an audio link upstairs, a gesture she appreciated. 'Death was simply and unequivocally due to multiple head injuries caused by a single gunshot wound. One shot through the left frontal lobe. Good shot too, I should say. My guess is that he was standing. The weapon, a small but effective firearm, calibre unknown 'til the labs do their stuff.'

'You're still of the opinion that he had little or no chance to defend himself?'

Stanton nodded. 'And certainly no chance of survival once hit with such accuracy. Shall we adjourn for tea?'

'No can do, Tim,' Daniels said apologetically. 'I've got to get going.'

Stanton was disappointed. 'Some other time perhaps?'

'Sure.' Daniels thanked him and quickly made her way out of the building, practically breaking into a run down a flight of stairs. She caught up with Bright as he hurried to leave the morgue via the back door. 'Guv? A quick word, if I may.'

Bright stopped walking and turned to face her. 'The PM gave us nothing we didn't know already?'

'That about sums it up,' Daniels said.

'Professional hit?'

'Possibly.'

'Time of death?'

'Between eleven and midnight, maybe a little after, just as we thought . . .' Daniels paused. 'Oh, and he'd recently had sex.'

'Lucky bastard.'

Daniels didn't react to his retort. She knew the poor bugger hadn't shared intimacy with Stella since the crash. Their relationship would never again resemble married life. He was now Stella's carer, not her husband, an insufferable situation for them both. Stepping to one side, they watched an undertaker's van arriving at a speed in the car park with less respect for its occupant than seemed proper. It parked near the back door of the morgue. Two men got out, unloaded a body, then disappeared inside with it.

Bright's car was nowhere to be seen.

'Can I drop you anywhere, guv? We can talk on the way.'

Bright shook his head, pointing at a second car approaching. He acknowledged his driver with a wave as he pulled into a vacant space beside the undertaker's van.

'Anything on the house-to-house?' he asked.

Daniels shook her head. 'Don't fret, guv. I have everything under control.'

'As I knew you would,' he said, a look of pride spreading over his face.

She wanted to ask him outright why he was shadowing her and tell him how his interference made her feel. Then a better question entered her head. 'You going to tell me why the ACC wants me on this case when he can't stand the sight of me?'

Bright moved towards his car, an avoidance tactic if ever there was one. Daniels followed him, hell-bent on getting an answer. As she arrived at the side of the car, he got in and wound down the window. She glanced at his driver, knowing she couldn't backchat in front of him.

'Then at least let me work both incidents, guv. Sarah's killer is still out there. We both know he'll kill again . . .'

17

He stared at the scissors he'd used to cut out the faces of the dead ones and thought about how easy it had been.

His mother had told him never to answer the door to strangers. If her mother had done the same, she clearly hadn't listened. Jenny's expression had turned from mild curiosity to terror when he produced the gun. Though why she was so surprised, he couldn't quite imagine. Hadn't she known it was coming? Hadn't he made her feel it? Watching her. Following her. Scaring her half to death.

He liked it best when they were women.

Liked it even better when she began to beg . . .

Like a dog.

Eyes like saucers as she inched away from him, screaming at first, then begging for mercy, pleading with him – tears running down her cheeks. She'd aged considerably from the image he'd been staring at for as long as he could remember; brown hair faded to washed-out grey, lines around her mouth like a cat's bum, ugly thin lips no longer smiling at him as they had done for so very long.

And then?

Then she began to calm herself, tried talking to him, pleading with him to stop and think about what he was doing – appealing to his better nature.

Ooops! Problem there . . .

So he lifted the gun and put her right back in her box. And, give her her due, she wound her neck in like a good little victim – just as he knew she would – until he mentioned his mother's name and the realization dawned.

Poor, dear, Jenny.

That'll teach her to choose her friends more carefully.

In his mind's eye, he still sees her as she used to be. Not as she was when he left her, covered in her own blood – the card sticking out of her cat's bum – dead eyes searching his face for the answer to a question she didn't live long enough to ask: what had she ever done to deserve such a sorry end?

Curiously, not telling her had given him the greatest pleasure of all.

18

Barring several emergency vehicles, the country lane was deserted. The darkness was illuminated by flashes of blue light and a felled tree was being hauled from the road by a crane. Soaked to the skin, a paramedic was doing his best to help the female casualty trapped inside. On the other side of the vehicle, under pressure from the medical team to hurry the job along, a fire crew were using cutting equipment to prise open the door, their job made worse by swirling, squally winds blowing red-hot metal fragments high into the air in every direction.

'Talk to me, pet . . .' The paramedic leaned in through the smashed window of the upturned car. 'Can you hear me?'

Jo couldn't move. Her arms – or was it her legs? – refused to obey her instructions. She must be having one of those dreams again, where she felt like she was awake when really she was asleep. When images weren't joined up and – no matter how hard she might try – she just couldn't open her eyes.

What was that?

'. . . whaaat's yououour naaaame?'

There it was again.

'. . . whaaat's yououour naaaame?'

Jo was really frightened by the moaning voice and the

high-pitched sound that hurt her ears. And she was cold. So very cold. And yet, her head was burning like it was on fire and something warm was crawling diagonally from left to right across her forehead, down and down over her eye and into her ear where it curled up and got bigger until it slithered away again down the right side of her neck to God knows where.

'She's in a bad way . . .' someone yelled. 'You've got to get in there now.'

Who was?

Jo couldn't see anyone. She couldn't see – full stop.

'Hold on, bonny lass . . .' a voice said. This one had a Scottish accent. 'We're going to get you out of there. Before you know it you'll be buying us a drink at the pub down the road.'

At last, the metal gave way and they were in.

Fire officers stepped back to allow the medical team in. Within no time at all they had Jo Soulsby out of the car and on to a stretcher. As critical seconds ticked by, they loaded her through the back door of a waiting ambulance. The senior paramedic worked quickly, placing an oxygen mask over her face and then hooking his patient up to a monitor which suddenly sprang into life.

Then, just as suddenly, it stopped.

No vital signs.

Nothing.

A waiting ambulance driver saw what was happening and slowly moved his hand across his throat. The paramedic scowled at him before attempting resuscitation, even though it seemed pointless.

19

Daniels burst through the door to the incident room, her stomach churning on two counts: Bright's refusal to level with her and the fact that she was in dire need of sustenance. It was time for the evening briefing and she'd been working flat out for the best part of fourteen hours.

'Sorry, sorry . . .' She held up her hands in apology and looked around the room. 'I could murder something to eat. Anyone seen Robbo?'

No sooner had the words left her lips, than DS Robson appeared. He produced a sandwich on a plate from behind his back and presented it to her waiter-fashion, a filthy tea towel draped over his arm.

'Enjoy your dinner, ma'am,' he said.

Greedily, Daniels took a big bite before assuming her position at the front of the room. She spoke with her mouth full, wondering what was keeping Gormley.

'Where's Hank?'

Blank faces stared back at her.

'OK, let's get on with it . . .'

The murder investigation team stopped what they were doing and paid attention. Daniels had no sooner started than the door opened and Gormley crept into the room like a naughty child coming late to assembly. She waited for him to take a seat before scanning the room, finding DC Brown from his crop of strawberry-blond hair.

'Any news on Jo, Andy?'

Brown shook his head. 'I've tried her home three times. Her office haven't seen her since late morning.'

'What time's she due back?'

'She's not, boss. She saw one client this morning, cancelled everything else and left.'

Daniels looked at him for a long time. 'They gave her my message?'

Brown nodded.

'What about her sons? You manage to get hold of them yet?'

'Not yet. Thomas is on two weeks' leave. I've got feelers out for James with the welfare department at Sheffield Uni. They're getting back to me.'

'And Jo's address is definitely current?'

'According to our records.'

'Check again. Personnel records are rarely kept up to date,' she reminded him.

'No, she definitely lives there,' Brown said. 'I checked with a neighbour. I also took a peek through the letterbox . . .'

He broke off, a curious look on his face.

'And?' Daniels pushed.

Brown looked embarrassed. 'There are two suitcases in her hallway, boss.'

Daniels stifled a grin as the squad began to mutter among themselves. She told them to settle down, then began pouring cold water on the implication that Jo Soulsby was about to make a run for it.

It wasn't her intention to sound overly dismissive, but somehow it came out that way. 'Oh, come on, where's your loyalty? This is Jo you're on about. Remember her? Intelligent, consummate professional, one of the good guys – our side of the law! If she *were* guilty, believe me she'd have legged it by now. She's got nerves of steel, that one. You've seen the scum she works with.'

'Yeah, Andy, button it. She's practically one of us,' Gormley added. 'This isn't an offence carried out in a fit of pique and it's certainly no domestic. It's too clinical. In fact, if it turns out a woman is responsible, I'll show my arse in Fenwick's window! How's that for confidence?'

Lisa Carmichael, sitting at the front, made a derogatory remark about Gormley's hairy arse being an affront to human decency, especially in the window of Newcastle's favourite department store. The squad chuckled as Hank feigned a sulk. But all Daniels could think of was two suitcases in a hallway. She moved swiftly on.

'The victim's mother can't take us any further. She's in her eighties and I wouldn't be surprised if the shock of losing her second son doesn't finish her off. Monica Stephens bothers me, though. I'm not sure she's on the level.'

Brown waved his briefing notes in the air to attract Daniels' attention. 'If Monica hails from Rotterdam might there be a drugs connection?'

'I wouldn't rule that out,' Daniels said. 'Or anything else for that matter.'

'I'll have the drugs squad check it out,' Gormley said.

'Good idea, Hank. Tell them it's urgent.' Daniels headed for the water cooler. She filled a plastic cup and took a sip before continuing. 'Monica claims she last saw her husband just after seven when he was collected by taxi. The charity dinner was in aid of Kidney Research. Apparently his brother died of acute kidney failure years ago and he's been fund-raising ever since. Is there any progress on that list?'

Carmichael spoke up. 'I managed to track down a man called Michael Fitzgerald, the MC at the dinner. He confirmed that Stephens did turn up. It was a big do by all accounts, with some very high-profile guests. I've got Fitzgerald compiling a list of everyone who was there.'

'He's taking his bloody time about it,' Daniels said.

'I know, I'm sorry,' Carmichael picked up the phone. 'I'll get on to him again.'

Daniels took another drink, perched herself on the edge of a desk and looked at the tired faces of her team. She couldn't afford to take her foot off the pedal for a second.

'OK, tomorrow morning I want you all in here at seven o'clock sharp. By lunchtime I want to know who Stephens sat with at the dinner, who he talked to, what time he left the Weston and his mode of transport home.'

The door to the incident room opened. A uniformed officer entered, apologizing for the interruption. She made a beeline for Robson. His eyes grew big as she passed him a note. It was the news he'd been waiting for: a message to say that his wife had gone into labour. Robson quickly got to his feet, announcing that he was about to become a father for the very first time. Daniels watched him struggle to put on his jacket.

'Just a minute,' she said, glancing at her watch. 'Where the hell d'you think you're going?'

Robson's jaw dropped. He stopped grinning.

Daniels waved him away. 'Only kidding, you idiot! Go on, get out of here.'

Before she'd even finished speaking, Robson was tripping over his own feet in the rush for the door. Then, realizing he'd left his mobile and his car keys on the desk, he ran back into the room to find them.

Daniels shook her head and turned to Gormley. 'Hank, you'd better drive him. He'll never make the hospital.'

20

On the high-dependency unit, Jo Soulsby lay motionless in bed, her head heavily bandaged, her face covered with abrasions. Sandra Baker, a pretty nursing sister, was checking a drip at her bedside. Jo opened her eyes ever so slightly. The nurse's image was blurred. It faded away to nothing as she drifted back to unconsciousness.

Hours later – *or was it days?* Jo couldn't possibly tell – she was wading through a confusion of thick muddy memories when a hand gently stroked her arm. Then came a voice . . . it sounded familiar, but Jo wasn't altogether sure to whom it belonged.

'Can you hear me? Mum?'

Tom Stephens' voice seemed faint and far away. Jo felt like she was being hauled back to consciousness through a keyhole. She opened her eyes, straining to focus. All she could see was a dark shadow looming above her, then little by little a profile began to register. Her eldest son was tall and blond with a tanned complexion and a striking resemblance to his father. He took her hand and looked deep into her eyes.

Jo's face was so bruised it was difficult to manage even the faintest smile. Her lips felt rubbery and numb, like she'd been anesthetized by a dentist. Her mouth was parched. She swallowed painfully and tried to answer. The noise that came out sounded nothing like speech.

'Don't talk . . .' Tom said. 'James is on his way. I thought he'd be here by now.'

No sooner had he uttered the words than the door burst open and – like an uninvited gatecrasher – James Stephens fell through it, stopping dead when he saw the state his mother was in. He was a paler version of Tom: tall, with ashen blond hair tied in a ponytail at the nape of his neck. He threw down his backpack and grinned nervously.

'Some people will go to any lengths to get attention,' he said.

Winking at Tom, James leaned over the bed and kissed his mother, cradling her injured face in his hands. Jo pointed at a water jug on the cabinet beside her bed. Pouring a small amount into a glass, he lifted it to her mouth and wiped a dribble from her chin with the sleeve of his jumper. His mother's voice was hardly audible when she whispered in his ear . . .

'You smell like a brewery.'

James pointed at his own chest. '*Moi?*'

Jo nodded, ever so slightly.

'Makes two of us,' he said.

Leaving her side to collect a chair from under the window-sill, James shot a worried look at Tom. But by the time he'd returned to Jo's side, his cheeky smile had reappeared. He placed the chair back to front at the head of the bed, straddled it and leaned forwards, placing his chin on his forearms.

He looked his mother straight in the eye. 'Let's get one thing straight: I haven't come all this way for a lecture, I get enough of those in Sheffield. I was worried about you. I had a few pints on the train to ease my nerves, that's all. Now I've seen you're perfectly OK, I promise to remain teetotal for the rest of my days. Deal?'

But Jo had already fallen into a deep sleep.

*

They left a message by her bedside to say they'd be back the following morning, drove home in silence and let themselves in. Tom headed straight for the bathroom. He was bursting for the loo. James went into the kitchen, took off his jacket and threw it over a chair.

His wallet fell out on to the floor.

He bent down to pick it up, filled with anger and regret.

The wallet was lying open, the photograph inside nearly as old as James was – its subject, an immaculately dressed man about town. He stared at it intently. Other fathers posed with children on their knee dressed in Paddington Bear pyjamas listening to stories to match. Not his. His father was an egotistical megalomaniac, a selfish bastard who didn't deserve to be in his wallet at all – never had – never would be again. He took the photograph out, tore it into little pieces and threw it in the bin.

'Old girlfriend?' Tom asked, entering from the hallway, coat still on.

'Something like that.' James sat down.

Tom followed suit. 'You OK?'

'Yes I'm OK!' James sighed loudly. 'Sorry, I'm knackered. You think the police are aware that Mum had been drinking?'

A worried look crossed Tom's face. 'D'you think she had?'

'Don't be so naïve!' James eyed him with disdain. 'She *reeked* of the stuff.'

An uneasy atmosphere descended like a thick black cloud.

Resting his right elbow on the table, James made a fist with his hand and used it to support his right cheek. Fleetingly, he saw his father – not Tom – on the other side of the table. The image spooked him. He rubbed at his eyes, willing himself to relax. A trick of the light, nothing more; it was getting late. On second thoughts, there was more than a passing resemblance: the hair on the back of Tom's hands, the shape of his fingers, the line of his jaw, his facial expressions . . . James ran a hand through his hair and yawned, acting cool while a ghost walked over his skin.

'What's up?' Tom said, reacting to the intensity of his brother's stare.

James looked away, too tired to engage in any meaningful conversation.

'James? What's wrong?'

'Nothing . . . I was up half the night and some dickhead with a computer game prevented me from getting any shut-eye on the train. I'm off to bed.'

'Not yet, I want to talk about Mum,' Tom said. 'She could be in real trouble.'

'Oh, lighten up!' James put his size elevens on the table, then removed them and stood up, scraping the chair on the hard wooden floor as he got to his feet. 'Just be thankful she didn't kill anyone, including herself. It was a fucking accident, that's all. Things'll be fine.'

'She never drinks and drives.'

'So? She made an exception. We all get bladdered some-times, even you.'

Tom's expression darkened. He reached into his coat pocket, pulled out a business card and handed it across the table. 'It was at the house when I got here,' he said.

James took the card, a frown slowly appearing on his brow as he read it. It was a police calling card, a handwritten mes-sage from DC Andrew Brown urging their mother to get in touch. He shrugged and stuffed it in his pocket.

21

Bright was struggling to make supper, stirring a pan on the stove. On the other side of the kitchen, the telephone rang and the kettle began to boil simultaneously. He stopped what he was doing and rushed over to attend to them. He answered the phone first – more out of habit than necessity – then pulled the whistle out, stopping the din from piercing his eardrums. It had to be said, he wasn't having a good day, at work or at home. Pouring water over a teabag already in a china pot, he barked his name into the phone.

A man's voice came on the line. 'It's Trent.'

'Trent who?' Bright said impatiently.

'Sorry, wrong number.'

The line went dead.

Bright looked at Stella, the woman he'd loved with a passion since the day they had met some thirty years before, now a shadow of her former self. 'Charming,' he said. 'You been up to no good, love? Guy called Trent on the phone, no manners, younger than me by the sound of it. Having a clandestine affair, are you? Would have to be a secret with a name like Trent.'

A tear rolled silently down Stella's cheek. She was at the kitchen table in her wheelchair, her frame shrivelled, her eyes fixed to a point on the far wall.

'Dinner won't be long now, love,' Bright said.

Of course it would be long! *It always was.*

Bright smiled at his wife, trying hard to mask his feelings. He wasn't cut out for domesticity in any form. He'd barely coped since the accident, was too proud – or was it too stupid? – to ask for help. He had struggled to keep up appearances both at home and at work when he was barely hanging on.

Pouring Stella's tea, he added water from the mains tap to cool the temperature, then tipped it into a child's beaker and lifted it to her lips, his thoughts turning to a little boy whose parents were relying on the murder investigation team to bring his killer to justice. And they damned well would, even if they had to work day and night to do it.

And still his wife continued to stare from those vacant eyes, trying to send a message she couldn't put into words. Bright followed her gaze to the cooker and looked on in horror as the unappetizing contents of the pan on the stove made their own way out, oozing over the edge into a congealed mess he knew would take hours to clean up.

'Fuck's sake!' he yelled, slamming his fist on the table.

22

Daniels' mobile bleeped.

A text from Bright: *Any chance you can swing by?*

She sighed. That was all she needed.

It took her around half an hour to reach his home. She patted his arm as she walked past him into the house. Stella was asleep in her wheelchair by the fire, wrapped up warm and cosy with a blanket over her knees. No hint of any major crisis here. And yet the guv'nor's grave expression told a different story.

Daniels had known for a while that her boss was a man under immense pressure. But tonight he looked ill and smelled strongly of alcohol.

He sat down, inviting her to do the same. 'She practically begged me, Kate.' He was losing his composure in a way she hadn't thought possible. Until now. 'I was getting her ready for bed, the usual routine: bath, teeth, she likes me to brush her hair . . . Then I realized the time and reached for her medication. She takes two pills at night, so I gave her them and water to wash it down with. Next thing I know she grabs my arm, her eyes pleading with me. I tell you, it bloody near finished me. You want a drink or something?'

'No thanks, guv . . .' Daniels glanced at Stella. 'She's bound to have good and bad days. She'll think differently tomorrow.'

'And if she doesn't?'

Stella seemed to be in a deep sleep, totally unaware of their conversation. But was she? Daniels' mother would sometimes repeat things uttered when she'd appeared to be at rest. God forbid the woman could hear them.

'You put her to bed . . .' Daniels said. 'I'll make us a coffee.'

The mess on the stove was the least of her worries when she entered the kitchen. It was the room of an obsessive: like walking into a 'live' incident room. Case notes and jottings were spread out across the kitchen bench, crime-scene photographs pinned to cupboard doors. Some were close-ups like the one she'd seen in his office – just a child's innocent face – others were more grotesque: wide-angled shots showing the boy lying in the rubbish skip, an arm and a leg twisted unnaturally beneath his body.

He'd obviously been tossed in after death.

Daniels' heart sank.

This explained the media frenzy, an outcry for police to throw every resource at the case and bring the killer to justice quickly to protect the region's children. What must the dead child's parents be going through? Was it any wonder Bright looked so ill? Combined with a difficult home life, this level-one case might tip him over the edge. It surely would if he insisted on shadowing her own murder enquiry as he had done up to now.

Scooping everything up, she dumped the lot in his old briefcase, which was lying open on the grubby tiled floor. Fifteen minutes later, wiping her hands on a tea towel, she surveyed a spotless kitchen. She poured Bright's now cold coffee down the sink and went upstairs in search of him, half expecting to find him curled up in bed with his wife, exhausted from his ordeal and the Jack Daniels he'd downed in order to cope with it. She found him sitting on a pink nursing chair at the bottom of the bed, just staring at Stella.

He heard her approach, got up and joined her on the threshold.

'I've got to go . . .' Daniels said. 'You going to be all right, guv?'

'She's going to be fine.'

'I was talking about you,' Daniels said quietly, searching his tired face.

Bright just looked at her. Gone was the bolshie bastard she worked with and looked up to. In his place was a sad, lonely man whose married life had been cut short, a man who inspired her to do her very best. Daniels hated seeing him like this and hoped he'd get back on track eventually. What other choice did he have?

She pulled on her coat. 'It wasn't your fault, guv.'

Bright swallowed hard. Clearly he thought it was. 'You take care, Kate. Remember, one minute you're on a high, next you're on your arse.'

Wasn't that the truth. 'Give it time, it's early days.'

Bright looked at her deeply, his bottom lip quivering as he glanced back at his sleeping wife. 'Stay, Kate . . . just for tonight.'

Daniels took a deep breath, momentarily wrong-footed. Christ almighty. Now she knew he was losing it. She gave him an awkward hug, patting him on the back.

'Look after her, guv.'

She turned away . . .

23

To Daniels' surprise, Bright turned up at her house early next morning. He'd had a shave but dark shadows under his eyes suggested he hadn't been to bed. As he walked into the house begging for forgiveness for the state he'd been in the night before, she detected a slight whiff of a cigarette.

A hint of what was to come perhaps?

Bright only ever smoked when he had a drink in his hand and, for a fleeting moment, Daniels wondered if he'd started the morning where he'd left off just eight hours ago and was about to say something they'd both regret. But she was wrong. His apology was grovelling and well rehearsed, which explained the nicotine hit so early in the day. She laughed when he mentioned an 'inappropriate request' to stay the night at his place, lightening the mood between them, putting him at ease as she poured him a coffee.

As far as she was concerned it never happened.

She gave her word that it wouldn't be mentioned again so long as he agreed to stop putting himself under so much pressure . . .

'You'll run yourself into the ground otherwise.' The smile slid off her face as a grim thought crossed her mind. 'Guv, who's looking after Stella?'

'Neighbour,' Bright said vaguely.

Daniels looked out at the darkness through black kitchen windows. 'At this hour?'

Bright registered the doubt. 'Don't fret, Kate. I'm not ready to lose Stella yet. Our neighbour is also an old school-mate. Salt of the earth, too. Up at the crack of dawn. Comes in every day at six. Never misses.'

They left the house together but in separate cars, Bright on his way to headquarters, Daniels en route to the incident room with a manpower problem to sort. She'd assembled a good team: a dedicated group she trusted to cross-reference each and every piece of information that came into the incident room, no matter how small or seemingly insignificant, with Harry Holt – a DS pushing fifty with almost three decades of experience under his belt – appointed as receiver, and Paul Robson as statement reader. But with the benefit of hindsight she knew she should've chosen differently where the latter was concerned. Robson's sudden departure on paternity leave was going to leave her short.

Driving into the city, she was forced to consider drafting in his replacement. Carefully sifting the possibilities in her mind, she eventually settled on a newly promoted ex-squad member, DS Patrick O'Doughty from Northern Area Command. Not that he had many statements to read as yet; so far the house-to-house had failed to turn up a single witness. Which didn't surprise her, given the Bonfire Night celebrations. The killer had been one of many thousands of strangers in the city for the occasion. She wondered if he'd planned it that way or just got lucky.

She entered the incident room with the intention of ringing O'Doughty's line manager. As with every murder she'd ever worked on, over-crowding was proving to be a problem. Typists, data-entry clerks and squad members were crammed together, sharing desks, frustrated by the lack of facilities afforded to their work. But they would manage in the end. They always did. In the wider scheme of things, space was less important than just getting the job done.

In her early years as a police officer, Daniels would gladly have worked for no pay – and often did. She believed that, for a woman, self-sacrifice was an integral part of reaching the top in any profession. Motherhood was the obvious example of what she'd missed out on in pursuit of her career. It was a decision she'd take again tomorrow if she had to.

As she'd just told Bright, life was too short for regrets.

Daniels' father suddenly entered her thoughts. A smile crossed her lips as she recalled her childhood, the afternoons spent watching cowboy movies with him. *Good times.* He'd nicknamed her Annie Oakley and teased her a lot. When they'd played make-believe, she was never the gunslinger – always the county sheriff. He'd once told her she was 'born to uphold the law'.

Little did she know that his comment would later split them apart.

She wondered if *he* ever had regrets. He was the one who had taught her to take pride in what she did, instilled in her a sense of devotion and commitment – good old-fashioned qualities that had moulded her into the impressive officer she was. He was the one who'd given her a strong perspective on right and wrong. Daniels swallowed hard. Her father had been an affectionate, hard-working, proud man with a great sense of humour – until she'd reached the age of ten and everything changed.

Ed Daniels was now a broken man whose emotions – even to this day – were still raw from the miners' strike. Memories of the bitter and bloody confrontation with the police on the picket lines, Scargill's troops versus Thatcher's, had not diminished. He'd never recovered his status as breadwinner for the family after his pit closed. It nearly killed him to walk out of the gate on the last day. When Daniels left school at seventeen with above-average grades and a burning ambition to join the police, he'd taken her choice of profession as a personal betrayal, refusing to give her his blessing. How long would it be until he forgave her for that? She'd always felt that she was born to be a detective, but now Stephens' death had changed things and, once again, divided loyalties weighed heavy on her mind.

There was a muddle of bodies around a desk in one corner of the incident room. As it slowly dispersed, Daniels was delighted to see DS Robson emerge from its centre. His wife had given birth overnight to a boy – Callum, named after a Scottish grandfather on his mother's side – weighing in at a healthy 2.85 kilos. The mood in the room was buoyant as people arrived for work and heard the news. They shook hands with Robson before taking their seats, aware that the new arrival would get less attention than it deserved. That came with the territory. It wouldn't be the first time pressure of work had prevented a proper celebration to wet a baby's head.

It wouldn't be the last.

'I'm not taking paternity leave just yet,' Robson said.

Daniels was taken aback. 'Oh?'

He smiled. 'I could tell you it's down to my enduring

professional integrity, but I'd be lying. Truth is, my mother arrived late last night. She's hell-bent on stopping for a fortnight. I've talked it over with Irene and I'm yours till she goes home. Irene doesn't fancy playing referee.'

Daniels tapped his arm. 'I'm delighted to hear that. We're run off our feet.'

Gormley sauntered over, adding his own congratulations, telling Robson that having a son would change his life for ever.

'In a good way,' he added. 'First sixteen years are the worst!'

Robson smiled. 'I appreciate the tip-off.'

Gormley's phone rang. He took it from his pocket and lifted it to his ear, leaving Daniels and Robson hanging. He listened intently for a few seconds, holding the DCI's gaze, then rang off thanking the caller for getting back to him so quickly. 'The drugs theory is a non-starter,' he said. 'Neither Interpol nor Customs and Excise have anything on their radar.'

Daniels shrugged – it was a long shot anyway.

She turned to Robson. 'Can you give us a sec, Robbo? Hank and I have something important to discuss.'

Gormley threw her a questioning look as Robson moved off. 'Something I missed?'

Daniels shook her head. 'Fancy getting out of here for a bit?'

'Er, aren't we a tad busy to go on walkabout?'

'It's important.'

'What is?'

'Not here,' Daniels said. 'Meet me at Sarah's in ten.'

She suddenly had his undivided attention.

Sarah's was known as a last resort.

24

Sarah's Café was just across the road. The place was a dive: dishes abandoned on tables, chairs strewn around at odd angles waiting to be put back where they rightfully belonged, the untidy mess ignored by a gum-chewing waitress – too busy on the phone to notice, too idle to care. They were sitting at a table by the window, each with an insipid mug of coffee in their hands. Gormley had no intention of drinking his and was getting impatient to hear what was too important to talk about in the station.

'Spit it out then,' he said.

Daniels sat for a moment considering the many motives for taking a person's life: rivalry for power or love, jealousy, greed, and the most potent of all – revenge. She looked at Gormley and took a deep breath. 'I know something, Hank. Something I'm duty-bound to disclose. Something that, for the time being, stays between the two of us – understood?'

'You're the boss.'

'Jo once told me, in confidence, that Stephens raped her.'

Gormley's eyes widened. 'What?'

Daniels knew she was on dodgy ground.

'And you chose not to disclose it because . . .?'

'I want you to check it out first.'

'She reported it?'

'No further action was taken. It was pre '91. No such offence if you were married. On the outside he was a model citizen, a church-going Christian with a social conscience. But behind closed doors, I gather he was a pig.'

'Am I missing something here?' Gormley picked up his coffee, grimaced, then put it back down. 'It's just . . . well, not to put too fine a point on it, revenge is a pretty strong motive!'

'Eighteen plus years ago, maybe . . .' Daniels thought it unlikely that a person would commit murder nearly two decades after the event. 'And we don't think this is a domestic, right? At least, that was the consensus yesterday when you were offering to moon us from Fenwick's window!'

'True,' Gormley conceded. 'But we can't ignore it.'

'I'm not!'

'Aren't you?'

'If she ever becomes a credible suspect—'

'Credible? In case you've forgotten, her ex is dead and she can't be found. Anyone else, you'd be getting the cuffs out.'

'Come on! Do you really believe someone in her position would jeopardize all she has worked for to wreak revenge on an ex-husband she hasn't lived with for years? I don't think so. I didn't say anything before because . . . well, at the risk of stating the obvious, would you want your personal life broadcast at the station? You know what the rumour squad are like . . .' There was an awkward silence between them. 'Don't look at me like that! I just . . . well, I see no reason to drag up her past. I think we should keep it to ourselves – for now, anyway.'

'You going to tell Bright?'

Daniels shook her head, mention of their boss a reminder of the state he had been in last night and his subsequent visit to her home shortly after six-thirty a.m. She glanced at her watch. He'd be at Fantasy Island by now – a commonly used nickname for force headquarters – no doubt facing a barrage of questions from the powers that be. More drama. More pressure. And scant reward for the time he was putting in. Top brass weren't remotely interested in his personal welfare. Target-driven bollocks was the name of the game nowadays. As far as they were concerned, Bright could be ready for a straight-jacket just so long as he got results.

Daniels paid the bill and led Gormley from the café. Her revelation about Jo's past was the only topic of conversation as they crossed the road to the station. Gormley was uncharacteristically subdued, probably weighing up how she would handle things if the shit hit the fan further down the line. She reassured him she'd take full responsibility should that happen. No way would he be implicated in any breach of protocol. 'You happy with that?' she asked as they passed through reception and made their way along the corridor to the incident room.

'Do I have a choice?'

'Of course.'

'Fine! Whatever you want. It's your funeral, not mine. Why should I give a shit when you don't?' He stopped at the door to the incident room and took a long deep breath, clearly pissed off. Then, finally, he let the matter drop. 'Want me to put some pressure on the Home Office? *They* might know where Jo is.'

'It's worth a try, but do it quickly. I want her found and I need to nail the sequence of events from the time Stephens left his apartment to the time of his death. Maybe he met someone either before or after he left the Weston. If he did, someone out there must've seen something.'

'And if it was Jo he met?'

'We'll deal with that if and when it arises.'

Gormley could see his boss was troubled. 'There's something else, isn't there?'

Daniels nodded. 'Monica claims she and Stephens hadn't had sex for a fortnight.'

'Is that right?'

'That's what she said. Someone had sex with him though, didn't they?'

'You think it was Jo?'

'Not likely, given their history.'

'But not impossible?'

Daniels felt a knot of tension settle in her neck. 'I really don't know what to think.'

A couple of hours and several phone calls later, Daniels was alone in her office when there was a knock at the door. Robson entered with Carmichael and Gormley in tow: a delegation, if ever she saw one. Good news, Daniels hoped. Both men sat down, inviting Carmichael to go first. 'Fitzgerald's list from the Weston.' She handed over an A4 sheet and stood back, waiting for a response.

Daniels gave the list the once-over, wondering why it was taking three of them to present this to her. There must be something else. 'Terrific, Lisa. Get on to that, will you?' She handed the list back. 'Talk to door security. See if they kept a record of who *actually* turned up, as opposed to who was invited.'

Carmichael was way ahead of her. 'Already have. As guests arrived, somebody checked their names against the seating plan. I've been working my way through it. I'm pretty sure of where everyone was sitting.'

'Unless they all played musical chairs,' Daniels said.

It was a gentle lesson never to take things at face value.

Carmichael was embarrassed. 'Why didn't I think of that?'

Daniels gave a considerate smile. 'Do what you can, right away.'

She waited for Carmichael to leave, but it soon became apparent that she wasn't going anywhere. The young DC shared a brief but knowing look with Gormley. Noticing the exchange, Daniels wondered what was holding her back. From the look of her, Carmichael was about to throw a spanner in the works. She took a deep breath, darting a second look at Gormley. He winked at her and nodded towards Daniels.

'OK, this must be good,' Daniels said. 'Something else I need to know?'

The hiatus provided her with an opportunity to take in Gormley's self-satisfied grin. Robson stretched his arms above his head and yawned, too tired to notice. He'd been up half the night and looked as if he was feeling it. He sat with his mouth open, waiting for Carmichael to speak.

'Stephens was sat with the Assistant Chief Constable,' Carmichael said, eventually.

You could have heard a pin drop as Daniels scanned the faces of each detective in turn.

'She's good, no?' Gormley said.

He crossed his arms over his chest, looking extremely proud of his underling, taking none of the credit for himself.

It was so like him not to rain on her parade. As a young officer, Carmichael needed all the praise and encouragement she could get in order to progress to the next level. Daniels was pleased to see Hank Gormley back on form.

'There's more . . .' Carmichael sat down, clearly on a roll. 'ACC Martin is no longer in the area. His secretary told me he rang in early this morning and took leave at short notice. He's scarpered to his holiday home up north. It took a while to track him down, but I got there eventually.' She grinned at Gormley. 'He's none too pleased with Hank.'

Daniels shifted her gaze. 'You spoke to him?'

Gormley nodded. But before he could open his mouth, Carmichael was off again.

'I found out that Stephens made generous donations to Kidney Research, sending his cheques directly to the Chairman. He insisted on anonymity, apparently. As far as the organization is concerned, he was quite an important guest.'

'Great!' Daniels glanced at the ceiling. 'A high-profile victim and a senior officer withholding evidence. Can it get any worse?'

Carmichael gave a little nod. 'Yeah, it can. Martin is the Chairman.'

'Which he failed to mention when questioned . . .' Gormley was paraphrasing the police caution and clearly enjoying himself at the ACC's expense. 'Something that we all very much hope he may later rely on in court.'

Carmichael and Robson both laughed.

'Unbelievable!' Daniels began thinking out loud. 'If Martin is so well connected to Stephens, then why keep silent about it? What the hell is he up to?'

'Maybe he's on the hey-diddle-diddle,' Gormley offered.

'Not funny, Hank. But I take your point. Get hold of the charity's books.'

Everyone stopped talking as Bright entered the room. 'Kate, there's been another shooting, a woman this time. I'm tied up. Can you deal?'

Daniels nodded. He handed her the details and left.

25

Twenty minutes later, the Toyota turned left at a signpost for Houghton-le-Spring. Moments after that, she pulled into an ordinary street that had recently become a crime scene. Jenny Tait's terraced house was already secure, taped off to keep the public out, with a uniform guarding the gate, a crowd of onlookers close by. Avoiding Gormley's smug expression, Daniels got out of the car and shook hands with Detective Superintendent Ronald Naylor of neighbouring Durham Constabulary who'd come out of the crime scene to greet her.

'Ron.'

'Kate.' Naylor swept his arm out, drawing her attention to a glut of police vehicles parked along the kerb. The insignia on the cars didn't match. His tone was friendly. 'Bit of a Mexican stand-off, wouldn't you agree?'

Daniels was a little embarrassed. 'Hank said it wasn't our patch, but the control room was having none of it.'

'Nasty business . . .' Naylor looked past her to the Toyota. He held up a thumb to Gormley, who nodded back and settled down in his seat for a nap. 'We don't get many of these round here. I've got no witnesses, no motive, no bloody idea where to begin.'

Daniels nodded. 'Sounds familiar.'

'Consider yourself stood down, Kate. Call you later?'

'Yeah, do that.' She was about to walk away when Naylor spoke again:

'If you come across any bodies with a prayer card stuffed in their mouths, give us a call, eh?'

Daniels felt the colour drain from her face as the image of Father Simon clutching a prayer card flashed to the forefront of her mind. 'Does a priest count?'

'Excuse me?'

'Remember the double murder last Christmas Eve at St Camillus church?'

Naylor nodded. 'How could I forget?'

'The priest with a bullet in his chest was holding a prayer card.'

Naylor bit his lip. 'Yeah well, he would be, wouldn't he? Tools of the trade and all that. You'd expect—'

'Keep me informed, Ron. I don't believe in coincidences.'

'You serious?'

'Very.'

Daniels got back in the car and sat for a while, scanning the faces of the crowd behind the police tape, wondering if a killer could be among them. She drove away, hoping against hope that Naylor's case might somehow be linked to her unsolved double murder, the one still giving her nightmares. What if the prayer card on Father Simon's body was a clue to his killer's identity and not merely a 'tool of the trade'? She made a mental note to call Naylor when he'd finished at the crime scene.

Gormley hadn't picked up on her excitement. He was sitting quietly, studying the list Carmichael had supplied earlier. 'Know a woman called Felicity Wood?' he said, looking up.

'Should I?'

'She's a brief at Graham & Abercrombie.'

'Don't think so. Why?'

'According to this list, she was sitting with Martin and Stephens at the dinner.'

'Was she now?'

'I know the name,' Gormley said. 'I just can't place it.'

Daniels made a right turn and then a left out of the housing estate and put her foot down, heading back towards Newcastle along a winding country road that cut its way through lush green countryside, hedged on either side by drystone walls. In parts, the stones had fallen away, exposing open pasture that seemed to go on and on. A canopy of bare branches met above the centre of the road, creating a strobe effect as she drove beneath it.

She slowed behind a caravan of vehicles: a farm tractor spewing mud from gigantic tyres; a single-decker with only one passenger on board; an impatient driver of a blue transit van who chanced his arm by straying from the kerb trying to overtake – irritating Daniels, who was bringing up the rear. She wondered if the maniac ever stopped to consider his own mortality as he put oncoming traffic in danger.

'Jesus!' Gormley said.

Daniels took her eyes off the road a moment to glance at him. 'What?'

'I knew I'd come across her name before!'

'The brief?'

Gormley grinned. 'She's a resident of Court Mews.'

'You sure?'

'Yep, saw her name on the action list this morning.'

'Then maybe we should pay her a visit.'

Daniels switched on her blue light, indicating her intention to pull out . . .

26

Felicity Wood was a power dresser with a superior attitude. She had on a pair of well-cut navy trousers, an off-white silk blouse and a pair of calf-skin, high-heeled, fuck-me boots, sharply pointed at the toe. Her outfit screamed a hefty salary, as did her lovely apartment. The view across the Tyne from the picture window was identical to that from the crime scene on the floor below. A small table in front of it bore the remains of a light lunch, set for only one person Daniels observed.

'Please sit down.' Wood picked up her wine glass. 'Would you like to join me?'

'Not for me, thanks.' Daniels hadn't come to get cosy. 'I'm sorry to interrupt your day off, but I'd like to know about your relationship with Alan Stephens.'

'We're . . . we were, neighbours.'

'Nothing more? You were his guest at dinner on Thursday night, were you not?'

'My firm contributes to many fund-raisers, DCI Daniels.'

'Is that what the ACC advised you to say?'

Wood bristled. Daniels had clearly hit a nerve. 'If you have a point to make to the ACC, I'd be grateful if you'd make it to him.'

'It'll be my pleasure.' Daniels noted the woman's anxiety as she forced a smile and reached forward to pick up the wine bottle and refill her glass. 'Forgive me for being so blunt, Ms Wood, but did you have sex with Alan Stephens on the night he died?'

'That's impertinent!'

'It's also a question that requires an answer.'

'Then no – not that it's any of your business.'

'You sure about that?'

Wood took a sip of her wine, meeting Daniels' gaze over the top of her glass. 'I think I'd have remembered.'

'Any chance you'd volunteer a sample of DNA?'

'Am I being arrested?' Wood said, with a smug raise of the eyebrow. Daniels had nothing on her and she knew it. 'Then there's your answer.'

'When you returned home from the Weston, you didn't see or hear anything unusual?'

'As it happens, I did. A loud bang . . . sometime around midnight. It seemed to come from inside rather than outside the building.'

'Did you investigate?'

'Do I look stupid?'

'You didn't think it worth mentioning before now?'

Wood lifted her glass, took another sip of wine and moistened her lips. 'I couldn't swear to it. It was Bonfire Night. It was noisy.'

'I see. Well, thank you for your time . . .' Daniels reached into her pocket, pulled out a business card and handed it over. 'If you think of anything else, I'd appreciate a call.'

She left the building and found Gormley leaning on the Toyota, which was parked on double yellow lines right outside Court Mews. When he saw her approaching, he binned his cigarette on the pavement and ground it out with his foot. Daniels glared at him, picked it up and handed it back.

'You speak to Wood?' he said.

'For what good it did – smarmy, self-opinionated cow.'

'So you liked her a lot.'

'And she's lying. Luckily for us, she's not very good at it.'

Gormley checked his fag end for burning embers and then put it in his pocket.

They got in the car.

'Let's swing past Jo's house one more time,' Daniels said.

27

They parked right outside Jo's house. As they did so, the curtains of the house next door inched open and an elderly lady peeped out from within. Daniels noticed a Neighbourhood Watch sticker in the window.

They got out of the car and made their way to Jo's front door. Gormley pressed the bell and stepped back. They waited . . . and when there was no reply Daniels pointed to the adjoining property.

'Let's try next door,' she said.

The elderly lady they'd seen at the window opened the door with the chain still secured. She was a fine-looking woman, around eighty years old: extremely alert with steely eyes and curly, cotton wool hair.

'Mrs Collins?' Daniels held up ID. 'May we have a word?'

The chain came off. 'Yes, yes. You people did that already. I'm old, not stupid. I know who you are.'

Daniels smiled.

The woman showed them into her living room and sat down in a high-backed chair. Daniels asked how well she knew her neighbour, Jo Soulsby. Mrs Collins told her not very well at all. The last time she'd seen Jo, she was getting out of a taxi in the small hours of Friday the sixth of November.

A matter of hours after the fatal shooting.

The fact that nobody had seen her since had Daniels wondering why.

'Can you be more precise on time?'

Mrs Collins thought about this before answering. 'Around one forty-five in the morning . . . I'd been listening to the *Night Shift* programme on radio, you see. Then I read for a while – an old P.D. James novel, *Death of an Expert Witness*; I'd bought it the day before at a jumble sale – so I do know how late it was.'

Gormley and Daniels smiled at one another, tickled by the programme title. Neither had heard of it – they were too busy with the real thing – but both had read the book.

'A fan of our colleague Commander Adam Dalgliesh, are you?' Gormley asked.

'Oh, yes,' Mrs Collins said. 'A real gentleman, just like my late husband.'

Daniels pushed on. 'Was Ms Soulsby alone?'

Mrs Collins nodded. 'I don't sleep well since my Jack died. I heard a car pull up and saw her getting out of a taxi. That's the last time I saw her. Is everything all right next door?'

'Nothing for you to worry about,' Gormley said.

They thanked Mrs Collins for the information and headed back to the murder incident room, stopping at Dene's Deli on Jesmond Road to collect something decent to eat – the best sandwiches around, as far as Daniels was concerned.

Back at the office, they grabbed a coffee and got stuck into their lunch: Daniels' Italian salami and organic sundried tomato and the 'special' Gormley had chosen, 'Last Mango in Paris': creamy crab, tuna and mango chutney. They'd just finished eating when Brown stuck his head round the door.

Gormley had asked him to trace Jo through her employers, but his efforts had so far drawn a blank. The Home Office official he'd spoken to point-blank refused to give out any details without first speaking to someone in authority.

'Understandable, I suppose,' Daniels said. 'Given the nature of her work, they're entitled to be cagey. She has to deal with some evil bastards. No doubt one or two might pay handsomely for her details.'

'Doesn't give him the right to treat me like a prat.'

'Did he?' Daniels took in Brown's nod. 'Well, we'll see about that.'

Just then, her phone rang.

'This'll be him now, I bet,' Brown said. 'I gave him your extension number.'

Daniels picked up. 'Murder Investigation Team.'

The Home Office official didn't ask who she was or bother to introduce himself, just demanded to know why the police were sniffing round one of their own. What was it Jo Soulsby had done? Did Daniels know she was a professional of high standing in her field? There were issues of Data Protection to consider . . . blah, blah. Daniels shook her head and raised her eyes to the ceiling, letting Brown and Gormley know that it was indeed the Home Office, holding the receiver half a yard from her ear as the man continued his tirade. He was speaking so loudly, they could hear every word.

Eventually, he stopped to draw breath.

'Have you any idea who you are talking to?' Daniels asked.

'Well, no, I assume . . .'

'Then piss off and stop wasting my valuable time!' She

slammed the phone down to a spontaneous round of applause from her two colleagues. 'Officious little prick!'

They got up and followed Brown back into the incident room. As Gormley peeled off, heading for the gents, Daniels eyed the photographs attached to the murder wall: Stephens, Monica, James . . . Jo.

Where the hell are you?

Daniels looked at her watch. She wanted an update from Ron Naylor, but it was too early to call him. His victim would have to be examined, first in situ, then transported to the morgue for a full post-mortem. Only then would Forensics get their hands on the card that had niggled her subconscious since she'd learned of its existence.

Two scenarios loomed large in her thoughts, neither of which appealed. Either way, Daniels knew she had a problem. If Naylor's case and the killing of Sarah Short and Father Simon weren't linked then there were two dangerous offenders on the run in bordering counties, a problem that definitely needed sorting. But if the opposite was true, then a serial killer who had eluded capture for almost a year was lurking out there somewhere – a situation that was so much worse.

28

He was in complete control. His weapons had opened many doors, allowing him to go wherever he chose – invited or not. He knew what he wanted and how to get it, though he had to admit he'd learned the hard way.

He'd left too many clues on the first tart he'd wasted, ended up captured within days. Twenty years on, every detail of his trial was etched on his brain like the tattoo on his head. That courtroom – hot and overcrowded – his fate resting in the hands of twelve strangers, none of whom dared meet his gaze. Each glance quickly whisked away when he looked at them, unfazed by the seriousness of his position, as exhibit after exhibit pointed an accusing finger in his direction.

The jury's discomfort was laid bare for all to see. When shown photographs of his victim, battered to a pulp like the whore she was, one woman in the jury box was even moved to tears.

Silly tart . . .

Nobody had asked how he felt.

And what about the two of them? He had watched them, huddled together in the public gallery, pretending to give a shit, like the day they put him in care for no reason he could think of – lied to keep him there – and went through the motions of supporting him. They disgusted him.

But he'd be leaving his parents till last.

Just why they'd spent that day snivelling and holding hands, he couldn't imagine. Her especially. She'd spent more time teaching Sunday school than taking care of him.

Fucking goody two-shoes.

She was only alive now because he'd decided not to kill her . . . yet. In any case, she was already dying of shame – the slow kind of living death people like her deserved. By the time he'd finished messing with her head, books would be written about his life, a film perhaps, with some A-list celebrity playing him, maybe even a sequel or a series on the box . . .

Sweet.

He could see it now – his name, their name – up in lights or plastered across every billboard in the country. She'd find that difficult to ignore. That's why he felt so angry. Any profiler worth her salt should have given the filth a lead by now, flagged up his record, his obsession with the God squad.

What the fuck did they think they were doing?

Why hadn't they joined up the dots?

29

Daniels looked around the room. Maxwell appeared to be working away quietly for once, his warrant card sticking out of his computer. She wandered over, taking in the soft-porn magazine he was doing his best to hide.

He nearly jumped out of his skin when she spoke to him:

'Neil, the Tactical Support Group are whining for some PDFs. Nip down to Admin and get some, will you?'

She didn't need any personal descriptive forms. It was just a ploy to get rid of him.

A smirk appeared on his face as he moved off probably thinking he'd got one over on her. What he didn't know was, she was about to do the same to him. As soon as he was out of sight, she took his seat and began searching the vehicle index. She had to work fast, scrolling down quickly, keeping one eye on the door for him coming back.

Her mobile rang again. She pulled it out of her pocket and gave her name, placing her elbows on the desk, supporting her chin with one hand, holding the phone to her ear with the other. Her eyes fixed on the screen – flitting here, there and everywhere – as she listened intently to the caller.

Shit!

She hung up and left the building without a word to anyone.

*

She decided to skirt the city rather than risk getting stuck in traffic, approaching the West End from the south side of the river. It took her a few miles out of her way but it was the right move. On the Gateshead side of the Tyne, she picked up speed, eventually turning right, crossing back over the river on the Redheugh Bridge.

On the north side of the river, Daniels turned left, headed up the West Road for a mile and a half, passing a sign for NEWCASTLE GENERAL HOSPITAL. A block further on, she turned right into the hospital grounds, screeching to a halt in a spot marked: AMBULANCES ONLY. She got out of the car and raced to the main entrance, quickly searching the information board before approaching the lifts. Her eyes darted back and forth between the two digital displays, but the lifts were taking too long, both stuck on the floor above.

Entering the stairwell, she took the stairs two at a time with her heart thumping out of her chest, the smell of disinfectant hitting her subconscious like a brick, transporting her back in time. Two floors up, she lost herself in the narrow hospital corridors, blindly running this way and that with no apparent goal in mind – even less direction. Then suddenly she was still.

The sign directly above her head pointed to the chaplaincy.

Disorientated, she walked on to a ward . . .

A priest was standing over a bed, administering the last rites. The person in the bed was a sick, pale version of Daniels herself.

'Mum?'

The priest spoke softly: 'Cleanse in thine own blood the sinners of the whole world who are now in their agony, and are to die this day.'

Daniels let out a scream, 'NO!'

But all she could hear was silence.

The priest didn't lift his head or stop praying. Her mother appeared to be sleeping peacefully. Daniels didn't want *him* there, neither of them did. They weren't ready for the end. Never would be. She grabbed the priest by the lapels, physically ejecting him from the room. His God allowed the innocent to die . . .

'Detective Chief Inspector Daniels?' When she got no response, Nurse Baker repeated herself. 'DCI Daniels?'

Daniels was staring at an empty bed, faintly aware of a woman's voice. She turned towards it as echoes of the past slowly began to subside. She could breathe again, pulled herself together and held out a trembling hand.

'That was quick!' the nurse said, shaking hands. 'I hardly had time to put the phone down. Come this way.'

They entered a room no bigger than a police cell. As they walked in, Daniels eyed a pile of case notes on the desk, got out her notebook and wafted it in front of her face.

'Do you think I could have a glass of water?' she said. 'It's really hot in here.'

'Tell you what,' the nurse said, 'how about a nice refreshing cup of tea instead?'

Daniels nodded. 'That would be great, thanks.'

'I'll let Mr Thorburn know you've arrived.' Nurse Baker left the room.

The moment the door closed behind her, Daniels was on her feet searching the case notes, but the file she wanted wasn't there. Cursing, she sat back down and waited impatiently for the nurse to return, her eyes eventually coming to rest on a tray of case notes stacked neatly on a shelf by the door, the name of the consultant pinned to the wall above it. Daniels leapt to her feet. Jo Soulsby's file was on top. Reaching for it, she stepped away again when suddenly the door opened and the nurse backed into the room with a tray of tea and digestive biscuits.

'Sorry it took so long,' she said. 'No milk, as usual. Had to borrow some from the canteen. Mr Thorburn is with a patient. He'll be along shortly.' She handed Daniels a mug of steaming tea. 'Can I help in the meantime?'

Daniels sat back down. 'How badly injured is Jo Soulsby?'

'Hard to say. She sustained a nasty bang to the head.'

'Can I see her?'

'If it was up to me, you could . . .' Baker looked unsure. 'I think you'd better speak to her consultant first.'

Daniels cleared her throat. 'She will survive?'

'Oh, she'll live, all right.' The nurse teased her hair round her index finger, dropping her voice to a conspiratorial whisper. 'CT scan shows no permanent damage. She has a convenient loss of memory, if you know what I mean.'

Daniels was irritated. The woman was acting like a newspaper hack protecting an exclusive. She half expected her to wink and tap the side of her nose.

'What makes you say that?'

The nurse was off again, leaning forward, dropping her voice a touch, hyping up the intrigue. 'They all do it.'

Daniels brow creased. 'Excuse me?'

'Drunk drivers,' Baker said curtly. 'Want my opinion, you should lock her up and throw away the key.'

Now Daniels was really rattled. 'So, you're not only a nurse but judge and jury too – very impressive. Well, for your information, Jo Soulsby is a colleague and a friend, so maybe you'd like to keep your opinions to yourself.'

Before the nurse had time to back-pedal, Daniels' mobile began to vibrate. She took it from her pocket, flipped it open and stood up.

Baker bristled. 'You're not really supposed to—'

Daniels held her hand up to silence her. 'What is it, Andy?'

Brown sounded excited on the other end of the line. 'I found her,' he said.

'Hang on a minute . . .' Daniels left the office and shut the door behind her. 'OK, go ahead. But hurry up, I'm busy.'

'Jo's vehicle was involved in an accident yesterday afternoon. She's in the General. I'm on my way over there now.'

Daniels stopped dead in her tracks. 'No! Stay put, I'm in the area. Anyway, it might be more appropriate for a female to respond.'

Brown sounded deflated. 'You sure?'

'Yeah, I'm on it.'

Silence.

Daniels could almost hear him sulking on the other end. Before he had a chance to start whining, she ended the call and walked back to the nurse's station. Baker still had a face like a smacked arse. There was no time for small talk.

'I need to speak with Jo Soulsby's consultant now,' Daniels said. 'Can you get him for me please?'

Baker was just reaching for the phone when the door opened and a doctor in a white coat entered. Thorburn was an unattractive man, at least a foot shorter than Daniels, arrogant and with an unfriendly attitude. He was standing ever so slightly on his toes to gain a little height.

'Mark Thorburn, neurologist. You wanted to see me?'

'DCI Daniels.' Thorburn's palm was cold and clammy. 'Thank you for seeing me at such short notice. I know you must be busy.'

'How can I be of assistance?'

Daniels wiped her hand on the side of her jacket, hoping he hadn't noticed.

'I need your assessment of Josephine Soulsby's condition,' she said.

'I'm afraid I can't divulge that.' Thorburn folded his arms across his chest. 'I have to respect patient confidentiality, Detective Chief Inspector. And not just because of the compensation culture in this country – though clearly patients feel justified in suing doctors if they so much as breathe on them these days – but because it's written clearly in black and white in hospital regulations. Much like the rules that bind you, I imagine.'

Here we go. Daniels fought the temptation to grab the pompous arsehole by the lapels and do him for wasting police time. 'So you've no objection to me telling Ms Soulsby that her ex-husband and father of her children is now a murder statistic.'

Thorburn raised his bushy eyebrows a notch, pushing his specs a little further up the bridge of his nose. He glanced sideways at Baker, who looked as though she was having more fun than she'd had in years. Daniels wondered how long it would take her to spread the word.

'That doesn't change things,' Thorburn said.

'I beg to differ. It changes things considerably. Nurse Baker here tells me Ms Soulsby has suffered memory loss.'

Thorburn's reaction was predictable. He scowled at Baker, who immediately went scarlet and began examining the floor tiles. Daniels didn't give a damn that she'd dropped the nurse right in it. She had her own job to do.

'Will she get it back?' she asked.

'She regained consciousness within hours, so that's always a good sign.'

'You didn't answer my question.'

'The prognosis is favourable,' he intoned, adding that he could never guarantee a full recovery. He spoke in terms Daniels didn't fully understand. It was like hearing a medical science lecture. As her eyes glazed over, he took the hint and stopped talking.

'Thank you. Now, is your patient fit to be informed of the death or not?'

The neurologist wound his neck in. 'I assume you've spoken to her sons?'

'We're still trying to locate them. I understand that neither is in the area just now.'

'Then your intelligence is flawed.' A smug, almost triumphant, expression flashed across Thorburn's face as he spewed out the last word: 'They just left.'

30

There was a slight lull in proceedings in the incident room. The majority of MIT were out tracing potential witnesses, a few others were assisting with the house-to-house. All were engaged one way or another in finding new pieces of the jigsaw that was Stephens' murder.

As statement reader, Robson remained anchored to the office. It was his job to ensure continuity as information came in. He was taking a well-earned break by the coffee machine when he noticed DC Brown sulking at his desk.

'What's up? Robson asked. 'You look like you're about to spit the dummy.'

'I just traced Jo to the General Hospital,' Brown said. 'Car crash, according to Traffic.'

'Is she OK?'

'Dunno, do I?'

Robson dunked a biscuit in his coffee and lost the end of it in the cup. 'Bugger!' he said. 'Shouldn't you be out there, following it up?'

Brown looked at him. 'You'd think so, wouldn't you? Only, when I rang to tell the boss I was on my way over there, she told me to stay put, said she was in the area and would deal with it herself.'

'So? She's got a lot riding on this one.'

'Yeah, well, Eddie just came on duty. He saw her screaming into the General like a bloody tornado over fifteen minutes ago.'

At a nearby desk, Gormley's ears pricked up. 'And your point is?'

'My point is, she was obviously already there when I rang, though she never said so.' Brown flicked a paperclip off his desk. 'Instead she made some poxy excuse about it being preferable for a woman to attend.'

Robson spooned a sodden biscuit from his mug, dumping it in the bin. 'Like I said, she wants to get it right. This case could mean a crown on her shoulder.'

'Bollocks!' Brown said. 'She never pulls the sex card, ever!'

Gormley dropped his head, sifted the papers on his desk, acting as if it was business as usual when really his mind was elsewhere. He could smell a rat from a mile away and was deeply troubled by what he'd heard.

31

At six twenty-five on the dot, two young men re-entered Newcastle General Hospital and joined the queue for the lift that would take them back to their mother's private room. If anyone cared to notice, Tom Stephens was the more troubled of the two. He was staring intently at the floor indicator as the lift made its descent, anxiety and impatience getting the better of him.

James nudged him in the ribs. 'You know her?'

Following his brother's gaze, Tom turned his head to the left where a woman standing a short distance away, someone James said he felt sure he'd seen before but right at that moment couldn't place.

The woman ignored their interest.

'She doesn't seem to know you,' Tom said.

James gave a little shrug – but still he continued to wrack his brains.

They entered the same lift, travelled up in silence and got out on the same floor, the familiar woman heading for the nurse's station, the two brothers peeling off towards the female surgical ward, never suspecting what catastrophe lay ahead. Mark Thorburn intercepted them before they had a chance to reach their destination and they were now eyeing him suspiciously in a quiet relatives' room.

The neurologist hadn't even got started when James noticed the woman from the lift approaching. She stopped short of the door and hung around in the corridor outside. Then, suddenly, his brain made the connection and his imagination went into overdrive.

'She's a copper!' James announced suddenly. 'She works with Mum.' He looked accusingly at Thorburn, putting two and two together, making five. 'Shit! Mum isn't . . .' He couldn't bring himself to finish the question.

Thorburn rushed to reassure him. 'No, no, nothing like that. Your mother is making steady progress. In fact, we've moved her from high-dependency.'

'What then?' Tom asked. 'Why can't we see her?'

There was definitely something Thorburn wasn't telling them. He shifted in his seat as if he had something awful to say but didn't quite know how to start.

'She is a police officer and she is here to see you,' he said, eventually.

Tom and James exchanged glances.

James felt in his pocket. Brown's police calling card was still there.

'Concerning what?' he said.

'She'd better tell you herself . . .'

Thorburn went to the door and invited Daniels in. As she entered the room, both brothers stood up. Thorburn fluffed the introductions, but it mattered not. Neither lad was remotely interested in a word he had to say. They were both too busy searching Daniels' face for answers.

James tackled her head on: 'Is my mother in trouble?'

'I hope not.'

'What the fuck does that mean?' he said.

'I have some bad news,' Daniels said softly. 'I'm afraid your father is dead.'

Tom's reaction was immediate. He began to sob un-controllably. The sound of a tea trolley passing the room was an incongruous intrusion on his grief. As it moved off, clattering along the corridor, Thorburn caught Daniels' angry expression. He got up, closed the internal window blinds and slipped quietly from the room, shutting the door behind him.

Daniels gave them a moment, then said, 'I'd like to tell your mother now—'

'No! I'll do it,' James cut in.

'I'm sorry, James. But, under the circumstances, I can't allow that.'

'Why not?'

'What circumstances?' Tom asked. 'And what's it got to do with the police?'

'Your father didn't die of natural causes . . .' Daniels paused, making absolutely sure the two men understood. 'Nor was it an accident. I'm sorry to have to tell you, but we've launched a murder enquiry.'

As Tom's hand went to his mouth, James' expression hard-ened. He bit his lip, fighting to keep his emotions in check. The DCI's words had stunned both brothers into silence. They sat down.

'There must be some mistake,' Tom said.

Daniels shook her head. 'There's no mistake.'

She'd seen the same reaction countless times. Denial was often the first response in situations like these. In the coming days he would process the information – eventually come to accept it.

Tom looked up. 'Does Monica know?'

The mention of their stepmother's name made Daniels' ears prick up.

James looked at his brother with disgust, his eyes cold and disbelieving. He rounded on him. 'Who gives a shit about Monica? It's Mum I'm concerned about.' Then, to Daniels: 'She'll be devastated. There was a lot of unfinished business when our parents split up. I don't think she ever really got over it.'

'That's private family stuff!' Tom blurted out.

'Why are you really here?' James fixed the DCI with a penetrating stare. 'Mum's not his next of kin.'

32

Rain thundered against the window pane of the private hospital room, but the patient lay in peaceful oblivion, hooked up to all manner of drips and monitors. Years of experience had taught Daniels that injuries, particularly ones from road-traffic accidents, often looked worse than they actually were. Even so, she hadn't expected to see quite as much swelling or bruising on her colleague's face.

Daniels stood for a while, contemplating the part of the job that every officer loathes, the part where the truth had to be told and told now – irrespective of the circumstances; a task made doubly difficult by knowing the woman personally. How could she justify heaping yet more suffering on Jo?

Did she have the right to hold back?

The report on the accident made scary reading. The attending Traffic officer had found black parallel skid marks snaking across the tarmac, a deep gouge in the embankment where Jo's BMW had taken off as she swerved to avoid a falling tree. Fortunately for her there was a gap in the drystone wall where it came to land on its roof. Otherwise, according to the experts, the crash would certainly have been fatal.

Daniels sighed.

Bending down, she unhooked a medical chart from the foot of the bed and tried to decipher Thorburn's scribbles:

unconscious when found, confusion on admittance, query cranium bleed, cardiac arrest.

Shaken to the core, but trying to keep a lid on it, Daniels went to the window and looked out over a forbidding sky. She wondered if Jo Soulsby would ever make a full recovery.

'Took you long enough,' a croaky voice said.

Daniels spun round and rushed to the bedside, taking Jo's hand in hers. 'You scared the hell out of me,' she said.

Jo attempted a smile. 'I'm touched you still care.'

'I'm not sure I should,' Daniels was in bits, the lump in her throat almost choking her. A single warm tear fell heavily from her right eye and landed on her cheek. She wiped it away with the back of her hand.

'Don't start blubbing, Kate. It really doesn't suit you,' Jo moaned. 'My head feels like shit. Would you . . .?'

As Daniels helped her to sit up in bed, the two women came very close physically, locked eyes briefly, a real sexual tension between them – so close and yet miles apart. It was an intense moment, interrupted by Nurse Baker, who looked in briefly. She checked a drip and then disappeared again, smiling at Jo as she left the room.

'See, it's not all bad,' Jo said. 'You know I'm a sucker for a uniform.'

Daniels didn't respond.

Jo forced a grin. 'Then again, you never could handle the competition.'

'Your sick sense of humour's still intact, I see . . .' Daniels pulled herself together, got serious: 'Your lads are waiting to see you.'

'Tell them I've no cash on me. That'll send them packing.'

Seeing that Jo was still uncomfortable, Daniels moved to support her body with one arm, while plumping up her pillows with the other. No sooner had she eased her back down than the combined effects of the medication and the effort required just to sit up took their toll. Jo was fast asleep . . .

33

A clap of thunder rumbled overhead as Carmichael drove out of the city, turning her wipers up a notch so as not to miss the turning.

Three miles further on, she reached the residential heart of upmarket Gosforth and the Victorian splendour of the Weston Hotel, set back off the A1. Though she'd never been inside, Carmichael knew it catered for the discerning business and tourist traveller alike – as long as they had deep pockets, from the look of the cars outside. Beneath a covered portico, a smart limousine was dropping someone off. There were no free parking spaces close to the entrance, so she drove round the back, pulling between some recycling bins and a stack of empty crates.

In the hotel's plush foyer, five businessmen were huddled together at a table near the window. Talking in low whispers, they looked more like a gang of thieves plotting their next big job than a group of corporate lawyers holding a business meeting. They looked up as an elegant woman swept in like a summer breeze, gliding to reception leaving the scent of her perfume drifting subtly in her wake. She was exquisitely dressed, might just have stepped off the cover of *Vogue*. The concierge jumped to attention, handed her a key, and accompanied her to an elevator that only went to the penthouse suite.

As the lift doors closed in front of her, she smiled briefly at the lawyers and then at the young woman who had just walked through the door. Carmichael was soaked to the skin, water dripping off her clothes and on to the floor, strands of bedraggled hair clinging to her red face. The contrast between the two women could not have been more obvious. Embarrassed by her appearance, Carmichael hurried to the desk where a member of staff checked her ID and took her in the service lift to a less salubrious part of the hotel, a small room in the warm basement far away from the eyes of paying guests. She was offered a towel to dry her hair and advised that the security guards she'd come to see would be along very shortly.

By the time they arrived, Carmichael looked a bit more like a detective and a little less like a drowned rat. She spent the next hour poring over Fitzgerald's list, checking the seating plan against invitations handed in at the door. One of the guards told her that security had been a major consideration at the prestigious event.

'No invitation meant strictly no admittance,' he said. 'Company policy, on account of the high-profile guests.'

Unconvinced, Carmichael threw a spanner in to test them out. 'But if someone turned up without an invitation – for argument's sake, someone *really* important – for a few quid you'd let them in, right?'

A fleeting look from one guard to another provided a truthful answer.

'Yeah, that's what I thought,' Carmichael said.

34

Lightning suddenly lit up Jo's room. Counting the seconds between the flash and the next crack of thunder, Daniels calculated that the eye of the storm was around five miles away – somewhere south of the river.

Jo stirred in the bed.

Daniels looked on, a deep sadness gnawing at her heart. They'd once shared so much more than a passion for solving cases. She wished things were different between them and thought of all the reasons why they were not. Nobody – not her father, not even Jo – had ever come before her ambition to reach the very top.

She had to speak to her now – she still had a job to do.

'Why didn't you tell me Alan was back?' she said gently.

It was a good question; one that had niggled Daniels from the very second she'd come across Stephens' body. Jo was many things, but it wasn't in her nature to be secretive. When push came to shove, she always told the truth. Like the day she ended their relationship because Daniels refused to 'come out'.

The worst day of her life.

Jo chose not to answer.

'You knew he was in the country?' Daniels pushed.

She waited for a response. Jo might have come up with any

number of excuses, but clearly she didn't want to talk. Well, she'd have to sometime, whether she liked it or not. Better to Daniels than to one of her colleagues.

'Talk to me, Jo . . . We found his body two nights ago.'

Jo shut her eyes and turned away, her emotions spilling over. Daniels had known it was coming. She got up from the bed and walked to the window, unsure of where to go next.

She spoke without turning around. 'Do you want me to get the kids?'

'No, I need to be on my own. I want you to go now.'

Daniels turned back to face her. 'Things are not that simple. I'm looking into Alan's death. You know I can't do that if anyone finds out about us.'

'Aren't you forgetting – there *is* no us!' Jo stopped talking as a second flash of lightning lit up the room, quickly followed by a rumble of thunder. The lights flickered on and off. The storm was getting closer. 'Oh my God! How did he . . .? Kate?'

Daniels looked at the floor.

'He was murdered!?' It seemed to take for ever for the news to hit home. 'You don't think I—'

'Don't be stupid!'

'You're not sure, are you?' Jo laughed, then filled up. 'You seriously think I might have put a bullet in his head?'

An unfortunate choice of words.

Being suspicious was in Daniels' nature, an integral part of who she was and why she was good at her job. But then again, so was a sense of fair play. Everyone deserved the benefit of the doubt. *Once.* Innocent until proven guilty, there was nothing wrong with that.

Daniels had no idea just how she'd managed to reach this

particular hard place, even less idea of how she could find her way back from it. She moved towards Jo, touching her arm gently.

Jo pulled away. 'Don't touch me! What's in it for you, Kate? Offer you a promotion, did they?'

Silence.

Jo smirked. 'Oh, that is priceless. They really know how to push your buttons.'

Daniels tried to stay calm, tried to think of the right thing to say – and got it wrong all over again. 'Look, taking this case has landed me right in it. Please, Jo. Listen to me—'

'No. You listen to me. Whatever you're up to—'

'I'm trying to protect you!'

'You sure that's why you're here?'

'Don't, Jo.'

'Why not? Your job comes first, doesn't it?'

'That's unfair!'

'What is it with you and the police force? It's just a job, Kate. It isn't real. *We* were real, you and me! We had something good, something other people would give their right arm for. But it wasn't enough for you, was it? Why d'you think I—'

Daniels cut her off. 'It'll be different this time, I promise.'

Jo wanted to believe her. 'Yeah, well it's a bit late now.'

Daniels failed to notice her press the buzzer for assistance until it was too late. Thorburn was first through the door, followed closely by Nurse Baker, Tom and James. She slipped quietly from the room – there was nothing more to be said.

35

The lights dimmed as the Metro train rattled into the tunnel. The woman seemed terrified, but he was just marvelling at human nature. She couldn't help herself watching his reflection in the black window, checking on the intensity of his gaze. He looked down at the *Evening Chronicle* someone had left on the seat and reread the article, his temper boiling in his gut.

> A murder enquiry continues following the discovery of a body at a prestigious Quayside apartment in the early hours of Friday morning. A police press official said that, until the results of a post-mortem are known, they are unable to confirm how the man died. We are led to believe that he has been identified. The Senior Investigating Officer, Detective Chief Inspector Kate Daniels, today appealed for witnesses to contact the Murder Investigation Team.

His agitation grew. He'd expected a visit by now and yet the silly cow was still pussyfooting around asking the public for help. How much bloody help did she need? What kind of SIO was she anyhow?

'She's not even a fucking superintendent!' he muttered under his breath.

*

The woman's heart raced. *What did he say?* Was he talking to her? He was probably one of them psychopaths she'd read about. He'd probably escaped from some mental institution, mistaken her for someone else.

God, help me!

Tightening her grip on her bag, she pulled her skirt down over her knees and looked around her. The carriage was busy. All young people. Heading out? Heading home? Laughing. Texting. Paying her no attention. Trains unnerved her. They always had. The Metro especially. She wished she'd left earlier and paid extra for a cab. The creep had been staring at her since the last stop, his eyes sliding over her, taking in every detail of her face, each button on her jacket, the cut of her skirt, her legs, her shoes. She didn't want to think about why he was examining her so closely, sizing her up, or what his intentions were. He was filthy and unshaven. Probably drunk or high on drugs, she thought. And yet, he had a presence, an awareness about him that suggested otherwise.

Avoiding his gaze, she shifted uncomfortably in her seat. But looking out of the window didn't help. For the second time in as many weeks, a power failure had plunged the north of the city into total darkness, creating chaos and cutting off twenty thousand homes. As the train sped along there were no references outside, no familiar landmarks, no moon, just the odd candle flickering in houses that backed on to the track.

Otherwise, only pitch darkness.

And those eyes . . .

The Metro slowed. He looked at her, a sneer almost. Should she move while she had the chance? Get off? Stay put? What if he followed her? Her body was frozen to the spot, refusing to obey her instructions. Too late. A buzzer sounded. The doors were closing.

Sighing, he glanced at the paper again, an idea forming in his head. Taking a pen from his pocket, he wrote her name on the back of his hand: Detective Chief Inspector Kate Daniels. Maybe they needed to get better acquainted . . .

Maybe . . .

He'd like that.

But for now he had only one thing on his mind. Shoving the newspaper on the floor, he slid his hand inside his pocket and grinned at the woman sitting opposite. Her face paled as he withdrew the scissors, toying with them, teasing her for a while, unchecked by anyone in the carriage.

Where was a guard when you wanted one, eh?

It had taken a while, but he'd traced his next victim. He'd trace them all eventually. Shows what an education can do. Classroom dunce to computer wizard in one stretch. Sweet. Didn't they realize he was a genius? He cut around Malik's smiling face. Still alive, but not for long. He held the picture up to his new friend and travelling companion. Fuck her! Tomorrow morning he'd be on his way. Crack of dawn. All the more special because it was a Sunday.

He winked at the woman.

Lucky for her he'd looked at it today.

36

Gormley was noshing a fry-up enthusiastically when Daniels caught up with him in the station canteen. There were no home comforts here. It was a no-frills refreshment area designed to get the punters in and out in the shortest possible time. Standards had dropped since the force had contracted out the catering. Daniels hadn't eaten a hot meal there for weeks. Opting for a cup of tea and a sandwich, she thanked the woman behind the counter and headed for Gormley's table.

He spoke with his mouth full. 'Any update on Jo?'

Daniels lifted the top off her sandwich and found that the filling was non-existent. As she shoved it away in disgust, Gormley leaned across the table and helped himself to the bread. He began piling beans on top of it, scooping up escapees with a fork.

She grimaced. 'Christ, Hank, how can you eat that?'

Gormley clearly had no idea what she was on about. Wiping a piece of bread around his plate, he continued with his meal as if it had been lovingly prepared by a gourmet chef. 'I hear she's in a hell of a mess,' he said. 'Someone on D Rota told me she flat-lined in the ambulance. That right?'

Daniels nodded soberly.

'Mind if I stick my oar in?' Gormley stopped chewing, pushed his plate away and wiped his hands on a serviette.

Daniels got the feeling that she wasn't going to like what he had to say. But she was too preoccupied with Jo to give it serious thought. Things were already just as bad as they could be. 'You need to watch your back,' he said. 'Andy's noticed you're on a mission, not delegating as an SIO should.'

'Well, Andy should mind his own business.'

He looked at her like a concerned friend would.

'What?' she said, biting his head off.

'This is your big chance, Kate. I'd hate to see you blow it.'

She met his gaze defiantly, checked her watch and swallowed the last dregs of her tea. 'Eat up. You can walk me back to the office. I've got an interview to conduct.'

Minutes later, Daniels entered an interview room with no windows, four chairs and a table with peeled-back Formica edges. Robson was hovering near the door and James Stephens was sitting at the table. Daniels smiled at the lad as she sat down too and relaxed back in her chair, trying to reinforce the fact that the interview was informal. It clearly wasn't working. James' customary bravado had deserted him: he was sweating profusely, tapping his fingers on his knees, eyeing a tape machine housed in a recess in the wall.

Sensing his anxiety, she pointed at the tape. 'Relax, James, it isn't switched on. You're not under caution. I just want to find out as much as possible about your father, then you can go. I imagine it's been a long day for you. You'll be keen to get home . . .'

James wasn't reassured. His eyes darted from Daniels to Robson and back again, before settling on a tiny camera mounted in the corner of the room.

'Can you please tell us when you last saw your father?' Daniels asked.

'About five years ago, give or take. Don't remember exactly.'

'That's a long time.'

'Not if you knew him. He was over here on business, condescended to see us for an hour, then he did what he did best and took off again – forgot we ever existed.'

'You didn't see him three years ago when Tom did?'

James instantly became defensive. 'So what?'

'Why was that?' Daniels pushed gently.

'I was busy.'

'Tom made time.'

'Tom's easily pleased!'

Daniels watched him like a hawk. The lad was so like his mother, she could almost feel Jo's presence in the room. And that unnerved her.

Robson sat down next to her. 'Don't piss about, James. We're just trying to find out who killed your father.'

'Biological father!'

'Whatever,' Robson said.

'Just making a point. Takes more than flesh and blood – know what I'm saying?'

'Fair enough.' Daniels registered the unhealthy family dynamics. Tom Stephens had been cagey about his brother's ambivalent relationship with the deceased. She wondered how deep that went. She smiled at James, trying to reassure him. 'Right now, I'm not too keen on my old man either.'

Sensing that she knew exactly where he was coming from, James calmed down a little, dropped his shoulders and some of his attitude. 'Look, my father was a prat. He treated my mother like shit and probably reaped what he sowed, OK?'

Daniels liked his style. In her experience of murder detection she'd learned that honesty was by far the best policy. Most killers she'd ever dealt with tripped themselves up by telling lies. Unless James Stephens had mastered the art of the double bluff, she thought it unlikely that he would speak about his father in such negative terms – if he had actually killed him.

She changed tack: 'And how is your relationship with Monica?'

'She's just another one of my father's tarts.'

'Why do you say that?'

'She wasn't the first. Probably wouldn't have been the last, either. Surprised you didn't know that already.' James looked at his watch. 'How long are you keeping me here?'

'I've told you, you're free to go at any time.'

'Right! I'm out of here. My brother's waiting.'

James' chair scraped the hard wooden floor as he got to his feet. Daniels and DS Robson followed suit. They didn't try to stop him from leaving but, just as he reached the door, Robson asked one final question.

'Just one more thing, James . . .' He waited for the lad to turn round. 'Where were you *exactly* on the night of November fifth, early hours of the sixth?'

'In Sheffield at Uni – you can check.'

Daniels nodded. 'We will.'

James walked out into the corridor, shoulders hunched, head down. Daniels switched her attention to the window, watching as he left the building by a side door. From where she was standing, she could see Tom Stephens waiting near the perimeter fence. He was leaning against an old VW, smoking a cigarette. When he caught sight of his brother, Tom took one last hit of nicotine and flicked the butt high into the air. It landed on top of a panda car, sending red sparks flying. They got in the VW and drove off.

Daniels turned to Robson. 'Walk me to my car, tell me what you think.'

They left the station via the same door as James, arriving in the car park just in time to see the VW disappearing down a side street.

'No love lost there, then,' Robson said. 'Between father and son, I mean. The younger one's particularly bitter.'

'That's families for you. Complete pain in the arse, if you ask me,' Daniels said, her thoughts turning briefly to her own father, whose respect she coveted and thought she deserved. These days, it was hard to imagine that there had ever been a father–daughter bond between them. As far as she was concerned, that was *his* loss.

Robson clammed up, unsure how to handle her sarcasm. They had arrived at her car. She reached into her pocket, took out her key and pushed the button on the fob. The locks clunked open and she climbed in, leaving the door ajar. Robson stooped down, ducking his head, his hands on the roof of the vehicle.

'You think James realized he just gave Jo a motive?'

Daniels looked past him, brooding.

Robson back-pedalled a little. 'I know we don't think she's involved, but it's *possible* she had something to do with it. We all have the capacity, given the right set of circumstances. She could have hired someone to do her dirty work for her. Let's face it, she has access to some pretty heavy criminals. Some who'd cut a person's throat for the price of a heroin deal.'

'Or else we are barking up the wrong tree entirely and it's not family related at all. Which is what I have been saying from the very beginning.'

'You're right. Don't know what I was thinking.' Robson blushed. 'On the subject of families, though, I've been meaning to ask, boss: How would you feel about being a godparent to Callum? Irene and I would love it if you would.'

There was a definite shift in Daniels' mood. There was a time she'd have been delighted – honoured even – but not any more. She didn't want to cause offence, but she wanted to be a godparent even less.

'Sorry, Robbo.' She started the car. 'I don't do religion these days. Not even for you.'

37

Next morning, Daniels arranged for some food to be sent in. It wasn't exactly Sunday roast, but it would see them through a busy day. Murder enquiries didn't stop just because it was the weekend.

Drawing her eyes away from the gruesome pictures on the murder wall, still feeling bad about turning Robson down so abruptly the previous night, she was about to have a conciliatory word with him when DC Carmichael called her over to have a look at something on the incident-room TV.

'Yes, Lisa. What is it?'

'Boss, take a look at this.'

Eyes fixed like glue to the screen, Carmichael stood poised, her thumb hovering over the remote control's pause button, waiting to freeze a precise image. Daniels joined her and the two stood shoulder to shoulder, observing CCTV footage as it followed a cycle from floor to floor, location to location, within the Weston Hotel.

'There!' Carmichael cried.

The screen was now still, frozen on a clear image of Felicity Wood and Alan Stephens exiting a hotel room, his hand planted firmly on her bum. Carmichael ran the tape on and picked up the couple as they made their way down the corridor to the lift. A sign above it clearly showed FLOOR 4.

Carmichael rewound the tape at double speed, then moved the cursor, zooming in on a door number: 429.

She looked to her left.

Daniels was beaming. 'Gotcha!' she said.

Just then the door to the incident room burst open and Bright walked through it, flicking his eyes backwards over his shoulder. Looking beyond him, Daniels saw Maxwell in hot pursuit, a film of sweat clearly visible on his brow, his face all red and blotchy.

'Guv, a word, if I may?' Maxwell was out of breath.

'Make it quick,' Bright said, 'the DCI is about to start her briefing.'

Maxwell hesitated before letting them have it with both barrels: 'The squad have been helping themselves to my biscuits and stolen coffee from my drawer. I want it back.'

Bright feigned serious concern. 'Is that right?'

'Theft is a very serious allegation, Neil,' Daniels was smiling. 'You should call a detective.'

'I am!' Maxwell snapped at them. 'I'm calling them all thieving bastards!'

As he stomped off in disgust, mumbling about their casual attitude to a criminal offence, Bright turned to Daniels.

'Interesting management strategy,' he said, struggling to contain his laughter.

She made a face. 'He asked for it.'

'And he certainly got it!' Bright grinned at Carmichael. 'Watch and learn, Lisa. Your new SIO clearly has what it takes. And you do, too, I reckon. In fact, you're both looking pleased with yourselves. Has there been an update on Soulsby?'

Daniels held back her annoyance. 'Her name is Jo, guv. And I think the term is, "as well as can be expected".'

'I stand corrected.' Bright stifled a grin. 'Shall we get on?'

With Carmichael there, Daniels couldn't challenge him. 'You're staying?'

'Thought I might sit in, if that's OK with you?'

'I'm surprised you have time.' Daniels hoped he'd take the hint and stop looking over her shoulder, but it seemed he just couldn't help himself. 'I heard you had someone in.'

'You heard right, but the sick bastard's not going to cough. First the brief screams for a medical review because our suspect's just been discharged from St George's – which, incidentally, came out in our favour – and then he insists on eight hours' sleep following six of interrogation.' Bright gave a little shrug. 'Suits me fine. The search team are doing a number on his client's house. I'm letting both buggers stew. ' He glanced at the murder wall. 'You going to fill me in or not?'

'Jo's movements remain unclear in the hours leading up to the murder.'

Still rattled by his interference, Daniels didn't offer more. She was pleased her guv'nor had made an arrest. Of course she was. If his suspect was charged, the whole community would rest easier in their beds. He'd get good press too: chance to be the local hero, the main man. Chance to remind everyone that he was the most successful detective the force had ever seen. He needed that. The only downside was that, if he didn't back off of her own investigation, she'd end up in the same psychiatric hospital to which he'd just referred.

'And her sons?' Bright pushed.

'The eldest, Tom, has been eliminated. We have unequivocal

proof that he was on a flight from Tenerife at the time of his father's death—'

'Word is, Robbo found two bags in her hallway,' Bright cut in.

'Don't you start! I'd hazard a guess at Tom's dirty washing, wouldn't you?' Daniels looked him right in the eye. 'Guv, you can't think Jo had anything to do with this.'

Bright raised an anything-is-possible eyebrow.

'Then you're a mile wrong.' Daniels smiled at Carmichael. 'Lisa just clocked Stephens leaving a room at the Weston Hotel with a woman from his apartment block.'

'Is that right?' Bright said. 'Well, things *are* looking up.'

'And Monica Stephens gave an account of her movements that doesn't quite add up,' Daniels added. 'There was no flight from Newcastle airport to London at the time of night she allegedly saw off Teresa Branson – who, incidentally, has gone AWOL. Repeated calls to her mobile phone have gone unanswered. Oh, and you might like to take a look at this . . .' She led Bright to a chart positioned a few feet away. Turning over the front cover, she revealed a circular seating plan resembling a huge green squash ball with a red dot at its centre. 'I'll let Lisa explain this. It's all *her* good work.'

Carmichael pushed her shoulders back, pleased to have made a good impression.

'The red dot indicates Stephens' position at the charity dinner,' she said. 'The surrounding green area represents the tables nearest to him. I've managed to identify every guest within this circle.'

'Excellent, Lisa.' Bright was impressed. 'What have you done to ensure all these witnesses are traced?'

Carmichael pointed towards the receiver's desk. 'Harry is fast-tracking actions as we speak, and detectives from Area Command are lending a hand to get through them ASAP.'

Hearing his name, DS Harry Holt looked up and threw in his contribution. 'If an action comes back unclear, guv, it'll bounce straight back to them.'

'Fair enough,' Bright said, turning back to Carmichael. 'You're certain security collected invitations from everybody?'

'That's company policy at the Weston, guv,' Carmichael said. 'I interviewed the security staff myself. No invitation was supposed to mean strictly no admittance.'

'But if someone made it worth their while, they'd turn a blind eye, right?'

'That was the impression I got. Security pay is poor.'

Bright nodded. 'And this was definitely the seating plan they used?'

'Yeah, but . . .' Carmichael glanced again at Daniels. 'They may have played musical chairs.'

Daniels grinned. *Carmichael was learning fast.* Turning to face the assembled squad, she raised her voice to gain their attention and pointed at Carmichael's chart. 'Listen up, everyone! I want you all to familiarize yourself with this plan.' Taking in the collective nod of heads, she noticed Maxwell attempting to sneak back in without drawing attention to himself. 'Neil, what's the state of play with the house-to-house?'

Maxwell turned beetroot. Being singled out was not something he'd anticipated. He promptly knocked his notes off his desk and scrambled around the floor on all fours trying to retrieve them – irritating Bright in the process.

'In your own time . . .' Bright rolled his eyes. Unable to resist an opportunity to pull Maxwell's leg, he added: 'You look like you could do with a shot of coffee, Detective.'

'No residents on the third floor of Court Mews heard or saw anything, guv,' Maxwell puffed, trying to gather papers and his thoughts at the same time. 'The fireworks display was well advertised and most had made arrangements to go out for the evening. We do have a witness at number 28: Mrs Kim Foreman—'

He stopped mid-sentence. When he looked up from the floor he was sweating profusely and his notes were all mixed up. The guv'nor towered over him, clearly out of patience. The rest of the squad weren't helping either; their gawking was making him even more flustered. Finally, he got his act together and stood up, scratching his left ear, something he tended to do when he was nervous.

'Mrs Foreman is a dancer at Rivaldo's nightclub. She began her shift at around seven and was due to work until closing on Thursday night, but she went home early—'

'Why early?' Daniels asked.

'Said she was feeling ill. Anyway, she remembers hearing raised voices, one male, one female, definitely arguing.'

Daniels wanted more. 'Exactly where does she live in relation to the victim?'

Maxwell bowed his head, trying his best to avoid eye contact with her and with Bright. It was obvious to everyone in the room that he didn't know the answer.

'I'll find out,' he said.

'Come on, man!' Bright said. 'You must have some bloody idea.'

'Have you not drawn up a plan?' Daniels asked.

Maxwell glowered at Carmichael, who was trying not to look smug. 'Not yet,' he said.

'That's not good enough!' Bright was almost yelling.

'Get it done, ASAP,' Daniels said quietly. 'Is there anything else?'

'No, nothing.' Maxwell's relief was obvious. At last they were going to move on to someone else and leave him alone.

Bright, however, was not done with him yet: 'I think you mean nothing else, *thank you, ma'am.*'

Maxwell looked as though he wanted the floor to open up and swallow him. He hung his head in shame, steeling himself for a blasting. There was a moment's silence and then Bright left the room.

38

Daniels was carrying a rolled-up plan of Court Mews as she entered the building with Bright in tow. The crime scene was crawling with SOCOs, who had obviously given the place a thorough going-over. They'd finished sweeping the living room, had just moved out into the corridor and now stepped to one side to enable the detectives to pass through.

In the living room, Daniels spread the plan out on the sofa. She studied it a while and then looked up thoughtfully. Bright could see she wasn't happy.

'Problem?' he asked.

'Nothing I can't handle.'

'You sure?'

'Every floor in this block is identical to this one. Kim Foreman claims she heard a heated argument going on at the time of Stephens' death. Felicity Wood – the woman caught on CCTV with him at the Weston Hotel – denies any knowledge of it. They live next door to each other on the floor above. As you can see, Wood's flat is *directly* above us and she reported hearing a loud bang just after midnight, which she thinks came from inside rather than outside the building.'

'The shot that killed Stephens?'

'Maybe.'

'Will she make a compelling witness?'

'Should do. She's a brief with Graham & Abercrombie. D'you know her?'

Bright shrugged. 'No. Do you?'

Daniels shook her head. She rolled up the plan, securing each end with an elastic band. For a split second, Stephens' body was back on the floor. Daniels put the plan down and let out a sigh. Working hard was one thing; keeping secrets was really taking it out of her. Fortunately, Bright hadn't noticed her stress.

'Did she investigate the noise?' he asked.

Daniels shook her head again. 'Odd, isn't it? You'd think that someone with the curiosity of a solicitor might have done. I know I would have. She thought it was too risky . . . her words, not mine. In fact, she wasn't very forthcoming at all, really. She seems reluctant to get involved, full stop.'

'I hope you put her in her place?'

'Give it time, guv . . . I'm not finished with her yet.'

Daniels walked to the window and looked out at the Millennium Bridge; a giant curved structure known locally as the 'blinking eye'. Her own eyes followed a large party of students making their way across the river to The Baltic, a converted flour mill, now a centre for contemporary art, the largest gallery of its type in the world. For a miserable November day, it was attracting a lot of interest. Daniels wondered if there was a special exhibition on. She and Jo Soulsby had been there many times. It was a favourite haunt of theirs. Most days it was crammed with an eclectic mix of lunching ladies, tourists, art buffs and shoppers. The food was excellent, the view from the rooftop restaurant stunning.

Bright joined her by the window. He looked at his watch.

'I'm bloody starving. Come on, I'll shout you lunch before we head back.'

'I can't, guv. I've got too much on.'

'We have to eat, don't we?'

'I said I'd meet Hank.'

They took the lift to the ground floor, left the apartment building from its main entrance and walked in silence to his car. Bright got in and hesitated before starting the engine.

'So . . .' he said. 'Want to share what's eating you?'

Daniels knew full well he wasn't referring to the case, but didn't let on. 'Just these conflicting statements, that's all.'

There was a wry smile on Bright's face. He hadn't been fooled for a second. He placed his key in the ignition and waited for the diesel indicator light to go off. 'Want me to go and interrogate them?' he said.

'Don't take the piss, guv. All I'm saying is that if Foreman heard an argument and Wood didn't, what does that tell us?'

He grinned. 'Wood's a bit mutton?'

His joke fell on stony ground; Daniels was in no frame of mind for frivolity. 'I think Wood was the one arguing,' she said. 'But who with? And was she the one pulling the trigger?'

'Why don't you bring her in?'

'I will – when I'm ready.'

'Any witnesses who might corroborate Foreman's account?'

'Only one: Mrs Close from number 25. Someone's on it.'

Daniels was impatient to get back. Sensing this, Bright turned his engine over. He pulled out of his parking spot and turned right along the river road. Heading west, he took a left at the roundabout to avoid a well-known bottleneck. Daniels approved. It was a route she would've taken too.

'Now . . .' Bright glanced sideways at her. 'What's really eating you?'

She mimicked him. 'You *really* have to ask?'

He kept his eyes on the road. 'You're still chewing about Sarah Short, right?'

'Who wouldn't be, with a psychopathic moron on the loose?'

39

He left the train invisible in a sea of strangers all shuffling towards the exit gate of platform 10b. As he walked towards it, he could see that the filth were out in force, automatic weapons at the ready, eyes searching for a terrorist with a darker skin than his.

Perfect.

He could slip in and out, do what he'd come to do, right under their very noses. Even as a kid he'd had the luck of the Irish, an uncanny knack of getting away with things when the chips were down. He smiled, reminded of all the times his mother had accompanied him to court, expecting he'd be put away, only to have to grin and bear it when – seeing his innocent face and puny frame – the magistrates had ordered the tossers in Probation to write reports, giving him *just one last chance.*

No shit!

Juvenile justice? Fucking joke, more like! If that wasn't permission to do it all over again, he didn't know what was. They might just as well have handed him the matches to start the fires, the knives, the guns . . .

This one felt warm against his hip.

He'd use it only the once.

His mother could no longer hurt him or fill his head with

the teachings of the Lord. If she thought she could still beat him into submission, she was sorely mistaken. He was much stronger than she could ever imagine. Who was fucking with whose head now? Killing those she held dear had given him a reason for living, a goal to aim towards, a foundation on which to rebuild his life, an incentive to survive two decades of being caged like an animal and cast out from society. And now he was back, ready to make up for lost time, willing and able to make the necessary sacrifices.

Just a little longer.

Until he reached the end of his cherished list.

Then he'd off his father right in front of her.

With a cocky swagger, he disappeared into a city of a million people, none of whom knew his name. He was ready to do his worst. Ready to begin a Jihad of his own; one guaranteed to bring about his own brand of paradise right here on the streets of Birmingham.

One bombshell.

One Muslim.

Sounds reasonable.

A racially motivated crime . . . that wasn't.

It cracked him up.

40

'I'm listening . . .' Bright said, negotiating a tricky left-hand turn.

'No, guv. If you were, we wouldn't be having this conversation,' Daniels said.

'What the hell does that mean?'

'OK, you asked, so I'll tell you. If you insist on overseeing this enquiry, I want out. I'm being kept in the dark and you obviously have no faith in me.'

'That is absolute rubbish and you know it.' Bright ran an amber light, just as it changed to red. 'You can do this job with your hands tied behind your back. The whole team aspire to be just like you – and why wouldn't they? There's nobody I'd rather see make it to the very top, Kate. You're the best detective I've ever worked with—'

'Oh, you remembered!' Daniels bit back. 'Yeah, well, I am the best, and that's precisely why I won't be undermined. I'm serious, guv. And if you don't like it, well, tough!'

Bright cursed as he missed the turning. They were both silent for a while. Daniels wished he'd get a move on. Hank was waiting for her back at the station and the atmosphere in the car was chilly, to say the least. All she wanted from her boss was a little honesty. Was that too much to ask?

Yeah, right! How hypocritical did that sound? Even in her own head!

Daniels looked out of the side window as they cut up off the Quayside and headed into the centre of town. She felt a pang of misery settle heavily in her chest. She'd been on the verge of telling Bright the truth, confiding in him, asking for his support, but at the last minute she'd lost her bottle and pulled back. She just couldn't do it. Instead, she'd dug a hole big enough to bury not only herself but her precious career as well. The way she saw it, telling her boss would've seemed more of a betrayal than not telling him. But he'd been her boss for ever – wouldn't he have understood?

Hell might freeze over first.

The station recreation room was nearly always empty at this time of day, serving as a quiet space where people could talk without fear of being overheard. For years Bright had used it to brainstorm difficult cases, preferring a less formal environment than an incident room bursting with distractions. Many cases had been broken within those four walls and – while the informality wasn't her personal style – Daniels had to concede that it was results that counted in the end.

It was a dingy space, strewn with all sorts of personal paraphernalia: make-up, books, magazines, discarded clothing. A full-size pool table in the corner had been abandoned mid-game. Bright picked up a snooker cue, set up the triangle in the appropriate spot and took his first shot, striking the cue ball hard, sending the others flying in every direction.

Gormley watched one ball dribble into a side pocket. 'That was a complete fluke!'

Bright eyed up his next shot and chose the harder of two options, confident he could pot it. 'So . . .' He drew back the cue. 'What's the story with the ACC?'

'He's on his way back from Scotland as we speak, apparently . . .' Gormley said. 'Rumour has it he wants my warrant card.'

Bright grinned, potting another ball in the corner pocket. He winked at Daniels and walked round the table, considering all the available angles. But after his show of concentration he missed the side pocket by a whisper. As Gormley stepped up to take his turn, Bright leaned against the wall, arms folded, feet crossed over one another – a serious expression on his face.

Daniels knew he was thinking about the fruit-bat in the cells. By the time they had got back to the station her guv'nor was chomping at the bit, ready to have another go at him. But the suspect's brief had disappeared, summoned by a High Court judge in another murder case, and now the interrogation would have to wait for his return.

'You think Martin has the balls to kill, guv?' she asked.

Bright gave the honest answer. 'Depends what's at stake, I suppose. You be careful what you accuse him of, Kate. He can be an out and out bastard when he wants to be. You cross him, he'll shaft you first chance he gets.'

Daniels wondered if that was why he was shadowing her case. Was he trying to protect her from an ACC who took pleasure in ending careers? Didn't he know by now she was capable of standing on her own two feet? Gormley's voice interrupted her train of thought.

'To hell with that!' he said. 'Martin knows something, and

I want to know what it is. He once told me I'd never make detective as long as I had a hole in my arse. Now it's payback time.'

Bright chuckled. 'Talking about arses, what time does he get in?'

'Skye's quite a drive,' Daniels said. 'It'll probably be sometime in the early hours.'

The Super had an evil look on his face. He snatched the mobile from his belt and scrolled through his phonebook. When Martin's name appeared he punched the call key and listened. The number rang out for a few seconds before switching to a voicemail service: *The mobile you are calling may be switched off. Please try again later.*

'This is Detective Superintendent Bright, sir . . .' Bright's tongue was firmly planted in his cheek. 'I need to speak with you urgently. A good time would be in my office at eight a.m. tomorrow, if that's convenient.'

Daniels winced as he hung up.

'What?' he said.

She grinned, checking her watch. 'C'mon, Hank. Playtime's over.'

'Fancy a jar down the pub later?' Bright said. 'Assuming I wind up my case.'

'I'm in,' Gormley said.

Bright looked at Daniels.

'I can't tonight, guv.' She pulled an apologetic face. 'I'm meeting Ron Naylor later and I've got a million things to do.'

Bright watched as she moved away, stopping at the coffee machine on her way out of the door. She dropped a fifty-pence piece into the slot. When nothing happened, she kicked the machine. Still no joy. She kicked it again, adding another dint to several others that were already there.

What was it that drew him to her? Her feisty personality, perhaps; her strong sense of right and wrong; or something altogether more basic than that? Her natural beauty? Her scent? The way her lips moved when she talked?

What the hell did Naylor have that he didn't?

Gormley looked at him. 'Your tongue's hanging out, guv.'

'Sorry . . . I was miles away.'

Gormley knew exactly where he was.

41

The phone rang on Harry Holt's desk. On the next desk down, Maxwell looked up, irritated by the interruption. He chose to ignore the phone; seconds later it went quiet.

Seconds after that, it rang again.

Brown's eyes conveyed contempt. 'You going to get that this time?' he said.

Maxwell didn't move. 'If it's important, they'll call back.'

'I think you'll find they just did!'

Shaking his head, Brown got up and answered the phone himself. He didn't immediately recognize the caller but the urgency in the voice of a young PC from Area Command was enough to raise his curiosity. He was desperate to speak to the receiver.

'Whoa, slow down.' Anticipating a long story, Brown grabbed a pen and paper, took a seat. 'Harry's in the bog, mate. You'll have to make do with me. DC Brown, how can I help?'

The caller cleared his throat. 'I've been given an action to interview a Mrs Close at Court Mews apartment block. D'you know anything about that?'

'No. But did you?'

'What?

'Trace the witness!'

'Oh, right, yeah I did. Mrs Close told me she travelled up in the lift with Felicity Wood at around eleven o'clock on Thursday night. As she searched for her key, the witness claims she heard Wood's high heels on the hallway above. Almost immediately, the lift went down, then came straight back up and she heard someone knock on the door to Wood's apartment. She *definitely* had company on the night of the murder!'

Brown stopped writing. He leaned back in Harry's chair, crossed one leg over the other and poured cold water over the revelation: 'Doesn't necessarily mean Wood was lying. Maybe someone got the wrong door? It happens.'

'Don't think so. Close was adamant the lift didn't go down again.'

Brown sat up straight, pressed the caps lock on the computer keyboard and entered the name: FELICITY WOOD. Immediately, a transcript of Wood's original statement popped up on the screen. As he studied the data, he thought back to a conversation he'd had with Daniels earlier in the day. She'd had a gut feeling that the solicitor wasn't on the level – it looked as though she was being proved right.

'OK, thanks, leave it with me.' Brown put the phone down just as Gormley walked in. 'You seen the boss, Hank?'

A roar went past the window as the Toyota sped away.

'I think you'll find she just left,' Gormley said.

42

She couldn't move. Something was holding her down, putting pressure on her right shoulder. She was cold: very, very cold. She could hear an awful grinding sound. Light flashing. Movement too. A hand pressing on her left hip. A voice, close and yet far away. Words, muffled and unrecognizable, as if spoken through a thick wet blanket.

Talk to me, pet . . .

. . . talk to me . . .

Jo woke in a panic. The sight of Daniels keeping vigil by her bedside was a clear reminder that her problems hadn't gone away. For several seconds, they just looked at one another, regretting the harsh words of their previous meeting.

'I had a dream . . .' Jo said. 'You'd bugged my room. Should I be talking to you while I'm in here?'

'Are all psychologists paranoid?' Daniels grinned and made a meal of looking furtively over her shoulder towards the door. 'Don't worry, I'm not wearing a wire. I'd show you, only I might get rumbled.'

'Spoilsport.'

An intense moment of regret . . .

Jo got serious. 'Why are you here? Come to ask me some more questions?'

Daniels noticed that the bruising round Jo's eyes had begun

to disappear. The shape of her face was returning to normal and she'd regained a little colour and a familiar twinkle in her eyes. She wanted to tell her she was there because she cared, because she had regrets, because . . .

Fuck it! She'd never listen. What would be the point?

'You know you'll be formally interviewed?' she said instead.

Jo swept a lock of damp hair off her sweaty face. 'By you?'

'No, not by me. I promise.'

As SIO, Daniels wondered just how she was going to keep that promise. How exactly *could* she justify dodging an interview with the prime suspect? She shoved the thought to the back of her mind.

'Right now I'm here as a mate, Jo. Not a Senior Investigating Officer. If there's anything you need to tell me, no matter what it is, now's the time. If . . .'

She broke off, couldn't get the words out. She'd asked a question she didn't *really* want to know the answer to. It was something she'd learned not to do very early in her police career. And now Jo was staring at her, looking through her, almost, as if she was an alien.

'Will you just listen to yourself!' Jo was angry again, but also disappointed. 'I hated him, you know I did. But not enough to kill him.'

'Even after what the bastard did to you? I could've killed him myself.'

Jo said nothing.

'You can see how it looks?'

'D'you think I need reminding? Even Tom and James have their doubts. I can see it in their eyes, even though they're trying to hide it. Please tell me they're not suspects too.'

Daniels was desperate to throw her a crumb of comfort. But James had lied about his whereabouts and, well, it just wasn't that simple. Gormley had recalled him for interview. 'You know how it works, Jo. As soon as their alibis check out, you'll be the first to know. Right now, I want to talk to you about the accident.'

'Like I said, I don't remember a thing.'

'Your car came off a road heading away from the coast towards the A1, just north of Morpeth. Your receptionist said you'd been to Acklington Prison on Friday afternoon for an interview.' Nothing was registering. 'One of your lifers nearing his tariff date?'

Jo's expression was blank.

Daniels fed her a little more information, hoping to prompt recall. 'He has a parole review coming up and his behaviour was causing concern, apparently. The Governor was thinking of shipping him back to Dartmoor but wanted the benefit of your advice before making the arrangements.'

'Which inmate?'

'Woodgate?'

'Oh . . .'

'You *do* remember him?'

'He's not easy to forget. He's not the most popular person on the planet. Look, I'm sorry, Kate, but it's like a black hole. I really couldn't say if I saw him or not. Didn't they find my BlackBerry after the accident?'

'I don't recall seeing it in the report I read. I'll check.' Daniels' spirits lifted. If she could help Jo to remember her last appointment at work – where she'd been, who with – perhaps they could work their way back to Thursday the fifth.

Some cognitive interviewing just might work.

Jo's face paled as Daniels' voice trailed off. It was as if the seriousness of her situation had suddenly hit home. She looked small and insignificant against the white sheets, like a frail old lady who didn't understand where she was or how she'd got there.

'I know you're scared,' Daniels whispered, 'but I'm not going anywhere. We're in this together. I promise.'

43

In Interview Room 2, James Stephens sat nervously waiting for the questions to begin. Gormley clasped his hands in front of his waist and studied the young man in front of him. He bore many similarities to his own son, Ryan; a son he might lose unless his marriage situation improved. Gormley's wife, Julie, had finally reached her limit: she'd had enough of playing second fiddle to his job, his working all hours, their cancelled social arrangements. She'd given him an ultimatum: take her and Ryan seriously or they'd move to the south coast to begin a new life without him.

Pushing away that worrying thought, Gormley turned on the tape deck and cautioned the lad. Seeing no reason to pussy-foot around, he launched straight in. 'Mr Stephens, is there anything you would like to add or change from the information you gave DCI Daniels when you came in to help us with our enquiries?'

James looked a little sheepish. He shook his head.

'For the benefit of the tape, James Stephens has shaken his head. Could you please answer the question?'

'No,' James mumbled. 'I've nothing to add.'

'You sure about that?'

'I said so, didn't I?'

'That's interesting. You see, according to Sheffield CID,

you weren't actually present at your Halls of Residence when you said you were.'

James shrugged.

Gormley wasn't taken in by the young man's bravado. His body language was giving him away: rapid eye movements, hands in front of his genitals, knee moving up and down as one foot continually tapped the floor. But even though it was obvious the kid was shitting himself with fear, Gormley knew he was no killer – he'd stake his pension and his reputation on it.

'So where were you?' he said.

James' eyes darted to the LED on the recorder.

'Look, son, I'd like nothing better than to sit here all evening talking to you, on account of the fact that my wife is a pain in the arse and I've got nowt special to go home for. But I'm betting you have more important things on, so why not do yourself a favour and just tell me the truth?'

James shifted in his seat. 'Technically, I was – telling the truth, I mean.'

'You're going to have to do better than that.'

'I *was* in Sheffield . . .' James looked like a little boy caught with his hands in the sweetie jar. 'Only . . . I haven't been entirely honest about my living arrangements.'

Gormley grinned. Hooking one arm over the back of his chair, he studied the lad's features more closely. There was definitely something in James' appearance that reminded him of his son. Perhaps it was the mop of blond hair, or maybe the piercing blue eyes. He couldn't quite put his finger on what it was, probably because he hadn't seen much of Ryan in recent weeks. He'd been too busy keeping his head down, staying out of the way.

James smirked as young men do when they're embarrassed. But there was some other emotion in play, one Gormley thought he recognized.

Conceit?

Pride, perhaps?

'Care to elaborate?' he pressed.

James chose not to answer.

Gormley sighed and looked at his watch. 'Interview terminated at seven fifty-seven p.m. . . .' He turned off the tape, relaxed back in his chair and shut his eyes. 'Wake me when you're ready to talk.'

The silence didn't last long.

'I was shagging my tutor, if you must know.'

Gormley opened his eyes. 'Then why the hell didn't you just say so, you idiot?'

44

Ron Naylor was waiting – as Daniels knew he would be – in The Living Room restaurant on Grey Street, as agreed. *He scrubs up well, for a copper*, she thought, as a waiter took her coat. Always the policeman, she knew he'd sit facing the door, careful never to turn his back on potential trouble – a useful tip drummed into them at training school that now came as second nature. Subconsciously or otherwise, he'd have clocked everyone in the place, could probably tell her what they had on, what mood they were in, and whether or not they were up to no good.

He smiled and stood up as she approached.

She sat down, couldn't help noticing that he'd ordered French wine, her favourite Sancerre La Fuzelle from the Loire Valley. 'You shouldn't have, Ron.'

'Thought you could do with a treat . . .' He poured her half a glass. 'You looked shagged out when I saw you yesterday.'

'Tell me about it . . .' Daniels took a sip of her wine, mulling over the day's events. After seeing Jo she'd rushed back to the MIR to check on progress; it had come as a relief when she heard that James Stephens had now given an account of his whereabouts on Thursday night, an alibi being checked out by Gormley as a matter of urgency. And the developing situation with Felicity Wood intrigued her; she'd tasked Brown to follow up on it, first thing in the morning. She put down her glass. 'Sorry I'm late, Ron. I was just about to leave when I got a call from the front office to go down there right away. Asian woman, really agitated, so the desk sergeant said, wanting to give me something. Couldn't speak a word of English by all accounts, just kept jabbing her finger at an envelope addressed to me. I thought it must be important.'

'And was it?'

'Never got chance to find out . . .' Daniels rummaged in her bag. Retrieving a brown envelope, she passed it over the table. Naylor looked inside and removed a crossed-out photo of a young Asian male. It was on flimsy, shiny paper with newsprint on the reverse; obviously a clipping from a magazine.

'Who is he?'

'Search me. I've never seen him before.'

Naylor studied the envelope, which was addressed for Daniels' personal attention in childish handwriting. He looked up. 'Maybe it's her son. Maybe she's seen you on the box and is trying to tell you he's gone missing.'

'It's possible, I suppose.'

'And there was no accompanying message?'

'No message, no explanation, just that.'

'She could be a crank,' Naylor suggested.

'Or, as you say, someone desperately in need of help.'

'She'll be back, if that's the case.'

'You're right. I'm starving, you ready to order?'

They called the waiter and ordered a fillet steak for him, sea bass for her, then got straight down to business. Naylor had brought along a photocopy of the crumpled card taken from

Jenny Tait's mouth for comparison to the one found in Father Simon's hands a year ago. They were similar only in as much as they were both prayer cards. Forensic examination had failed to establish any further link between them.

'I know what you said about coincidence...' Naylor said tentatively. 'And I know you want to get the bastard that killed the priest and the young lass from your village, that goes without saying. But I can't see it myself. I mean, if he wasn't a priest—'

'If he wasn't a priest, you'd be jumping up and down!'

'Exactly my point, Kate. Look, if we found a murder victim with a stethoscope round his neck, it would *only* be odd if he was a plumber, not a doctor.'

Daniels knew what he was getting at – of course she did – but that didn't stop her arguing her corner until their waiter arrived with food. They sat in silence for much of the meal, contemplating the significance of the prayer card – at least, that was what Daniels was doing. Now that the card was on her radar, she kept hoping it would somehow lead to a result so that she could finally close the book on the Corbridge case – give David and Elsie Short some peace. But was she just clutching at straws? Naylor noticed her push her plate away, no longer hungry.

'Penny for them,' he said.

'I'm sorry, Ron. This double murder got to me, it's still getting to me – I know that. And not just because these people are close to home, but . . . well, just because they deserve justice and I've got nothing to give them. After all this time, we still don't know if Sarah was attacked because she witnessed a murder, or if Father Simon was murdered because he stumbled upon her being raped in his bloody church.'

'Hey, come on . . .' Naylor reached across the table and put his hand on hers. They'd known each other for years; always platonic, never anything other than good mates. 'Head down, bum up. You'll get whoever did this eventually, you know you will—'

She didn't wait for him to finish. 'Assuming for one second that Sarah witnessed Father Simon's murder, and not the other way round, then the card isn't the only common ground. The MO is exactly the same. Jenny Tait and Father Simon were both shot in the chest, remember.'

'True. But half the murders we investigate are shootings these days. It's like the OK Corral out there. Except this isn't Tombstone, Arizona.' He paused. She usually appreciated his cowboy references. But not tonight. 'It's not just that, though, is it, Kate? I'm sensing something more. C'mon, what is it?'

Daniels sighed heavily, lifted her wine glass to her lips. 'Maybe I just need a few days off to recharge the batteries, get my focus back . . .' Naylor was no fool. Daniels could see that he wasn't buying it. She quickly changed the subject. 'Why did you never marry, Ron?'

'No point.' He wiped his mouth on a serviette. 'You want a sweet, coffee . . .? The night's still young.'

Daniels shook her head. 'I've got to—'

'Dash, I know.' Taking out his wallet, he caught the eye of a waiter and wrote an imaginary bill on his hand. 'If you think about it, you just answered your own question. I've seen too many relationships go tits-up. Marriage requires two people in them, not just one. I'm too busy most of the time. That's my excuse – what's yours?'

Daniels didn't have one.

At least, not one she could tell him about.

45

He hid outside in the cold night air, still as a statue, head cocked back slightly, peering through the narrow glass panel in the door, trying to make sense of what he could hear. The muffled voice of another person in the flat? No: a radio presenter and gentle music.

The coast was clear.

Jamil Malik was asleep on the sofa with just a dim light for company. The anticipation of what he was about to do to him felt like sexual arousal. He'd waited long enough. Silently he turned the handle, pushed open the door, heart racing slightly, hands damp with sweat, eyes firmly focused on his prey. He moved forward on to the threshold, aiming the beam of light at Malik's face.

Malik sat up, shielding his eyes, his voice hardly audible.

'What do you want? Get out of my house!'

Lowering the torch, he reached deep into his pocket and drew out his weapon, touching Malik's lips with the tip of the barrel to silence the cunt. It worked. A sharp intake of breath was followed by irrepressible weeping and a patch of piss growing big around Malik's crotch.

He gestured for him to kneel on the floor. Malik did as he was told, joining his hands together, pleading for his life as a carriage clock on the mantelpiece struck midnight.

Perfect.

His forefinger began to squeeze the trigger, then he swung round as he saw movement out of the corner of his eye. He relaxed again as a toddler padded across the carpet, rubbing his eyes with one hand and trailing a threadbare teddy along the floor behind him with the other. Panic seized Malik. He tried to push the boy away, but the child clung to him, alarmed by the tears running down his grandfather's face.

Malik pleaded for the boy's life.

'Kill me! Kill me!'

He smiled.

There was a God, after all.

'What's your name?' He spoke the words gently, bending down, gesturing for the toddler to join him. The boy blinked, still wary of the stranger. So he made a silly face until the child began to giggle, his little milk teeth gleaming in the torchlight. 'Come, see what I've got. Bang, bang.' And then to Malik: 'Let him go, and he lives.'

Malik understood. He released his grip, allowing his bony fingers to slip from the child's pyjamas. But still the boy hesitated. And then, as only a child can, he slowly came round and walked towards their guest, his innocence and trust plain to see. Malik was praying now, praying for all he was worth.

The sound of his prayers – any prayers – was like a red rag to a bull. He wanted it to stop, but he knew yelling at the old man would alarm the child.

And still Malik prayed aloud, hands joined, eyes closed.

His anger rose, then fell away as Malik's prayers faded into the background, replaced by others more terrifying than he could ever have imagined, spoken by a voice that transported him back to a room, equally dim and dingy, to a mother forcing him to his knees to beg for the Lord's forgiveness for his sins.

He tried to focus on Malik's hands, but he could only see *hers*.

She was yelling at him now, her hands parted from prayer, raised high above her head. Blows rained down on him as he cowered, defenceless.

And then he saw the red mist. Rage took over as he remembered that Malik and his mother had once been close friends. And suddenly he knew what to do. Turning the weeping child round to face his grandfather, he placed the gun in his tiny hand and guided his fingers on to the trigger. Applying gentle pressure, he felt the child's body jerk backwards as the gun went off. Malik fell and the boy ran to him.

Job done, he placed the calling card on the floor . . .

And walked away unperturbed.

46

The day had passed in the blink of an eye. There had been some interesting developments that Daniels felt sure would help her find the person responsible for Alan Stephens' death, but not enough to get Jo Soulsby off MIT's radar altogether.

After leaving Naylor, she hadn't driven straight home. Instead she'd taken a short detour past Francesca's Restaurant on Manor House Road. Jo had told her that Tom and James were heading there after an evening visit to the hospital. Her suggestion. Her shout. Anything to stop her sons grabbing a takeaway, she'd said. And, right enough, their battered VW was parked directly outside.

Daniels slowed the Toyota to walking pace and did a quick recon, just in case. She could see through the window that the place was heaving, could even smell Italian herbs as she drove slowly by. The brothers were sitting at a table near the door, a menu in Tom's hand and a fresh pint of beer in front of each of them.

Perfect timing – she was free and clear.

Within minutes she'd been home and changed. Now walking to her front door, dressed in motorcycle leathers and carrying her helmet, she wondered what the hell she was doing. After a moment's hesitation, she let herself out and locked the door behind her. The Yamaha Fazer 600 was already outside. She climbed on and rode off into the night, pulling the visor down over her face.

It wasn't a long journey. She'd be there in a few minutes, if the cars in front would get their act into gear instead of cruising up and down, checking out the talent. Osborne Road was in an area that had undergone a transformation in recent years. Bars had sprung up all over the place, many attached to big hotels with terraces out front leading directly on to the tree-lined street. They all had cool names: Blanc, Bar Polo, Osborne's, Spy, Bar Berlise. The clientele were well catered for with tall tables, patio heaters and wind breakers – just as well, given the lack of clothing being worn on a cold winter's night.

Despite the throaty purr of the Fazer's engine, laughter and music faded in and out of Daniels' head as she slowly negoti-ated round a group of kids making their way across the road, taking less care than they ought. Arriving at her destination, she came to a stop directly opposite Jo's house. She didn't dismount, nor lift the visor on her helmet, just sat astride the machine for a second or two, watching. The place was in total darkness. With a remote, she opened up the garage, rode in and killed the engine. She dismounted, unzipped her jacket and pulled out a torch.

Leaving her gloves on, she entered the house.

There were signs that Tom and James had been there: dishes left abandoned on the kitchen table, washing-up in the sink, a newspaper open at an article reporting on Alan Stephens' death. Daniels moved through the house quickly, her anxiety rising. If she was discovered creeping around in the dark, there'd certainly be a lot of explaining to do. But she soldiered on, convincing herself that she was trespassing for all the right reasons – ostensibly to prove Jo's innocence, though what she was expecting to find was anyone's guess.

She found nothing untoward.

Returning to the kitchen, Daniels opened up the bin and shone the torch inside. Unable to make out what she was looking at, she lifted segments of a torn-up photograph on to the work surface. Piecing them together, she made an image of Alan Stephens. Gutted, she gathered up the pieces and returned them to the bin.

She got back on her bike and left.

47

The minute hand on the dial of an eighteenth-century longcase clock moved forward a notch. For over forty-five minutes, Brown had been reading magazines in the smart waiting room of solicitors Graham & Abercrombie, situated on Grey Street – some would say Newcastle's finest example of architecture.

Brown knew about clocks; his grandfather used to repair them. The one he was staring at was a fine example, worth around twelve thousand pounds, give or take. It was made of mahogany, inlaid with brass, a typical eight-day longcase with five-pillar movement striking the hour on a bell. Thankfully it had only done this once while Brown had been sitting twiddling his thumbs. But it was gone ten o'clock and he had other calls to make.

Fed up with waiting, he stood and approached a middle-aged woman who was typing on a computer keyboard at the reception desk. She wore a pink cardigan fastened to the neck with tiny silver buttons. Her bifocals sat lower than the bridge of her nose, her hair was slicked back, her head tilted slightly to one side as she listened through a modern earpiece.

He stared at her intently. 'Miss, I haven't got all day.'

She didn't look up. 'Shouldn't be long now . . .'

Brown stood his ground, putting the woman off. She

stopped typing, removed the earpiece and spoke high-handedly with an accent he couldn't quite place, except it was nowhere in the North East.

'I already told you, Ms Wood is in conference with a senior partner and cannot be disturbed . . . for anyone.' She smiled. 'It's more than my job's worth to—'

'Then please tell her that her presence is required at City Central police station in connection with a murder enquiry.'

The receptionist's smile dissolved. 'I'll check how long she'll be.'

'How kind.'

No sooner were the words out of Brown's mouth than a side door opened and Wood appeared. She ushered him into an office to die for, a huge room with large Georgian windows facing south over equally fine buildings across the street.

'Please be brief, I'm very busy.'

'With respect, I'm here in connection with a murder en-quiry, madam. It'll take as long as it takes.'

Wood walked round her desk and sat down, placing a physical barrier between them. 'I've already had a conversa-tion with your boss, PC Brown. What is it this time?'

'DC Brown. Just one or two questions . . .'

She waited.

'I've come to see if you have anything to add to your origi-nal statement.'

Despite her best efforts, Wood couldn't hide her anxiety. 'I'd have let you know, if that were the case.'

Brown exhaled through his teeth. 'Then we have a dilemma. You see, we have a witness who claims you had company on the night of the fifth. Yet you failed to mention that when questioned. Of course, the witness could be mistaken . . . but she seems pretty sure.'

He didn't think for one minute that the solicitor would take his word for it right off – he *was* a policeman, after all. And he was right. Wood made no comment, but he thought he saw a slight increase in her facial colour. It was hardly detectable, but there nevertheless.

'What witness?' she asked eventually, trying not to sound remotely worried.

'So it's true then?'

'It most certainly is not!'

The solicitor took a deep breath, embarrassed by her sudden outburst. She smiled at him through perfect teeth. Brown formed the opinion that she was a woman who could wrap most men around her little finger with that smile. Well, it wouldn't work. Not this time. She *definitely* wasn't his type.

'I was alone all evening,' Wood said. 'Your witness is mistaken.'

'Thanks,' Brown smiled. 'That's all I wanted to know.'

Now she was worried. A look of panic crossed her face like a dark shadow. It was obvious she hadn't expected to be let off quite that easily. In fact, she looked totally bemused.

'That's it? You waited all that time for the answer to one simple question?'

Brown walked away without another word, pleased with himself for putting Felicity *'Up Herself'* Wood in her place after keeping him waiting so long. As he turned to close the door behind him, he allowed himself a moment to savour the guilty expression on her face.

48

The garage forecourt was busy as Assistant Chief Constable Martin filled up his Jaguar. In his peripheral vision he could see his wife, Muriel, taking another swig from the flask of Bombay Sapphire she'd concealed in her bag before they set off.

He got out his wallet and headed inside to pay.

Just as he got to the door, his Barbour jacket began to vibrate. By the time he took out his phone, the caller had rung off. Martin pressed the recall button, keeping one eye on Muriel as two German bikers entered behind him. One of them began complaining – in his native tongue – about the lack of refreshment facilities on offer. It was a cheek to call it a service station the other one said.

This was Britain, what did they expect?

Martin was fluent in five languages: French, German, Spanish, Dutch and Russian, all acquired at Cambridge with a view to securing a job as an interpreter for the Foreign Office. Quite why he'd changed his mind in favour of policing wasn't clear, even to him. Except that it had opened up the more exciting option of working for Interpol at their headquarters in Lyon.

Until Muriel came along.

The ringing tone in his ear stopped and Martin stared at the phone display. The signal had dropped out. He tried again. As he waited for an answer, Martin thought about his dreams of international policing and how they had come to nothing. His one and only claim to fame was that he was the youngest officer in Britain ever to reach the rank of Assistant Chief. His failure to make Chief Constable needled him more than he cared to admit.

More customers entered. He stepped back in the line, allowing them to go first, and in the process caught sight of his reflection in a mirrored panel that ran down the side of a shelving unit displaying cheap sunglasses. He didn't like what he saw: he had dark circles under his eyes and was sporting a five o'clock shadow.

Martin was in a foul mood. He'd intended to make the journey down yesterday but only made it as far as the Skye road bridge, which was closed due to strong winds. The ferry across Loch Alsh, the only other route connecting the island to the mainland, had been suspended, resulting in several hours of delay and an enforced night in a lumpy four-poster in the only available B & B. His wife had been giving him earache the entire journey and he was four hours late for an appointment with Bright.

Too bad – the bastard would just have to wait.

When Felicity Wood came on the line, she sounded frantic. Her speech was so hurried he could hardly make out what she was saying.

'Wally, thank God. Can you talk?'

'If you're quick, Muriel's in the car.'

'I had the police here. They know! I'm really worried.'

Martin forced himself to breathe as the sight of half a face flew into his head. Blood on white walls. Bits of brain and bone on the floor. He was finding it difficult enough to cope, without Felicity's anxiety making matters worse.

'Calm down,' he said. 'Are you in the office?'

'Yes, and I'm bloody scared. I want you back here.'

'I'm on my way. And stop panicking. I could get time for this.' Martin flushed as the Germans stopped talking and turned to look at him, intrigued by his conversation. He moved out of the queue and stood with his back to them, lowering his voice. 'You didn't tell them anything?'

Silence.

'Felicity?'

Wood stopped snivelling. 'I'm not sure I can keep up the pretence. And why the hell should I? I've done nothing wrong.'

'For Christ's sake, calm down!' Martin whispered through clenched teeth. A horn blasted outside and he looked out of the window; Muriel was furiously tapping her watch, urging him to get a move on. On the other end of the phone, Wood started to cry. The Jaguar's horn blasted again. 'Look, I've got to go. I'll sort it, I promise you. I need to find out what they know and what they think they know. I've got somebody on the squad. Don't worry. Just sit tight.'

49

It had been a long shift. Bob George had been driving his taxi since six a.m. He was about to knock off for lunch when a call came over his radio; something to do with urgent police enquiries concerning a fare he'd picked up the previous Thursday night. He thought little of it. Calls from the law were a regular occurrence in his profession. In fact, if he was honest, he'd been expecting their call.

Dropping a gear, he drove on, cursing under his breath. Fearing a possible law suit, should an accident occur, his boss had forbidden drivers to use or even carry mobiles in his cabs. Some did. But George didn't think it worth the risk. The pay wasn't bad. And he figured that working for a prize wanker was better than not working at all.

Parking his cab on double-yellow lines on a busy street in the city's east end, he dashed into a phone box that stank of stale sweat and worse. The names and telephone numbers of prostitutes he knew covered every available surface, written in permanent ink. Some even had pictures, graphic descriptions of what was on offer. He noticed that Joy and Brandy only came as a pair these days.

Jamming his foot in the door to let in some air, George held a hand against his free ear and spoke loudly against the traffic. He gave his name, the company he worked for, and asked to speak with Detective Sergeant Hank Gormley. When eventually he came on the line, George had to shout down the phone to make himself heard. They arranged to meet and rang off.

Less than half a mile away, Daniels sat in her Toyota watching the offices of Graham & Abercrombie.

Her entire morning had been spent fighting with admin and filling in bloody forms to keep the wheels on her SIO's wagon turning: sanctioning overtime, signing off on expenses claims, compiling budgetary reports . . . Tasks that wouldn't advance her investigation in real terms, but essential if she was to avoid it grinding to a sudden halt. When Brown got back from his interview with Felicity Wood, Daniels had seized upon the opportunity to leave her desk and follow up the lead in person.

And there she was: the woman herself, definitely rattled and dressed to kill, hurrying from the building and climbing straight into a taxi that had just pulled up outside. Daniels waited for the cab to pull away again, then tailed it for a short journey across town until it stopped near the entrance to Exhibition Park.

The solicitor got out, paid the driver and told him not to wait.

Keeping a close eye on her target, Daniels entered Exhibition Park a little way behind Wood. She was clearly in a hurry, rushing along a tarmac path for a hundred yards or so, arriving at the boating lake where ACC Martin was waiting for her. He was dressed in civvies and was not looking his best. Daniels kept them under observation, recording their clandestine meeting on a tiny state-of-the-art video camera. As Wood and Martin parted, they kissed.

Daniels made a call: 'Hank, meet me at Paul Hope's office. Fifteen minutes.'

The interior walls of the Northern Counties School for the Deaf were covered in examples of fingerspelling and signing resources for the deaf. One of the organization's volunteers, Paul Hope, was the accredited go-to 'expert witness' in video transcription, able to lip-read so well that he could provide hard copy for use as evidence in criminal cases. Daniels and Gormley had consulted him many times before.

The three of them were sitting together in one of the classrooms watching a silent video. Daniels was manipulating the controls, while Gormley took notes. Hope was staring intently at the two figures on the screen: Wood and Martin. They appeared to be arguing.

'She's talking about the police,' Hope said. '"They know . . ." Rewind please.'

Daniels hit rewind.

'"They know I had company when Stephen was killed?"' Hope peered at Martin on screen. '"Say nothing. If this gets out, I'm finished . . ."'

'You certain, Paul?' Daniels asked.

'Pretty much, or something very like it.'

Gormley stopped scribbling, looked at Daniels excitedly.

'I'll check – go back again.' Hope waited for Daniels to rewind the footage. 'Yep, definitely: "You mean we are?" And he says if he'd meant that, he'd have said it.'

On screen, Martin turned his back.

Daniels grimaced. 'Shit!'

The camera focused on Wood, who was by now clearly agitated.

Hope was off again: '"No, of course not. I did what we agreed."' He watched carefully as Martin turned towards the camera, running his hand through his hair.

Daniels got in on the act. '"Pull yourself together?"'

Hope smiled. 'Very good!'

She grinned. 'Didn't get the last bit, though.'

'"You're a bloody solicitor, aren't you?"'

Gormley raised a hand, inviting a high five. Daniels obliged. Things were looking up.

They thanked Hope for his help and went back to the car. Gormley took out his notebook and began flicking though it.

'This'll wipe the supercilious smile off Martin's face,' he said.

'Beats an orgasm.' Daniels' grin was as wide as the Tyne.

'Beats two.'

The phone rang and Daniels picked it up. Hearing Robson's voice, she put the call on speaker:

'. . . Mrs Collins asked if you'd pop in.'

'Hope she's got cake,' Gormley said. 'I'm bloody starving.'

Daniels dug him in the ribs. 'She say why, Robbo?'

'Only that it might be important.'

She rang off and took a sharp right, heading east along the West Road. The route took them past the General Hospital, reminding her of Jo. Not that she needed reminding: the woman had never been far from her thoughts since the day they met.

An image of Francesca's flashed through Daniels' thoughts, her slow drive-by last night making absolutely sure Tom and James Stephens were safely out of the way before raiding their mother's home. Having obtained Jo's permission beforehand, technically it wasn't a burglary. Even so, Daniels couldn't help feeling a tad guilty.

Mrs Collins opened the door before they had time to press the doorbell; evidently she'd been waiting for them. They followed her through into the living room. Gormley took a seat, but Mrs Collins remained standing and so did Daniels, hands clasped behind her back. It was her intention to keep the visit brief.

'I've not seen Mrs Soulsby yet,' Mrs Collins began, 'but her sons have been coming and going. I'm a Neighbourhood Watch volunteer, you see, so I notice these things.'

Gormley stifled a grin and looked away.

Mrs Collins tapped her walking cane hard on the wooden floor to regain his attention. It had the desired effect. Like a naughty schoolboy in the headmistress's study, Gormley sat up straight in anticipation of a dressing-down. It didn't take long to arrive.

'This is not a joke, Detective. I'll have you know we play a vital role in crime reduction. Your job would be much harder without us.'

'We appreciate that, Mrs Collins.' Realizing he'd blown his chance of cake and cuppa, Gormley looked genuinely downcast. 'However, we are really very busy just now, so unless there's anything else . . .?'

Aside from wasting our bloody time . . .

Gormley stood up, keen to be on his way, but Mrs Collins

wasn't quite done. She pointed at the chair with her stick and held the pose until he sat back down again.

Daniels was unable to make up her mind whether the feisty octogenarian was an extremely helpful witness or a lonely old dear who just needed someone to talk to. In the end she decided probably a bit of both.

'As a matter of fact there is something else . . .' Mrs Collins began.

Gormley smiled, trying his very best to look interested.

Fuck! Daniels' heart sank as a horrible thought occurred to her. Watching Mrs Collins closely as she sat down and made herself more comfortable, Daniels' fists were so tightly clenched behind her back she thought she might draw blood. This pillar of the community was about to disclose an unscheduled, if not suspicious, visitor to the house next door.

How the hell would Daniels explain that one to Hank?

'Her boyfriend's been here too,' Mrs Collins said finally.

Gormley and Daniels shared a look.

'Not that we were ever introduced,' the old lady said. 'He used to stay over a lot, though, turning up at all hours of the day and night. I thought they'd split up, but he was back here last night. Not for long, mind. No point. There was no one home.'

'Does he have a car?' Gormley asked.

Mrs Collins shook her head. 'One of those motorbike contraptions. Awful things. Parked it in her garage, which struck me as odd, bearing in mind she wasn't there.'

Gormley's smile dissolved. He glanced sideways at his boss.

Daniels held her bottle, staring straight ahead, not a flicker of guilt on her face, her mind racing back to the times she'd ride into Jo's garage, pull her bike on to its stand and dismount. Then she'd wait for Jo to press a buzzer on the wall, closing the up-and-over door and shutting out the street. Only then would Daniels remove her helmet, put it on the seat and shake her hair free. Only then would they kiss – two people passionately in love.

Like ice-woman, Daniels froze Gormley out, her eyes firmly planted on the old lady who continued to elaborate until, finally, she ran out of steam and things to say.

'Did you get the registration number?' Daniels asked casually.

''Fraid not,' Mrs Collins was crestfallen. 'My eyes aren't so good nowadays.'

'Never mind.' Daniels managed a smile. 'If he turns up again, give us a call.'

They said their goodbyes and Mrs Collins saw them off the premises.

The detectives walked to the car, a hostile silence between them.

'Drop me at The Bridge,' Gormley said as they got in. 'I've got an appointment with a taxi driver and a beer.

50

Bright's day had begun well. He'd known all along that he had the right man in custody, despite protestations to the contrary from the suspect's brief. Confronted with CCTV footage showing the offender leading his victim away from a Bonfire Night gathering, the scumbag had finally coughed. Now he'd been formally charged with the murder of an unfortunate and much-loved little boy.

Word travelled fast . . .

Bright found himself mobbed by reporters as he left the office to watch his offender being arraigned. His mobile hadn't stopped ringing on the way to court. More journos. More questions.

They all wanted just one thing: a name.

Assistant Chief Constable Martin was conspicuous by his absence at the full-blown press conference that followed, keeping a low-profile for once, allowing Bright to take centre stage in front of the nation's media. This raised an eyebrow or two among local journalists and prompted questions from the floor on which Detective Superintendent Bright refused to be drawn. But later, off the record and off camera, he was at pains to make it clear that he had no idea why the ACC wasn't there to offer condolences to the bereaved family.

Although a major result for the murder investigation

team, celebrations in the office were understandably low key. Bright's investigation team were fathers too, their respect for the child's family outweighed any wish to sink more than a jar or too in the police club afterwards.

It seemed ungracious to party.

They'd been in the bar for less than an hour when people began to drift off home and Bright began to drift downhill. So what if his offender was facing a lengthy stretch in prison? What fucking good would that do? Bored and alone with nothing to do and no one left to talk to, he began brooding over Stella and decided to take himself off to The Bridge to sink a few more bevies and generally wallow in his grief alone. Only to be hauled out an hour later by Gormley, who just happened to have chosen the same pub for an informal interview with a taxi driver Daniels had been trying to trace.

Some bollocks to do with Stephens, no doubt.

They walked back to the station together, a heavy atmosphere between them. In all the years they'd worked together, Bright had never seen Gormley in such a bad mood. He assumed Hank was festering because *he* was behaving like a complete prick, meddling in Daniels' case. But when he'd asked him why he was so down in the mouth, Hank had just clammed up.

Daniels was almost at her office door when the pair of them showed up. She'd been hoping to nip in, grab her things and head off to the hospital, but it looked as though a clean getaway was now out of the question. Judging by Gormley's expression, her face must have registered her disappointment on seeing them, but she'd regained her composure before Bright had time to notice.

'Congratulations, guv,' she said. 'Cracking result. Been celebrating, have you?'

'Good news travels fast . . .' Bright peered at her through bleary eyes and held her gaze for a little too long. He grinned as only a drunk can, his lips refusing to obey his command. 'Stick with me long enough, guys, and you might just learn something.'

'Take no notice – he's pissed! I just dragged him out of The Bridge,' Gormley said crossly. Opening the door, he stood back, rolling his eyes as Bright forgot his manners and walked in ahead of Daniels. 'Nice one, guv!'

'Oh, sorry.' Bright sat down in Daniels' chair and put his feet up on her desk.

Smiling uncomfortably, the DCI went straight to a side table and put the kettle on. Gormley took a seat with his back to the door, shaking his head at the state their guv'nor was in.

Blissfully unaware of the concern he was causing, Bright looked around the orderly office as if he'd never seen it before. His eyes scanned the desk and shelves for the usual personal odds and ends, but here there were no photos of loved ones, no clues to a life outside the job. Again and again his eyes came back to Daniels as she stood with her back to him, spooning Harvey Nicks coffee from a tin into a cafetière, then pouring water on it. A delicious aroma began to fill the room.

'Here! Get this down you.' She handed him a mug. 'You're a bloody disgrace!'

The sound of her voice made him sit up and take notice. He looked past her, distracted by movement in the corridor. Following his gaze, she turned to find Maxwell lurking outside, his nose in a filing cabinet, curiosity getting the better of him. Daniels moved round the desk, closed the door and sat back down, unable to tell whether Gormley's unease was down to Bright's condition, or Mrs Collins' revelation earlier. If the latter was true, he wouldn't want Bright around while he boned her about it.

Paranoia was setting in.

Gormley relaxed back in his chair and loosened his tie, avoiding direct eye contact. 'My meeting with Bob George didn't quite go according to plan,' he said.

'Bob who?' Bright looked at him, frowning comically.

'Our elusive taxi driver,' Gormley reminded him. 'Get this – and I'm quoting now: "Before you ask, I never touched her, OK?" Those were his first words.'

Daniels narrowed her eyes. 'What?'

'He thought we'd traced him in connection with Jo, not Stephens.'

'What?' Bright and Daniels said in unison.

'Yep. You couldn't make it up.' Gormley put down his coffee. 'It seems the firm he works for responded to our call to trace drivers working a late shift on the fifth, early hours of the sixth, right . . .' Gormley paused, making sure they were still with him. Bright and Daniels nodded. 'Well, when the call went out, George jumped to the wrong conclusion entirely. I was confused myself when he started banging on about some woman he'd picked up from town at one thirty in the morning—'

'Wait! Now you've lost me,' Daniels interrupted him, mid-flow. 'What makes you think this woman was Jo?'

'That's the easy bit,' Gormley said. 'George wrote down her address and the exact time he dropped her off. Said she was

acting weird and he was worried in case she made any allegations against him later.'

Daniels frowned. 'Yeah, right. I expect women do that all
the time. Sounds like a man with a guilty conscience, if you
ask me.'

'No . . .' Gormley shook his head. 'The way he tells it, he was
just covering his own back. And, for what it's worth, I believe
him. He said Jo was in one hell of a state physically: her tights
were all ripped and she was freaking out over something. He
described what she was wearing and the timing of the drop.
What he told me ties in exactly with the statement Andy took
from Mrs Collins. What's more, he'll make a bloody good witness, too. It puts Jo no more than a mile from the crime scene
at the relevant time – or there and thereabouts.'

'In other words a ten-minute walk.' Bright blew out his
cheeks, filling the room with the stale smell of beer and
cigars. He got up, began pacing up and down, the combina-
tion of strong coffee and Gormley's words sobering him up
and – from the sounds of it – setting his imagination off and
running. 'Right! I don't buy this amnesia crap. You don't
interview Soulsby again in hospital, you hear me, Kate? If she
didn't kill Stephens, maybe she knows who did.'

Daniels tried to get a word in: 'Guv, I really think—'

But Bright wasn't finished. 'Psychologists have contact with
undesirables, it's what they do. As soon as she's discharged,
I want her in here under caution. In fact, I intend to have a
crack at her myself.'

Daniels saw Gormley's jaw bunch as Bright rode rough-
shod over the discussion without a thought for her position as
SIO. He seemed to be on the verge of saying something when

Bright slapped him hard on the back, congratulating him for his efforts, hardly stopping to draw breath.

'Do we know when she's due home?' he asked.

When Daniels failed to answer, Gormley did it for her. 'Couple of days, tops.'

Daniels suddenly felt claustrophobic. She wanted Bright to stop, wanted to turn back the clock. How the hell had she got herself into this mess? More importantly, how was she going to get herself out of it?

'Excuse me a sec . . .' she said, getting up. 'Need a pee, won't be long.'

Walking out of her office, she made her way along the corridor to the women's rest room. Fortunately for her, it was empty when she reached it. She went in, locked the door behind her, turned on the tap and lifted the clear, cold water to her face with cupped hands. As she raised her head from the bowl, the image reflected in the mirror wasn't pretty. She looked pale and gaunt, her brown eyes underlined with dark circles. A million uncertainties flooded her head. So many questions, none of them with answers: Could any of it be true? Was Jo really capable of murder?

Wasn't everyone?

But why hadn't she seen it coming? Would she, could she, stand by her now?

The Kate Daniels who came bursting through her office door looked and sounded a lot less defeated than the one who'd slipped out five minutes earlier. Ignoring Bright, she fired off a direct question to Gormley:

'Did you find out the answer to the original enquiry? Was

Bob George the driver who picked up Alan Stephens from the Weston?'

A glint appeared in Gormley's eye. 'It just so happens he did. He says he dropped Stephens off some time before midnight, picked Jo up almost two hours later.'

Daniels turned to Bright. 'Then we have ourselves a contamination problem.'

51

'Things still tough at home?' Daniels said.

At a signpost for Tynemouth, she pulled off the central motorway heading east, fully expecting to get stuck at a notorious bottleneck before reaching the coast road. Fortunately, she met no such hazard. New traffic lights had made a big difference in recent months and the road ahead was clear. She glanced to her left. Bright was slumped in the passenger seat, staring straight ahead, deep in thought.

Either he hadn't heard her or he'd chosen to ignore the question.

'Take some leave, guv. I can cope.'

'And do what, take Stella dancing?'

His words stung. 'Guv, I'm sorry, I didn't mean—'

'I'm just tired, Kate. I'll get over it . . .' Bright ran his left hand through his hair and let out a frustrated sigh. 'Look, I didn't mean to bite your head off. It's me who should be sorry.'

'Don't be. I've got broad shoulders. Take after my boss, remember?'

'You've been a great help to me in recent months, I don't know how to—'

'Guv, I'm just worried about you.'

'Don't, Kate. Please, I couldn't handle your sympathy.'

He fell silent again as they passed through a short tunnel and up a slight incline. Cars in front began to apply their brakes at the sight of speed cameras, accelerating as soon as they were able without danger of a £60 fine and three points on their licence. Daniels did likewise, deciding to let the matter drop. Now was not the time to try and talk some sense into her boss. She wondered how long he'd been drinking and wished he'd seek counselling from Occupational Health.

Jo was out of the question obviously, more's the pity. A: They didn't get on. B: She was a prime suspect in *her* – now their – current case.

Daniels' eyes shot to the clock on the dash. *Visiting time.* She could make it if she hurried. But the man sitting next to her had expressly forbidden it. How could she tell Jo that she wouldn't be visiting again? As she mulled over this latest dilemma, the miles rolled silently by, neither of them in a mood for chat. When they arrived at Bright's house, she realized she'd been on automatic pilot, with barely any recollection of the journey.

The curtains were drawn and a light was on as they pulled up outside. Stella's part-time carer had obviously been busy, hopefully managing to feed her and get her settled down for the evening. Just as well, Daniels thought. *He* was in no fit state to look after his wife's needs. Not tonight, anyway. She killed the engine but he made no attempt to get out of the car, just swivelled his body round to face her.

'We won a salsa competition once, Stella and I.'

Daniels smiled, unable to imagine him tripping the light fantastic. 'You kept that quiet, guv. How long have we known each other?'

'Repeat it and you're off the squad,' he said.

She tapped the side of her nose. 'Your secret's safe with me.'

'It better be.' He looked towards the house, his expression morphing into one of dread.

'Want me to come in, guv?' She cursed as her phone rang. The display showed RON CALLING. 'Mind if I take this? It's Naylor.'

Bright held her gaze for a little too long, shook his head and got out of the car, bidding her goodnight. Daniels watched him trundle heavily up the path to his front door and let himself in without a backward glance.

'Yeah, Ron. What's up?'

'You're not going to believe this . . .' Naylor's voice sounded a little shaky. 'We've got ourselves another one. Birmingham, this time. Guy called Malik. Same MO – well, a shooting, at any rate. And the same signature: a prayer card left at the scene.'

52

Daniels could hardly contain herself as she drove to the hospital with Ron Naylor's words ringing in her ears: another crime scene . . . another corpse . . . another prayer card. The latest victim was a middle-aged Asian named Jamil Malik. Although considerably older now, Naylor was sure it was the same man in the magazine cutting hand-delivered to the station for her specific attention the day before by an agitated woman who hadn't hung around long enough to be seen.

At the time, they hadn't been able to decide if she was just another bloody crank or someone in real trouble; some poor soul who had neither the guts nor the language skills to make herself heard. Now Daniels was wondering if someone altogether more sinister had put her up to it. Had she been forced into making the delivery and then fled, fearing further questions? Had Father Simon's and Sarah Short's killer surfaced after all this time? Was he taunting her? Telling her to follow her gut instinct? The idea that at last she might be on to something filled her with joy. But before she could follow that up, she had something equally important to do . . .

Withholding information was one thing; direct disobedience was altogether more serious, especially when your guv'nor was Superintendent Bright. Even though they enjoyed such a close working relationship, he was not a man to cross.

Daniels entered the hospital lift, aware that, if Bright found out where she was, her promising career was as good as over. But he'd given her no choice. She needed a breathing space to work out what to do next. The only way to get it was to persuade Jo to play for time.

As she exited the lift on the second floor the air seemed rife with hospital gossip. Nurse Baker was chewing the fat with a junior doctor outside her office door. When she caught sight of Daniels, the nurse flushed, stopped talking and looked at her watch. Her plastic smile didn't fool the DCI.

Not for one second.

'Visiting time's over,' was all Baker said.

Sensing the tension between them, the doctor made a hasty retreat. The usual preferential treatment for fellow emergency service personnel didn't apply here; Nurse Baker was in no mood to offer concessions. Daniels forced a smile, prepared to eat humble pie to get back in her good books. She'd never been good at amateur dramatics, but put on her best begging face and said apologetically:

'I'm *really* sorry, but it's vital I see her. It can't wait, I'm afraid.'

'Well, it'll have to . . .' Baker threw back her shoulders, letting Daniels know who was in charge. 'She's resting. You'll have to come back later.'

Daniels swallowed her pride. 'Look, I know we got off on the wrong foot. It was my fault entirely. I, I was stressed out, concerned for my colleague. My apologies. Two minutes, that's all I'm asking, then I'm out of here.'

'Two minutes!' The nurse tapped her watch. 'Not a minute more!'

Sleep under the influence of drugs was one continuous nightmare, controlling Jo's subconscious, making her see things she didn't want to see. A black shadow hovered above her head and an indistinct image of a man covered in blood was lying on the floor. He got up and moved towards her. She tried to move away but was pinned to the bed by her sheets, hair stuck to her head in sweaty strands, eyelids glued shut. And still the figure approached. Out of focus, but getting closer . . . clearer . . . closer . . . clearer. Alan reached out to touch her, smiling through bloody teeth. His lips were moving but no words came out. If they did, Jo couldn't hear them.

Daniels studied the twisting, writhing form on the bed, tormented by whatever ghosts were invading her dreams. Nervous of waking her suddenly, she waited by her side until, as if sensing her presence, Jo stirred, forcing open her eyelids as if someone had sewn them together with invisible thread.

The tension in Jo's body subsided when she saw who was standing over her. 'They gave me a painkiller,' she said, wiping sweat from her brow. 'I went out like a light. I had an awful dream about Alan. It was horrible.'

Daniels sat down and took her hand. 'Are you properly awake?'

Sensing the change in Daniels' mood, Jo nodded uncertainly.

'I need you to listen to me – we haven't got much time. There've been developments. You're to be interviewed under caution. You say nothing, do you hear me? Nothing at all. Get a solicitor right away. Plead ill health. Anything to buy time. Can you do that?'

Another nod. 'I don't understand. What developments?'

'I haven't got time to explain. Trust me, Jo. If they can link you to the crime scene, we're in deep shit and there's not much I can do about it.'

Despite the seriousness of the situation, Jo's face suddenly relaxed. She smiled at her visitor with her eyes as well as her mouth, the way she used to when they were together. It stopped Daniels in full flow.

'What?' she said.

'There's hope for you yet . . .' Jo filled up. 'You just referred to the police as *they*, as if your colleagues had suddenly become public enemy number one, the opposition, a force to be reckoned with.'

Daniels hugged her. 'When are you going to realize that I'm on your side?'

The Toyota raced out of the hospital grounds. Daniels turned left, flooring the accelerator and heading into town. It had been a long day – she desperately needed to crash – but three prayer cards in separate locations loomed large in her mind as she drove along: Birmingham, Durham and, before that, St Camillus.

There had to be a connection.

Naylor's contention that a man killed in Birmingham was the same Asian male whose photograph she'd shared with him only yesterday filled Daniels with both horror and excitement, sweeping away feelings of exhaustion, replacing them with relief. If Naylor was right, this could open the door to a potential breakthrough in the Corbridge case; the enquiry that still dogged her, despite her best efforts and those of MIT. After almost a year of painstaking work they had failed to get a result, and remained unable to offer closure to those left behind.

For a moment or two, Daniels was back at St Camillus, fear gripping her as she took in the scene. Then her mind flew forward several months to her face-off with Bright in his office, his galling statement that the Corbridge enquiry was well and truly dead in the water.

No way!

Not as long as she drew breath, it wasn't.

Anyway, Naylor was now on board.

Two of them couldn't be wrong.

Could they?

Back in the MIR, Daniels didn't bother going to her office, just took off her coat and slung it over the back of Gormley's chair. Reaching into her bag, she took out the cutting of the young Asian male, scanned the image and sent a copy, via email, to both Ron Naylor and her counterpart within West Midlands Police, DCI Vic Nichols. Next, she placed the cutting into an evidence bag – together with the envelope it had come in – and sent them off for forensic examination.

Now all she could do was wait.

53

DC Neil Maxwell yawned. Five hours' sleep was all he'd managed and it was nowhere near enough. He'd felt decidedly groggy when the alarm went off and since then his day had got progressively worse. Scanning grainy CCTV images for hours on end wasn't the most stimulating of tasks. Bored to death with it, he leaned back in his chair and put his feet up on a desk, then quickly removed them when he heard someone coming. He sat up straight, glad for the interruption, especially when he saw who was striding into the room.

Sensing his eyes on her, Carmichael pointed at the footage running, ignored, on his screen.

'You might want to rewind that, Neil,' she said.

Maxwell mumbled something crude under his breath and hit pause. Then restarted it again without rewinding, wondering what it was about him Carmichael didn't like. She looked really pleased with herself today – more so than usual – as she made a beeline for DS Robson, who was sitting at a desk a few yards away.

Robson looked up as she approached.

'This just came in, Sarge.'

Carmichael handed over a message that had just arrived from the East City police office. It was addressed to the murder incident room and marked: *For the urgent attention of the SIO.* Robson's eyes opened wide as he read it. He handed it back, nodding toward the receiver's desk.

'Give it to Harry,' he said. 'I'll get on the blower to the boss.'

Just a few miles away, Daniels checked her rear-view mirror and signalled that she was pulling in. As she slowed down, the boy racer behind blasted his horn, made a disgusting hand gesture and sped off. She took his number before answering her phone.

'What is it, Robbo?'

On the other end of the line, Robson sounded more excited than when his wife gave birth to their son. 'Our lucky day, I hope,' he said. 'Some punter took a firearm into the east end nick around an hour ago – a 9mm semi-automatic knock-off pretending to be a Browning.'

'Could it be ours?'

'Absolutely. It's gone off for analysis.'

'Good. Anything else?'

'There is . . . but I'm guessing you won't want to hear it.'

Silence.

'Boss?'

'Yeah, I'm listening.'

'The gun was found less than a hundred yards from Jo's office,' Robson paused for a second to let the information sink in. 'ACC Martin has obtained warrants for her home and place of work.'

Meltdown.

It was the worst possible news and it hit Daniels like a brick. 'Who the hell told him?'

'Dunno, he just . . .'

She lost Robson's voice as an HGV sped by, hardly registered what he was saying as her thoughts turned to Jo, tuned back in to hear something about Gormley executing a warrant to search Jo's office.

'. . . the guv'nor wants you to do likewise at her home . . .' Robson stopped to take a breath. 'Boss, you still there?'

Daniels no longer felt like the boss, much less the Senior Investigating Officer. She opened her window to get some air and made a mental note to find whoever was responsible for contacting the ACC and bone them for going over her head.

'Robbo, I'm losing you . . . my battery's low.'

She hung up.

54

It was a closed community with a high crime rate, an area of the city where role models came at a premium and doors slammed in the faces of the police. Gormley pulled to the kerb outside a semi-detached house, its windows protected by heavy iron bars and closed-circuit television security cameras above the front door. He got out of the car with Brown in tow and locked it securely, hoping it would still have four wheels by the time they got back.

A couple of young kids skateboarded across the road in front of them, nearly coming to grief as a double-decker bus swung round the corner in a huge arc, its driver shaking his fist, receiving two fingers in return. The kids hopped back on their boards and skated off laughing. Gormley remembered the days when he'd have clipped them round the ear and taken them home for worse from their parents, a time when being a policeman counted for something more than just a big fat lump sum at the end of thirty years – enough of a pension to live on for the rest of your days.

Brown pushed open a rusty iron gate in dire need of a lick of paint. The garden was awash with all kinds of rubbish: pizza boxes, chip wrappers, abandoned cans and bottles chucked over the wall without a second thought. As he depressed the bell push with his thumb, the word WANKER right in his eye line, Gormley wondered whose bright idea it had been to situate the Regional Psychology Service here.

'Respect agenda, my arse!' he said.

Brown pulled a face. 'Did I miss something?'

Gormley shook his head. Blair's 'respect agenda' had left so little trace, what was there to miss? 'Just thinking out loud.'

A woman's voice came over the intercom. 'Yes!'

Brown held up his warrant card to the CCTV camera. 'Police.'

A buzzer sounded and the door clicked open. They passed through an outer hallway into a narrow corridor, Gormley leading the way. There was a reception desk at the far end where a middle-aged receptionist sat behind thick protective glass, which was just as well, given the clientele. It was Scumbag Central; a side bench was lined with a bunch of them slumped with their legs outstretched, effectively blocking the narrow waiting area. Some were reading, some listening to iPods, the rest just staring blankly at the opposite wall. The nearest one, Gary Henderson, didn't bother to move as they approached.

'Shift!' Gormley said, in no mood to be messed around.

Henderson nudged Forster, the next man down, who had his head in a magazine, and then sniffed at the air artificially.

'What's that smell, d'you reckon? Shite, pig shite, or just pigs?'

Forster grinned but kept his head down, not wanting to get involved. Gormley smiled reassuringly at the receptionist, figuring she'd have witnessed one or two fights in her time. With the likes of Henderson it was usually a case of when, not if, things would kick off. The wimp on the right was far too old for the shaved head and tattoos he was sporting under thinning hair. Gormley ignored him, eyeballing Henderson instead, bending over him and placing his hands on the bench either side of Henderson's thighs.

He leaned in close, so close their faces nearly touched. 'I said shift!'

Henderson smirked.

Gormley swung back his foot, kicked both men's legs away and then carried on to reception. The woman behind the desk was practically beside herself, eyes darting past him, expecting more trouble as he made his way towards her.

'I'm Detective Sergeant Gormley, this is DC Brown. We need a word.'

The receptionist put her hand out, expecting Gormley to pass his warrant card under the narrow gap of the security window. Instead, he pressed it against the partition, making her examine it through the glass. In all his time in the force he'd never let go of his most prized possession and wasn't about to start now. She peered over the top of her spectacles, comparing him with his ID. The man in the photo was much younger than the man standing in front of her, but she could still tell it was him. Then Brown produced a search warrant and shoved it beneath the window.

'We need access to Ms Soulsby's office,' he said.

The receptionist unfolded the piece of paper and took for-ever to read it. When she looked up, she shrank back from the glass, highly agitated. Henderson was on his feet and walking towards them.

Gormley swung round on his heels. 'Move and I'll break your arm!'

Henderson backed off, holding up the middle finger of his right hand. As they were buzzed through a door marked PRIVATE, Brown cautioned him to sit down and show some respect.

They found Jo's office at the rear of the building on the ground floor. Apart from bars at the windows, it was a pleasant enough room: a large mahogany desk in the centre, a comfortable chair, solid-wood bookshelves housing professional manuals, with a small selection of children's books on the bottom shelf.

They spent over two hours searching before returning to the front desk. Gormley thanked the receptionist for her cooperation while Brown gave her a list of items they were taking away: Jo's desk diary, her laptop, a mobile telephone receipt and several other documents they thought they might need.

'We may need to come back,' Brown warned. 'We'll also need a copy of Ms Soulsby's current caseload.'

'Is that *really* necessary?' the receptionist said.

''Fraid so.'

The woman logged on to her computer and typed a command. The printer reset itself, then sprang into action, spewing out a list of sixty or so names. Brown wondered if the people on it would be referred to as clients or patients. Either description was too good for the scum they'd met on their way in.

55

Daniels spent the next few hours trying to find out more about the Malik killing. Naylor had no news. So, instead of waiting for them to come to her, she rang the Birmingham SIO directly. But it was a fruitless exercise. DCI Nichols was about as much help as a chocolate fireguard. Or so it seemed initially . . .

'It looks very like him.' Nichols was referring to the cutting she'd sent. 'I'll get back to you on that as soon as.'

Daniels took a deep breath and counted to ten.

'As soon as' didn't fill her with confidence.

'Any witnesses come forward in the house-to-house?' she asked.

'Not one, despite our best efforts to allay their fears. I'm sorry, Kate. We've got bugger all.' As he paused for breath, Daniels could hear the buzz and chatter of a busy incident room in the background. 'Locals aren't willing to get involved on account of the MO. Can't say I blame them. They're terrified. It's hard to imagine what was going through that cruel bastard's head when he used a child to pull the trigger.'

Daniels' ears pricked up.

Maybe Nichols wasn't such a divvi after all.

'You have evidence to back that up?' she asked.

'Indisputable: the boy's fingerprints were on the gun and

there was gunshot residue on his hands. Can you believe that? It's a first for me, I can tell you! And the last, if I have anything to do with it,' he added.

Daniels had to admit this modus operandi was a first for her too. Nichols' final comment was hopeful, but it lacked any real conviction. He was in no position to offer guarantees to her or the community he served. There was no magic wand either of them could wave in cases like these. All the more reason to work as a team. Thanking him, she asked him to keep her posted and rang off.

Carmichael wandered over, frustration showing on her face as she informed her boss that she'd struck out too. 'Forensic tests on the weapon found near Jo's office will be some time coming. There's a backlog of cases of equal importance, so I'm told.'

'Is there now? Well you get straight back on to them with another request. I want a comparison test between my gun and the one used to kill Jamil Malik – and I want it now!' Carmichael nodded. She was already walking away when Daniels called after her: 'Lisa, don't bother. I'll make that call myself.'

Picking up the office phone, Daniels made the call and then left the building asking Carmichael to hold the fort.

Fifteen minutes later, she entered Jo's house to find SOCO crawling all over it. An officer dressed in a white forensic suit acknowledged her with a nod, stood up and handed over two clear evidence envelopes.

'I found that in the waste bin in the kitchen,' she said pointing to the first.

Daniels held it up in front of her face. It contained a

MARI HANNAH

torn-up photograph, which came as no surprise to her. Then she held up the second. 'What's this?'

'Demand for unpaid university tuition fees, in which Alan Stephens is named.'

'Where was it?'

'In one of the bedrooms upstairs, stuffed under a mattress.'

Daniels' jaw went rigid. She pulled out her phone and made a call. 'This is DCI Daniels. I need to ask you a few more questions.' She listened. 'Obviously, or I wouldn't be asking.' She rolled her eyes at the SOCO. The person she'd called was trying her patience. 'I'll be straight there.'

There was an atmosphere in the room. Monica Stephens' normally calm manner seemed to have deserted her all of a sudden. She appeared nervous, was fussing with cushions on a new sofa, trying her best to avoid eye contact with Daniels.

'And you didn't think it worth mentioning before now?' the DCI asked.

Monica looked up. 'Alan resented having to pay after the boy reached eighteen.'

'I take it you didn't agree with him?'

Monica sighed. 'No, I didn't. James had just begun his second year at university, but Alan wouldn't listen. He said *he'd* left school at fifteen and it hadn't done him any harm.'

Daniels was disgusted. 'And James found out?'

'Naturally . . .' Monica clasped her hands together and put them in her lap. 'He rang here, ranting and raving. My husband had already put Thomas through university and James resented being treated differently. Alan refused to see him, refused to reconsider. They had an awful row. I'm not sure what James said to him, but I've never seen Alan so angry.'

Monica got up, walked to the window, and looked out. With her back turned, Daniels couldn't help noticing that the room had been transformed in the last few days. Maybe now that Alan Stephens was dead his mother would reap the benefits of his considerable wealth.

The DCI pressed on: 'Is there anything else you omitted to tell me?'

Monica turned. 'What star sign are you, Detective Chief Inspector?'

Daniels didn't reply.

'Alan was a Scorpio through and through.'

'Meaning?'

'If someone hurt him, he hit back twice as hard. He hid it well most of the time, but Alan had a cruel streak, make no mistake. He threatened to disinherit the boy.'

'Only James?'

Monica nodded.

'In whose favour?'

Monica met her gaze head-on. 'Your guess is as good as mine. Who knows what a serial philanderer has up his sleeve?'

Daniels shook her head. 'Why didn't you tell me this before?'

'I'm not in the habit of washing my dirty linen in public, are you?'

'All the same . . .'

Monica looked guilty now.

'I'm sorry,' she said. 'I should've told you about Alan's affairs.' She paused for a moment collecting her thoughts.

'James is such a sweet boy under all that bravado. I know he blamed me for his parents' break-up, but deep down he knows I wasn't responsible. I didn't want to be the one to point the finger of suspicion at him. He didn't . . . well, I'm sure he had nothing to do with his father's death.'

'I wish I could be so sure.'

Daniels spent another half-hour with Monica. Only when she was absolutely sure the woman had nothing else to give did she leave the house. Walking back to the car, she called Gormley on his mobile and told him what she'd just found out: 'Stephens had a new will drawn up, cutting James out altogether.'

'Had he signed it?'

'Monica's not sure . . . at least, that's what she says.'

'That gives James a reason to kill him. Her, too, considering his infidelity. Maybe she wanted out before Stephens chose to move on permanently.'

Gormley paused. Daniels could hear traffic noises in the background. It sounded like he was crossing a very busy road. Then he was back on the line.

'Isn't it time you let Bright in on Jo's little secret?'

Daniels kept walking. 'See you tomorrow, Hank.'

56

Vehicles were like ghostly shadows on the road into town. Daniels drove slowly and carefully through a thick blanket of fog, conscious of a colleague who, just two years ago, had lost her life in a pile-up on the M6 motorway during similar weather conditions. She'd been on the way to collect her child from university and bring her home for Christmas when her car ploughed into the back of a slow-moving bus.

The thought made Daniels shiver.

She was feeling rough today, her sleep having been disturbed more than once by curious dreams she couldn't understand. She'd tried to settle herself down again and get some kip, but it was useless. In the end she just gave up, got up, had a shower and set off for work well before dawn. Relieved when the Toyota finally passed beneath the security barrier at the station, Daniels parked the car and let herself into the building via the back door. Her silent entry to the incident room startled a cleaner engrossed in her work.

'Jesus, I nearly jumped out me skin!' the young woman said in a soft Geordie twang. She was pretty, mid to late twenties, oval face, brown eyes and auburn hair pulled back tightly into a high ponytail – a hairstyle Maxwell cruelly referred to as a Croydon face-lift. 'You want me out of here? I'm just about done.'

'No, you carry on. I'm sorry, I didn't mean to frighten you.' In all her years in the police force, it was the first time Daniels had considered how spooky it must be for a civilian to work in a murder incident room alone, especially at such an ungodly hour. She pointed to her office. 'You finished in there?'

The girl nodded, then turned away, tiptoeing across the wet floor with her mop and bucket, the smell of disinfectant lingering in her wake. As she set about creating order from chaos, Daniels did likewise. The squad wouldn't be arriving 'til seven. She had an hour and a half head start. Closing the door behind her, she slipped off her coat, put on the kettle and waited for it to boil, then made herself a mug of coffee as black and as bitter as her mood. She alone was to blame for her professional dilemma – didn't need reminding how inappropriate her actions had been – but, bizarrely, those same actions had cemented her loyalty to Jo, and she liked the way that made her feel.

Maybe there *was* still hope for them.

But this was no time to indulge in fantasy.

Putting her personal feelings aside, Daniels tried to organize her thoughts, prioritize the many things competing for attention in her head. Alan Stephens may have possessed a 'cruel streak', according to his widow, but it was *her* duty to find the person or persons responsible for his death, to see that he got justice. It mattered not that he was a bad father, a despicable bully who'd humiliated Jo during their marriage – and Monica, too, by the sounds of it. Whatever Stephens had done in life, he certainly didn't deserve to have it taken away so violently. The dead deserved a voice and, whether Daniels liked it or not, she was his.

There were four Post-it notes stuck to her computer screen: one from Bright reminding her to submit her expenses claims and budget projections by the end of the day, the other three from her father. *Screw him.* She threw them in the bin. She had more important things to do. Picking up the phone, she rang the front desk. 'This is DCI Daniels. Fetch me CCTV footage of reception for Sunday night. I'm particularly interested in . . .' *What time was it?* 'Around seven. Yes, that's right . . . Yes, now!'

Hanging up, she logged on to her computer.

Within minutes, a civilian worker she recognized knocked gently on her door with a disk in her hand and a scowl on her face. Daniels thanked her for the disk, apologized for snapping at her on the phone, and promised to return it in due course. When the girl had gone, she put the disk into a computer slot, fast-forwarding the footage until the counter on the bottom right-hand corner of her screen showed six forty-five p.m.

She settled down to watch.

On screen, the door to reception opened and a surly-looking thug walked in: a regular visitor to the station, she recognized him immediately. The duty officer reached under the front desk, pulled out the sign-on register and leafed through it. At the appropriate page, he turned the book around. The offender signed it and walked off without a word. As he left the building, a woman in a burka entered holding up an envelope and pointing at the front, just as the desk sergeant had described.

Daniels sat back, rapt, watching the silent exchange. The desk sergeant reached out for the envelope, but the woman withdrew it from him, again jabbing her forefinger at the name on the front. The officer gestured towards a bench behind her and turned away to pick up the phone. When his back was turned, the woman stood up, dropped the envelope on the counter and left the building hurriedly. Daniels rewound the footage and then ran it again, freezing the image and zooming in on the figure in the burka . . .

The envelope . . .

Her hand . . .

Or was it *his*?

Jesus! He's got some nerve.

She immediately rang Ron Naylor, making no apologies for getting him out of bed. They arranged to meet later and then she turned her attention back to the Stephens case. Seconds turned to minutes, minutes to hours, and it was almost four in the afternoon before she lifted her head again.

Sitting back now, she was aware of telephones ringing, detectives hypothesizing, arguing the case on the other side of her office door. She could hear Gormley spouting off about lack of forensics in the case. Brown threw his thoughts into the mix, pointing to the growing body of circumstantial evidence against Jo Soulsby. He wouldn't yet describe it as compelling, but he agreed with Bright. Soulsby was beginning to emerge as the only real suspect.

If Daniels was honest with herself, if it hadn't been Jo she'd have been inclined to agree with them. Not this time, she thought, looking out of the window at the last dregs of the sun on the horizon. This time, she was determined to prove them all wrong. Somewhere in the city streets below, the *real* killer was out there.

57

He'd looked at it again today.

The shop doorway stank of piss and offered little shelter from the pouring rain. He smiled as a patrol car cruised by, its female occupant giving him the once-over before driving on, presumably with more important things to do.

How wrong could a person be?

Her colleagues were no nearer catching him now than they had ever been. He was already planning his next move and the pigs were the least of his worries. He was hungry for the scissors, impatient for the next cut, but Number Six was proving harder to track down than the others and a little more diligence was required.

It wasn't a race, he reminded himself; he was in it for the long haul, content to savour the moment, congratulate himself on his achievements so far.

He had all the time in the world to find Dotty.

Patience is a virtue! a caustic voice echoed inside his head.

Her fucking voice, the one that refused to go away, the one that made him cringe, affecting him deeply, waking him, sweating and crying in the night, her finger wagging in front of his face as he cowered beneath the covers. He'd been hearing it a lot lately. But, just as there was no hiding place for him back then, there was none for them now.

His smile faded . . .

Anger boiled inside him as something came to him in a flash. He could've, perhaps should've, taken the opportunity when he'd had it: asked Malik where his next target was, or Jenny, for that matter. They'd have known. And if they'd refused to spill, he'd have enjoyed torturing them until they squealed. He could still ask his mother, but that would give the game away. He wanted to drip-feed *her*. Let her hear of their deaths through the grapevine, bit by agonizing bit, until the cruel bitch knew he was coming for her.

No, he'd find Number Six and he'd do it alone.

Up at the second-floor window, he could see Detective Chief Inspector Kate Daniels staring out, concentration etched on her face. It gave him a warm feeling to think that, right at that very moment, they were thinking of each other, like a couple of lovesick teenagers too shy to make the first move, yet whose every waking moment was spent waiting for the day when they would finally get it together.

Sooner or later she'd realize that his victims were all God people, and then she'd be gagging to make his acquaintance.

Oh, how he longed for that day.

58

'DCI Daniels' phone . . . hello? . . . Daniels' office.'

Jo hadn't anticipated Gormley answering the phone. Flustered, she covered the speaker, trying to decide what to do next. She considered ringing off, but she needed to talk. And nobody but Kate Daniels would do.

Maybe he wouldn't recognize her.

'I need to speak to DCI Daniels right away,' she said.

'Jo?'

'Yes, it's me . . .' She wished he'd just fuck off and get Kate, even though she knew it was part of his job to field the DCI's calls. 'Can I speak to her or not?'

'Hang on. I'll see what I can do.'

The line clicked. As Jo waited, she imagined Gormley striding off into the bowels of the busy police station, tracking his movements in her mind's eye, until suddenly he was back on the line.

'Jo?'

'I'm still here.'

'I'm sorry, she was here a minute ago but she just left. Is there anything . . .?'

Jo put down the phone.

Ten minutes later, a bell rang indicating the start of visiting time. Through the open blinds on her door, she watched people passing her room bearing gifts: flowers, fruit, biscuits, balloons on a string. Jo closed her eyes and snuggled down in bed, then opened them again when she heard a gentle knock at the door. Excitement faded to disappointment when her visitor entered, for no other reason than she'd hoped, prayed, that Kate Daniels would come.

Kirsten Edwards smiled at her through perfect teeth. She was a striking Irishwoman with auburn hair, green eyes and the figure of someone half her age. She wore well-cut clothes, brown suede boots and carried an expensive handbag to match. Over her other arm was an enormous bouquet, a mixture of white lilies, carnations and roses that must've cost a fortune. She stood for a while, examining her surroundings – the bedclothes, the chair, the jug of warm water – and looking decidedly uncomfortable, as if her very presence in the building would cause her to catch some awful disease. Then, visibly steeling herself, she approached the bed and placed the flowers on Jo's lap.

Jo felt ugly compared to the vision of loveliness embracing her, filling her nostrils with the heady scent of Agent Provocateur. Then, over Kirsten's shoulder, she caught sight of her preferred visitor, hovering anxiously outside the door. Their eyes met briefly, then Daniels gave a little wave and walked away, causing Jo to burst into floods of tears as she disappeared from view, knowing Kate had risked *everything* to visit.

Misreading her sorrow, Kirsten pulled away and sat down on the chair beside the bed. Handing Jo a tissue, she waited for her to compose herself. 'Poor you,' she said. 'For what it's worth, these places give me the creeps too.'

'I didn't have a lot of choice.' Jo dried her eyes. She wanted to leap out of bed and race down the corridor before Daniels reached the lift, to let her know before she left the hospital, for what she assumed would be the final time, just how much she appreciated her support. But she knew that in her present state she wouldn't make it past the door. Instead, she sniffed at the bouquet and put on a brave face. 'These are lovely, Kirsten. Thank you so much.'

Baker popped her head in, caught Kirsten's attention and tapped her watch.

Kirsten raised a perfectly shaped eyebrow. 'The obergruppenführer says I've got five minutes, tops. She says you're overtired and need to rest. Doctor's orders, apparently.'

'You think she's bad, you should meet the night sister!' Jo managed a weak smile.

Kirsten tried to mask her distress at Jo's injuries but she couldn't quite manage that. 'I can't believe it . . .' she said, her eyes scanning every bruise, every graze on Jo's face. 'You looked absolutely fabulous on Thursday.'

Jo said nothing for several seconds.

'You saw me on Thursday?'

59

The wine bar was busy with partying customers all talking at once. It was subtly lit with a wooden floor and a distinct Mediterranean feel, the walls adorned with now-defunct covers of long-playing records. There was plenty of low seating and high stools at the bar, all of which were taken.

The waitress emerging from behind the bar had to be Kirsten Edwards. Daniels was sure it was the same woman she'd seen at Jo's bedside earlier in the evening, only now her hair was tied up and she was dressed in jeans, a silk shirt and high-heeled boots. Daniels wondered if Jo and this stunning woman were now, or had ever been, an item.

'Ms Edwards?' Daniels said.

The waitress nodded, scanned the bar and held up a finger. 'One second . . .' Her voice trailed off as she took in a female customer's hand raised in the air. She had a word with the barman before approaching Daniels with her hand extended. 'You must be Kate Daniels.'

'Yes, I am.' Daniels didn't waste any time. 'I take it you know why I'm here?

'Jo explained everything. Can I get you a glass of wine, soft drink, coffee . . .?'

Daniels shook her head, wondering if 'everything' meant *everything* or whether it was just a figure of speech. She decided to chance her arm: 'What is your relationship with Jo, exactly?'

Kirsten was a little taken aback. 'Is that relevant?'

Daniels let it go. 'Can you confirm you were together on Thursday night?'

'We were out together, yes. Me, Jo, and four friends from university. She wasn't keen to go at first. Reunions aren't really her style. She and I get together now and then, but the others had drifted apart. You know how it is.'

Daniels knew exactly how it was. She hadn't kept in touch with any of her school friends – could hardly remember any of their names – and social networking definitely wasn't her style. Kirsten raised an arm, attracting the attention of a staff member, and pointed at some abandoned glasses with a disapproving look on her face. As the barmaid scurried off to collect them, Kirsten turned back.

'Sorry, I have to keep on top of them or the place would be a tip,' she said, a wry smile appearing on her face. 'You're wondering why a law graduate is waiting tables in a wine bar, right?'

Daniels had been wondering no such thing. She was too busy reflecting on Kirsten's relationship with Jo. This wasn't the woman who had come between them. But were they just good friends? Or had things moved beyond that?

She played along. 'My apologies, I'm not usually that obvious.'

'I own it and several others like it,' Kirsten explained.

'I'm impressed,' Daniels lied. 'What made Jo change her mind?'

Kirsten smiled, almost flirting. 'I can be quite persuasive, Kate.'

60

In the morning, she drove straight to headquarters, having rung ahead to warn Bright she was on her way. But when she got there, he wasn't in his office. His bag-man told her that he'd gone out for a walk to clear his head. Wondering if that was a metaphor for having been drunk the night before, Daniels thanked him and left the building.

She found him in the grounds, watching a company of new recruits marching on parade. The dog handler with him acknowledged her with a nod and moved off, a young German Shepherd biting at his heels. Feeling her presence as she arrived by his side, Bright commented on how quickly his twenty-five years in the force had passed by. She found herself agreeing with him – her own fifteen years had gone in the blink of an eye. He turned and looked at her intently. For a moment, she thought he was going to say something *really* personal, but instead he warned her against treading on certain toes. He didn't have to spell out who it was he was referring to.

'I'm damned if I'll treat him differently just because he happens to be a senior officer,' Daniels bit back. 'Martin's definitely lying, guv. And I'm hell-bent on getting to the bottom of it.'

'He's also the ACC,' Bright reminded her. 'Why d'you think we're not having this conversation in my office?'

'That makes no odds, does it?' A pause. 'Well, does it?'

'All I'm saying is, take care in the way you go about it – unless you fancy traffic duty for the rest of your days. I know it might not always be apparent, but your career matters to me. It always has.'

'I appreciate that, guv.'

'Good. Now, what else is happening? We any further forward?'

'That's why I'm here. I now know where Jo was until around midnight on the fifth. I need time to follow it up, trace other potential witnesses. It shouldn't take long.'

Bright listened carefully to what she had to say. Daniels told him about the reunion, about the statement she'd taken from Kirsten Edwards, the need to find the others to corroborate her story. For a while he remained silent, but she could see from the look on his face that he was doing the maths.

'Midnight, you say?'

Daniels nodded soberly. She knew what was coming.

'Then if the taxi didn't pick her up until around one thirty, an hour and a half is unaccounted for.'

'That's why I need to—'

'That's time enough to commit genocide, let alone kill Stephens!'

Daniels drove back to town in double-quick time. On reaching the incident room, she headed straight for Gormley's desk and asked him to join her in her office. She walked in ahead of him, threw herself down on her seat and waited for him to shut the door before speaking.

'Any progress on Monica Stephens' alibi?' she asked.

'Airport CCTV caught her and her mate arriving around nine twenty-five; Monica leaving alone at eleven forty-seven; Teresa Branson boarding a plane around the same time. Her trip was a round robin by the way, Helsinki, London and back to Newcastle. They're both in the clear . . .' Gormley sat down. 'You OK?'

'I'm fine.'

'You don't look fine.'

She sighed – and spent the next few minutes sounding off about Bright and his blinkered approach to the case. 'He's being bloody ridiculous! Why can't he see it?' Then, realizing how inappropriate it was to rubbish her boss, even to Gormley, she clammed up. 'I'm sorry, Hank. This is *my* problem, not yours. Forget I said anything.'

He was quiet for a moment, then he tried placating her, telling her he completely understood how tough it was, living in Bright's shadow while having overall responsibility for the case, adding the obvious reminder that she didn't have a lot of choice in the matter. She felt bad about burdening him, even though she knew she could count on his discretion. She could trust Gormley with anything, even her life, but it wasn't *her* life that nagged at Daniels' thoughts at that moment. One by one, suspects were being eliminated and there was now a real possibility that Jo, or her youngest son, could end up charged with murder.

Jo would never get over that.

'His opinions have certainly divided the squad,' Gormley said, his voice interrupting her chain of thought. 'Ask around. Some are starting to think she's guilty, others are just as sure she's not. But I warn you, whether you like it or not, the balance is starting to tip.'

'It has to be someone with a grudge,' Daniels said, her thoughts turning to James.

'Yeah, well, who'd bear more of a grudge than an ex-wife!' Gormley said, picking city muck from his fingernails.

Reaching into her drawer, Daniels pulled out her make-up bag, producing a nail file that she slid across the desk. 'Here, these are so good you can buy them in the shops.'

Gormley laughed, began filing harshly as if he were sawing wood.

'We're looking for a psychopath,' Daniels said. 'That hardly fits Jo, now, does it?'

A grin crept on to Gormley's face. He waggled his right hand from side to side as if it were touch and go. 'Psychopath, psychotherapist . . . Is there a difference? As I said, the evidence is stacking up.'

'Circumstantial. It has no substance. I'm worried, Hank. James—' Her phone rang loudly, startling her. She lifted the receiver. 'Daniels . . . what? . . . when? Any idea where it was taken? OK, Vic. Thanks for letting me know.'

Daniels hung up, momentarily lost in thought.

'Problem?'

'Probably . . .' Her eyes shifted to the phone. 'That was DCI Nichol, West Mids. A member of Jamil Malik's family has positively identified the photograph delivered to me here at the station. He's no idea when or where it was taken, even less idea of anyone who might have held a grudge against his cousin – who, incidentally, he described as a good man, a man of religious integrity.'

'Christ!'

'No, not Christ, Hank. Just a man of religious integrity . . .'

She mimicked Gormley's funny face and then got serious again. 'Raise an action to trace the source document of that photograph, date, place and any other info.'

It was a tall order, but one Daniels hoped would bear fruit. A light tap on the door made them look up. Robson entered looking pleased with himself. He pulled up a chair and sat down.

'We've had a positive result from the ballistics lab on the weapon,' he said.

'Was it our gun?' Gormley asked.

'Yeah, but it's clean.'

Daniels wanted more. 'As in, it has no prints, or hasn't been used before?'

'Both. By the way, did you see Maxwell before he went out?'

Daniels shook her head. 'Why?'

Gormley's sawing began irritating her. She leaned across the desk and grabbed the file back before he ruined it completely. He pulled a face, took a box of matches from his pocket and carried on sawing his nails. He didn't look up as he spoke.

'Maxwell came up trumps for once?' he asked.

Robson grinned. 'As a matter of fact, he did. I didn't want to believe it, but CCTV doesn't lie. Jo Soulsby *was* on the Quayside at a little after twelve fifteen.'

'We already knew that,' Daniels said. 'Kirsten Edwards—'

'Running?' Robson cut her off.

Gormley stopped admiring his manicure as Daniels exploded in a fit of frustration. 'Is *anybody* observing the chain of command around here? Why wasn't I told straight away?'

Robson went red. He pointed to the ACTION tray on her desk. She pulled it towards her and found Maxwell's report on top – right where it should've been – along with a CD-rom in a plastic case.

'Hasn't that numpty ever heard of the telephone?' she said.

Robson made his excuses and left the room.

'It's not like you to shoot the messenger,' Gormley said, his voice full of concern. 'You sure you're OK, Kate?'

Daniels looked up from the report. 'I told you, I'm fine!'

'Your hands are trembling.'

'I skipped breakfast. Don't worry about it.'

Aware that he was examining her closely, Daniels continued reading Maxwell's report until her eyes spotted something that lifted her spirits. She took the disk out of its box and put it into her computer. Intrigued by her upbeat demeanour, Gormley got up and walked round the desk so that he could see what she was finding so interesting. He watched her run the disk on to a specific time, zooming in on Jo's face.

She was scared to death.

Gormley glanced sideways, a puzzled look on his face. Daniels ignored him, running the tape again until ACC Martin walked into shot. Then she looked at him, as animated as he'd seen her in days.

'It's enough to make you born again,' she said.

61

'I have no intention of answering your ridiculous questions!'
ACC Martin walked round his desk and sat down in a high-
backed leather chair. He didn't invite Daniels to sit. 'I suggest
you get back to work.'

Daniels stood her ground. 'With the greatest of respect—'

'Which, in my book, means the exact opposite!' Martin cut
her off.

She was unable to hide her amusement – unwise, given his
vindictive reputation. The ACC was right of course, she had
no respect for him – not one ounce.

'Are you deaf? I said, get out of my office!'

'I'm afraid I can't do that, sir. Unless you'd prefer to answer
to an internal enquiry. That would be a bit awkward, though,
don't you think?'

'I'd be careful, if I were you, Daniels. Carry on like this and
I shall be looking for your replacement.'

'Is that a threat, sir?'

'It's a promise!' Martin pushed out his chest, sat back and
clasped his hands in front of him. 'If you can't do your job
properly, I know plenty of men who can do it for you.'

Daniels resisted the temptation to walk round the desk and
kick the sexist pig in the balls. The ACC was sweating profusely, his face almost as red as the tie he was wearing. He was

old school: a bully who thought he could do and say whatever he liked and get away with it. He'd once thrown a telephone directory at her, followed by the phone itself.

'You've never been able to cope with strong women, have you, sir?' Daniels enjoyed watching him squirm. He might be a bastard at work, but she knew that his wife ruled the roost at home. Muriel Martin had a reputation for becoming verbally abusive under the influence of alcohol and had caused him deep embarrassment at police functions in the past. 'Or any women, come to think of it. Right now I'm guessing I represent all you dislike about my gender. But sexual discrimination is against regulations in the modern police service. Comments like that could land in you in an awful lot of trouble these days.'

Bulging veins pulsed at his temples. For a moment, Daniels thought she'd have to duck. But on this occasion he didn't lose his cool altogether. He just sat there, glaring at her, trying to psyche her out.

'I'm warning you, Daniels. Repeat that allegation and you'll be sorry—' He broke off, looking her up and down. 'Might I remind you that it would be your word against mine and, in case you hadn't noticed, I outrank you by some considerable degree.'

Daniels was undeterred. 'At the moment, you do. But keeping quiet would be a neglect of duty, sir. Some would see it as an attempt to pervert the course of justice. It might not go down too well with the Crown Court – or the disciplinary board, for that matter – when they hear of your failure to cooperate in a murder investigation. Why *were* you on the Quayside on the night Stephens died?'

'That's none of your damn business!'

He got up, walked to the door and held it open. Daniels stayed right where she was, holding an envelope aloft. Intrigued as to what it contained, Martin retraced his steps and snatched it out of her hand.

'This had better be your resignation!' He opened the envelope, sifted through photographic stills of his clandestine meeting with Felicity Wood in Exhibition Park, then looked back at her. 'Is this supposed to scare me?'

'It should. It's inappropriate to discuss a live case with a witness.'

Martin tore the stills in half and flung the pieces at her. 'They prove fuck all!'

'No. But the transcript of your conversation with Ms Wood is quite illuminating. It looks to me like you're screwed.' She held his gaze for just a second longer. 'By the way, so was your girlfriend – by Stephens at the Weston Hotel, a hastily arranged quickie, apparently. Thank you for your time, sir.'

Martin was practically apoplectic as she left the room, slamming the door behind her. He walked back to his seat, picked up the phone, dialled a number and sat tapping his fingers on the desk as he waited for an answer. He didn't bother to introduce himself or keep his voice down.

'What the fuck is going on? I've just had that bitch Daniels over here asking stupid bloody questions.'

The voice on the other end of the line was quaking.

'You were seen on CCTV near Stephens' flat, sir . . .'

In the corridor outside, Daniels stood stock-still, her heart beating out of her chest. The ACC's voice sounded muffled through the door, but, fortunately, she could still hear every word as he continued his tirade.

'Why the hell didn't you let me know, you useless piece of shit!' he barked.

Maxwell?

It didn't please her to think that Martin had a member of MIT in his pocket. But Daniels couldn't resist a little smile. She waited for him to slam down the phone before taking a small recording device from her pocket. She switched it off and left the building through a side door. *Every cloud . . .*

62

Puzzled, Gormley put down the office phone. He watched Daniels closely as she marched back into the incident room, her face set in a scowl. He picked up the mobile lying on the desk in front of him, contemplating whether or not to make another call. Mind made up, he keyed in a number, then got up and followed her to her office, pocketing the phone as he walked through the door.

Daniels ignored the muffled sound of a mobile ringing in her desk.

'Problem?' she asked.

'The receipt I found in Jo's desk drawer matches the phone found in her car. It isn't registered with a service provider and it's only been used to call one number, which isn't registered either. Tell me that isn't suspicious.' Gormley pointed at her desk. 'Aren't you going to answer that?'

Daniels looked at the desk drawer, then back at Gormley.

Just then, the phone stopped ringing.

'Tcht . . .' Gormley gave a shrug. 'I'd better get on.'

Returning to the incident room, he didn't go directly to his work station. Instead, he lingered a moment outside her office and made another call, watching as she opened her desk drawer to remove a mobile phone which began to ring in her hand. She looked up guiltily, meeting his gaze through the glass panel of her door. He glared at her, shaking his head as he returned to his desk and yanked his coat off the back of his chair, feeling absolutely gutted. Her 'thing' with Jo Soulsby hadn't reached his radar until Mrs Collins raised his suspicions a couple of days ago when she mentioned the mystery motorcyclist turning up at Jo's house.

Daniels could've confided in him then, but she had chosen not to.

Gormley felt utterly betrayed.

'Thanks for trusting me,' he mumbled as she arrived by his side.

The frosty atmosphere between them was drawing the attention of others in the incident room. Conscious that half of MIT were listening in, Daniels apologized with her eyes and dropped her voice to a whisper.

'Please come back to my office, Hank. Let me explain, it's the least I can do.'

Gormley turned on his heels and walked away without another word.

'Hank?' Daniels sighed. 'Hank, where are you going?'

Gormley spoke over his shoulder. 'No idea.'

He was outside in the street by the time her Toyota caught up with him, trundling along, hands in pockets, head bowed in silent contemplation.

Daniels wound down her window. 'Hank, stop!'

He kept walking.

'Hank, I'm sorry.'

He ignored her.

Frustrated, Daniels put her foot first on the accelerator and then braked sharply, pulling up a few yards in front of him. She jumped out of the car and leapt on to the pavement in order to block his way.

'I'm ordering you!' she yelled. 'GET IN THE DAMN CAR!'

Within minutes they were face to face in a busy underpass, cars and lorries flashing past in both directions. Traffic noise. Exhaust fumes. Road rage. A distant siren. The odd blast of a horn as drivers made fun of their childish argument.

'Take your head out of your arse, why don't you?' Gormley yelled above the deafening din. 'Just *think* about what you're doing. You stuffed up – and for what? You're always banging on about professional integrity bollocks, loyalty to colleagues—'

'So on this occasion I set a lousy example,' Daniels bit back defiantly. Leaning against a graffiti-covered wall, she crossed her arms defensively, then uncrossed them again and began pacing up and down. She turned towards him. 'Jo is a colleague, too, don't forget. I was trying—'

'Spare me the excuses, Kate. You should've come clean, and you know it!' Gormley stuck a finger up at a driver giving them grief. 'The job tolerates gays these days. Didn't anyone ever tell you that?'

Daniels reacted as if he'd slapped her. She stopped pacing and just looked at him hard, her face twisted in anger. '*Tolerates*? What sort of a word is that?'

'You know what I meant.'

'Yeah, next you'll be telling me it promotes them too! Well, fuck you!'

'You may as well. You fucked everyone else!'

Daniels took a deep breath and counted to ten. In dire need of a drink, she persuaded him to go with her to The Bridge.

*

Ten minutes later, they were deep in conversation, sitting in a quiet corner of the bar, tempers now in check, a couple of much-needed drinks in front of them.

'Old habits die hard, Hank.' Daniels had the weight of the world on her shoulders. 'How could I front up, just because they moved the goalposts?'

'You're scary, you know that?' Gormley spread his hands. 'It's just a job, Kate!'

Daniels looked at him. Jo had used those very same words to her once.

Gormley took a packet of cigarettes from his pocket, decided that now was perhaps not the best time to leave her alone while he went outside for a quick fix, and put them away again.

'Remember Ben Carter?' he said.

She didn't answer, though from the look of her she knew what was coming.

'He was ambitious, too. Lost his wife, his kids . . . The morning he dropped dead, Bright walked over to the duty roster and wiped his name off the board.' Gormley licked his finger and drew a horizontal line in the air. 'That was it. Poor sod wasn't even cold and he was just another vacancy. You think you'll be any different?'

Daniels looked away.

'You only get one life, Kate.'

'Don't lecture me, Hank. I know what's at stake.'

'Really?' Gormley shook his head. 'You just don't get it, do you? It's 2009, for Christ's sake! Gay, straight – who the hell cares?'

'No. You're the one doesn't get it!' She took a deep breath.

'On the face of it, people are all very nice, Hank. It's cool to have a gay friend; every self-respecting liberal should have one. But scratch beneath the surface and believe me it's a different story. The Church isn't the only establishment that denies homosexuality. No. The glass ceiling's hard enough to get through without making matters ten times worse.'

Gormley lifted his pint and took a long drink. He was beginning to understand. She was welling up now and he shifted seats so he could sit next to her.

'Come here . . .' He put his arm around her, hugged her close. 'So, who else knows?'

She pulled back. 'Are you mad? It would be professional suicide to say anything now. I may as well screw her on Martin's desk with the Chief watching.'

Gormley smiled at the image. 'Nobody?'

'No, well . . . my father.'

'And?'

Daniels swallowed hard. 'He doesn't want to know me.'

'Then he's a fool.' Gormley was aware that her relationship with her father was difficult. Not from anything she'd said. It was what she hadn't said that had given him that impression. On the rare occasions she'd mentioned her home life, she'd spoken with great affection of her mother. Until now, he'd never really understood why. 'He'll come round—'

'Don't, Hank.' She was thoughtful for a moment. 'Ironic, isn't it? Jo and I are history, have been for months.'

'Then why?'

She made a face. *Why d'you think?*

63

They re-entered the incident room to find the murder investigation team gathered round Bright, who seemed to be conducting an unofficial meeting. Daniels knew they were in trouble. She'd been ignoring his calls for the past two hours.

'Where the hell have you two been?' Bright said, looking up. 'A witness came forward who works in a dry cleaner's. She claims Jo left a bloodstained coat there on Friday morning that matches the one the taxi driver described in his statement. I think her alleged loss of memory is nothing more than a ploy to deceive us. I know that's difficult to believe, given the fact that we have worked with her in the past, but we can't ignore the evidence.'

Daniels was stunned by the news. What had begun as a small seed of doubt in her mind was fast becoming a strong suspicion. She began to question her own judgement: had she taken the case for the promotion, or to protect a woman she still loved? Trying to avoid Gormley's interest, she fiddled with her briefcase, keeping her head down and her thoughts on the subject of Stephens' sexual brutality. Hadn't a motive for murder been evident from the start? Hadn't it weighed her down from the moment she'd recognized him? The answer to both questions had to be *yes*. But she still couldn't believe that this was a case of unfinished business.

'Is that wise, guv?' she said. 'She might not be medically fit.'

'I'll get the Police Surgeon to examine her first,' Bright said. 'What's up? Worried I might upset the Home Office?'

'No, I couldn't give a shit about them, but . . .' Daniels scanned the room. 'Am I the only one round here who has any doubts? You all know her as well as I—'

'OK, try to imagine you *don't* know her personally. Then take away her qualifications, and what do you have?' Bright scanned the faces of his team. No one spoke up. 'Exactly! A woman with a big fucking grudge, that's what. And now we have enough to arrest her, so I suggest we get on with it.'

Daniels shook her head. 'I hear you, guv. But I think it's too soon.'

'The boss is right,' Gormley jumped to her defence. 'Don't forget there are others in the frame.'

Bright laughed. 'Yeah, they're queuing up.'

'James Stephens dropped out of uni two days prior to his father's death. *He* still has no alibi,' Gormley said. 'And he has one hell of a motive, given Stephens' refusal to support him financially.'

Daniels placed a hand on Gormley's shoulder. 'Yes, he does, Hank. But Sheffield CID spoke with James' tutor this morning. He was telling the truth about their affair, and she swears he was with her at the relevant time.'

It came as no surprise to Gormley to hear that the lad was innocent. A blind man on a galloping horse could see it, if they took the trouble to look. He swung round to face her. 'That still leaves Martin! Remember him? Funny blue uniform, scrambled egg on his epaulettes?'

'Guilty as sin,' Bright said. 'But only of wasting police time.

He was lying to protect his reputation. Didn't want his lovely wife Muriel finding out about his extra-marital activities. She's a bit of a bunny boiler, is our Muriel. Of course, rumour has it, she already knows.'

He grinned, letting them all know he was responsible for that. Daniels eyed him with disdain. They both knew there was more to it than that. She strongly suspected that the ACC had heard the gun go off, may even have entered Stephens' apartment before Monica arrived home. But she knew she'd never be able to prove it, no matter how much she might like to. In the end, she'd had no choice but to let the matter drop.

'So it was him that Kim Foreman heard arguing with Wood.' Gormley took in Daniels' nod and didn't wait for a reply. 'Well, if *she* heard the gun go off, then so did *he*, the tosser.'

'He must've done,' Daniels said.

Gormley was sulking now. 'Well? What are you going to do about that?'

Bright shrugged.

Daniels thought of the insurance in her pocket. She had enough on the tape to put one over on Martin, enough of a lever to get a crown on her shoulder. But that was for another day. She could see Gormley was furious and there was an uncomfortable exchange between them she hoped others hadn't seen. He was sending her a clear message: you've got to tell him now!

She knew he was right.

It was now or never.

'Guv . . . There's something else you should know.'

Her tone of her voice not only had Bright's attention but also the rest of MIT.

'Could Hank and I have a private word in your office?'

Knowing it must be important if it had to be said behind closed doors, Bright got to his feet and led them upstairs to mission control. As they all sat down, Daniels took a deep breath, looked him in the eye and just came right out with it.

'Jo once told me confidentially that Stephens raped her during their marriage.'

Silence.

Bright's face paled. He looked accusingly at Gormley, then back at Daniels, his jaw clenching as if he were about to explode. But beneath the anger there was also a look of deep disappointment, as well as bewilderment as to why she'd kept him in the dark. Fearing his next question, Daniels got in first.

It was time to make up the truth.

'And before you ask, the answer is no. Hank wasn't party to the conversation.'

'Why wasn't I informed?' Bright held on to his temper, just.

'It was my call, guv. I'm telling you now.'

'Not good enough!' He waited.

'If I'm told something in confidence—'

'Still not good enough. Try again. Jesus, Kate! Have you lost your mind?'

Daniels didn't know what to say. So she didn't say anything at all, just left the room, slamming the door behind her. Bright flinched as it damn near came off its hinges and then he rounded on Gormley.

'What the hell is wrong with you two? This is the result you've been waiting for, right? What we've all been waiting for. We're a team, aren't we? The Three Must-get-beers!'

'Yeah, that'll be right, guv. Teamwork! You and Kate are both good at that.'

Then he walked out too, leaving Bright baffled as to what was *really* going on.

Seconds later, Gormley was at Daniels' side as she made her way back down the stairs and along the corridor to her office.

'You OK?' he said, after a while.

She glanced sideways. 'What do you think?'

'For what it's worth, I think he's barking up the wrong tree.'

'I know he is.'

'To be that certain, you'd have had to have killed him yourself. You didn't—'

'No, of course not, you idiot!' She stopped walking, and faced him head-on. 'And by the way, Jo's impending arrest isn't our only problem.'

'Oh, goody.' Gormley's tone was sour. 'What is it this time?'

'Martin has a snout in the squad.'

'Maxwell?'

Daniels shrugged. 'He's the obvious weak link. Just keep your eyes and ears open. And don't worry about the ACC. We have ourselves a keepy-back.'

In her office, she delved into her pocket, pulled out the tiny recorder and pressed play. Martin's voice sounded muffled on the tape: *What the fuck is going on? I've just had that bitch Daniels over here asking stupid bloody questions . . .*

'All to protect the woman he loves,' Daniels said, stopping the tape and removing it from the recorder.

'See, you do have something in common . . .' Gormley just couldn't resist the temptation to have a pop at her. 'Can you live with the hypocrisy?'

'I think I can manage.' Daniels threw the tape into her bottom drawer and locked it with a key. 'Depends how far I'm pushed.'

64

The atmosphere was about as tense as it could get. They had been waiting for a good few minutes; Jo Soulsby and her solicitor, William Oliver, on one side of the table, Detective Superintendent Bright on the other, all of them wondering what was keeping Daniels. Keen to get the interview under-way, and growing increasingly angry, Bright looked at his watch and let out a frustrated sigh. He wasn't prepared to start until he was good and ready to do so, but, a few minutes later – spurred on by complaints from Oliver – he picked up the internal phone and punched the number for the incident room.

'Have you found her yet?' he asked.

Oliver tapped the dial on his own wristwatch, making a show of his growing impatience. He was a small, stern-looking man in his late forties – Jo Soulsby's friend and brief for over twenty years. He could have done without the delay, not to mention the ridiculous allegation against one of his dearest friends. He flinched as Bright barked into the handset.

'Well, where the bloody hell is she?'

Oliver glared at him. 'Superintendent, I have other clients to see. I think we've waited long enough, don't you?'

Bright ignored him, his thoughts with Kate Daniels. She'd been acting out of character lately and he'd let it go. But her absence this morning with no notification – let alone explanation – was unforgiveable, a liberty too far. Even though he had a soft spot for her, he knew he'd have to pull her into line. Forced to proceed without her, he turned his attention back to the phone.

'Get Carmichael in here, now!' he said.

He hung up.

Daniels slipped quietly into the observation room. Through a two-way mirror, she could see that the interview had been going on for a while: statements, exhibits, crime-scene photographs lay on the table, along with plastic beakers and a jug of water she knew from experience would be warm.

Lisa Carmichael appeared to be savouring her first experience of sitting in with the guv'nor who was poised like a cheetah waiting for that split second when the moment was right to pounce. Oliver, on the other hand, seemed far from impressed. In fact, he appeared to find Bright's approach extremely tiresome. Sighing loudly, the solicitor whispered something to his client, using his hand to shield his mouth, before replying on her behalf.

'My client has already answered your question, Superintendent. Did she not just state that she has no knowledge whatsoever of how that photograph came to be in her bin?'

Bright moved on. 'CCTV puts you on the Quayside shortly after midnight, Mrs Soulsby. Where were you between leaving the reunion and getting into a taxi at one thirty?'

He paused, inviting Jo to tender an alibi.

None was forthcoming.

Oliver intervened. 'Can we just stick to the facts?'

Carmichael's eyes flitted from Oliver to Jo and back again.

She rested her forearms on the table so she could read over Bright's shoulder, no doubt grateful that Daniels had been 'inexplicably delayed'.

'Mrs Soulsby,' Bright continued, 'we have a witness who will testify that you were in a dirty and confused state when you arrived home. Can you explain that?'

'I can't help you.' Jo turned her head away, unaware of Daniels' presence in the room next door. The two women were looking straight at each other on opposite sides of a party wall. Bright glanced at his notes and fired off another question, giving Jo no time to dwell on the last.

'OK,' he said, 'the weapon used to kill Alan Stephens was found close to your office. Do you wish to comment on that?'

He relaxed back in his seat, using his steely eyes to intimidate Jo.

The silence in the room was deafening.

'Superintendent!' Oliver damn near exploded. 'You can do better than that, surely? I asked for evidence! Have you found gun residue on my client or her clothing?' He waited for Bright to respond. 'No, I didn't think so. Your question is irrelevant. I'll let you in on a little secret: that gun was discovered closer to *my* home than it was to Ms Soulsby's office. Are you going to arrest me, too?'

Carmichael was enjoying the battle. She was getting the lesson of her police career. Bright wasn't in the least put off by Oliver's sarcasm. Sensing her adulation, he loosened his tie and revved up for the kill, pushing a package in Soulsby's direction.

'Do you recognize this? It's your coat. The one you took to the dry cleaner's within hours of your ex-husband's death.'

Jo chose not to answer.

'Refusing to comment will do you no good in the long run, as you well know. This is your opportunity to set the record straight.'

Jo watched Bright pour himself a beaker of water. He took a sip, letting his comment linger a while in everyone's mind. She was frustrated with all the questions. The man asking them was not someone she had much time for. And she knew the feeling was mutual – they'd never seen eye to eye. By reputation, he was apparently good at his job, a detective others – including Kate Daniels – tried to emulate.

Did he really think she looked like a killer?

Jo thought about this for a while. She had to concede that most killers she'd ever come across looked like your average person. They bore no distinguishing features, marking them out from the rest of society. Most went about their business just as she did: working, spending time with family and friends, eating, drinking, sleeping . . .

Suddenly very tired, she wanted the interview to come to an end so she could go home and climb into bed. She was innocent, and Bright had no evidence to prove otherwise.

'I haven't lived with him for years . . .' Jo pinched the bridge of her nose, meeting her accuser's eyes across the table. 'You know that to be the case, Superintendent. What reason would I have to kill him?'

'I'm coming to that,' Bright said confidently, keeping his trump card up his sleeve for just a moment longer.

*

On the other side of the party wall, Daniels' face was red with anger and frustration. She knew what was coming and cursed her guv'nor under her breath. She could remember sitting where Carmichael was now. Watching Bright in action that first time had seemed amazing. It felt like only yesterday, not some ten years ago. He was skilled at interviewing suspects, knew instinctively which buttons to press and how hard to press them. He'd taught her so much: how timing was almost as important as the evidence itself, spotting the precise moment to turn the knife. That was the key to getting a confession. Tripping the suspect up, forcing them to make the mistake that would put them inside for a very long time. But with all that was going on in his life, Daniels began to wonder whether he was losing his touch.

Couldn't he see he was getting it wrong?

Despite the police surgeon's assertion that Jo was fit to be interviewed, Daniels suspected she was still traumatized by the accident. Bright would make mincemeat of her and nothing Oliver could say or do would stop him. He was on the brink of asking another question when he was interrupted by a knock at the door.

'Come!' he yelled, glancing at Carmichael.

From her position in the observation room, it was clear to Daniels that they both expected *her* to come walking through the door. She grew anxious when Robson entered, carrying a package of some kind, which she assumed must be another exhibit, something vitally important to the case.

'For the benefit of the recording, DS Robson has entered the room.' Bright couldn't mask his disappointment. He got to his feet, joining Robson in a corner. They stood with their backs to Daniels, talking in low whispers. She couldn't see their faces, nor hear what was said, but their muted conversation didn't last long.

Dismissing Robson, Bright took the package. As he turned back to the others, Daniels detected a familiar look – a triumphant look that put the fear of God into her. He approached the table and sat down, fingering the package in his hand before placing it very deliberately on the table, halfway between himself and Jo. This piece of drama was calculated in its intent, a classic method of raising the stakes and putting the suspect under pressure.

'Mrs Soulsby, have you ever visited number 24 Court Mews?'

'It's Ms Soulsby . . . and no, I have not.'

'Are you certain about that?'

'Absolutely.'

'So you have *never* been in Alan Stephens' apartment before?'

'That is what I said.'

'Are you familiar with the term "provable lies"?'

'You patronizing bastard! You know I am!'

Picking up the package he'd so carefully and theatrically placed in the centre of the table, Bright opened it to reveal an unremarkable and commonplace photo frame with a mounted picture of Alan and Monica Stephens inside. He held it aloft so that Jo and Oliver could see it clearly.

'For the benefit of the recording, I'm showing Ms Soulsby exhibit FMD0811, a photograph . . .' He paused for effect. 'Have you ever seen this before?'

'No.'

'Any idea who the subject is?'

'Alan . . . and his current wife, I presume.'

'Explain to me how your prints came to be on this photo frame.'

Jo faltered, processing this. 'They can't have been!'

Jo stared at Oliver and shook her head. The solicitor remained poker-faced and said nothing. There was a short pause as Bright let the gravity of the information sink in.

In the viewing room, Daniels sat down. She felt so betrayed, it was hard to concentrate, even harder to accept what she'd just heard. The fingerprint bureau had produced the trump card: irrefutable evidence that Jo had visited Stephens' apartment, if not on the night of the murder, then at some time in the past. She'd given Jo every opportunity to take her into her confidence. Whatever the reason for her silence, Jo had created yet another blindside for Daniels to deal with.

Didn't she know that whoever knows the truth has the most power?

Bright was staring at Jo across the table, savouring his moment of victory, letting his suspect reconsider her position. He shuffled a few papers and stood up. As he walked away from the table, Jo appeared to relax a little. She obviously thought the interview was over.

Daniels knew it wasn't . . . *not in a million years.*

'In the past, you alleged that Alan Stephens raped you, is that correct?'

Bright said it matter-of-factly, as if he'd been talking about something inconsequential like the wintry weather outside. It was done for a purpose and left Jo visibly stunned. Turning her face away from him, she looked towards the two-way mirror separating the adjoining rooms. Looking hurt and betrayed, her anger was so near to the surface it very nearly brought tears to her eyes as she sensed Daniels watching the proceedings.

She turned back to face her accuser. 'That's a lowballer, Superintendent. Pity your lot weren't a bit interested when it happened. I could have done with your support.'

Bright pushed a little harder, unconcerned with her distress. He was enjoying himself, playing to the audience, an audience of one. From the look of her, Carmichael sensed their suspect was near to breaking point.

'You hated him, didn't you?' Bright waited. 'DIDN'T YOU?'

In the observation room, Daniels flinched, urging Jo not to let him wind her up, wondering when Oliver was going to start earning his big fat fee.

As if he'd read her thoughts, Oliver suddenly spoke up. 'That is quite enough! You're now being hostile, Superintendent. My client needs a break.'

Jo was seething, struggling to keep a lid on her temper. Daniels noticed that her face had lost its colour and her lips had gone pale. They always did when she was angry.

Then she began to fight back. 'You're a bully, Bright – just like he was,' she said. 'Yes, I hated him. I hated him with a passion, if you must know. But there's no law against that.'

She locked eyes with him across the table, holding his stare until he looked away. Bright placed the framed photograph back inside the envelope it had arrived in, smiling to himself as he did so.

'This alleged rape sounds like—'

'HE DID RAPE ME!' Jo yelled.

'Of that I have no doubt,' Bright said, his tone more sympathetic. 'That's why you killed him – for revenge. Isn't that the truth of it?'

Jo's jaw hardened. She didn't answer.

'You were seen on the Quayside at the relevant time in a dishevelled state.'

'Yes . . . no . . . I don't know. I told you, I can't remember.'

'The murder weapon was found near your office.'

Oliver insisted they take a break.

Bright ignored him and rounded on Jo. 'The victim is your ex-husband, a man you claim raped you and readily admit you hated. You deny being in his apartment, yet we discovered your fingerprints inside. I think you killed him and you're pretending to suffer from a loss of memory because you have no other option. Josephine Soulsby, I will be formally charging you with the offence of murdering Alan Stephens, contrary to common law . . .'

Jo's admission of hatred resonated in Daniels' mind long after she'd left the observation room. She made off quickly down the corridor to avoid bumping into her boss. It didn't surprise her that Jo hadn't completely broken down. She'd vowed never again to allow herself to be bullied and had risen from the ashes of domestic violence a much stronger person. Today she'd proved that, giving as good as she'd received under extreme pressure.

The murder investigation team had their heads down as Daniels re-entered the incident room. Seconds later, she felt a light jab in the back. Turning round, she came face to face with Bright. He didn't look best pleased.

'You'd better have a good excuse, Kate. Going AWOL in

the middle of a major incident is not to be recommended. You and I need to talk . . .' He sighed, searching her eyes for a moment. 'We're going for a drink, if you'd like to join us.'

'Think I'll pass, if it's all the same to you.'

'Suit yourself.'

As he stormed off with Carmichael in tow, Daniels picked up her bag and followed suit, slamming the door behind her, drawing the stares of the majority of those in the MIR.

Gormley approached Maxwell's desk. 'What was that all about?'

Maxwell shrugged his shoulders. 'If you ask me, she's losing it.'

Through the window, Gormley saw the Toyota racing away.

65

Being first to tell Jo's sons what had happened to their mother seemed the very least Daniels could do. Thomas and James sat motionless in Jo's living room, unable to take it all in. There were tears, expressions of disbelief, outpourings of anger.

And sarcasm from James. 'This *is* a wind up, right?'

There was an awful silence as Daniels shook her head, not quite knowing what to say. A million questions followed: Is she all right? Where is she now? Can we see her? How often can we visit if she's remanded? How do you go about it? Can we take her stuff? What's Oliver doing? What the fuck is going on?

Daniels leaned forward and spoke gently. 'I'm going to stick my neck out here. But I must warn you, I'll deny ever having said anything if what I'm about to tell you is repeated. Understood?'

Responding to the gravity in her voice, Tom and James both nodded.

'I do *not* believe that your mother killed your father . . .' Daniels wondered if she was digging her own grave. 'And I will do everything in my power to prove it. You have my absolute word on that.'

'Then why?' It was almost a wail from Tom.

Daniels sighed heavily. 'Most of the evidence against her

is circumstantial and I'm not at liberty to discuss it with you. You'll have to speak to her solicitor about that. All I can say is that it amounts to enough to sustain a charge of unlawful killing. She'll appear at the magistrates' court later today.'

When she got home, Daniels had a shower, put on a robe and went back downstairs to the living room. She poured herself a large gin and decided to put on some music. Her index finger trailed along her CD collection, each disc a reminder of a specific point in her life: Joni Mitchell, Neil Young, Jackson Browne, her mother's favourites she'd listened to from an early age. James Morrison, James Blunt and David Gray, whose lyrics and voice had moved her to tears the first time she'd heard him sing. And, last but not least, the Dixie Chicks Jo loved so much.

A little grin appeared on Daniels' lips, reminded of Jo's reaction to her music collection the first time she'd visited the house. 'All your taste is in your mouth,' she'd said, making them both laugh out loud. She glanced around at her books, her art, much of it influenced by Jo. In pride of place were three limited-edition prints; deeply atmospheric images captured by French photographer, Marc Riboud, Jo had bought as a birthday surprise – misty mountain landscapes she would treasure for the rest of her days. They were beautiful, sensual, much like the woman who'd bought them.

Daniels felt a pang in her chest.

They'd met at a mutual friend's party, a casual introduction like any other. Except right from the off it was obvious they might become close friends. Always the detective, she'd spent the evening keeping her ear to the ground, listening in to other people's exchanges, picking up snippets of gossip here and there, while giving little away of herself. In her experience, people – partygoers in particular – were often fascinated to find that she was a DCI on a murder investigation team. And so it proved when some of the guys began pulling her leg, begging to have their collars felt should they misbehave under the influence. She'd taken it on the chin and smiled politely, even though she'd heard it all before. And afterwards, when she'd turned around to speak to Jo, she'd disappeared without a trace – like Cinderella before the clock struck midnight. Daniels supposed that she'd returned to the bosom of a family living close by because, during the evening, there'd been talk of sons, an ex-husband, baggage.

With no way of knowing if they'd ever meet again, a curious disappointment had gnawed away at her subconscious for weeks afterwards. And then she'd arrived at work one morning to find Bright in a foul mood, spouting off about the police service moving in the wrong direction, specifically about the drift from methodical, intelligence-led detection to more modern methods of catching criminals. He'd promptly put her on standby to meet a new recruit, some academic being forced upon the department by top brass, who, he said, didn't know their arses from their elbows.

When Jo Soulsby walked through the door of the crime unit and introduced herself as Northumbria's new criminal profiler, Daniels' heart had inexplicably leapt. For a few tense moments, she'd been unable to formulate speech. They were an item within weeks, working together, living separately, but soul mates all the same.

And since they had split up . . .?

The truth was, Jo's departure from her life meant she'd had lost something very precious. *And now she wanted it back.* The moment the door had closed on their relationship, her whole future had vanished into thin air. She hadn't had a decent night's sleep since, never went to parties – hardly ever ate out. What would be the point? Without Jo to share in that special intimacy there was, well, nothing. And so she'd thrown herself into work and resigned herself to life as a single person.

Maybe that was to be her destiny.

Daniels finished her gin. Deciding that music would only make her weepy, she turned off the lights, went back upstairs and curled up on her bed with the TV on. The next few hours were a blur. She must've dozed off, because she woke with a start when she heard a man's voice. It turned out to be a BBC News 24 presenter outlining government plans for yet another wind farm development for the Northumberland countryside – an environmental protection initiative that had drawn a raft of objections across the county. Ordinarily she would have paid attention, but at three twenty-five in the morning, she had no energy to care.

She was about to kill the set when the piece ended and Jo's picture appeared on screen. Her arrest and remand in custody had made the national news. Daniels listened intently to the voice-over as the studio cut away to an outside broadcast showing Tom and James Stephens emerging from Newcastle Magistrates' Court with William Oliver, straight into the path of the waiting media. Riveted to the TV, salty tears welled up in Daniels' eyes as her personal nightmare was transmitted to the nation. In all her life, she'd never known such loneliness.

On the screen, Oliver held up a hand to quieten a jost

ling crowd of photographers and journalists, then gave a brief statement: 'Ms Soulsby has been remanded in custody pending her trial at the Crown Court on a date to be fixed. She will be contesting this matter and we have no further comment to make at this stage.'

Blinded by flashbulbs, the three men then fought their way to a waiting car.

As they were driven away at speed, the anchor man reappeared in the studio. Daniels turned off the set and threw the remote across the room. It smashed against the bedroom wall disintegrating as it hit the floor, the shattered pieces symbolizing her life and her career. If she wasn't careful, she'd be back walking the streets quicker than she could say 'uniform'.

66

'It's a long way down . . .' He forced the kid's head closer to the railing, making him look over the edge at the people below – so small they looked like ants. The kid couldn't struggle with the gun sticking in his ribs, loaded and ready to blow him away; the same weapon the little runt had nicked to order and brought back hoping for some monetary gain.

Big mistake.

His last?

Probably . . .

Do these street kids never learn?

Passing motorists continued to ignore them, whizzing by in both directions just a few feet behind with no interest in what they were up to. Probably thought they were tourists taking advantage of the river view, the famous bridges, the heart of a city locals called The Toon. By the time anyone stopped and got out of their car, the little twat would be toast and he'd be long gone.

He'd never offed one in public before and thought it'd be a blast.

'Cat got your tongue?' he said.

Silence.

'It's Friday the thirteenth today,' he said. 'Unlucky for some, eh?'

'Kiddin', aren't ya?' the kid said, suddenly full of bravado.

His eyes glazed over with sheer joy. 'Do I look like I am?' he chuckled.

'You wouldn't dare!'

The kid was really spooked now, his face set in a scowl, a dribble of sweat running down his cheek. Or was it a tear? He glanced nervously along the pavement, then at the twenty-five-metre drop to the road below. Even if he broke free, there was nowhere to run to, nowhere to hide. And he'd be as good as dead if he jumped from the point where the river ran beneath them.

He kissed the little shit, laughing as a driver hooted his horn.

'You queer or sommat, mate?' The kid flinched, expecting some kind of retribution, but when he didn't get slapped or hoyed over the railings for his cheek, he seized upon the opportunity to worm himself a deal: 'Money's not the only currency, know what I'm saying? Let us go and I'll give ya a blow job for free. Best you'll get round here by a long chalk. Two, if you want, but that'll cost extra . . . prob'ly.'

This one had a bit of spunk, at least, he thought. Sad to think he was about to have a tragic accident, or decide to take his life, like the rest of the sad bastards who'd leapt from the Tyne bridge over the years. One of his mates was talked down once after a concerned member of the public saw him teetering on the edge. Swaying back and forth, back and forth, in two minds whether or not to end it all. Fuckwit chose life that night, before rocking himself off on a line of coke.

Shame.

Not.

He took a deep breath of fresh night air, excitement growing inside him. He shut his eyes for a moment, visualizing throwing the little scrote from the parapet. Watching him free-fall past the northern pier before crashing to earth, his body twisted and contorted by the impact, taking out some of the ants below. Passers-by would hear a solid thump, or maybe a splat, as the kid hit the ground like a squashed tomato, exploding in a spray of red. To his knowledge, no one had ever survived the fall before. He looked at the lad again, imagining his skinny frame twisted on the ground, distorted and grotesque, lifeless eyes staring back at him, blood oozing from every orifice.

'Time to say goodbye!'

'Gan on then,' the kid said bravely. 'Get it over with, if you're gunna.'

'Tcht, tcht. That's no way to talk to your elders, now, is it?'

'Sorry.'

He was, too. He could tell that just by looking at him. Was it really necessary to kill him? Not strictly. The lad had no idea of his identity – what possible threat did he pose?

'Thing is, son. I just don't like loose ends,' he said. 'Nothin' personal.'

'I got no problem with that,' the kid said, sniffing snot up his nose, wiping tears on his sleeve. 'Wanted by the buzzies meself, arn I? Don't take risks 'less I have to, neither. Won't tell no one, promise.'

'Really?'

The kid nodded. 'Really.'

He relaxed the gun a little and the vice-like grip on the kid's shoulder. 'How do I know I can trust you? Think carefully on it, mind. You need to give me the right answer if you're gonna save your skin.'

'You can trust me, honest. I swear on my mother's life.'

Silly boy.

A lull in the traffic and he was gone.

67

Her mood mirrored a depression in the weather. It had been over three weeks since Jo's arrest and her reputation was in shreds following local and national coverage of the case. Daniels had made it her business to read every press article. Some portrayed Jo as a cold-blooded killer who'd planned and carried out an execution. It was a cracking good story from a press point of view, one they resurrected time and again, whenever there was a lull in more newsworthy stories.

It was all bollocks.

And still she hadn't heard from Jo.

For the first time in her career, Daniels had withdrawn into herself; she'd begun maintaining her distance from the squad, working to an agenda of her own. It had to stop. Keeping her own company had never been her style. The murder investigation team were getting restless – she could see it in their eyes. Half of them were busy putting the file together for the CPS, the rest already working another case, assisting Detective Inspector Fowler's team on the unsolved murder of a well-known prostitute.

Daniels stood alone, isolated and unsure, observing the squad from her office door. Willing herself to enter, she wondered when – *if* – she would recapture the same level of enthusiasm for her job she'd enjoyed prior to Jo's arrest.

Where the hell was that dedication to duty on which she'd built her reputation, that passion for policework she just couldn't live without?

On the far side of the incident room, a telephone rang out loudly and Robson picked it up. With the receiver held between cheek and shoulder, he made like he was rocking a baby in his arms. Gormley, who was standing nearby, nodded his understanding and left him to it, crossing the room to the coffee machine, deep in thought. Sensing Daniels' eyes upon him, he looked over in her direction, his glum expression lifting when he saw her standing there.

He smiled, held up a polystyrene coffee cup, inviting her to join him. Daniels shook her head and went back into her office, unable to summon up the emotional energy to face him just yet. It was results she needed, not small talk. As she reached her desk, her mobile beeped. She pulled it out of her pocket and sat down to read the text message that had just come in from Bright. It contained only two words:

She's gone.

Stella's death at a relatively young age brought Daniels abruptly to her senses. She left the office immediately, telling no one, not even Gormley, where she was off to. She drove straight to Bright's home and rang the bell. There was no answer at the door and she couldn't see inside, front or back, because the curtains were drawn. At first, she thought Bright was hiding away. But then she noticed his car wasn't on the drive.

She pulled out her phone and rang his bag-man.

'I'm looking for Bright,' she said. 'Any ideas?'

'None. I thought he was with you.'

Daniels knew the young DC very well. It was obvious he hadn't yet learned of Stella's passing. If he had, he didn't mention it, and neither did she.

She hung up.

Where the hell was the guv'nor?

Her guts churned as she recalled the last time he'd done a runner. One week after his devastating car accident he'd returned home to collect a few personal items to take back to London, where Stella lay on a critical-care ward. Daniels had arranged to meet him away from the office and got worried when he failed to show. She eventually found him in a pub, too drunk to stand, sobbing into a glass. She'd never seen him cry, before or since, nor mentioned the incident to another living soul.

Was history now repeating itself?

But if Bright didn't want to be found, then why text her? Deciding it was a genuine cry for help, she called his number again and again. When he didn't pick up, she got back in her car and toured his favourite haunts, putting the phone on redial. Two hours later, she spotted his car outside the Gibraltar Rock – a seafront pub in Tynemouth – doors unlocked, keys dangling from the ignition, all manner of confidential police documentation on the dash. Scooping it up, she shoved the lot in the boot and locked the car, pocketing the keys as she entered the pub.

Bright was propping up the bar in the back room, his reaction to his wife's death sadly predictable, his aggressive attitude less so.

'Go away,' he said as she drew up a stool.

He asked for another beer but was refused. The barman was clearly uncomfortable, but stopped short of asking them to leave. Daniels told him not to worry – she'd sort it. Then she asked for a moment's privacy, promising she'd have the 'problem' removed . . .

'By the law, if necessary.'

Bright scoffed, turned towards her, trying to focus. 'I said, get lost.'

'And what are you going to do if I don't? Go it alone? Sink enough alcohol 'til you can no longer speak, let alone feel – like you did last time? Stop answering your phone and push me away? Go for it, guv! Didn't work last time.'

He didn't answer.

He'd never change – Daniels knew that.

But *she* could.

Cliché or not, life *was* sometimes far too short. Her mother was the obvious example, and now Stella: two lovely people, cruelly taken before their time. You just never knew the minute when disaster might strike. It wouldn't be the first time that death had become the catalyst for change. And it wouldn't be the last.

Somehow she managed to persuade Bright to leave. Helping him into the Toyota, she took him home and dumped him on the couch to sleep it off, alerting his neighbour to look in on him later.

Daniels went home too.

Now, sitting cross-legged on her bed – no longer prepared to put off the inevitable – she was trying to pen a letter to Jo. But the words wouldn't come. How *could* she explain her decision to compartmentalize her life? Why was it so important to reach the very top in her career? What did she have to prove and, more importantly, to whom?

It was tempting to blame her father for the trouble she was in, but, if Daniels was being perfectly honest, the responsibility lay with her. So what if he hadn't shown her enough affection, or told her, just once, that he was proud of her achievements? That was *his* problem, not hers. No. No matter which way she dressed it up, *she* was the one making all the wrong decisions. She'd chosen to lead a double life, and now she was paying the price.

And so, unfortunately, was Jo.

The words on the page smacked of lame excuses. She screwed up the sheet of paper and threw it on the floor, where it landed among several other failed attempts. She started again just as BBC's *Crimewatch* began.

68

Yanking the ring-pull off his can, Gormley took a long swig of beer as the camera zoomed in on Kirsty Young. The Scottish presenter was looking particularly attractive tonight in a crisp white shirt and black jacket, her tousled hair hanging loose around her shoulders, her long legs crossed.

When she launched into an appeal for information into the murders of Jenny Tait and Jamil Malik, Gormley's ears pricked up. He knew Daniels would be watching too. She was convinced there was a link between those murders and the Corbridge case – young Sarah Short and Father Simon – even though she couldn't yet prove it. He was inclined to go along with that. Why else would the killer have sent *her* a cutting of his next victim? Why hadn't he sent it to Naylor, the detective in charge of the Tait investigation?

Perched on a tall stool, a grave look on her face, Kirsty told viewers: 'Police need your help with these two brutal murders. We're joined in the studio by senior detectives from Durham and West Midlands and, as always, we have a team of operators ready to take your calls. First, though, let's hear from Detective Superintendent Naylor of Durham Constabulary . . .'

Gormley smiled and took another swig from his can. In his dark suit and conservative blue tie, Naylor resembled an older version of football legend Alan Shearer. He seemed perfectly at ease, and there was a definite presence about him that said: *Don't-fuck-with-me.*

Reaching for the remote, Gormley turned up the volume.

'Yes, that's right, Kirsty. We now know these two cases are linked. In both incidents, a Catholic prayer card like this one –' Naylor held up a card '– was left at the scene.'

Gormley put down his beer and grabbed the phone. Keeping one eye on the set, he dialled Daniels' number.

She answered almost immediately.

'You got the TV on?' he asked.

'Yeah. Seems Ron got the thin end of the wedge.'

'You're kidding, aren't you? I've waited all my life for a case like that!' Gormley squashed his empty beer can, placed it on the floor and picked up another. Yanking the ring-pull, he took a long drink. 'You think this appeal will do any good?'

'You want the truth?'

'Shouldn't you be there?'

'Why?'

'Er, hello? Hand-delivery photos of the deceased!'

'Ron and I discussed that . . .' She sounded distracted. 'He thinks we should keep it to ourselves for the time being and see what gives. If we put it out for general consumption now, we'll likely attract the cranks, weirdos and copycats. He's got a point, actually. Neither of us wants an *I'm Jack* scenario.'

Gormley considered this for a moment. The furore over the 'Ripper' hoax had reared its ugly head not so very long ago, almost thirty years after it had derailed the hunt for Peter Sutcliffe, the real Yorkshire Ripper. The hoaxer had since been jailed for eight years – and rightly so – because thousands of innocent men across Wearside were questioned unnecessarily, wasting precious time and resources, resulting in detectives in Yorkshire taking their eye off the ball.

'D'you think there'll be others?' Gormley asked.

'Warning photos? Who knows? I really don't know what to think any more.'

'You sound like you need a drink!'

'Jesus! Why is it that men think a drink is an answer to everything?

Daniels looked back at the TV where an image of Jenny Tait was being replaced by a picture of her house, now a crime scene. She hadn't meant to bite Gormley's head off. He'd been a brick in recent weeks: fielding her calls, covering for her while she ran round and round in circles, trying to find evidence that would prove Jo's innocence, never once complaining.

He chuckled. 'You talking about me, or men in general?'

'You, my father, Bright . . . need I go on?' Daniels covered the speaker with her hand as a sob caught in the back of her throat.

'Kate?

Daniels couldn't speak. In the television studio, a large man she'd never seen before was invited into shot by Kirsty Young. A new caption appeared at the bottom of the screen: Detective Chief Inspector Victor Nichols – West Midlands Police.

'Kate, what's wrong? Apart from the obvious,' Gormley added soberly.

Daniels turned down the sound. 'Stella—' She broke off, unable to hold on to her grief any longer.

There was a short pause as Gormley put two and two together.

'Christ! Why didn't you say?'

'He's devastated, Hank. Completely fucked up.' She glanced down at the pad on her knee, at the screwed-up letters on her bedroom floor, her mind flashing back to the interview between Jo and Bright, two of the dearest people she knew, both rocked by events of recent weeks. Where would it all end?

She pressed a button and the phone went dead.

Fuck!

The lardy geezer on screen was pissing him right off now. What did the arsehole want, an Oscar? DCI Nichols was Mr Sincerity, that's for sure. He was standing right next to Kirsty Young, pointing at a photo of the rag-head, his voice all serious, like he gave a damn.

Yeah, right!

No mention of the hotshot toddler so far – *his* finest hour.

No mention of Daniels either.

It really wouldn't do.

Two victims?

They're 'aving a laugh.

Discounting the one he'd offed as a lad, his tally was a fuck sight more than that. And he wasn't finished yet. Oh, no! Not by a long chalk. His list was good and long, his game plan well rehearsed. Shame a few had gone to meet *Him* a little early. Couldn't help that now, could he? No arguing with natural causes now, was there?

Plenty more where they came from.

His fist closed around his scissors as a bitch copper on screen had the gall to move on to another case – some bollocksy burglary – botch job, too, by the looks. Now who'd give a shit about that? Raising his arm, he brought it down, slamming his fist into the table so hard the scissors stuck fast and he had to use both hands to free them.

They hadn't heard the last of him. Not yet.

69

Daniels was trying to concentrate on paperwork, but her mind kept straying back to her visit with Jo, now only a matter of hours away. And then she needed to drop in on David and Elsie Short – and her father? – Bright, too, if she could possibly manage it.

What was she thinking? She had to manage it. Never mind that she'd just about reached her limit after weeks of juggling the demands of her new role as Acting Superintendent – Bright having been on compassionate leave since Stella's funeral – as well as her continued campaign to disprove the case against Jo, which had to be conducted in her own time and beneath the ACC's radar.

The rap of knuckles on wood was followed by Robson's head appearing round the door. His eyes were like piss holes in the snow, his shirt could have done with ten minutes on an ironing board, and he had the look of a man in the grip of a monster hangover. She could swear he'd worn the same clothes yesterday. It wasn't like him, and it worried her. Now she came to think about it, he'd been looking pretty miserable for weeks. But she had neither the time nor inclination to indulge that thought. She gave him a list of things to do, told him she would be incommunicado for the rest of the day, then grabbed her things and left the office.

She made it to Low Newton Remand Centre within the hour, entering the prison with a feeling of trepidation – and no idea she'd be walking out again less than ten minutes later. Or, to be more accurate, *running out.* Back behind the wheel of the Toyota, she fumbled with the ignition key in her desperation to get as far away from the place as fast as she possibly could. Whatever preconceptions she may have held before visiting Jo, she could never, ever, have anticipated what would happen inside that grim visiting room.

What had already happened.

Had it been possible to floor the accelerator, she would have. But a prolonged cold spell meant that the surrounding fields and meadows were white with snow, and the winding lane that was her only exit was like a bobsleigh run in places. So she crawled along, in slow motion almost, with Jo's hushed voice echoing in her head: *It's too late to make it right, Kate. I won't be sending you another VO. I just wanted to tell you to your face.* As soon as she'd said her piece, Jo had risen to her feet and signalled to a female prison officer to escort her back to her cell. She hadn't faltered once, nor did she cry; it was as if she'd rehearsed what she had to say. And her words had cut through Daniels like a knife.

She didn't mean it. How could she possibly?

Slowing down at a crossroads, Daniels turned left on to the A1. Heading north now on freshly gritted roads, she picked up speed, steeling herself for more misery to come. If she could have put off her visits to David and Elsie Short, and the guv'nor, she would have. But cancelling wasn't an option.

No matter how bad she was feeling right now, she knew they would be feeling much worse.

It was already dark. She'd been on the road for an hour and was now heading north west across country. Leaving the dual carriageway, she crept past the turn-off for her father's cottage, craning her neck to see if his car was parked in its usual spot. It was. Despite their differences, she knew he'd be furious if he found out she'd gone by the road-end without calling in. Especially on Christmas Eve.

She checked the clock on the dash . . . no time . . . and ploughed on.

Ten minutes later, the road narrowed at a thirty-mile speed-limit sign. The countryside gave way to housing on one side, then on both. The marketplace was on her left as she drove into Corbridge and parked up, her hands clammy on the steering wheel as she looked towards the church and thought back to the night she went in to light a candle and discovered two bodies.

Notwithstanding her recent personal crisis, Daniels' failure to bring the killer to justice had been, and still was, the disappointment of her career. What could she say to the parents of Sarah Short on this, the first anniversary of their daughter's death? What words could she use that wouldn't sound like empty promises?

Until her untimely death, Sarah had been a young woman with a brilliant future ahead of her. It was a sad irony to think that she had aspirations to work in criminal law after completing her degree at Oxford. Her murder had robbed the Shorts of a loving, intelligent child in the very prime of her life, and

Daniels hadn't been able to offer them even the small consolation of justice for her killer.

She got out of her car knowing that the individual responsible would surely kill again. Engrossed in her thoughts, she pulled up sharply as a man stepped into her path, less than twenty metres from St Camillus' gate. They did a little dance, as people do when they get in each other's way. Finally he moved politely to one side and stood to let her pass. She sighed, angry at her reaction to a total stranger.

Just past the churchyard, the Christmas tree was another reminder of her gruesome find twelve months ago, transporting her back to that night and the harrowing weeks that followed. MIT had thrown every resource into solving the case yet failed to turn up a single witness. It was as if a spaceship had beamed the person responsible in and out of the village.

No . . . there were no words that could convey the sorrow she was feeling, or give hope of a result in the near future. The best she could offer the Shorts was her personal reassurance that the case would never be closed. The last time she'd seen them, they'd begged her for that. It was their right. And Daniels intended to see it was respected.

Every surface in the cosy room was taken up with photographs of Sarah Short as a happy child and teenager. Some showed her posing with her parents, and Daniels was shocked by the contrast with David and Elsie Short as they were now. Both had aged considerably in the last twelve months. David's hair was almost white now and he'd lost a lot of weight, particularly from his face. His hands were shaking as he placed a second cup of tea down on the table in front of him.

'We lit a candle at church today,' he said, looking up.

'David!' Elsie glared at her husband.

'I'm sorry, Kate,' David said, realizing. 'That was insensitive. I'd forgotten how . . . what you were doing, when you found . . .'

His voice trailed off – he couldn't bring himself to finish the sentence.

'How can you still believe?' Daniels said. 'I just know I couldn't.'

'Go home, Kate,' he said gently. 'Make it up with your father. He needs his only child. From the state of you, I'd say you need each other.'

Daniels got to her feet. 'I've got to go.'

David and Elsie stood up too, taking it in turns to give her a hug.

'You're welcome in our home anytime, Kate,' Elsie said, grabbing Daniels' forearm as she turned away. 'You promise the case will remain open?'

'It was never closed, Elsie . . .'

Daniels dared not share her suspicions with the Shorts, tell them that their daughter might have been murdered by a serial killer being hunted down by two other forces. What if she were wrong? She couldn't risk raising their expectations on a doubtful outcome. No – that would be totally wrong.

'I'll see if I can organize a reconstruction, televised appeal, something that might jog someone's memory.'

David and Elsie appeared to accept this and followed her to the door to say goodbye, their fingers moving closer together and joining as they watched her walk away.

On the way back to the Toyota, Daniels sensed eyes on her.

Raising a hand, she turned, expecting to see David and Elsie on the doorstep. But they were nowhere to be seen. Her eyes swept the market square . . .

Nothing.

The narrow streets were deserted.

The graveyard too.

Back in the comfort of a new set of wheels, he slid a little further down in his seat and continued to watch her. Why was she staring at the tree? Was she thinking about Number Two – or the good Catholic girl he'd taken just for fun? He smiled. Daniels looked exactly like she did on the telly, only taller and more beautiful.

He'd known she would be here tonight. Couldn't say why, he just did.

She swung round, as if sensing his presence. Even as a silhouette against the moonlight, he could tell she was uneasy. Her eyes were all over the place, chasing down shadows in the snow. He'd already started without her, his dick hard and massive in his hand, thoughts of getting under her skin fuelling his fantasy. Unzipping the fly of his jeans to ease the pressure, he came looking straight into her big brown eyes, ejaculating a warm pool of hot semen on to the passenger seat.

70

Daniels drove away from Corbridge with a heavy heart, pained by David and Elsie's loss. She envied those who were looking forward to spending Christmas with their families, exchanging gifts, partying, making the most of precious time off. Without any of those distractions, she planned to throw herself into her work. But first she had to see Bright – and she wasn't looking forward to it.

She found him in the pub where they'd agreed to meet. He was too consumed in his own darkness to notice that she was also grieving: for Sarah, for David and Elsie Short – for a lost relationship of her own. Although he hadn't said as much, she was sure he suspected she was in some kind of trouble.

They talked about Stella in terms they never had before. Daniels thought it curious how death seemed to bring out the little anecdotes, the secrets, the joys, the pain, the closeness – or lack of it – people had shared with the recently departed. On the outside, at least, his suffering was over. He seemed to be holding up well, maintaining a stoical veneer, but deep down she knew he was hurting and blaming himself all over again. When he abruptly changed the subject, it was obvious he'd said all he could bear to on the subject of his late wife.

'How did it go with David and Elsie?' he said.

'Not good,' she told him, adding that she planned to revisit their daughter's case.

She was taken aback by the flare of anger this aroused in him. It was, after all, still a 'live' case, with a dangerous killer still at large.

'You've got to stop obsessing about it, Kate,' he said, slamming his empty glass down on the table. 'I told you before, that case is so cold it's practically frozen. And if that offends you, well, I'm sorry, but that's just the way it is. You have absolutely no evidence that the card in Father Simon's hand is in any way connected to the other two murders, and until you—'

'I accept that, I do. But David and Elsie are barely coping. How do you expect them to rest while their daughter's killer remains on the loose? All I'm asking is a chance to look through the evidence again, for my own sanity as much as theirs. What possible harm—'

'I appreciate your concern, really I do. But we threw every resource – human and financial – into that incident for months. So, unless new evidence has come to light—'

'How dare you!'

Kate's raised voice had most of the other customers turning round to see what was happening.

Bright moved closer and dropped his voice. 'I'm sorry, Kate. You have to understand that it's not personal, it's just the hard reality of being an SIO. Something you'll have to get used to, sooner rather than later.'

Daniels knew he was right, but less than an hour ago she'd been listening to the Shorts describing how, at times when they least expected it, their grief kept smashing over them like some giant wave that swept everything in its wake, leaving them feeling battered and raw and alone – just as *she* was feeling now. Bright too, if only he'd acknowledge it.

Why was he always so bloody stubborn?

Why was she?

'They practically begged me, guv. I'd have thought that you, of all people, would understand their loss, today of all days.'

Bright held his hands up, too drained to argue with her.

'I'm sorry, guv. I shouldn't have said that. My apologies.'

'OK, OK! I know when to quit. Rework the damn case, if you must. But I warn you, there's no more money, understood? And you take your proper leave first, you hear me? You're not yourself.'

'I intend to,' she lied. 'And thanks, guv. You've no idea what it means to—'

'Yeah, yeah.' Bright got.to his feet. 'Same again?'

Without waiting for an answer, he set off for the bar. She wished now she'd never agreed to come for a drink with him; wished she'd called time on what had been a ghastly year for both of them. When he looked over his shoulder, she took out her mobile phone and lifted it to her ear, even though there was nobody on the other end. As he turned his back on her, she pocketed the phone, gathered her bag and coat from the back of her chair, and made a beeline for the bar.

'Don't bother with mine, guv.' She put twenty quid on the counter and gave him a peck on the cheek. 'I'll catch you later. I've got to go.'

He looked crestfallen. 'Will I see you . . .'

But she was already halfway through the door

71

Two exhausting days later, with her meticulous attention to detail driving her mad, Daniels closed the Corbridge file with Bright's words ringing in her ears. He was right. The case *was* dead in the water. She'd found not a shred of evidence that might have been overlooked, nothing at all that would take her any further. But still the card in Father Simon's hand nagged at her subconscious.

She just couldn't get it out of her mind.

Removing her warrant card from her computer, she sat back in her chair, rubbing her aching neck and wondering how she would tell David and Elsie Short. As she recalled her last visit to their house, Jo entered her thoughts. There had been no further contact between them and she was desperate for news.

Daniels looked out of the window. While she remained stuck in this limbo of utter despondency, outside her window, life was somehow continuing as normal. A couple passed by, their arms around each other, laughing and carrying on without a care in the world. Walking behind them was a teenager wearing just skinny jeans and T-shirt. She must be frozen without a coat on.

Daniels sat bolt upright in her chair.

Breathe. Breathe.

The girl in the street had brought to mind an inconsistency, something she hadn't thought of before. Daniels' hands fumbled with her warrant card as she tried to slot it back into her computer. She typed a command and waited until the investigation into Alan Stephens' death popped up on screen. Drumming her fingers on the desktop, she dared not let herself believe that what she'd seized upon had any significance at all.

C'mon, c'mon.

It seemed to take forever for the relevant page to load, then finally it appeared on screen. Daniels was right. Despite Stephens' murder having taken place in November, items taken from Monica Stephens did not include any outdoor garments. And, if this was the case, it was tantamount to a major cock-up for the murder team, and for statement reader DS Robson in particular. It might even prove to be the breakthrough she'd been hoping for. It was all there in black and white – right before her eyes.

How could they all have missed it?

Daniels keyed Gormley's number into her mobile.

He answered right away.

'Hank, we have a problem: Monica Stephens' coat was never retrieved for forensic testing. I need to re-interview her right away.'

'You're kidding!' He sounded half asleep. 'Have you tried to reach her?'

'I'm about to, but I want to check CCTV footage from the airport first. You going to be in later?'

'Yeah, I'll be here. Me, Santa and a crate of beer. Let me know what gives.'

She hung up.

Using the internal phone, she rang the exhibits officer and asked him to pull the relevant evidence box, then immediately set off downstairs to collect them. The box was waiting for her when she got there and she signed it out and carried it straight to the new murder suite. Selecting a disk marked – *Interior: Newcastle Airport* – she settled down to watch. Within seconds, Monica Stephens and Teresa Branson walked into shot in an airport lounge – and both were wearing coats.

Daniels fast-forwarded the tape to the end, until Monica disappeared off screen through a large revolving door. Then, inserting the second disk, Daniels picked up Monica leaving through the same door, still wearing her coat, stopping briefly at a pay booth before making her way to the short-stay car park. Moments later, her car drove away.

Daniels was a firm advocate of the cognitive interviewing technique; a verbal probing method allowing the interviewee to think aloud. She'd used it to unlock witnesses' memories many times before and was hoping that it would do the same for Monica in the comfort of her own home.

Stephens' widow was at home when Daniels rang. She agreed to be interviewed even though it was Boxing Day. What else was there to do that mattered any more, she'd said, adding that Bank Holidays were for families and hers was now gone. Alan might not have been a saint, by any stretch of the imagination, but he was all she had and she missed him dreadfully. She'd only remained in the country on account of his elderly mother, delaying her plans to move back to Holland until the New Year. Daniels drove straight there.

Stephens' mother seemed to know why she was there and disappeared into the kitchen leaving the two women alone to talk. Taking a digital recorder from her pocket, Daniels turned it on, mindful that she was collecting evidence for use at a later date. She urged Monica to close her eyes, relax, and try to recall every detail of that evening, from the moment she left Court Mews to take Teresa Branson out for dinner to her return home and the discovery of her husband's body. Listening intently to every word, every hesitation, Daniels watched as the colour drained from Monica's face when she revisited the horrific memory.

Although she'd already established that Monica had been wearing a coat, Daniels still needed to hear her confirm it and was careful not to put words into her mouth.

'What were you wearing that night, Monica?'

'Brown pants, boots . . . a camel coat and scarf.'

'You definitely had a coat on when you returned home?'

Monica nodded.

'Keep concentrating,' Daniels said gently. 'You're doing *really* well. Now, tell me what you're seeing.'

Monica's bottom lip quivered. 'The door . . . the front door.'

'Is it open, or closed?'

'Slightly ajar.'

'Push it open . . . see what's inside.'

Monica opened her eyes wide and stared intently at the floor. 'I found something . . . in the hallway. I'm not sure what it was.'

'Take your time.'

'I remember bending down . . . no, I'm sorry, it's no good.'

'Try to picture it.'

'A letter? Writing on a card . . . a business card, perhaps?'

Oh my God! Daniels felt the colour drain from her own face. 'Did you pick it up?'

'No, yes . . . I thought Alan . . . I thought he must have dropped it on his way in.'

Images of prayer cards flashed before Daniels' eyes in quick succession: in Father Simon's hands, in Jenny Tait's mouth, next to Jamil Malik's twisted body and in Ron Naylor's hands in full view of a *Crimewatch* audience.

'Monica, this is *very* important: what did you do with it?'

The Dutch woman's hand instinctively touched her pocket.

Daniels felt herself getting hotter, wished she could crack open a window, get some fresh air. But this was no time to interrupt such an important interview. In her mind's eye, Monica walked further into the flat, found her husband dead on the floor and fled the scene to Salieri's restaurant next door. Staff called for an ambulance and, finding her in a state of shock, the paramedics whisked her off to hospital before the police arrived. Her coat was left behind – returned to her after the event – since given away to charity.

Now the race was on to find that coat . . .

72

It was getting dark as Daniels pulled on to the driveway and parked the Toyota behind Gormley's car. With a bottle of whisky in one hand and a thick folder in the other, she got out and walked to the front door, using her elbow to ring the doorbell. When no one answered, she assumed it wasn't working and hammered on the door with the side of her fist. It was yanked open by Gormley, his face poised to remonstrate with his noisy visitor, his anger lifting the second he saw who it was.

'Sorry, must've fallen asleep,' he said, opening the door wider.

Daniels' mind was doing somersaults as she tried to make sense of what she now knew. 'Careful what you wish for, Hank. Naylor's case and ours are definitely one and the same. And I'm not talking about Sarah Short or Father Simon here, either. I'm talking about Alan Stephens!'

Gormley was puzzled.

Daniels pushed right past him into the house. Even in her preoccupied state of mind she couldn't miss the distinct lack of Christmas in the living room. One present, beautifully wrapped, sat alone on the sideboard, unopened, the gift tag made out: *To Julie, with love.* Daniels was curious to know where Gormley's wife was at such a pivotal moment in the calendar, but was too afraid to ask. She turned to face him as he arrived by her side.

'I just took Monica through a cognitive interview,' she said. 'She *did* have a coat on that night. And what's more, she remembered seeing a business card on the floor as she entered the flat.'

Gormley shook his head. 'Not true. I was there when SOCO did a sweep of the crime scene. I'm telling you, there was no card.'

'Not in the flat, no. Monica told me she found it in the hallway and picked it up, thinking Stephens had dropped it on his way in. Seconds later, she found his body and legged it. She thinks she put it in her coat pocket—'

'*Thinks?* That sounds like a definite-maybe to me.'

'What if the killer put it there deliberately, Hank?'

'Whoa, slow down. I'm half-cut here and you're making my head hurt.'

'Be serious!' Daniels said. 'What if it wasn't a business card at all, but a Catholic prayer card?' They both sat down. She waited for a response but, for once, Gormley didn't have a slick one-liner. He sobered up right there and then. 'There's an evil bastard on the patch, Hank. Some God squad freak, by the sound of it. And serial killers don't just stop – it's not in their pathology.'

Silence.

Then laughter through the window. An explosion outside. Someone was letting off fireworks, a poignant reminder of the night Alan Stephens died. Not that Daniels needed one. That date was not one she'd forget in a hurry. It was likely to remain imprinted on her brain for evermore. From start to finish, her first case as SIO had been one bloody nightmare. And still was.

'Oh, do me a favour,' Gormley scoffed, reacting to her glum expression. 'Monica hasn't got the coat any more, has she?'

Daniels shook her head. 'Gave it to Kidney Research. Couldn't bring herself to wear it again. I'm recalling the squad and I'll get Lisa on the coat first thing tomorrow morning.'

Even as she said it, she knew it was a long shot.

'On a Sunday, in the Christmas holidays!' Gormley's shoulders dropped. 'Don't fancy your chances.'

Daniels couldn't allow his misgivings to derail her. They weren't home and dry yet but her recent discovery had filled her with hope and expectation. She was sure he felt it too. And soon Jo would be home.

73

Carmichael pulled slowly to the kerb outside a large grey warehouse guarded by a chain-link fence. Beside the gate was a large sign: *KIDNEY RESEARCH – Please Give Generously*.

As the crow flies, it was less than a mile and a half from the incident room in a rundown area on the south side of the Tyne. Carmichael didn't think it would be long before the land, once a thriving industrial estate, was snapped up for redevelopment as much of Gateshead Quayside had already been. The adjacent building, demolished long ago, had only the footprint remaining; the ground it once stood on was over-run with weeds, with long tufts of brown grass poking through where the concrete had cracked. The only reminder of its existence was an old bench that lay abandoned on its side: wood rotting, planks missing, but a tiny brass plate still attached.

She got out of her car, craning her neck to read the inscription: *DONATED BY ALUN ARMSTRONG*.

'A former worker,' a voice behind her said.

Carmichael turned to see a stout man in his late fifties with wavy grey hair, gentle eyes and a ready smile.

'Ken Carruthers . . .' He held out his hand. 'I hate to admit it, but I've been here longer than the bench. I've worked for the charity for twenty years, been warehouse supervisor for ten.'

'DC Carmichael. Thanks for seeing me. Sorry to drag you out.'

'No problem. Tell you the truth, I hate Christmas. Just don't let on to the wife.' Carruthers smiled. He made a meal of looking over his shoulder, where a woman was waiting in the car. 'I have to warn you, mind, it's a tall order. The words *needle* and *haystack* spring to mind.'

Carmichael forced a smile. It was not what she wanted to hear. A month had gone by since Monica Stephens had donated her coat to the charity. In all honesty, she didn't hold out much hope of ever finding it.

'You're lucky in one way: we're closed for two weeks over the Christmas period.' Carruthers nodded towards the building. 'You'd better come inside.'

They crossed a yard lined with recycling containers. As they walked, Carruthers explained how heavily the charity relied upon the local community to supply them with items for resale. 'You wouldn't believe how much people chuck away,' he said, taking a remote-control device from his pocket and pushing a green button.

In front of them, a galvanized steel curtain began to move slowly upwards. As it passed eye level, a mountain of plastic bags came into view.

Carmichael's face dropped. 'Jesus!'

'See what I mean?'

'And there's no way of knowing where each bag came from?'

The curtain came to a halt with a heavy thud.

'Or how long they've been here, I'm afraid,' Carruthers said. 'You'll have to search each and every one.'

74

Bright had risen early, determined to kick off his first day back at work with a more positive outlook – albeit without Stella. But a lot can happen in just two hours. A dressing-down from the ACC had put paid to that. And the atmosphere between the two officers was as bad as it had ever been.

'Tell me you're not serious!' Martin yelled.

'DCI Daniels is certain, sir . . .' Weary of standing, Bright shifted his weight from one foot to the other and glanced at an empty chair, hoping his boss would take the hint and invite him to sit.

He was out of luck. Martin just glared at him.

'I've contacted Soulsby's brief and he is trying to arrange an application for bail.' Bright's eyes scanned Martin's face. It looked as though he must have shaved in a hurry that morning: his face had more nicks than a butcher's block, and a tiny piece of bloodstained tissue was stuck to his neck, giving the impression that his pristine shirt collar was torn. 'It was the very least I could do, given the doubt over her guilt.'

'Jesus Christ! That woman's reputation hangs in shreds and we – *you*, are wholly responsible. This is a public relations nightmare.' The ACC looked past him towards the closed door. 'Where the hell *is* Daniels, anyway?'

Bright had to stop himself from answering with: *How*

the hell should I know? Daniels had been a law unto herself in recent weeks, distracted by work and whatever else was going on in that head of hers. Even after Stella's funeral, when he'd invited his colleagues back to the house, she'd made her excuses and rushed off early, having stayed just long enough not to appear insensitive. It wasn't like her. He felt like a pig, hitting on her when Stella was alive, and wondered if his behaviour that day had changed the dynamics between them for good. It hadn't been his finest hour.

He sighed – he should've waited to make his play.

'Well?' Martin yelled.

'The DCI is busy making further enquiries and mobilizing the squad. I believe the Tactical Support Group are gearing up to help in the search for the coat as we speak.'

His words made Martin even more irate. 'Get out!'

'Sir.'

'Oh and, Bright . . .'

With his back turned, Bright winced. He knew what was coming and steeled himself for another tirade. Letting go of the door handle, he turned to face his boss.

'You make bloody sure the press don't get wind of this until I'm good and ready to speak with them,' Martin said.

'It's too late for that.'

'What d'you mean, too late?'

Martin looked as if he was about to explode. Bright wished the floor would open up and swallow him whole but decided, after a moment's hesitation, that honesty was the only way to go.

'They're already camped outside, baying for blood,' he said. 'The nationals are wetting their knickers for the story and they're prepared to pay handsomely to get it.'

'What? They'll crucify us! Who the hell tipped them off?'

'Who do you think?' Martin knew as well as he did that William Oliver was a solicitor who liked his name in the papers and his face on Sky News. 'I assure you it wasn't one of ours, sir.'

'Oh really!' The ACC bit back. 'Well, I'll give them a bloody exclusive, Bright! And believe me, heads *will* roll. And yours will be one of them, just in case you're in any doubt.'

In the MIR, the atmosphere was a little less tense. Some of the murder investigation team were nursing hangovers when they arrived at work, regretting the excesses of the Christmas break. Others were happy to be there: rest days cancelled at short notice meant an opportunity to work overtime. With double pay and time off in lieu on offer, even Maxwell was glad of the opportunity to work.

'You come to give me grief too?' Robson said as Gormley approached.

Gormley walked straight by, took off his jacket and hung it on the back of his chair. He sat down at his desk, in no mood for small talk, particularly with Robson. But his colleague failed to take the hint.

'The boss'll be chuffed,' Robson said, the trouble he was in momentarily outweighed by his enthusiasm for Jo's imminent release. Only then did he take in Gormley's scowl and realize he was in for the high jump. 'Where is she?'

Gormley glanced in the direction of Daniels' empty office. He shrugged. 'Maybe she's gone to make sure that the CPS don't oppose her release. Although I'd like to see them try! She's got a lot of time for Jo. So did we all, until your ridiculous cock-up.'

Robson's grin slid off his face. 'Hank, about the coat business—'

'Save your excuses, man.' Gormley pulled his chair closer
to his desk and logged on to his computer. 'What's done is
done. You weren't the only one to blame.'

Robson knew he was referring to Bright, who, for some
reason, hadn't yet made an appearance. 'Has anyone contacted Jo's sons?' he asked timidly.

'Oliver's taking care of it.'

Feeling for his pocket, Robson pulled out his mobile, which
had already switched to voicemail. He collected the message,
then asked: 'Is your mobile switched on?'

'Why?'

'That was the guv'nor.' He pocketed the phone.

'And?'

'He sounds frantic. He's been trying to reach you.'

Gormley shrugged. He had ignored a number of calls that
day. Since the news got out, his pocket hadn't stopped vibrat-
ing. 'Yeah, well, he can wait. It was *him* got us into this mess.'
He wondered whether Bright felt guilty at all. 'If he'd listened
to the boss, Jo might not have spent the past six weeks inside.
Can you imagine what that would do to someone like her?'

'He wasn't firing on all cylinders, what with Stella—'

'Yeah, well, we've all got problems. But we still have a job
to do. And *some* of us manage to do it properly.'

Robson looked at the floor. 'He's on his way in, wants all
hands on deck and a debrief from the boss as soon as possible.'

'He'll be lucky,' Gormley moved off. 'I'll see if I can track
her down.'

75

'I am grateful to Your Lordship for hearing this bail application . . .' William Oliver glanced at the man seated in a high-backed leather chair. The judge looked splendid in his red robe and black sash, which was tight around his chest on account of a long-standing weight problem; sweating profusely from the heat in the courtroom, he took off his wig and wiped his brow. Oliver cleared his throat before continuing: 'M'lord, as you are aware, my client, Josephine Soulsby, has been incarcerated at Low Newton Remand Centre on a very serious indictment of murdering her ex-husband Alan Stephens, pending a hearing at this Crown Court.'

'Yes, Mr Oliver. I am familiar with the case.'

Daniels was sitting on the police bench, willing the two men to get on with it. She'd already lost time – twenty-four hours, to be precise – because no judge was available to hear a bail application yesterday. But, all things considered, she counted herself lucky that she'd found a court – any court – sitting at this time of the year. Fortunately for her, a big case due to finish before the holidays had run on and the sitting judge had insisted that those involved proceed with closing arguments without further delay.

Who said the wheels of justice were slow to turn?

She looked across the courtroom to the dock, where Jo

was on her feet, eyes front, flanked by two prison officers. She looked pale and gaunt, a fresh bruise beneath her left eye. Directly opposite her, a young female stenographer sat with her hands paused over keys in readiness to resume typing. The woman looked sideways as the courtroom door opened. Four barristers entered, acknowledged the judge with a nod and quickly took their seats, glaring at Oliver because he'd somehow managed to nip in and gain His Lordship's attention during the short adjournment of another important case.

Finally, Oliver decided to get a move on. 'M'lord, new evidence has come to light of which the police had no prior knowledge. This leads them to believe that the death of Stephens was the work of a serial offender and not my client. If Your Lordship so wishes, Detective Chief Inspector Kate Daniels is in the courtroom and will verify this under oath.'

The judge smiled at Daniels, considering.

She got to her feet, identified who she was and indicated her willingness to give evidence should he wish to hear it. In her peripheral vision, she was aware of Jo's gaze shifting in her direction. The judge took his time deciding whether or not to call her to the witness box, then he made a downward movement of his hand: a 'sit' command, like a handler signalling to a dog.

'Very well,' he said. 'I'll take your word for it, Mr Oliver.'

Daniels sat.

The judge put down his pen, his stern voice booming out over the heads of those assembled in Court 8. 'As I recall, however, there is the small matter of a partial fingerprint found at the scene. Of itself, such a discovery does not prove guilt beyond any reasonable doubt. But it was presented as "irrefutable evidence" before the magistrates' court, was it not?'

Daniels had been expecting him to pick up on that point. She looked across at Jo, who still had no explanation to offer the court as to how it got there. Daniels' stomach was in knots. Bail wasn't a foregone conclusion, even with the corroboration of the statement she had recently obtained from Monica Stephens.

'It was indeed, Your Lordship,' Oliver said confidently, 'but I urge you to release Ms Soulsby while further enquiries are undertaken. The Crown Prosecution Service do not intend to oppose this bail application. They are, shall we say, keen to avoid any further miscarriage of justice.'

'I am pleased to hear it,' the Judge said. 'Do you have anything further to add?'

'Only that my client is a professional woman of previous good character, willing to surrender her passport and submit to any bail conditions you may feel obliged to impose. She poses no obvious risk to herself and others. A pity the same cannot be said for the man who charged her in the first place.'

'Detective Superintendent Bright is not often wrong, Mr Oliver,' the judge warned.

'Yes, well, might I respectfully suggest that on this occasion he was, shall we say, wide of the mark. His overzealousness resulted in Ms Soulsby losing her liberty unnecessarily – a traumatic event, I'm sure Your Lordship will agree, for both herself and her family. I have it on good authority – from Assistant Chief Constable Martin, no less – that an urgent enquiry into this matter is now underway.'

Oh God!

On the press bench, a junior reporter Daniels knew was scribbling furiously. He worked for a local newspaper, the *Journal*. She wondered if he'd agree to leave Bright's name out of his article if she gave him something else in return. Suggesting that the buck should stop with Martin might do the trick. After all, the more senior the officer, the more papers it would sell. It wouldn't be the first time a journalist had mixed up two names – an easy mistake to make in the heat of the moment, she thought. Especially if she promised to make it worth his while. She made a mental note to have a word on the way out.

'Quite so, Mr Oliver,' the judge said. Looking over his steel-rimmed spectacles, he addressed the barrister acting for the Crown. 'Anything to add, Mr Cartright?'

Cartright got to his feet. 'No, M'lord.'

'Very well. Bail is granted on three conditions . . .'

Oliver's chest rose. He let out a sigh of relief, so loud it was audible at the front of the courtroom. Waiting counsel turned round and smiled insincerely at him, keen to get back to their case.

As the judge continued to read out the conditions, Daniels smiled to herself and scribbled down the result.

Jo Soulsby was free.

He remained seated as the judge left the court and prison officers escorted Soulsby below to the cells. Daniels had an expression on her face he didn't quite understand. Given her spectacular mistake, he'd have thought she'd have been crapping herself now.

So how come she was smiling?

With no progress on Dotty's whereabouts, he'd been filling his time by watching, waiting, getting better acquainted with the DCI. Following her here had been a stroke of genius. He'd slipped into the public gallery behind all the other sad bastards with nothing better to do than stick their noses into other people's business. During the delay while the female usher cleared the court of all interested parties from the bail hearing, the woman to his left stopped making notes and went back to her crossword, the one to his right got stuck into a crime novel. It tickled him. He wanted to lean across and tell her she was sat next to the real deal, just to see the look on her face.

Daniels left her seat and came within a few feet of him as she crossed the room. Inhaling her perfume as she walked by, he could've reached out and touched her, they were so close. The thought of touching her was enough to give him a hard on.

She was having a quiet word with a young guy on the press bench now. They were so obviously in cahoots: definitely a you-scratch-my-back-I'll-scratch-yours type deal going down.

The police made him sick sometimes. *He* was the one that was newsworthy, not Soulsby, not Bright – and *certainly* not Daniels. She was fucking hopeless, when he came to think about it. He hoped she'd be a better screw than she was a detective.

The reporter was nodding, a wry smile on his face as he reached into his top pocket, pulled out a business card and gave it to her. She did likewise, then walked away.

Well, he had cards too. Only his said *goodbye* and not *hello*. He chuckled.

'All rise!' the usher said loudly.

The door at the back of the court opened and the judge re-entered.

The woman on his left hastily substituted her puzzle with a notebook; the one on the right shut her novel; a John Grisham bestseller, he noticed. The front cover depicted a man in silhouette, backlit by a street lamp, a shadow on the wall behind him, the title emblazoned across the bottom of the cover in white lettering: *The Partner*.

And then it hit him like a brick.

Was this why Daniels looked so relieved?

Jesus, it was!

Fuck – they were partners.

This was so bizarre you couldn't make it up. First he offs a guy that turns out to be his psych's ex – another controlling female who thought she could push him around. Then, in a cruel twist of fate, she goes down for it, leaving him free to carry on as before. When her name got splashed over all the newspapers and he realized she was once married to Stephens, he just about pissed himself laughing. Which fuckwit said there's no such thing as a coincidence?

And now it turns out that the woman who should be hunting him down is shagging the bitch! What would ACC Martin and Superintendent Not-so-Bright make of that?

76

They looked like a bored married couple, breathing the same air, occupying the same hard wooden bench, sitting side by side with a big space between them, facing forwards, not speaking – each acting as if the other wasn't there. An hour earlier, Bright had summoned her to his office, having received an anonymous tip-off – a letter, hand-delivered to the gatehouse at HQ – alleging an inappropriate relationship between her and Jo Soulsby.

By all accounts, the ACC had received an identical copy.

Daniels was gutted. Was this a disgruntled colleague out to make trouble? God knows it had happened before as she'd risen through the ranks. But how and when had they found out about her relationship with Jo? She knew Gormley wouldn't have said anything. And Jo certainly wouldn't. Then again, she'd been to hell and back lately. In a moment of madness, maybe she'd confided in someone with a grudge against the police. A bloody parking ticket was enough to set *some* people off on a crusade.

After all she'd lost, the news was out.

It had all been for nothing.

She could've lied to Bright. But her recent weird behaviour had given her away. The guv'nor was no fool and – figuring that she was about to meet her end – she decided to do so with dignity and front up there and then. She owed him that much. He'd taken it well, under the circumstances, accepting that the relationship was over and had been for some time, accepting too that Daniels had tried to tell him on more than one occasion since the enquiry began. But as she replayed their conversation in her head, she still felt like a traitor with her head on the block.

'I feel like such a tit,' Bright said, out of the blue, without looking at her. 'Asking you to stay the night.'

'Forget it, guv. I have.'

'You could've said—'

'You didn't ask.'

'You didn't offer.'

Daniels rolled her eyes. 'And why would I do that?'

Bright let out a sigh. 'My gaydar never *was* any good.'

'That's just the sort of comment—' Daniels stopped talking as a pretty secretary let herself out of the Assistant Chief Constable's office. She held up her hand, indicating five, and walked off down the corridor.

'He wants someone's head,' Bright said. 'For the cock-up mainly, but this other stuff too. Seems to think yours and mine will do nicely.'

Daniels just stared at the wall opposite, unsure how she would handle it. She decided to play it by ear, wait and see what Martin had in mind for her, and take it from there.

'The personal stuff is down to you,' Bright continued. 'But don't worry, I'll take full responsibility for the rest.'

Now Daniels looked at him. 'I'm *not* worried,' she said.

The secretary was back and showed them into Martin's office. He was sitting at his desk with an open file in front of him. Daniels recognized it as a personnel file – most probably hers – and braced herself for what was coming. Bright walked round one side of the desk, leaving her exposed, standing to attention directly in front of the ACC, shoulders straight, hands behind her back, feet slightly apart.

Martin sat forward, interlocking his fingers, resting his chin on his hands, his elbows on the desk. He observed her for what seemed like an age, enjoying his moment, playing up to his nickname: the smiling assassin.

Daniels met his gaze defiantly.

'This is very impressive . . .' He tapped the file in front of him. 'Seven Chief Constable's commendations. Two compliments. Exemplary conduct all round. Not a mark or a blemish to be found. Until now . . .' He paused for effect. 'You seem to have shot yourself in the foot, Daniels.'

'Have I, sir?'

He sat back, hands behind his head, looking her up and down. 'Weren't you telling me that a relationship with a suspect in a murder enquiry is against the rules? What was it you said? A neglect of duty? An attempt to pervert the course of justice?'

A flicker of a smile crossed Daniels' lips.

Martin glared at her.

Bright shook his head – almost imperceptibly – warning her not to push it.

'I'd like to help you out here, Daniels. I really would. But you seem to have an attitude problem bordering on insubordination . . .' The ACC locked eyes with her. 'You think you're so smart, don't you?'

'I don't think, sir. I know,' Daniels said. 'You see, I actually have proof, whereas you have nothing more than a flimsy piece of paper from an anonymous source. I wouldn't get the blue forms out just yet, because if I'm going down, then so are you.'

He spent the next half-hour haranguing her, baiting her, trying to trip her up. Daniels stood her ground until he ran out of steam, incensed by her resolve. And in all the time she stood there taking it, Bright never said a word either for or against. But she felt his support, didn't need telling whose side he was on.

'Get her out of here!' Martin yelled.

Bright led Daniels out of the office, down the corridor and out into the fresh air.

'You better get your shit together, Kate. He's not finished with you yet – not by a long chalk.'

'I couldn't care less!' Daniels kept walking.

'That's not true and you know it.'

'Isn't it? Jo went to prison because *he* wanted the enquiry to go away, and that's the truth of it. What I'd like to know is, what's he got on you?'

Bright went quiet. As they reached her Toyota, the doors clunked open. They got in. Daniels started the car and drove off, stopping at the main entrance to enable the gate officer to check her vehicle's security disc, then drove on as the barrier lifted and he waved her through.

'I'm still angry with you for charging Jo without consulting me first,' she said.

'If you hadn't gone AWOL—'

'Yeah, well, now you know the reason for that. A: I never thought there was sufficient evidence. And B: Well, how *could*

I interview her, guv? You can see my problem. And what Robson was doing during the enquiry, God only knows!'

She turned right, heading towards Ponteland village, intending to pick up the A696, the fastest route back to the city.

Bright tried to make amends. 'Look, none of us can turn the clock back, so the best we can do is find Stephens' killer—'

'I think you should apologize to Jo first, don't you?'

'OK, I will. But she still lied about being in his flat!'

'There'll be an explanation for that, I'm sure.'

At least, Daniels hoped there would . . .

77

They made good time and twenty-five minutes later Daniels
parked the Toyota in her usual spot. On a mission to prove
her point, she bypassed the incident room and went straight
downstairs. She had one aim in mind as she pressed the bell
for attention.

The exhibits officer appeared at the counter almost immediately.

'I need the evidence box for the Stephens enquiry, right
away,' Daniels said.

He disappeared. Seconds later, he was back carrying a large
box. He waited as she signed for the item, then he turned
away.

'No, can you stay? I want you to witness this.'

'Oh?'

'Trust me,' Daniels said. 'I'm a detective.'

The officer smiled, retraced his steps and leaned on the
counter as she put on latex gloves. Taking an evidence bag
from the box, she checked the reference number on the side
before breaking the seal, then lifted an item free: an unremarkable, commonplace frame with a mounted photograph
of Alan and Monica Stephens inside.

Alan James Stephens. D'you know him?

Gormley's words reverberated round Daniels' head. It was

then she realized she'd seen the picture before, had looked at it in Stephens' flat on the night he died, the photograph that had set off a chain of events too terrible to contemplate back then. Laying the frame face down on the counter, she opened up the back, discovering almost immediately that there was more than one photograph inside. With the officer looking over her shoulder, she used the very tips of her fingers to lift them out. There were two photographs, stuck together in one corner. She carefully teased them apart.

The exhibits officer moved in even closer, intrigued at what they were about to find. Discarding the photograph of Alan and Monica, Daniels discovered another underneath, a pristine photograph of two little boys, most definitely Tom and James Stephens.

Thanking the exhibits officer, she handed back the evidence and headed straight upstairs to Bright's office. He was standing by the window looking rather sombre as she entered without knocking. He turned at the sound of the door opening and glanced at his watch.

'Be quick, Kate,' he said. 'I only have a few minutes – Martin's been inundated with calls and wants me back at headquarters.'

She sat down. 'Just so we're clear, the exhibit you were so concerned about – the photograph with Jo's prints on – is unsafe.'

'What?'

'Forensics lifted a partial fingerprint from the back of the frame but found no corresponding thumb print on the front. Doesn't that strike you as odd, if Jo had handled it?' She glanced at Stella's photograph on his desk. 'May I, guv?'

He nodded.

Daniels leaned forward and feigned picking it up with her right hand without actually touching his most prized possession. 'See what I'm getting at? I can't prove it, but the way I figure it is this: Stephens took the frame from the marital home when he and Jo separated. When he lost touch with his sons, he reused the frame to hold a picture of Monica instead. You clean the glass, right? Who cleans the back?' She paused – half expected him to rubbish her theory outright – but he just looked at her, coolly considering what she'd just told him. 'He was a twat, guv. He was too tight to buy a new frame. He just put his new life on top of his old one.'

'Faaantastic!' Bright exhaled loudly. 'That's the one bit of hard evidence we have, the only reason I get to keep my job and my pension.'

Despite his interference in her case, Daniels almost felt sorry for him then. Since Stella's death he'd been looking rather ropey. He'd been drinking too much and she knew he was struggling to cope.

'I appreciate that makes it difficult for you,' she said. 'But it might help your situation in the long run. Martin knows *why* you decided to charge Jo. But now he needs to placate her.'

Out of the corner of his eye, Bright noticed his car arriving outside. He held up a hand to his driver, letting him know he'd seen him, then turned his attention back to Daniels. 'Even if you're right, I'd like to know just how you think that helps my case with Martin. He's just looking for an excuse to throw the book at me.'

'Then admit we made a genuine mistake.'

'*We?* Don't you mean—'

'This is no time to apportion blame, guv. I know Jo better than you do. If she sees we're being transparent, she won't make a fuss. Martin will be expecting a complaint as well as a long and protracted enquiry. If he sees you making an effort to avoid one, well, let's put it this way, it can't do you any harm. My guess is, Jo will want to move on with her life, just as you do, just as Martin does. I take it you won't be opposing her return to work?'

'I hadn't thought about it, but no,' Bright said. 'It's more a question of whether she still wants to collaborate with us, isn't it?'

78

Bright was a proud man; man enough to do his own dirty work. His meeting with Martin had gone reasonably well. He knew that, because his warrant card was still in his pocket and the egg on his face felt a little less obvious.

Daniels' ploy had worked. The ACC had responded well to her damage-limitation strategy. Now all Bright had to do was to put things right with Jo. Pulling his notebook from his briefcase, he checked the address twice – 45 Kings Gate – and tapped gently on the door.

At eye height, he was facing a tiny spyhole. He stood up straight, pushing back his shoulders in case anyone on the inside was checking him out. Seconds later, a dishevelled young man opened the door and leaned against the door jamb, one foot crossed over the other. Despite the time of year, he was wearing just a T-shirt, ripped jeans and flip-flops. He had long unkempt hair and a lit cigarette hung from his mouth.

Bright felt conspicuously disadvantaged. He had no way of knowing which one of Jo Soulsby's sons he was looking at. He'd interviewed neither. He reached for his ID.

'Mr Stephens?'

A male voice yelled from inside the house. 'Who is it?'

James Stephens shouted over his shoulder. 'Police!' He

turned to face Bright, sweeping hair from his handsome face. His voice hardened. 'I assume that's who you are?'

'Yes, I'm Detective Superintendent Bright.'

'What do you want?'

James flicked what was left of his cigarette out into the street in an act of defiance. It flew right past Bright's left ear before hitting the pavement beyond, sending sparks flying. A second man came to the door and stood shoulder to shoulder with the first. There was no doubting that they were brothers. All the same, Bright had to be sure. He couldn't chance another cock-up.

'You are James and Thomas Stephens?' he asked.

The two men glanced at one another.

'Come to arrest someone who's actually done something wrong?' Tom mocked. 'Or maybe you came to tell us the good news this time? Don't bother, we already heard.'

'Is your mother home?' Bright asked.

James snapped: 'You've got a nerve!'

He was about to shut the door when Jo Soulsby appeared behind him. She bristled when she saw who was standing on the threshold and quickly pulled her sons inside. Tom walked away without another word, but James stood his ground.

'It's OK, James,' she said. Her son withdrew and went back inside. Then she turned her attention to Bright. 'Something I can do for you, Superintendent?'

'It seems I owe you an apology.'

'I think that's an understatement, don't you?'

Bright pulled a bottle of wine from his briefcase. 'Peace offering. Can we talk?'

They went inside. Bright sat down in the living room, his

DCI's suggestion to front up and take what was coming ringing in his ears. From the look on Jo Soulsby's face, he doubted that even the most profound apology would put things right between them. He was prepared for a blasting, and it didn't take long to arrive . . .

'I don't like you, Bright. You're a bully.'

'So you keep telling me.'

'I detest bullies, even ones with their hearts in the right place.'

He sensed that all was not lost. 'If it's any consolation, I understand how you must feel.' He broke off as Jo's eyebrows arched in amazement. The softly, softly approach clearly wasn't working. 'You've every justification—'

'To complain? Damn right, I have.'

'Oh, fuck it!' Bright leaned forward, pulled an official-looking document from his briefcase and handed it over. He felt strangely relieved, having faced up to her, even though he suspected that the complaint form he'd just given her would be winging its way to the Chief Constable within the next twenty-four hours. 'I never *was* any good at grovelling. Whatever action you decide to take is fine with me. But I want you to know, it wasn't personal.'

'Oh, it was personal, all right! Why don't you have the balls to admit it?' Jo glanced at the form and set it down on the table between them. 'You've always resented my involvement in what you see as police business.'

There seemed little hope of reconciliation now. Maybe too much water had gone under the bridge. Bright looked at the floor, suddenly gripped by mixed emotions. He wanted to hit back at her, yell at her, tell her he now had another reason to resent her. Finding out that she'd been where he wanted to be had knocked him sideways. How could he compete with a woman, for Christ's sake? A relationship with Daniels was no longer an option for him and he was gutted by that thought. So much so, he was finding it hard to hide his hostility.

Picking up on this, but not the underlying cause, Jo damn near bit his head off. 'Trouble with you is, you're blinkered, a dinosaur in the modern-day police service. If you woke up, you might realize that we, I, have a contribution to make. Together, we might even make a good team.'

She had a point. Bright took her comments on the chin. She had every right to express her opinion and wasn't the first to tell him he was territorial, set in his ways, resistant to change. Other formidable women had said as much, more than once, as he recalled – including Stella and Daniels. Sensing Jo's anger subsiding, he chose his words carefully.

'Well, now we've cleared the air, can we bury the hatchet and start again?'

Jo sighed.

'Fair enough.' Bright wanted to explain away his negativity as healthy cynicism, but was worried he might antagonize her even further. 'I hear what you say and I accept that I'm old school. Will you at least meet me halfway and accept that I was just doing my job?'

'I know that.' Jo sat back in her armchair, crossed her legs and met his gaze head-on. 'I also know you've put away some evil bastards over the years. Kate Daniels says she owes . . . well, let's just say she has a lot of time for you.'

'The feeling is mutual,' Bright said.

79

Daniels heard their murmurs before they realized she was there. *Rumour has it heads are going to roll, I heard the guv'nor got a right bollocking from Martin . . . Bet the boss is bloody furious . . . Yeah, well watch out. What goes up usually comes down – and we all know what that means.* Rather than alert them to her presence, she remained on the threshold of the MIR, watching her team getting ready for potentially the most serious case any of them had ever been involved in.

Gormley was standing by the murder wall, carrying out her instructions to reinstate the Stephens enquiry so they could go back to the beginning and start the case afresh. Carmichael was diligently working away at her computer and Robson had his head down too, probably trying to blend into the background, given his spectacular and very public recent blunder. But Maxwell had his feet up, a mug of coffee in one hand, the *Sun* newspaper open on the desk in front of him – happy to carry on collecting the Queen's shilling for as little work as possible. Infuriated, Daniels stormed over to him and ripped the paper away.

'Right, I've had enough. Clear your desk!' she said.

'What?' He didn't think she was being serious, but it soon became apparent she was. Maxwell flushed, looking round the room for support. Found none. The rest of the squad simply turned their backs and got on with their work.

'You heard. You're off the squad, as of now. I can't afford any passengers on my team, and you've been warned about your conduct often enough.'

'I was having my bait!'

'Do you see anyone else taking a break?'

'You can't do that!' Maxwell protested.

'I just did,' Daniels said. 'Now get your kit together and piss off.'

'Boss, I—'

'OUT!'

As Maxwell scurried off, the eyes of MIT were on Daniels, wondering who would be next to feel the lash.

'Lisa, I *need* that coat. Don't come back until you find it.'

Carmichael logged off, gathered her belongings and made a quick exit.

'The rest of you, get back to work. And this time, do your jobs properly!' She held a piece of paper aloft. 'This is a list of urgent actions. Nobody goes home until they're complete, understood?' She scanned the room, finding Robson. 'Robbo, I'm replacing you as statement reader. I'd like to see you in my office as soon as you've finished whatever it is you're doing.'

Robson turned crimson, taken aback by the public humiliation. From the look on his face, he'd expected his dressing down to take place behind closed doors. Daniels scanned the room, could see that her decision was unpopular – the squad didn't know where to look – but she had no intention of changing her mind. It was a hard lesson, but a vital one. It would act as a reminder to them all.

'Well, what are you all waiting for?' she yelled.

She went back to her office and closed the door behind her. The euphoria she'd felt at Jo's release had been short-lived. Jo had refused Daniels' visit to the court cells while bail forms were being organized, and declined the offer of a lift home, opting instead to go with Oliver.

Daniels was desperate to speak to her, but she still refused to take her calls.

There was a gentle knock on the door and she beckoned Robson in. He looked anxious as he closed the door behind him and 'assumed the position' on the opposite side of her desk – hands behind his back, feet slightly apart.

'I take it I don't need to *explain* why I'm replacing you?'

'No, boss. But if I could just say in my defence—'

'Can I just stop you there? As far as I'm concerned, you have no defence.' She glared at him. 'How the hell could you miss such a vital piece of evidence, Robbo? It's basic procedure! You wear a coat in the winter, don't you?'

Robson was perspiring badly: dark wet patches appearing around his armpits, a thin film of sweat visible on his brow. 'Lots of lasses don't, especially down the Quayside,' he said lamely.

'Don't get flippant with me!' Daniels snapped back. 'This was a mature, affluent woman from Rotterdam, not some tart on the pull! You screwed up big style, and you know it!'

'I understand why you're angry—'

'I very much doubt that.'

He obviously had no idea what on earth she was on about. *Why should he?* Daniels thought to herself. *I was the one hiding the truth from him, from all my colleagues, from the whole wide*

world. What right have I to expect any of the squad to under-
stand? But that didn't excuse his incompetence.

'I'm not looking for a scapegoat,' Daniels said. 'This is a
major investigation and I can't risk another cock-up. Besides,
you deserve what's coming. I hope you're you man enough to
take it?'

Robson didn't answer.

'Go on, get lost.'

'Boss . . .' He pushed back his shoulders and stood tall. 'I
appreciate you not taking me off the squad altogether. I know
I'm in the wrong and I'm prepared to take full responsibility
for my actions. I'd like a chance to make it up to you, though.
I'll do whatever it takes.'

The silence in the room was deafening.

Daniels cleared her throat.

'We'll see . . . Now get out of here before I change my
mind.'

80

At the end of a very long day, Gormley was the last man standing in the incident room. With just a desk lamp for company, he was scanning a Police National Computer printout on his desk. He ticked off a name, then reached down and pulled out the corresponding file from a large box on the floor by his feet. The label on the front cover proclaimed: LIFE LICENSEE – PETER BATES.

'Unfortunate name, young Master Bates!' Daniels read over his shoulder, making him jump. He'd been so engrossed in his work he hadn't heard her approach. He put down his pen and leaned back in his chair.

'You shouldn't creep up on people,' he said.

'Talking of creeps, you found anything?'

'The PNC threw up a list of possibles: some lifers, violent recidivists . . . you name it, they're on here. And some even fit the profile.'

'Religious freaks included?'

Gormley nodded.

'How many?'

'A few – it seems the Church has a lot to answer for.'

'You got that right.'

'What is with you and the Church?'

Daniels pulled up a chair and sat down, suddenly feeling

the need to explain herself. Maybe it was time to get it off her chest. 'When my mother was dying, I caught a priest giving her the last rites before she was ready . . . I think she heard him too.'

'Kate, I'm *so* sorry—'

'She died the next day . . .' Daniels' eyes began to well up. She looked at the floor and then quickly pulled herself together. 'Anyway, that's all in the past.'

'You sure about that?'

She knew what he was getting at. It wasn't something that would ever go away, but it was something she'd have to learn to live with . . . eventually.

'Want to talk about it?'

She shook her head, pointed at the printout on his desk. 'How far have you got?'

'Not as far as I'd have liked.'

'Well, let me know what you come up with.' She could see something was bothering him, was beginning to regret having burdened him with her troubles. 'What's wrong?'

'You sure we should be cross-referencing the PNC list with Jo's client list? If I find anything, it'll make her look *more* guilty, not less.'

'I'll take that chance, Hank. She didn't do it. The evidence will prove it.'

'OK. You off home now?'

'D'you need me to stay?'

'No, you go ahead. I'll not be long behind you.'

The moment she got home Daniels dashed upstairs and changed into a pair of running shorts and a T-shirt. But after one look at the exercise bike that had been gathering dust in the corner of her study for the last few weeks, she was checking her watch and changing her clothes again, this time reflective gear more suited for a run outdoors, beanie hat and gloves. Picking up her iPod and earphones, she set off.

The air was fresh as she ran down her street and out on to the main road, turning left a few minutes later, skirting the edge of Jesmond Dene, a Victorian park covering acres of woodland, presented to the city in the late nineteenth century by local philanthropist, Lord Armstrong. Had it been daylight, she would've taken in the beauty of this hidden gem: the network of paths and bridges, the waterfall, the mill, all enclosed within a deep narrow valley. The fabulous scenery drew locals and tourists in droves – five minutes and yet a world away from a thriving party city.

Daniels had been jogging for a good half-hour when she pulled up on a street corner, began running on the spot. Looking across the road, she saw that the light was on in Jo's house. She checked her watch – 23.04 – in two minds whether to knock. She was about to do just that when she spotted some movement from within: Kirsten Edwards was walking into the living room with a glass of wine in her hand. She was in conversation with someone not visible from the street, animated, smiling, in a really good mood.

Daniels jogged away as fast as her weary legs could carry her.

81

The journey into work was more chaotic than normal. Overnight temperatures had dropped, freezing the snow into ice and causing a series of accidents across the region. Gormley was already hard at work, sitting alone in the incident room with his radio on. He'd left home extra early, missing the worst of it, but officers from outlying areas were going to have problems getting in. As the traffic report ended, he glanced out of the window just in time to see the Toyota pull up outside.

He watched Daniels get out and cross the car park, curious to know if she'd spoken to Jo since her release, whether there was any likelihood they'd get back together and, if they did, whether his boss would choose to make it public this time or carry on letting her career take precedence over her life. Moments later, she entered the room displaying renewed vigour, her attitude confident and businesslike, no hint of angst on her face. No one seeing her would suspect that her life was anything but perfect.

Gormley smiled to himself.

The two of them were not so very different after all.

Half an hour later, she began addressing a depleted squad at a hastily arranged briefing to bring them up to speed. 'OK, we can't wait for the others any longer. Firstly, can I remind those of you who are here that the offender we are seeking is dangerous, disturbed and most probably armed. He is not, I repeat, *not* someone you tackle without backup. Is that clear?' She paused, making sure they all understood. 'Pay particular attention to anyone who has a connection to, or problem with, religion. Hank is trawling through the national database for any known offenders who might fit the bill. Robbo, I want you on CCTV this time round.'

'I'll get on to it right away,' Robson said, managing a weak smile.

Daniels had to admit it, his attempt at cheerfulness was impressive. Such a laborious task would normally land on the desk of a much more junior squad member. Not to worry. Robbo had been in the job long enough to know that it was part of his penance, the natural order, the way things were done in the murder investigation team.

'I want the rest of you to review each and every piece of evidence.' She ignored a collective moan as it reverberated round the room. 'And I do mean *everything*! Make no mistake, our man is clever. He's already killed three times that we know of. It's possible there are other bodies that haven't yet been found, other unsolved cases where the link has yet to be established . . .'

She nodded to Carmichael, who got up and pinned two crime-scene photographs side by side on the murder wall next to one of Alan Stephens. The first was of a middle-aged, white female, lying on her kitchen floor with a gaping hole in her chest, her lifeless eyes wide open, a card stuffed in her mouth. The second was of an Asian male, also on the floor, his knees bent beneath his body, a gunshot wound to his head, a card on the floor beside him.

Carmichael sat back down.

'You're all familiar with Alan Stephens, but this . . .' Daniels pointed to the photograph of the white female '. . . is Jenny Tait, the Durham case. And this . . .' she moved her hand across to the photo of the Asian male '. . . is Jamil Malik, who was found murdered in his flat in Birmingham, a day after his photograph was hand-delivered to this very building by someone we suspect was a man wearing a burka. It was specifically addressed to me.'

The squad began to chatter excitedly.

'I'm sorry I've had to keep this from you, but it was a case of the fewer people who knew, the better. It is, however, a development that leads me to conclude that the person we're looking for either has links with this area or to a case of our own.'

Daniels paused, letting the information sink in.

'Until we find Monica Stephens' coat and, more importantly, the card she claims she found at the scene, we cannot conclusively link Alan Stephens to these other two victims. However, there is a possibility – and I stress only a *possibility* at this stage – that whoever killed these people may also be responsible for the double murder in St Camillus church last year. A single prayer card was found at all three crime scenes: Durham, Birmingham, Corbridge. Same MO, same signature. For those of you without GCSE Maths, that makes five victims in all.' Daniels held up a prayer card, passed it on, watching as it journeyed round the room until everyone had seen it and she had their full attention again. 'The sick bastard is toying with us, trying to tell us something. Ironically, the person best placed to help us find this individual is the colleague we arrested and charged with murder. For obvious reasons, Jo Soulsby cannot assist us this time.'

Seeing a tiny chink in Daniels' armour, Gormley got to his feet. 'What we *do* know is that Stephens, Tait and Malik were all born locally or lived on our patch at some time in the past. And, before you ask, the same goes for the victims in our un-solved double-murder case. It's down to you to find the link and pinpoint the time-frame.'

'Remember, there is no such thing as *random* selection . . .' Daniels was back on track. 'The geographical location of the crime scenes is less important to our killer than his choice of victim, so you can safely assume he's not acting on impulse. It would appear that he's put himself out to find these people, so they must have something in common with him, and/or with each other. Somewhere along the line, this is all tied up with religion, so keep your eyes and ears open at all times.'

At that very moment, Daniels felt strangely close to the offender she was hunting. Though operating on opposite sides of the law, she could identify with him on more than one level. Hadn't her own loss of faith been so profound it had very nearly tipped her over the edge? The only difference was that the killer was projecting his rage outward, while she was internalizing hers. Was she searching for a mirror image of herself, she wondered, someone so traumatized that they'd gone beyond the pale? In her mind, she matched their simi-larities. They both felt justified in what they did. Both were determined to succeed. And Daniels strongly suspected that they both found the thrill of the chase more satisfying than the end result. There were no winners where murder was concerned.

Just losers.

A uniformed officer was holding her hand up at the back of the room. 'What time-frame are we talking about, ma'am?'

'That's yet to be precisely determined,' Daniels said. 'It's looking like the late eighties. Maybe they all spent time together in a children's home, went to the same church, same school . . . Remember, three forces are currently searching for the answer to that very question, and murder investigation teams right across the country are also on alert. I will be liaising with the other SIOs – Naylor from Durham and Nichols from Birmingham – and their respective teams will no doubt be in touch with you lot occasionally, although officially we have yet to be "ruled in". Unofficially, we're all of the opinion that a link exists. So I want full cooperation with our colleagues in other forces. This is not a points-scoring exercise. Our *only* priority is finding this killer before he claims another victim.'

82

The weather was playing its part. It was bleaching down again; a good excuse to tighten the drawstring of his hood without attracting unnecessary attention to himself. He'd bought his ticket online and entered the bus depot unseen – feeling lucky – with one aim in mind. He saw the unattended ruck-sack almost immediately, slipped his arms into the straps and hopped on the Kendal bus just as it was about to pull away. The theft was a risk worth taking. There was a hot drink and food inside, enough sustenance for days if he eked it out. Sliding his hand further inside the deep front pocket, he found maps and something resembling thin foil, folded into a small neat parcel. Further still and he hit the jackpot.

The warehouse was now sectioned off into manageable chunks. Under Carmichael's watchful eye, the Tactical Support Group – a team of twenty officers – were rummaging through bag after bag, paying meticulous attention to what was inside. She could see on their faces how bored they were.

Carmichael was bored too.

And cold.

It was freezing in the warehouse and she couldn't feel her feet. And it looked as though Ken Carruthers was going to be proved right: at this rate, the process of combing through the mountain of black plastic bags would drag on for weeks. Her mind wandered off to a warm incident room where many of her colleagues were getting stuck into the enquiry in a more meaningful way. An enquiry that could turn out to be the biggest and most notable the Northumbria force had ever seen. She wanted to be more involved – and she would have been, if Daniels hadn't insisted that she come down here to keep up the pressure on the TSG, even though it was far from certain that their search would turn up the missing coat.

Ken Carruthers wandered over and stood next to her. He was wearing a knee-length sheepskin coat, gloves and hat with the earflaps turned down. Good move, Carmichael thought, making a mental note to dress more appropriately tomorrow.

And there would be a tomorrow . . .

And the day after . . .

And the day after that.

Carmichael was sure of it.

'Nothing doing?' Carruthers said.

''Fraid not,' Carmichael blew on her hands and stamped her feet, which were numb with cold. 'We knew it was a gamble. An expensive one, but a gamble nevertheless.'

'How long will they keep searching?'

'For as long as it takes.'

'You want a coffee or something?' He pointed upwards, towards an office in one corner of the warehouse. 'It's a little more comfy in there.'

'If it's all the same to you, I'll have mine with the lads. It helps to keep up their morale.' She pointed at a green Waitrose bag on the floor. 'Got my auntie to make them a nice lemon drizzle cake. Secret family recipe. Should earn me some brownie points. I'll keep you a bit, if you like.'

Carruthers smiled, patting his stomach. 'I can already taste it,' he said.

She watched him move off in the direction of his office, which was situated on the mezzanine floor above, accessible via a reinforced steel staircase. It was virtually a glass box on stilts with a good view over the warehouse. A warm fire. Coffee. Maybe even biscuits.

Just then, Carmichael heard a shout. Looking in the general direction of the call, she saw a TSG officer standing a little way off, holding his left hand in the air.

The signal could only mean one thing . . .

His actions resulted in his supervisor rushing over to examine the coat he'd found. Heart pounding, Carmichael made her way towards them. But before she got close enough to see for herself, the supervisor shook his head, frustration showing on his face.

It wasn't the one they were looking for.

He slept . . .

Not well. She was waging war on his subconscious again, yelling like a woman possessed by the devil, her face contorted with hatred. She towered above him, ordering him to kneel on the floor, say his prayers and beg for the Lord's forgiveness.

He cried . . .

She brought the stick down on his shoulder in the same place as yesterday, the gag in his mouth muffling his screams. He turned his face away, towards the locked door. She'd stopped yelling now. A bad sign. When he dared look up, her eyes were black with rage. It was already the third time today she'd done the thing she called *discipline*.

He scuttled across the floor as she raised the stick above her head again. Shutting his eyes tightly, he hoped one of her friends would knock on the door and then she'd leave him to go into the room for her meeting. Today was Tuesday. They always came on a Tuesday. Never missed. But the doorbell didn't ring. Any moment now the stick would come crashing down.

He waited . . .

And woke with a start, feeling black and blue. He was breathing heavily and there were beads of sweat on his face. People were staring now. That same accusatory expression he'd seen in her eyes minutes earlier. What for? What the fuck were they all looking at?

Through the window, a thick mist hung – as if suspended in mid-air – obliterating the upper slopes. The single-decker bus snaked its way around the frozen lakeside, heading for the middle of nowhere.

Just two miles from Dorothy Smith's house, a bell sounded. Three middle-aged walkers stood up. He made his move, tagging along close behind like he was one of them.

As if!

It would take more than a stupid rucksack to make him like them. They were nothing: nil, zero, zilch.

As for Dotty, she was only special because he'd chosen to kill her today.

83

By close of play, the Murder Investigation Team looked some-
what deflated. Reviewing a case for the second time was never
going to be easy, and Daniels knew she'd have to work even
harder to keep them motivated in the days ahead. From her position in the doorway, she studied Gormley, his head buried in a
pile of files. He looked up as she approached with her coat slung
over her arm; his eyes were bloodshot from having read all day.

'Is that the last one?' she asked.

Gormley nodded. 'And we've got jack shit.'

He sounded fed up. Daniels moved a little closer in order
to read over his shoulder. Written on the inside front cover
of the file were the words, CONFIDENTIAL: LIFE LICENSEE
JONATHAN FORSTER. And in a number of boxes beneath
were the offender's personal details, written in capital letters
in thick black pen:

PRISON NUMBER:	K67889
SURNAME:	FORSTER
FORENAME(S):	JONATHAN
ALIAS:	FOSTER, JOHN
SEX:	M
HEIGHT:	188 CM
COMPLEXION:	SWARTHY

HAIR COLOUR:	BROWN
EYE COLOUR:	GREY
BUILD:	STOCKY
SHAPE OF FACE:	SQUARE
BIRTH PLACE:	NCLE/TYNE

Gormley turned the page, showing her Forster's previous convictions.

Daniels eyed the list. 'He sounds like a nasty piece of work.'

'He is. But he's not our guy. It's not his style.'

'OK, grab your coats everybody. Let's call it a day.' Daniels watched the squad pack up and move off, saying goodnight as they filed out of the door.

Gormley stayed put. 'Think I'll hang around for a bit.'

'I'm not taking no for an answer,' Daniels said. 'Put it away – I said it's time to go.'

As he muttered his dissent, she leaned over him, closed the file, opened up his bottom drawer and threw it in. She knew he was avoiding going home, so she asked him to go for a quick drink, at which point he stood up and put on his coat, wrapping a petrol-blue scarf around his neck.

'You sure you want to be seen in the boozer with an old man like me?' he said.

'Do you see a queue of younger ones?' Daniels slipped on her coat and did up the buttons. 'Anyway, I always tell people you're my dad.'

Gormley grinned as they headed into the corridor. Just then the phone rang. He looked at Daniels, his step faltering.

'I'd better just get that.'

She shouted for him to leave it and walked out the door, turning off the lights.

The warehouse had still not given up its secrets. After a very long day, Carmichael caught the eye of the TSG unit leader and mouthed the word *Sorry*.

He gave her a wry smile. 'You look it.'

'Ten more minutes?' She put her hands together, pleading for his patience.

'OK.' He made a face. 'But the drinks are on you if we find it.'

She left him to it, returning to Carruthers' office on the floor above to make a few calls. She was still on the phone half an hour later when the unit leader radioed his men to wrap it up. He'd hardly finished giving the order when an indistinct, but definite, shout came from the far end of the long corrugated shed. Carmichael glanced through the observation window. Probably another false alarm. There had been umpteen similar shouts since the search began. None of them had come to anything. She would never admit it – at least not to the industrious TSG – but she held out little hope of ever finding the coat.

Turning away again, she carried on with her conversation, oblivious to the heightened excitement going on in the warehouse below. Several men were making their way towards one officer who was standing still with his arm raised in the air. There was some discussion between them, then everyone turned their attention to Carruthers' office.

Carmichael was at the viewing window, but with her back to the glass.

The unit leader got on the radio. 'Lisa, you might want to get down here.'

Turning to look at them, Carmichael hung up the phone. Within seconds, she was running down the stairs as fast as her legs would carry her, her grin widening by the second.

A muddle of officers parted to let her through.

'Is it the one?' she asked.

The TSG leader looked up. 'Think so. The rest of the stuff in the bag fits. You're going to need to take out a mortgage at the pub,' he teased.

Putting on a pair of latex gloves, Carmichael bent down to take a closer look. The designer label was right, it was a full-length cashmere coat matching Monica's description – stylish, camel in colour, with two front pockets and a chic slit up the back. The right-hand pocket was empty. She took a deep breath, teased open the left, and could hardly believe her luck when she saw there was something inside.

'Fuck me, Danny – I think you're right!'

The TSG officer grinned.

Taking a small pair of tweezers from her bag and expertly attaching them to one corner of a small card, Carmichael lifted it free and dropped it into an evidence bag so she could examine it in more detail without fear of contamination. On one side was a picture of a saint with writing underneath: *S. Camillus De Lellis*. On the reverse, there was a reference to St Camillus, *Universal Patron of the Sick and Dying*. Underneath was a small prayer, beseeching the Good Lord to grant eternal happiness.

Carmichael felt like she'd already found hers.

Finnegan's was an old-fashioned long bar with more standing room than seating. It was packed to the rafters with off-duty officers, many of whom were watching an overhead TV. A

European football game was at stalemate with only seconds left on the clock. Gormley glanced at the screen just as a goal was scored. The ball thundered into the net, giving the goal-keeper no chance.

As the ref blew his whistle, the whole place erupted. Chairs scraped the hard wooden floor as fans hurried for the late bus and the noise level peaked as excited conversations merged with one another before dying to a steady hum.

Gormley acknowledged the barman with a nod, then pushed the only available bar stool towards Daniels. She sat down facing him, supporting her cheek with one elbow on the bar.

'Why d'you say Forster's not our guy? Not that I brought you out to talk shop.'

''Course not.' Gormley ordered a dry white wine and soda for her and a pint of Theakstons for himself. 'He's a scumbag, plain and simple. Likes to rape young girls – at least, he did when he was sixteen. He's got no recent form, but give him time. He's only been out two years.'

'Why is he on the list if his profile doesn't fit?'

Gormley shrugged.

'Where does he live?'

'West end. I was only halfway through his file when you kidnapped me. You sure you don't want me to work on? I'm happy to—'

'You want the night shift now?' Daniels accepted her wine from the barman and took a sip. 'Tomorrow's fine, Hank. You're no good to me if you burn yourself out.'

'You're right,' Gormley said drily. 'I can't wait to get home.'

She opened her mouth to say something, then shut it again as a young woman pushed in between them. As the barman took her order, Gormley noticed some football fans vacating a table near the door. They left the bar and made a beeline for it. No sooner had they sat down than Daniels' pocket began to chirp.

'Jesus! Mobiles really bug me sometimes . . .' She took out her phone. 'I'm going to start switching the damn thing off.'

Gormley grinned. Clearly she wasn't irritated enough to ignore it.

'Yeah, Lisa. What's up?'

Gormley took a long drink and used the back of his hand to wipe excess froth from his top lip. The pub door opened, letting more punters in, the noise of passing traffic forcing Daniels to cover her free ear – a mixture of excitement and disbelief crossing her face as she listened.

'You're kidding me? . . . You sure? . . . No, don't. I'll meet you there in ten.'

She hung up.

Gormley was more than a little intrigued. 'Come on then, spill. From the look on your face, I'd say at least some of that was good news.'

'We got lucky.' Daniels picked up her wine. 'You're not going to believe this, Hank: the TSG found the coat.'

'And the card?'

She was too stunned to answer.

'Kate?'

'Sorry?'

'The card?' Gormley pressed. 'Did they find it?'

Daniels just stared at him, a list of names running through her head: Father Simon, Sarah Short, Jenny Tait, Jamil Malik . . . and now Alan Stephens. 'It's him, Hank! Just how many people has this maniac killed?'

84

Getting there had been a cinch. Much less problematic than he'd expected, given the prevailing weather conditions. He didn't know how, when, if, he'd get back to Newcastle tomorrow, but that was the least of his problems. He'd come here to do a job on her and planned to stay until it was done. Assassination was his new best friend – the only one he could rely on. Like a drug to his system, it sent a rush of pleasure through his whole body. He needed a hit now.

Almost two months had gone by since Number Five. And in that time he'd missed his little ritual:

The guns . . .
The cards . . .
The scissors . . .
Especially the scissors.

Now here he was, primed and ready. But there was no sign of Dotty.

He'd been waiting in the shadows for hours, working himself into a lather, thinking of all the trouble he'd gone to, tracking her down – and for what? The house was in total darkness. A little cottage with a little gate; a little path leading up to a little front door for the little bitch he'd come to see. She was exactly like his mother, making him wait 'til she was ready. He didn't like it then and he didn't like it now. What was he supposed to do, hang around in the freezing cold for ever?

He consoled himself with thoughts of that other bitch being hauled over the coals by her bosses. If only he could have had a ringside seat to watch the fallout after his little intervention. She'd probably been taken off the case by now. Though he hoped not. He intended to introduce himself to Daniels. Maybe to both of them, now the other dyke had received a get-out-of-jail card. He smiled: *that* would certainly float his boat. Or should he take Soulsby out first? That way he wouldn't have to share.

He'd never been good at sharing.

The snow was falling heavily again, falling silently to earth in the picture-postcard garden, a reminder of Corbridge, in many ways. Should he break in and wait? Move on to the next one? Fuck, no! That would spoil everything! No! Dotty was Number Six. Not seven. Number SIX. That's just the way it was – plain and simple – the way it had always been. *They* had decided that, not him.

85

'Who?' Gormley said. 'What you on about?'

Daniels looked at the mobile phone in her hand, resisting the urge to call Carmichael back, to check that she'd heard her right and hadn't been dreaming. She pulled her chair closer to the table and dropped her voice to a whisper.

'It's him, Hank. He killed them all! The TSG just found the proof.'

'Yes!' Gormley punched the air in celebration, his enthusiasm wavering as he saw Daniels' brow crease.

'The card came from St Camillus,' she said. 'Would you credit that?'

Overriding his objections, Daniels sent Gormley home and walked back to the station alone. She went straight to the exhibits room to examine the recovered items and make sure they'd been properly logged, then she sent Carmichael packing too.

Daniels was too wired, too excited for sleep after the latest revelation. She wandered into the incident room and stood for a moment looking around. Despite the introduction of HOLMES – Home Office Large Major Enquiry System – a computerised programme that replaced the antiquated manual process of compiling and cross-checking data, murder enquiries still generated mountains of paperwork and much of it had landed on Gormley's desk.

Turning his desk lamp on for company, she sifted a few files that were sitting there, skimming through some, ignoring others. Then she opened his bottom drawer and took out the file she'd thrown in earlier, the one he'd been reviewing before she'd dragged him off to the pub.

Spreading it out on the desk she wondered what it was about this 'scumbag' that had triggered his inclusion on the PNC list. Forster was a lifer, yes. But he'd been captured within days leaving forensics all over the place and had absolutely nothing in common with the cold-blooded, calculated killer she was seeking.

Gormley was right: his profile simply didn't fit. She scribbled a note for Gormley and stuck it to the front of the file:

Waste of bloody time. Don't bother going over it again.
  See you tomorrow.
  Kate

86

She glanced sideways at the Dutch woman, feeling guilty for having doubted her. Whatever misgivings she may have had about Stephens' second wife, Daniels knew that none of Jo's problems had been her doing. Monica was not responsible for Jo's incarceration – Bright was.

They had hardly spoken on the way to the exhibits room. And now, Monica waited patiently as Daniels scribbled in a ledger, asking the exhibits officer for some privacy. They watched him disappear into the back office, and then Daniels took a large transparent bag from a box he'd left on the counter.

Monica took her time studying the garment inside.

'Can you say with absolute certainty that this is your coat?' Daniels asked after a while. She already knew the answer. The coat was foreign, for a start, and Carmichael had discovered a card in the pocket. Still, it was vital to go through the motions of identification.

Monica nodded.

'Are you completely sure? It's very important. I can take it out, if you like?'

'May I?' Monica pointed at the bag. Daniels handed it to her. 'Yes, definitely . . .' Monica indicated a mark on the lapel and used her hand to smooth out the cellophane so the DCI could see it more clearly. 'You see the pulled thread there? I did it on one of the flowers for the war dead.'

'A poppy?'

Monica nodded.

Daniels lifted out a second evidence bag containing the card itself. 'And this?'

On seeing the card, Monica broke down, as if the sight of it brought back the full horror of that night. Daniels had expected as much. She held Monica's trembling hand and offered to get her a drink of water.

'No, I'm OK,' she said. 'Just give me a moment.'

Daniels sighed. 'I know how difficult this is for you, Monica. Believe me, I wish I didn't have to put you through it.'

Taking a deep breath, Monica reached for the card. She examined it closely, rotating the bag so she could view both sides. 'It looks exactly like the one I found on the night . . . the night Alan was killed.'

'Are you absolutely certain?'

Monica gave an emphatic nod.

On the floor below, Gormley was being given a hard time. He hadn't had a proper conversation with his son in weeks and Ryan wasn't at all happy. As Gormley listened to the tale of woe coming from the receiver clamped between his shoulder and ear, he began doodling on a sheet of paper: the cartoon head of a boy, a cute cat, a house, a cross . . . Suddenly he sat up straight, staring at the doodles.

A cross, a bloody cross.

'Look, Ryan, I've got to go . . .' Gormley winced. 'No, of

course you're important to me . . . that's really unfair, son. You know I do. Look, I'll call you back, I promise. No . . . I *will* call you.'

He hung up.

Forster's file was still lying in his bottom drawer where Daniels had thrown it the night before. He lifted it out, opened the inside front cover and scanned the personal information boxes. Then he scanned them again, just to make sure.

He picked up his mobile.

It was beginning to feel like a very long day, as far as Daniels was concerned. After seeing Monica off, she had gone directly into a strategic case conference, convened at short notice in the major incident suite upstairs. It was chaired by Assistant Chief Constable Martin and involved top brass from two other forces – Durham and West Midlands – as well as a senior officer from the National Crime Faculty. The subject up for discussion? Linked murders and which force should take the lead role in the investigation.

In other words: *Who's going to foot the bill?*

Despite Martin's fervent opposition, it had been decided that Northumbria should have the honour. Daniels couldn't tell which upset the ACC most: the cost of the enquiry, or the fact that this would put her firmly centre stage in the case of her career. If she hadn't been so preoccupied with the case she might have relished the moment.

As they filed out of the meeting, she was intercepted by Gormley.

'You get my text?' He was buzzing with excitement as he brought her attention to a file in his hand. 'Forster's our man!'

ACC Martin brushed past them, shooting looks. Turning her back on him, she set off down the corridor with Gormley in tow.

'I thought you said—'

'I know what I said, Kate. But I was wrong. C'mon, we've got work to do.' They took the stairs quickly, heading for her office. 'You know when something niggles you – you don't know why, it just does?' Gormley stopped walking as they reached her office door. Opening the file, he turned the page, pointing at a photograph of Jonathan Forster. 'Well, if this is who I think it is, I met him in the waiting room at Jo's office. He was a wimp. His mate was behaving like a prick. I wanted to kick his head in, but I restrained myself.'

'That was big of you . . .' Daniels held the door open and ushered him in. 'You sure it was Forster?'

Gormley sat down. 'I'd bet my last pay packet. I rang Jo's receptionist, but the dozy cow couldn't remember – which surprised me, given the fact that the other guy was itching for a fight.'

'Didn't she check her records?'

'Yes. Forster definitely had an appointment that day. See these . . .' Gormley pulled out two very similar photographs and handed them to Daniels. 'One is from our own database, the other is a photographic copy that was in one of the files we seized from Jo's office. On both of these he's got hair, right?'

'So?'

Gormley reached for a pen and paper, began drawing as he talked. 'He's changed his appearance, Kate. That's what threw me. When I met him, he had a shaven head and a tattoo underneath the hairline, like this . . .'

He showed her his drawing of a crucifix.

'There's no mention of it in his file,' Daniels said.

'Exactly my point! Take a look here . . .' Gormley produced another sheet of paper. 'This is a photocopy of the inside front cover of Forster's prison file. Every physical description is listed, *including* distinguishing marks. But if his tattoo was hidden by hair, it wouldn't have been noticed.'

'And therefore not recorded.'

Gormley grinned. 'Exactly.'

'Most pond life have tats. They copy each other on account of the fact that they have no imagination. Crosses are common. It's religious symbolism, but on its own it's not enough.'

'Then we'll just have to find something that is . . .'

They split the file in half and worked late into the night, the hands of the clock winding their way slowly and painfully round the dial. Daniels sighed loudly. Sick of reading, she sat up straight, casting her tired eyes across the litter on her desk: empty sandwich cartons, spent coffee cups and several crisp packets – all cheese and onion. Gormley looked up briefly and then went back to his reading. His capacity to keep going amazed her. Using a paper knife as book marker, she flicked through the remaining pages to see how long it would take her to finish. Right near the back there was a typed report. Her eyes homed in on familiar handwriting, a scrawled reference to a conversation between Jo and one of Forster's juvenile counsellors.

'Hank, listen to this. It's in Jo's handwriting.' She began reading aloud: '"Mrs Forster is a profoundly religious woman and Jonathan resents this deeply. Paradoxically, this led him, at sixteen, to have a crucifix tattoo engraved under his hair-line. A definite attempt to piss off his mother, who, the social worker tells me, is now terrified of him."'

'Yes! Oh, you little beauty!' Gormley rushed round the desk to see for himself. 'Maybe there *is* a God, after all!'

Daniels re-read the note, feeling suddenly energized.

'It's a religious link, no doubt about it,' she said.

'I'm telling you, Kate, this guy makes Dennis Nilsen look like a boy scout.'

'I don't doubt it. But you said yourself, he's a sadistic rapist. This recent spate of killings are hardly his style. Apart from Sarah, who I can't help thinking just got caught up in something she had nothing to do with, our victims are all middle-aged men and women. They weren't interfered with. He just shoots them. End of.'

Gormley's determined expression was hard to argue with.

'Trust me,' he said. 'Forster's our man.'

87

As they waited to gain entry to the Regional Psychology Service, Gormley had time to notice a new addition to the graffiti on the door. Under the word WANKER someone had taken a thick-tipped permanent marker and added SPERM DONORS REQUIRED.

He glanced sideways. 'You *sure* you want to do this without talking to Jo first?'

The door clicked open before Daniels had a chance to answer.

The receptionist was waiting behind her security screen. She gave a welcoming smile as they walked in. Daniels explained why they were there and detected a slight reluctance from the woman. But she made no fuss; just directed them down the corridor, even offered to make them a cup of tea.

When they reached Jo's office, Daniels stopped short of the door.

Gormley gave her a second. 'You *really* want to do this?'

'I do, OK? She'll kill me when she finds out, but that's *my* problem, not yours.'

They entered the office and put on the lights.

'I'll take the desk,' Daniels said. 'You start with the filing cabinets.'

They had only just got started when the door flew open and

Jo stormed in. The room temperature seemed to drop several degrees as the three of them stood there, no one knowing quite what to say. Jo was dressed casually in cords and a sweater, her hair tied back carelessly, leaving wisps hanging loose around her face. She was obviously well and truly hacked off.

'Ever heard of search warrant?' she asked.

Daniels bit her lip. In her wildest dreams she hadn't expected to meet her like this. She wondered why the woman on reception hadn't warned them Jo was in the building. You could cut the atmosphere with a knife. Gormley removed his hands from the drawer he was searching, made his excuses and left.

'Well?' Jo barked. 'What the hell d'you think you're doing here?'

'We have a warrant—'

'Which you know perfectly well has now expired!' Jo walked to the filing cabinet and slammed the drawer shut. 'Could you not have had the courtesy to call me first?'

'I've been calling you for days.'

Daniels moved towards her but Jo stepped away.

'I'm not ready to make nice, Kate.'

A little grin appeared on Daniels' face. 'Not Ready to Make Nice' was the title of one of their favourite Dixie Chicks songs, the one they used to play when they'd had a row and neither of them wanted to back down.

Jo went and sat at her desk, leaving Daniels isolated in the middle of the room.

'You going to tell me what you hope to find here?' she asked.

Feeling a little bit silly and a lot sad, Daniels said, 'Can I at least sit down?'

Jo nodded towards a chair.

'The truth is, I'm not sure.' Daniels sighed. 'One of your clients is beginning to emerge as a likely candidate for Alan's murder and at least two others. He's our best suspect yet, but I don't really understand him and I need to, if I'm going to catch him.' She pulled a folded sheet of paper from her pocket – the photograph Gormley had copied from Forster's police record – and handed it over. 'I know you're officially barred from working on the case, but MIT need your help, Jo. I need your help. He *is* still on your caseload?'

Jo nodded, her expression darkening. In the time she'd been supervising Jonathan Forster, she'd formed the opinion that his was a case where 'life' should have meant just that. For the last two years, she'd tried to peel back the layers of his past, to get beneath his thick skin, to talk some sense into him – show him that he could so easily take a different path . . .

She'd been wasting her breath.

Within the confines of her office, he'd emptied the contents of his polluted mind, worn his sentence like a badge and re-fused to see beyond his own twisted logic. If he *was* involved, then Daniels had a problem.

'You'd better make yourself comfortable,' Jo said.

It was a clear warning that they were in for a long session. Daniels called Gormley on his mobile and told him she'd meet him back at the office. Jo rang her secretary, told her not to disturb them and asked for a pot of coffee, then fetched Forster's file from a grey filing cabinet behind her desk. There was no question of doctor/patient confidentiality here.

There was no time to lose.

Daniels relaxed a little. It felt good to be on the same side once again. But before they got down to business, she had something important to say about the events of the past few days. It was the first chance she'd had to talk to Jo face to face and she didn't know when she'd get another. Jo sat down again, curious as to what was coming.

From the look on Daniels' face, something was.

'Bright knows,' she said bluntly.

'About us?'

Daniels nodded.

'How?'

'What makes you think I didn't tell him?'

'Did you?'

Daniels flushed. 'Anonymous letter, delivered to HQ with a copy to Martin. Thought I should give you the heads up, in case—'

'They won't say anything to me,' Jo said calmly. 'I'd like to see them try!'

'No . . . I don't suppose they will.'

'What did you tell them?'

'I told Bright the truth. We *were* involved, but not any more.'

'Bet that went down well. And Martin?'

'Has no proof whatsoever. Let's just say I'm not his favourite DCI right now. You told me it would come back and bite me on the arse, and now it has.'

'And you're still alive? Still in the job? Well, goodness me!'

So the subject was now closed, and they were no closer to resolving their differences. Daniels was convinced she'd be blackballed from going any further in the job. But somehow that didn't seem to matter any more.

Changing the subject, they got down to business and talked about Forster for nearly two hours, going over his psychological assessment in minute detail. The information Jo provided was pure gold; the picture she painted guaranteed to put the fear of God into most right-minded people.

'. . . as I said, he has all the characteristics of an anger rapist. It's not unusual for attacks to increase in severity over time.'

'Whether or not they involve a sexual element?' Daniels queried.

Jo was thoughtful for a moment. 'His attack on the young girl he killed was horrific and unpremeditated, but the source of his anger was definitely his mother.'

'And now what? He's displacing his anger?'

'Possibly . . . his perception of women is that they're whores: hostile, self-centred, disloyal. Rejection is an obvious trigger for guys like this. They become enraged and strike out whenever their masculinity is threatened. Don't underestimate him, Kate. He might look and act like a wimp, but he's an evil little shit, make no mistake.'

'But why would he be killing men as well as women?'

'You're the detective. I'm sure you'll work it out.'

'Please, Jo. I'm struggling here.'

'I don't have all the answers, Kate. You know that. The guy's been locked up for over twenty years! Who knows what nasty things have happened to him during that time. Such a prolonged period of incarceration might have sparked off a fury the magnitude of which we can only guess at. People change – even damaged ones – and not always for the better.'

'OK . . . thanks for the insight.' Daniels gathered her stuff. 'I'd appreciate it if you kept this meeting between the two of us. Bright will go nuts if he finds out I've discussed the case with you.'

Jo reacted as though she'd been slapped. But Daniels was already rising to her feet and hadn't seen it. She was half expecting Jo to embrace her when she stood up too and was caught off guard by her angry tone.

'Shame *you're* not capable of change!'

Daniels was lost for words.

Jo marched over to her filing cabinet, replaced Forster's file, then went to her bookshelves, the top three of which housed hundreds of professional journals she'd collected over the years. On a shelf lower down, one book in particular caught her eye: Jean Piaget's *The Child's Conception of the World.* As she watched Jo remove it from the shelf, Daniels' stomach lurched at the sight of the front cover, which featured a child's drawing of a little girl with lots of freckles. Jo opened the front cover. Inside, there was a personal inscription, beautifully crafted by its writer.

She brought the book to Daniels and handed it over, still open.

It was a moment of real heartache for Daniels as she stared at her own handwriting. She had bought the book many years before. Knowing nothing of psychology, beyond that which she'd observed on the city streets, she'd loitered for ages in the bookstore, agonizing over which book to buy. In the end, it was the freckles that tipped the scales. How Jo had laughed when she found out.

Well, she wasn't laughing now.

'Take it!' she said. 'I won't be needing it any more.'

Their moment of closeness had dissolved without trace. It was a cruel way of saying their relationship was over. For good.

Devastated, Daniels slipped the book into her pocket and left.

88

Daniels was staring out of the window. Gormley suspected she hadn't told the whole truth about her meeting with Jo earlier. She was brooding about something. He didn't know what, but suspected it had little to do with the case.

A knock at the door surprised them both. Maxwell poked his head in, asking for a second of their time. Daniels beckoned him in, curious to know what he wanted. Since his transfer to another team, he hadn't been seen for dust. She wondered if he'd come cap in hand, thinking he could get his old job back. If so, he didn't have a hope in hell.

'What do *you* want?' She didn't wait for an answer. 'If you're sniffing around for Martin, you're wasting your bloody time.'

Maxwell's brow creased, as if he had no idea what she was on about.

'Well? Spit it out, now you're here.'

He handed her a disk. 'I found more footage of Jo Soulsby while working on another enquiry . . . I think you should take a look at it, boss.'

'Where the hell have you been?' Gormley snapped. 'Haven't you heard the news?'

'She's been bailed, Neil,' Daniels explained. 'Expects to be cleared of all charges. Given that she's done nothing wrong, why would I be remotely interested in whatever's on this disk?'

Maxwell hesitated. 'Because she was in another part of town, being dragged up a back alley by two thugs.'

Complete silence.

Oh my God! Daniels felt sick. Outraged. She couldn't quite believe what she was hearing. Maxwell had drawn her a picture she just couldn't get out of her head.

Poor, poor, Jo.

What she must have gone through.

Daniels was close to losing it, unable to conceal her disgust.

'. . . I couldn't actually see what happened,' Maxwell continued. 'But it doesn't take a lot of imagination to fill in the blanks. I only wish we'd found it sooner. To be raped by Stephens was gross, but to suffer at the hands of two morons in the street, well, it doesn't bear thinking about. She's innocent, all right.'

Gormley stood up, about to usher him from the room.

Daniels put her hand up to stop him. 'No, Hank. It's OK, this is important. It ties up a lot of loose ends, explains why Jo hung around in town, her blocked-off memory, why she was in a state when the taxi picked her up.'

She didn't really know what else to say. What to think. Maxwell was an unlikely source of closure. Gone were the smart-arse remarks, the snide glances. It was as if this latest shocking revelation was too awful even for *him* to contemplate. His lips were moving again but Daniels didn't hear a word of his apology, the shame he felt for the way he'd behaved, his request to be given another chance.

89

Daniels had been sitting in her vehicle for a good half-hour, observing the entrance to the Regional Psychology Service. In that time, the door had opened only twice, allowing a couple of women back out on to the street.

According to the receptionist, Forster was still inside. Daniels couldn't bear the thought that he was probably in a room with Jo, sharing the same air, when she now had knowledge that he might conceivably have killed her ex. Wondering how she was coping with that, Daniels glanced at her watch. Forster's weekly reporting was scheduled to last just half an hour.

He'd be out any second now.

While she waited, the conversation she'd had with Jo following Maxwell's revelation that she'd been attacked reverberated round her head. After several attempts to call her, Jo had finally answered her phone. But she point-blank refused to discuss the thugs in the alley; refused to be a victim again. The police hadn't been interested when she reported Stephens for rape. As far as she was concerned, they had nothing more to say to one another. Then the phone went dead.

Daniels willed the door across the street to open again.

It did.

She put her hand to her earpiece. 'Here we go.'

A scruffy man left the building, hesitating at the gate just long enough to light a cigarette. He set off along the road with an arrogant strut, picking his nose as he went, wiping his hands on the back of his jeans. It was the first time Daniels had seen him in the flesh, though something about him struck a chord. He was a very different person than the one Gormley had described. Not a wimp frightened of his own shadow, but an arrogant, cocksure lowlife with an evil look in his eye.

Gormley's favourite saying popped into her head at the exact same time it came out of his mouth: *If it looks like shite . . .*

'. . . and it smells like shite,' Gormley said, 'then it's probably shite.'

Daniels smiled.

Although it was getting dark, the streetlights were good enough to make the identification. She got out of her car, making sure she wasn't seen, conscious that Forster might very well be armed. She followed at a safe distance. It looked as though he was heading for the address Jo had given her. He turned right off the main road, in no hurry, stopping to pass the time of day with a young boy coming the other way, a glance over his shoulder forcing Daniels to retreat into the shadows of a shop doorway. She caught his reflection in the glass and thought she saw something change hands. Her earpiece confirmed that Gormley had seen it too.

'Probably an arrestable offence . . . want me to pick him up?'

Daniels spoke quietly into her sleeve. 'Negative, Hank. We want to get the bastard for something much bigger than a poxy heroin deal. But first, we need proof. Something concrete we can act on. We can't risk this thing going tits-up a second time.'

As if sensing their interest, Forster looked back over his shoulder again, then took off downhill towards the entrance to Brandon Towers, a block Daniels knew well. Built in the sixties to combat overcrowding, it had since become home to many of the region's criminals, the socially disaffected and the downright unfortunate. The exterior walls were covered in graffiti, the whole place in need of pulling down.

Forster went in through the main entrance. Daniels stood a while, considering what to do next. She gave Gormley permission to return to base, watched him drive off, and then turned away.

Ten floors up, Forster stood well back from the window and looked down on the street, watching the good detective walk back in the direction of her car. He raised his gun, lining her up in his sights and feigned a shot. BANG!

90

Monday 4 January was the start of the working New Year and Bright was struggling to come to terms with the fact that his glittering police career was crashing around his ears. He wasn't coping without Stella; the woman behind the great man, the woman without whom he'd never have made it this far. Throughout their long and happy marriage she'd smoothed the ups and downs, supported him through the good and bad moments – always willing to take a back seat.

How he wished she'd been in that seat on the night of their accident.

He sat up straight, cupping his hands together in front of his chest. Looking around him, he could see that he wasn't the only one flagging; his team were suffering too. Daniels looked particularly jaded this morning. He didn't know why, but he had the distinct impression she was deliberately trying to avoid him.

Well, he'd see about that.

She turned as he approached her at the coffee machine. 'Want one, guv?'

'No, you're all right,' he said.

He was on the verge of suggesting they step into his office for a private word, when in walked Ron Naylor.

'Phil. Kate.'

Bright felt instantly angry, but his anger turned to smugness as he watched Naylor give his DCI a winning smile. The rumour about her sexual preference obviously hadn't reached Ron yet. It would. Martin would make sure it did.

Bright found himself smiling. Maybe Naylor still thought he was in with a chance. Why else come all this way during a major investigation?

'How's it going this end?' Naylor asked.

'Not good, I'm afraid.' Daniels held up her polystyrene cup. 'Coffee?'

'No thanks, I'm wired enough already.'

Bright observed him closely. On the outside at least, his Durham counterpart didn't seem in the least bit stressed. In fact, quite the opposite. How the hell did he manage it? Year after long year. No respite from a Godawful job with not enough time off, even less reward. Bright was sick of it. Maybe it was time to knock it on the head, take his pension pot and tend his garden.

'Word is, ACC Martin wants your guv'nor's gonads for his wall,' Naylor said to Daniels, his tongue firmly in his cheek as he had a laugh at Bright's expense. 'Finding this serial killer is the only way he gets to keep them, I hear.'

Daniels glanced at Bright, then back at Naylor. 'I'm a glass half-full girl myself. If we make an arrest before your lot, I think our guv'nor might still end up with all his bits intact.'

'Game on, then!' Naylor was flirting with her.

'Indeed,' Daniels grinned. 'Shame we're now in the driving seat, eh?'

She was referring to the fact that Northumbria had been

designated as the lead force, on the basis that their patch seemed to have a particular significance for the killer. Most of the victims had lived in the region at one time or another. Now all MIT had to do was find out what else linked them together.

'*Touché!*' Naylor tapped her shoulder. 'I'll leave you to it, then, Kate.'

Bright waited until he was gone. 'Er, can we get back to work now?'

'We're doing all we can, guv. You can throw as much finance and as many resources at this case as you like, but the Forster link just isn't happening for us. Churches and care homes have already been ruled out. And if Andy doesn't come up trumps at the Education Department then, to put it bluntly, we're screwed.'

He looked past her as the door opened and Brown walked in. Watched by a dozen pairs of eyes, he walked across the room shaking his head. He'd obviously drawn a blank.

With his whole future now hanging in the balance, Bright looked gutted. Daniels had little sympathy for him, but neither did she want him to lose his job. She hadn't seen him this wound up for ages and flinched as he bellowed angrily at the squad.

'Does *anyone* have a clue?'

There were red faces all round. No one said a word.

'Come on, think!' he pushed.

'We've narrowed down the time-frame a bit, guv,' Gormley piped up in defence of the squad. 'If it's any consolation, West Mids and Durham haven't got a clue either.'

'It isn't!' Bright snapped. 'So why don't you pull your bloody fingers out and give me something concrete!'

Daniels put down her coffee. 'Guv, can I have a word?' They retreated to a quiet corner. 'Look, we're not going to get anywhere if we start losing our tempers. I absolutely refuse to be beaten on this. I've never given up on a case in my entire career and I'm not about to start now. And neither have you. Alan Stephens can't speak for himself. His widow is relying on us to do his talking for him. We can only do that if we stick together. We owe her one. It's the least we can do.'

Bright mumbled an apology and something about flushing his career down the bog. 'I agree with you,' he said. 'We should work as a team. And if you can save my arse, too . . . well, that'll be a bonus.'

'OK, I've had my bollocking from the DCI,' said Bright, getting the briefing back underway. 'Anyone *not* happy that this area is the key?' There was no response. 'Good. At least we agree on something.' Bright directed his next question to Gormley: 'All three victims were living here, when?'

'Between eighty-five and ninety,' Gormley replied.

'And Forster is the only person thrown up by the database who we know had a thing about the Church and the opportunity to kill all three?'

'Yep.'

'What year was he sentenced?'

'Eighty-eight. October,' Daniels said.

'OK, that fits with the timeline . . .' Bright was calm again. 'Assuming for one second it *is* him, what's his motive?'

'Maybe he's offing the jury,' Carmichael spoke up. 'Apparently, he went down screaming revenge at the end of his trial. I read that somewhere yesterday.'

Bright raised an eyebrow. 'Is that right?'

Carmichael went beetroot. Everyone was staring in her direction. Even Daniels appeared to be considering the possibility. *Was everyone nuts?*

'What?' Carmichael said. 'I wasn't being serious!'

'It's as good a motive as any other.' The comment came from someone at the back. 'Improbable, but not impossible for him to have traced the jury, I suppose.'

Gormley raised his eyes to the ceiling.

'She's got a point . . .' Brown said. 'Juries get nobbled all the time.'

'Yeah, before or during a trial, not after,' Daniels chipped in. 'And not this far down the road. Come on, guys! He'd have to possess an amazing memory, for a start.'

Robson's entry into the room interrupted her train of thought. He took one look at the expressions on their faces, realized his timing might have been better and quickly took his seat. Carmichael leaned in close, filling him in on developments.

'Maybe he had an accomplice,' Brown then suggested, 'someone sitting in the public gallery with an axe to grind.'

'Wait, wait, *wait*!' Bright was off again. 'Assuming he got hold of the names, it's stretching it to think he could find the jurors after all this time.'

'Not in this day and age, guv . . .' Carmichael pointed at the laptop on her desk. 'That stint I did on cybercrime with the fraud squad taught me just how much personal info people post online nowadays. You wouldn't believe it. Conmen can work out a date of birth in less than ten minutes from a name and a bloody star sign, apparently! Addresses are easy, once they have that. If web data can be used to obtain passports, it can be used to find people too.'

Bright smiled at Daniels, buoyed by Carmichael's knowledge and enthusiasm.

Daniels smiled back. 'She's right, guv. A stranger these days isn't someone you meet in the street, it's anyone with a personal computer or smart phone.'

'There are newspaper archives, for a start,' Robson added. 'Not to mention social network sites: Facebook, MySpace, Friends Reunited, Google . . .'

'Ask the audience, phone a friend . . .' Gormley mocked. 'You lot are barking mad. Facebook! Sadbook, more like.'

Robson gave him a friendly dig in the ribs. 'Don't take the piss, Hank. You're a technophobe . . . That means a dinosaur, in case you didn't know.'

The mood in the room had lifted. Daniels couldn't remember the last time she'd witnessed such camaraderie within MIT. She waited for them to settle down before asking Carmichael to carry on.

The young DC pushed back her shoulders, ready to take up the challenge. 'I might not find every one of them, but I reckon I'd come up with some. With no other leads, it's worth a try.'

Bright rubbed at the stubble on his chin. 'Go for it, Lisa. We've got sod all else. Robbo, get me Forster's court file, a transcript of the trial and anything you can get your hands on. Let's give Forster a whirl and see where it takes us.'

The Moot Hall had been the preferred court for many High Court judges since the early nineteenth century. Robson remembered someone telling him it had taken nearly seven years to build and cost less than a hundred thousand pounds. He couldn't calculate how much that was in today's money as he rushed up the steps to the splendid front door heading straight for Court One.

It was a magnificent courtroom with solid-oak furniture that had been stained with tea to bring out the natural colour of the wood. Fine desks were inlayed with leather and the dock area was surrounded with lead and brass railings, polished to perfection.

Sally, the legal administrator, was waiting for him. She was an old friend, curious to know why he needed a file dating back to the late eighties. She was a little awkward in his presence and he couldn't understand why.

They'd been great pals, back in the days when they were both studying Law at Durham University with aspirations to become barristers. He'd forgotten their one drunken night of passion during a lock-in at the student bar. They'd not seen each other in ages and neither their relationship nor their adolescent dreams were important to him any more. Having explained why he was there, he sat down to wait.

The entire team looked round nervously as the door opened. When it wasn't Robson, they relaxed again. Carmichael's theory was a long shot, but it had raised their expectations and Daniels felt compelled to rein them in.

'Hold on, let's not get ahead of ourselves,' she said. 'We have motive and opportunity, but not an ounce of proof.'

Bright smiled. 'You ever get sick of always being right?'

'Oh, you noticed!' Daniels grinned back. 'And think about

it, guv: if all three victims *were* jury members, then nine others need tracing and protecting.'

The door opened again. This time it was Robson, soaked to the skin and out of breath. The focus of everyone's attention, he took off his dripping coat and handed a hefty court file to Bright. The room held its breath as he opened it, his hopeful expression quickly dissolving into a frown.

Deflated, Daniels went back to her office, unable to face propping up her boss for the umpteenth time that day. It was high time he managed without her. Gormley joined her seconds later, armed with cans of coke and crisps. There was no sign of *his* enthusiasm wavering, not in the slightest. In fact, his upbeat manner filled her with hope.

Setting one can on her desk, he threw her a bag of cheese and onion crisps and sat down in the opposite chair.

'Pretend it's Starbucks. Skinny Cinnamon Dolce Latte with a Very Berry Scone.' He sniffed the coke tin. 'Mmm, smells good.'

Daniels laughed out loud, hungry all of a sudden. She tore open the crisps and stuffed a handful into her mouth. She couldn't remember the last time she'd eaten.

'Still think it's him?' she said, her mouth full.

'Absolutely.'

'Right, I want you to retrieve each and every document that so much as mentions him, going right back to the day he was born. I want school and social-enquiry reports; prison, police and medical records . . .'

'It'll take time.'

'Never mind that, just do it! I've got a good feeling, Hank.'

They clinked their cokes, suddenly in a good mood.

'Happy New Year!' they said in unison.

91

It took longer than she'd anticipated to gather the documentation: several days and scores of man-hours to assemble a mountain of paperwork, the most comprehensive profile of an offender MIT had ever seen. Daniels instructed them to begin with the most recent stuff and work their way back, but they soon tired of wading through Forster's life of crime and began questioning her strategy. There were mumblings of dissent: *Hope she's right . . . We could be wasting our time . . . Eggs in one basket didn't work last time.*

After several hours' reading, she knew just how they felt. The page in front of her was dancing, the words merging into thick black blobs, so she sat up straight, taking a break, stretching her arms above her head. Out of the window, a pale blue cloudless sky offered brief respite from the four walls of her office. Two gulls caught her eye. A joyous sight, they soared high above the rooftops, gliding effortlessly on the wind heading for the coast.

Shutting her eyes, Daniels suddenly felt a wave of regret. She'd never again walk on a beach with Jo, never look into those pale blue eyes or share the ecstasy of a perfect mate. It was time to accept that they would never be together.

Jo would argue they never had been.

Pushing away the suffocating emptiness she'd been feeling

the past few days, Daniels wiped her cheek with the back of her hand. On the other side of her battered desk, Gormley had his head down, oblivious to her sadness – or so she'd thought. Without lifting his head, he extended his arm, handing her a handkerchief.

'Don't!' he said. 'You'll set me off.'

Daniels managed a grin. She jumped as her phone rang. She lifted the receiver. 'DCI Daniels.'

'It's me. Can you come round?'

'What, now?'

'Yes, now!'

Daniels hung up. 'I've got to go out,' she said.

Her excitement evaporated when she discovered that the invitation was strictly business, not pleasure. Jo had done some checking, and turned up some dead files on Jonathan Forster she felt Daniels needed to see.

They were sitting in her living room, Jo cross-legged on her sofa, reading from a psychological assessment on her lap. 'I'm quoting now: *From when he was quite young, he used to kill small birds and rodents just for the fun of it.* End quote.' Jo looked up. 'There are several references to similar behaviour over the years, some I knew about, some I didn't.'

The extract made Daniels' blood boil. 'If that isn't an indicator that he'd turn out to be an evil shit, I don't know what is.'

'He's a creature of habit, Kate. This repetitive behaviour doesn't surprise me.' Uncrossing her legs, Jo stretched them out on the couch. 'He was a jealous, overbearing child, prone to tantrums if he didn't get his own way. As a juvenile, he got

his rocks off perving through windows, graduating to inde-
cent exposure, sexual assault, rape and, finally, murder.'

'Sounds like a right control freak,' Daniels said.

'Correct. He *has* to dominate and control. That's what
makes him so dangerous.' Jo dropped the report into a box
on the floor, where it landed with a solid thump. 'If he *is* your
man, then it's this need that turned him from rapist to killer
in eighty-eight.'

A pile of files with yellow Post-it notes marking the sections
Jo wanted to discuss sat on the table between them. They had
only got through half of them and there was still a way to go.
As Jo picked up the next one, Daniels rubbed her tired eyes
and then suddenly had a light-bulb moment.

'Creature of habit, you say?' She leapt from her seat and on
to the floor, began searching the box of dead files.

Sensing a change in atmosphere, Jo lifted her head. 'Don't
keep me in suspense,' she said. 'What are you looking for?'

'Hang on, it could be nothing.' Daniels found one particular file, opened it and shuffled through several pages as she
spoke. 'Didn't you tell me that he had some kind of religious
magazine in his possession when he was released on life licence? *True Faith*, something like that?'

'Close!' Jo laughed. '*True Faith* is the Newcastle United
fanzine, you idiot!'

Daniels laughed too.

'It was *Living Faith*,' Jo said. 'Why?'

'There's a note in here somewhere . . .' Daniels went back to
her search. 'Here it is!'

She pulled out a short scribbled note, handwritten on an
A5 Probation letterhead. Her heart raced as she noticed the

date: *10th October 1988* – the day Forster got life. She re-read the note quickly, unclipped it from the file and handed it to Jo.

> *10th Oct, '88*
> *For the attention of Reception Officer, HMP Durham*
> *Ref: Jonathan Forster*
>
> *Following the passing of a life sentence today, I attended the cells to carry out a post-sentence interview and risk assessment on the above prisoner, having first spoken to his parents, neither of whom felt able to face him personally.*
>
> *I sought special permission from the Senior Prison Officer on duty to hand over two items: a small crucifix and a religious magazine. His parents hope that these items will give him guidance in the dark months and years to come and assist him to come to terms with what he has done.*
>
> *Forster accepted the items from me, but refused to speak about his sentence. When I pressed him, he became abusive and I terminated the interview. <u>No risk assessment was carried out</u>, therefore I recommend that he is placed on suicide watch until seen by a member of the medical staff. His parents have also asked that you refer him to the prison chaplain at the earliest opportunity.*
>
> *Matthew Spencer – Crown Court Liaison Officer*

Daniels suddenly felt charged with electricity. The hairs stood up on the back of her neck and goose pimples covered her skin. Several images flashed through her mind, vying for her attention: a woman in a black Burka, a photograph of Jamil Malik, the magazine cutting she'd passed across the table to

Naylor at the Living Room restaurant. She looked at the letter again. Could this be the break she'd been looking for? It could so easily have been discarded soon after it was written, or become detached from the file over time.

But it hadn't.

And that excited her.

'Well!' she said. 'What do you reckon?'

'You're thinking the photo of Malik could have come from the same magazine?'

'Got any better ideas?' Daniels said, wounded by Jo's disbelieving tone.

'You *do* know his mother never visited throughout the two decades he was inside?'

'There you go! What was it you said about men like him? Can't cope with rejection in any form? Our backs are against the wall here, Jo. If it *is* the same magazine – a gift from a mother who doesn't love him – isn't it possible that it has become a symbol of his hatred over the years?'

'Anything is possible where the human psyche is concerned,' Jo said. 'But what would that have to do with Alan and the others?'

'Honestly? I haven't got the first idea.' Daniels thought for a moment. 'You told me that Alan was a bit of an evangelist in his youth. Maybe he featured in the magazine, wrote an article for it, who knows? Maybe Jamil Malik did too. His cousin said he was deeply religious. What if the photograph *was* cut from this magazine?'

'This has really got you going, hasn't it?'

'I need to chase it up, find out who publishes *Living Faith*, how often and whether Forster received it on a regular basis during his sentence. I'll get Gormley to check if it's mentioned elsewhere in the system.' Daniels stood up, began pacing up and down. She could read Jo like a book, could see she was far from convinced. 'Look, when I was a custody officer, if I took possession of a magazine in someone's property I would write down *Living Faith* magazine and the issue date. If it was pristine or dog-eared, I'd write that down too.'

'That's because you're Polly Perfect. Not to mention – personality wise – ah, let me see . . .' Jo began counting on her fingers '. . . borderline obsessive/compulsive, anal retentive, possibly manic depressive, oh, and . . .' She touched her lip. 'Did I mention paranoid?'

Daniels grinned. 'So, I'm screwed up!'

'What's your point?'

'That *is* my point. I'd do it because it's professional to be exact. A good custody officer might write "one church magazine"; a crap one would write "one magazine". . . See what I'm saying?' She didn't wait for an answer. 'I'm amazed it was mentioned at all, but thanks to some other "screwed-up" professional, maybe we just got lucky.'

Jo smiled. 'You're really good at this detective lark, aren't you?'

Daniels flushed. *Yeah, but at what cost?*

Their business concluded, Jo excused herself. Daniels gave Gormley a quick call to set the ball rolling, leaving instructions for someone to collect Forster's parents first thing next morning to help with their enquiries. She hung up and was pleasantly surprised when Jo reappeared with an open bottle of wine and two glasses.

'You can stay for a drink?'

Daniels couldn't: she had far too much to do. 'That would be nice,' she said.

Jo put on some music, a Dixie Chicks album: *Home*. They drank and made small talk, avoiding the elephant in the room until the lyrics of one particular song hit home: 'I Believe in Love'.

Daniels swallowed hard as Jo looked intensely into her eyes from across the room, the words of the song affecting them both. 'I've got to go,' she said.

On the doorstep, they kissed and said their goodbyes.

It was a fleeting moment of intimacy.

But it was a start . . .

92

From the window, Daniels watched the Traffic car arrive at speed. Two officers got out and opened the back doors. Forster's parents looked fragile as they stepped from the vehicle. They shuffled across the car park as if they were entering a village hall for a coffee morning, the old man greeting everyone by tipping his trilby hat.

Gormley put down the phone and let out a frustrated sigh.

'No joy?' Daniels said, turning to face him.

He shook his head. 'According to the librarian, *Living Faith* was discontinued years ago. It was an amateur publication, written by some obscure prayer group, apparently – all faiths, all denominations. They don't have any copies on file and no idea where we might find one.'

'Damn! Well, nothing else we can do for now – let's see if Forster's parents can help . . .'

The meeting had been going on a while. Right from the start it was clear that Forster's parents hadn't grasped the seriousness of the situation. Worse still, their collective elderly brain cells were unable to recall passing *Living Faith* to Matthew Spencer on the day of their son's trial.

It was a bitter blow.

Daniels hoped she wasn't wasting her breath as well as her

precious time. From the blank expressions facing her, she'd formed the opinion that Mrs Forster was probably her best bet in terms of providing the information she required. Drawing her seat a little nearer – engaging the old lady face to face – she tried not to sound patronizing.

'I don't mean to rush you, Mrs Forster. But I can't stress how vital it is that we trace the person who wrote that magazine . . .' Daniels paused. 'Is there anyone, anyone at all, who might remember? Perhaps someone you know who might have kept a copy?'

Mrs Forster looked at her husband, then back at the DCI. 'I'm sorry, dear . . .'

Daniels stood up, frustrated once again. 'OK, thank you for your time.'

'We appreciate you coming in,' Gormley said. 'I'll arrange for an officer to—'

'There is someone!' Mr Forster suddenly spoke up. 'Though I'm not entirely sure she lives round here any more.'

Daniels sat down again with renewed anticipation. *Maybe the old codger wasn't as dim as he looked.* Mr Forster patted his wife's hand gently and bit his lip, the skin round his watery eyes creasing into a million wrinkles as he beamed at them from across the table.

'You remember, dear . . .' He looked at his wife. 'The kind lady, the one who used to bring along those wonderful rock buns with the lemon peel we all enjoyed so much. Jennifer, wasn't it?'

The atmosphere in the room was heavy with expectation. Daniels was on the edge of her seat, but the old couple appeared to be in a fog of nostalgia – in no hurry to aid their enquiries any time soon.

Tickled by the memory, Mrs Forster gave a little giggle. 'He's right you know – delicious, they were. Trust a man to remember something like that. My mother always said that the way to a man's heart—'

Daniels cut her off – she'd had enough. 'Jennifer? I need a surname.'

Mr Forster cleared his throat. 'Jennifer Wright – or was it Wight? I'm sorry, Detective Chief Inspector Daniels . . . I'm not entirely sure.'

'No, dear, not Wight,' Mrs Forster volunteered. 'It was Tait. That's right: Jennifer Tait.'

It was a eureka moment.

Daniels wanted to scream with joy but her mouth felt suddenly dry. She didn't need to look at Gormley to see that he was just as excited as she was. The atmosphere between them was charged with electricity. Crime-scene photographs flashed before her eyes: a middle-aged woman lying dead on her kitchen floor, hand outstretched, begging for help.

Poor, dead Jenny Tait was beyond helping them now.

Pushing away the image, she decided not to upset the couple by telling them their former friend was dead, or burden them with the knowledge that they'd proved the vital link between their son and a victim of homicide. They would learn that soon enough. Daniels gestured towards the door with a flick of her head. Gormley understood. He rose to his feet immediately and ushered them from the room, apologizing for any inconvenience their visit to the station might have caused.

Two minutes later he was back.

Bright followed him in and pulled up a chair. 'Any luck with Darby and Joan?'

'Couple of oddballs,' Daniels said. 'Next to useless as witnesses.'

Gormley played along. 'What she means is, they don't know what day it is, guv.'

'Shit!' Bright exclaimed. 'They haven't seen their son?'

Gormley winked at Daniels.

Realizing he'd been had, Bright pulled a face. 'You bastards!' He sat down and listened carefully as Daniels paced up and down, talking ten to the dozen, hands never still. He laughed out loud when she got to the part about the lemon peel. He didn't know why, but he had reason to believe she'd been missing of late, lost in her own darkness. He hoped he wasn't responsible.

Assistant Chief Constable Martin's call to her mobile had come out of the blue as she was on her way to work. Assuming he wanted to discuss her arrest and remand in custody, and not her affair with Kate Daniels, she was completely surprised when it turned out that he needed her professional expertise as a profiler.

It was the first time she'd been back to the station since her arrest and her confidence deserted her the moment she set foot inside the building. Checking in with the desk sergeant, she made her way to the second floor where she'd arranged to meet the ACC. She loitered a while outside the office, feeling utterly unprepared to resume her duties. Surely, if she changed her mind, Martin would understand? Then, finally, she convinced herself she had to start somewhere.

After all, she'd done nothing wrong.

Taking a deep breath, she was about to tap on the door when Carmichael entered the corridor from the stairwell. After a moment of awkwardness, the young DC stuck out her hand and smiled, said something about no hard feelings, adding that the murder investigation team, her especially, was pleased to see her back.

'I'm pleased to be back,' Jo said, then covered her discomfort with a little humour. 'I've never been one to bear a grudge, Lisa. Well, not for long, anyway.'

As Carmichael moved off, Jo heard familiar voices as the door to the incident suite opened further down the corridor. Bright, Gormley and Daniels walked through it, completely unaware of her presence.

'So . . .' Bright addressed Daniels directly, a big smile on his face. 'Now you're back to your old self, where do we go from here?'

Daniels looked puzzled. 'Why are you asking me?'

'Because, as SIO, it's your call,' Bright said. 'And this time I guarantee there'll be no interference from me.'

'But Martin said—'

'Until I'm told otherwise, I'm still in charge here, Kate. That means I make the decisions about who does what. Consider yourself in the driving seat.'

Daniels welled up. 'You mean it, guv?'

He smiled.

'I don't think she's up to it,' Gormley said, poker-faced. She punched his upper arm and he made his eyes go big, put his teeth together, grinning like a ventriloquist's dummy. 'What do you want me to do, boss?'

Daniels wasted no time. 'Tell Andy to get down to Brandon Towers right away. I want that place under obs at all times. If he sees Forster, he's not to approach him. He doesn't know we're on to him and I want to keep it that way. When you've done that, alert the firearms unit. I'm sick of running round in circles. Let's get him locked up.'

Bright winked at Gormley. 'She's bound to get the next rank now.'

His words were like music to Daniels' ears. Her joy was cut short, however, when she noticed Jo standing a little way off. Her unspoken message was loud and clear: *some things never change.*

93

The sun peeked out from behind a cloud, reflecting on the windows of Brandon Towers. Brown looked up at the building, wondering if any one of the hundreds of offenders living there had clocked him. For the third time in the past half-hour, his radio crackled into life.

Daniels was getting impatient. 'Any luck with the target, Andy?'

Brown pushed a button on his radio. 'Negative. Not a murmur, boss.'

'OK, I'm going in. Armed response is standing by, so no heroics. If he shows, give me a shout. We can't afford to lose him.'

The tenth-floor corridor was dimly lit and covered in graffiti.

Daniels listened at the door to number 36. Silence. She looked around . . . no one coming . . . and deftly picked the lock. The door creaked as she pushed it open. Stepping over junk mail on her way in, she crept along the hallway, pulling on latex gloves, listening to the sound of music coming from the adjoining flat.

Porn covered the living-room walls. What little furniture there was in the room was frayed and worn. A computer on a desk had been left on, beside it a shot glass and an empty vodka bottle lying on its side. In the opposite corner, a heavily soiled armchair made Daniels recoil at the thought of the gross acts that might have caused the staining.

At the back of the flat, the small kitchenette stank of rotting food. The bin was overflowing and dishes were piled high in a sink of greasy brown water. There was a half-eaten sandwich on the bench. Daniels put pressure on the bread with her hand. It was fresh . . .

Forster hadn't been gone long.

Daniels could hear her own heartbeat as she returned to the living room, wondering how long she had before he came back. She worked quickly, searching the drawers of the desk, finding nothing but more porn, unpaid bills and a bit of dope. There weren't many places to hide the magazine, if indeed he felt the need to hide it at all. She scanned every available surface, her eyes finding the filthy armchair again and again.

It wasn't a task she relished, but it had to be done.

Crouching down beside the chair, she was about to lift the cushion when she heard it. A voice – hardly audible – but a voice nevertheless.

A faint whisper, nothing more.

Daniels swung round, training saucer-like eyes on the door. Then she relaxed again, scolding herself for losing her bottle.

In the adjoining flat, Forster sat back in his armchair and smiled to himself.

She thinks I'm just in her imagination.

He pinched himself.

No . . . I'm definitely here.

He watched her carry on with her search, lifting the cushion gingerly.

Bingo!

Taking hold of the filthy magazine with two fingers, Daniels headed back to the desk. She set it down flat, studying the front cover before turning it over and scrutinizing the back. Using the tip of a pen, she lifted the first page, conscious of spoiling prints. On each of the first five pages, some faces had been removed very carefully and precisely. Her eyes shifted to the left; lying on the desk was a pair of scissors he'd probably used to cut them out. As she read the associated articles, the realization dawned . . .

Oh my God!

Focusing on the holes where the dead ones used to be, she worked quickly, turning over several more pages, finding other faces ringed in thick red marker pen.

'Their time will come, Katie.'

The whispering voice was the most chilling sound Daniels had ever heard. Resisting the temptation to run, she stared at the dancing image of the screen saver on the computer in front of her. Just inches above the screen, she saw it – a tiny red light on the webcam. Feeling the colour drain from her face, she leaned towards the camera lens, looking straight at it, and almost puked as she realized he was watching her remotely.

Sick bastard! He was good . . . he was very good.

Daniels felt a chill run down her spine as the music from the adjoining flat suddenly stopped. In a split second, she grabbed the mouse and launched the camera, bringing up a tiny screen – just in time to see it shut down at the other end.

She reached the safety of the transit van in double-quick time. Brown immediately called for backup and made her a hot, sweet mug of tea. It tasted awful, but she drank it down anyway. It hadn't yet stopped her hands from shaking, but she thought she could feel it doing its job.

The sound of Gormley's voice on the radio was comforting, even though he was giving her such a hard time. 'You should've known better!' He sounded out of breath. 'Andy said he'd never seen you so spooked.'

Daniels gave Brown a look. 'Did he, now?'

Brown turned crimson and looked at his feet.

'I'm serious, Kate!' Gormley yelled. There was some background noise on the radio; the muffled sound of someone arguing, perhaps? Daniels couldn't make out who was speaking or what the conversation was about. Gormley probably had his hand over the mouthpiece. Then she heard another sound. High heels on a solid-wood floor?

'Kate, are you listening to me? That bastard might have killed you.'

'Well, I've still got all my arms and legs, so none of that matters now, does it? I tell you, Hank, technology is brilliant for scum like him. As long as he leaves the webcam switched on, he could be spying on us from Timbuktu or from the comfort of an armchair on the other side of a party wall.'

More muffled conversation.

'I rest my case!' Hank said.

Through blacked-out windows, Daniels could see several

police vehicles arriving. Officers began piling from vans: some armed, some with sniffer dogs, all fired up with the hope of finding Forster before he managed to slip away.

'Hold on, Kate . . .' Gormley was calm now. 'There's someone here wants a word in your shell-like.'

'Just a sec, Hank,' Daniels cut him off. 'Andy, tell them to seize the computer and get it to Carmichael right away.'

Brown hesitated, in two minds whether or not he should leave her alone.

'Go on! What are you waiting for?'

'You sure you're OK?'

Jo's frantic voice came over the radio. 'No she's not OK, you idiot! You stay right where you are and use your mobile, you hear me? Andy?'

Brown made a face.

Daniels raised her eyes to the ceiling, not knowing who to speak to first. 'Oh, for God's sake! Andy, do as I say! Jo, butt out! This is strictly a police matter. Put Hank back on!'

Jo ignored her. 'Kate, listen to me. You can't take risks with Forster.'

Daniels waited until Brown was clear of the van. 'Jo, what's your status?'

'What do you mean?'

'Is this radio secure?'

Jo took a moment, presumably to check with Gormley. 'Yes, go ahead.'

'Then get used to it. It's what I do. What do you care, anyhow?'

94

Brown's backside was numb. It was the third consecutive night he'd spent in the back of the transit van, keeping pointless observations on the front door of Brandon Towers while a colleague did the same at the back. In that time, he'd witnessed a dozen or so criminal acts and public order offences: exchanges of money for drugs, two assaults, four incidents of criminal damage and five separate acts of urinating in a public place. Just now he wished that he could do the same himself.

Checking his watch, comforted by the fact that his replacement was due, he began counting down the minutes 'til he could go home to a warm bed.

Friday, 15th January arrived with a hard frost and brilliant winter sunshine, sweeping away the gloom of the past few days. A search of Brandon Towers had led to the conclusion that Forster was clever and sophisticated. Having escaped from the tower block via an old maintenance shaft, he had now gone to ground.

In the murder incident room, DC Lisa Carmichael was on the phone making enquiries. Daniels suspected that the outcome was a foregone conclusion. She didn't have to wait long to have her suspicions confirmed.

'OK thanks, you've been a great help.' Carmichael put the

telephone receiver back on its cradle and shook her head. 'Forster's not signed on with the DSS.'

'And the close protection team?'

'Report a no-show with Jo.'

'Figures . . .' Daniels sighed. 'He could be anywhere, doing *anything* – which is why we need to go the extra mile to find him. Hank said you'd managed to locate copies of the magazine?'

Carmichael nodded.

'Same issue?'

'Complete set,' the DC said proudly. She shivered. 'This guy gives me the creeps, boss. We've nicknamed him *The Editor* for cutting out those articles. I reckon he must've thumbed that magazine a thousand times.'

'Call him what you like as long as you're as good at locating people through unofficial channels as he is.' Daniels put a hand on her young DC's shoulder. 'You're doing brilliantly, Lisa. People are in grave danger and I need your expertise to get him off the streets. Think you're up to it?'

Carmichael nodded enthusiastically. 'I'll give it my best shot.'

Lisa worked tirelessly, with surprisingly quick results. Within hours she'd found a reference to Alan Stephens in a local newspaper's archive: the article reported his appointment as fund-raising director for Kidney Research – a role he'd accepted just days before his death. Although his address hadn't been printed in the publication, Daniels didn't think it would have taken a resourceful offender like Forster very long to find him.

Two phones rang simultaneously.

Carmichael and Daniels both picked up.

A few minutes later, Daniels ended her call. 'OK, keep me posted.'

'I'll tell her.' Carmichael rang off too.

'Tell me what?' Daniels said.

'I had someone in technical support give Forster's computer the once-over. He's definitely been tracking his victims via the Internet. They already sent me a batch of deleted files; information he dumped in his recycle bin thinking he'd got rid of it permanently. He's not clever enough to realize we have ways of retrieving data from his hard drive. Jenny Tait's retirement was among the second batch of recovered files. She'd had a long career as a nurse, apparently, devoted her entire adult life to looking after others. It's sickening, when you think about it.'

'Ironic, isn't it?' Daniels said. 'Forster was practically illiterate when he went inside. The education department targeted him for specialist help, extolling the virtues of his right to read and write. Later, they praised his new-found computer skills, held him up as some kind of success. If you ask me, they just made him more dangerous.'

'That's rehabilitation for you.'

Daniels pointed at the *Living Faith* magazine on Carmichael's desk. 'He's been staring at the pages of that magazine for the past two decades planning this. Don't take this the wrong way, Lisa, but I want you to forget the ones we know are dead already. It's too late to help them now. Try and trace the targets ringed in red. Forster's finding his victims somehow. Either he's been hacking into government databases, or there's information about this lot in the public domain. By the way, don't waste your time looking for Dorothy Smith – she's just been reported missing.'

Leaving Carmichael to her work, Daniels turned her attention to Forster's parents. On the surface they seemed nice enough, and yet they'd abandoned their son when he most needed them, a copy of *Living Faith* their only gift to him in over twenty years. No doubt it had been passed on with all good intentions, yet in a bizarre twist of fate, their gift had kick-started an unhealthy obsession which had culminated in the deaths of innocent people. Years of frustration and resentment had gone into creating the monster that Forster had become – and all because he'd been ignored, overlooked. This wasn't some halfwit scrambling around in the dark; Forster was clever, imaginative and thorough – his plan well rehearsed and meticulously constructed over a lengthy period of time.

Typing a command on the keyboard in front of her, Daniels brought up a list on screen. She updated the outstanding action to trace Dorothy Smith with just two words: RE-PORTED MISSING. The list made chilling reading:

SUSAN THOMPSON:	DECEASED (Natural Causes)
SEAMUS DOWD :	ACTION – TRACE
ALAN STEPHENS (Newcastle):	VICTIM (Deceased)
JENNY TAIT (Durham) :	VICTIM (Deceased)
JAMIL MALIK (Birmingham):	VICTIM (Deceased)
DOROTHY SMITH (Cumbria):	REPORTED MISSING
NATHAN BAILEY:	DECEASED (Natural Causes)
FRANCES COOK:	ACTION – TRACE

IAN COCKBURN (Australia):	SAFE AND WELL
KEVIN BROUGHTON:	DECEASED (Natural Causes)
MALCOLM WRIGHT:	ACTION – TRACE
MAUREEN RICHARDSON:	ACTION – TRACE

Gormley wandered over and stood behind her. He was having trouble getting used to a pair of bifocals, a recent acquisition. He hadn't been able to put off the evil day any longer and had finally owned up to failing eyesight. Tipping his head back slightly, he peered at the screen to see what was making her look and sound so glum.

'What's up?' he asked.

'Pound to a penny the bastard's got another one . . .' Daniels pointed to the screen. 'Dorothy Smith hasn't been seen for days. My guess is she's already dead. Cumbria force is joining the hunt. Which is good – we need all the help we can get.'

'Welcome to the party,' Gormley said drily, pulling up a chair. 'So, assuming Dorothy Smith *is* dead and Ian Cockburn is far enough out of harm's way, that only leaves four.'

'Three,' Daniels corrected him, updating the list again. 'Malcolm Wright is safe and well in Cherbourg. He's scared shitless. The French authorities are making arrangements to babysit him.'

'They better hurry up.'

'That's what I told them.'

They sat in silence for a moment, studying the computer screen.

'Hmm . . .' Gormley was troubled.

'What?'

'Leaving aside those who have died of natural causes,

there's a pattern here. He's killing them in order: Alan Stephens, Jenny Tait, Jamil Malik . . . and now Dorothy Smith is missing.'

'You're forgetting Seamus Dowd.'

Gormley looked up at Dowd's name. 'Maybe he's dead but we just haven't found his body yet. Or Forster hasn't traced him yet – which wouldn't surprise me, given that we can't.'

Daniels looked down at the list again. 'If you're right, then Frances Cook is next.'

Forster smiled to himself as his fingers flew over the keys, typing a message next to her name on the School Reunion website.

> Hi Frankie!
> Can't believe we lost touch after leaving school. It'd be great to see you again. I'm in Berwick at the weekend, if you fancy meeting up. You probably don't even remember me. I re-member you though!
> Virtual hugs . . .
> JJ xx

95

Something was still troubling Gormley as he entered Forster's flat. In the living room – *if anybody could actually call it living* – two Scenes of Crime Officers were conducting a second painstaking search. Dusting powder was everywhere and one officer was busy tipping the entire contents of Forster's desk into an evidence bag.

Gormley acknowledged them both, then moved on, allowing them space to get on with the important job of finding any clue that might lead them to Forster. Stepping over items left abandoned on the floor, he entered the bedroom, where another SOCO was running a gloved hand along the inside of an empty chest of drawers. Cupboard doors were hanging open and in some places the floorboards were up; nothing short of what he'd expected to find. The room was a complete shit-pit: soiled sheets covering a saggy double mattress on the floor; empty bottles and an overflowing ashtray on an upturned beer crate doubling as bedside table; and dirty clothing scattered everywhere.

Walking back to the living room, the soles of his shoes stuck to the filthy lino with each step. The stench in the flat was getting to him, despite the open balcony door. The officer on her hands and knees looked up as he arrived.

'Find anything useful?' he asked.

She didn't bother removing her disposable dust mask, just shook her head and went back to work. Stepping out on to the balcony, Gormley lit a cigarette. Leaning against the railing, he looked out over the cityscape, savouring a brief moment of peace and quiet. In the foreground, a lovely old church sat incongruous amidst seven tower blocks, its huge carved doors boarded up against the vandals and piss-heads. The word 'Godforsaken' jumped into his head as he wondered how long it had been since any cleric had set foot in the place.

He took another long drag on his cigarette, his elbow shifting on the vertical support of the safety rail as he moved his arm. On closer inspection, it was more like a piece of heavy-duty scaffolding pole than anything else, with a grille attached to stop small children falling through – an absurdity, given its dangerous condition. Crouching down to examine it properly, he noticed that a T-shaped coupling had come loose. Not for the first time, from the look of it. Pulling the top off, he saw a roll of papers hidden inside. He dug them out and was horrified when he realized what he'd found.

Despite several attempts to contact Daniels and umpteen messages left on her voicemail, she still hadn't called back. This left Gormley with no alternative but to take matters into his own hands.

He drove straight to Jo's office at breakneck speed. Entering reception, he came face to face with Henderson, who glared at him through drug-fuelled eyes.

'I'd sling my hook, if I were you, pal,' Gormley said.

Realizing that the DS was in even less of a mood for fun

and games than he'd been the last time they met, Henderson backed off.

'Buzz me in, please,' Gormley said to the receptionist.

Seconds later, he burst through the door to Jo's room unannounced. She was sitting by the window with her head in a file, dressed casually in a pair of snug-fitting jeans and a petrol blue cardigan, matching the pumps on her feet. Her hair hung loose around her shoulders and she looked a little pale but otherwise more like her old self. Barring a touch of lipstick, she wore no make-up. She looked very different from how she had at the station.

'I'm busy, Hank. Can this wait?'

'No, I'm afraid it can't,' he said, grabbing her coat and bag.

Ignoring her protests, Gormley escorted her from the building, put her in his car and drove away at speed. It was raining hard, the windshield wipers moving quickly and noisily, and Jo's complaining was making his head ache. Only when he explained that she might be in grave danger did she put a sock in it, though not for long. Insisting he pull over, she demanded to know what the hell he thought he was doing.

Gormley took his foot off the accelerator, stopped the car and turned to face her.

'On whose authority am I being taken in?'

'Mine!' Gormley snapped. He couldn't stop himself being angry with her, even though he had no real cause. 'And you're not being taken in – not to the station, anyhow. I need to get you to a safe house.'

'What makes you so sure I'm at risk?' she said.

Gormley reached into his pocket, removed the rolled-up photographs he'd found hidden on Forster's balcony. As Jo unfurled the images of her and Daniels kissing on her door-step, her hands began to shake.

'He's been watching me at home?'

Gormley saw the panic set in. He wished he'd kept quiet. She'd been through hell, and now he was adding to her distress. He'd have liked to offer some comfort, but didn't know how.

'Don't worry,' he said. 'He won't get to you. I'll make damn sure of that.'

'Does Kate know?'

'Not yet. But if I don't protect you, she'll string me up by my balls. So, are you going to give me any more grief, or what?' He paused. 'Have you two been in contact today?'

'No, why?'

'You're friends . . .' Gormley looked out of the window, avoiding eye contact and choosing his words carefully. 'I just thought you might have.'

Jo's eyes narrowed. 'She told you, didn't she?'

'Only when she had to, when I forced her because she was wrecking her career.'

'You resent me, don't you?'

'D'you blame me? You landed her right in the shit.'

'That wasn't how it was!'

'Wasn't it?'

'No, Hank. Kate and I had something special. It was her idea to keep it secret, not mine. That's why it didn't last. She's only got herself to blame. I certainly didn't ask her to compromise her position on the murder investigation team. She did that all by herself!' Glancing again at the photographs, Jo looked as though she could do with a drink.

Now Gormley thought about it, he could do with one himself.

Daniels was stunned to hear of the discovery. She needed authorization for a safe house and had absolutely no idea how the hell to get it without disclosing the evidence to Bright. If he saw the photographs, he was bound to think she'd lied about her relationship with Jo being over. And there was no question that they could form part of a criminal case in a public court of law.

That would *definitely* finish her career.

'Jo's in danger how?' Bright asked, creeping up behind them.

Daniels jumped. 'Guv! You scared me half to death!'

'I found a photo of Jo in Forster's flat,' Gormley said, thinking on his feet.

'You're joking!' Bright whistled. 'C'mon, let's see it then.'

A tense moment.

Daniels smiled uncomfortably at her boss. Convinced that the shit was about to hit the fan, she braced herself for a dressing-down. Keeping Bright engaged in conversation, she glanced over his shoulder, her eyes following Gormley to his desk. He looked back at her, spreading his hands in a gesture that said: *What the fuck do I do now?*

Turning his back on them, Gormley opened his desk drawer. After a quick look around to ensure that nobody was paying him any attention, he cut one of the photographs of Jo and Daniels in two. Aware that his actions, if discovered, would result in kissing his pension goodbye, he slipped one half in his pocket and took the other half to Bright.

The guv'nor looked at it briefly then gave it back. 'Is that it?'

Gormley shrugged. 'What were you expecting, a Page Three pose? He's a dab hand with the scissors, this freak.'

'Close protection it is, then,' Bright said.

He had no hesitation in financing the safe house. Which was just as well, Gormley told him, because Jo was already there. They assigned two officers to stay with her round the clock and agreed that Carmichael should keep her company through the day and work remotely from there.

'I'll take the night shift,' Gormley volunteered.

'Good idea.' Bright glanced at Daniels. 'She's practically one of us, after all.'

Daniels felt like smacking and hugging him at the same time. It was painfully obvious that he was trying his best to make amends.

Then he went and spoiled it.

'With any luck, it might get us back in the ACC's good books,' he said.

'Fat chance!' Gormley smirked.

As Bright walked away, Daniels put her hands together and mouthed the words: *Thank You.* Gormley winked at her, using his fingers like scissors. She smiled and blew out her cheeks. *That was a close call.*

The isolated bastle house was located to the north west of the Northumbria force's area, deep within Border Reiver country. The police regularly used it as a safe house. With its metre-thick stone walls and built-in fortifications it was perfectly constructed for keeping unwanted visitors out.

While Daniels and Gormley peered over her shoulder, Carmichael logged on to a familiar website. She placed a cursor into a search box and began typing out a name:

Forename: FRANCES
Surname: COOK

On the advanced search page, she highlighted a box for the United Kingdom and Ireland, pressed the enter key, then looked up at Daniels.

'Age?' she asked.

'Fifty-seven.'

Carmichael highlighted the appropriate age range and pressed the enter key again. The screen jumped and up popped a negative result.

'Shit!' she said. 'No matches fit the criteria.'

Daniels had an idea. 'Try a younger age range.'

Carmichael gave her an odd look. 'Boss?'

'Trust me, Lisa. Women lie about their age as they get older. It's a well-known fact. You'll understand when your turn comes.'

As Carmichael scrolled down to the next age range, Daniels glanced across the room. Jo looked completely at ease sitting near a wood-burning stove with her head in a book, her socked feet toasting by the fire. Satisfied that she'd be safe here, Daniels turned her attention back to the computer as Carmichael pressed the enter key again. Processing the search didn't take long. Within seconds, four matches appeared on screen.

Daniels' smile said it all. 'That's the most likely candidate . . .'

She pointed to a set of details in the list. *'Frances Cook. UK Member. Ex-pupil of Gosforth High School. Now living and working in Berwick.'*

'Perfect!' Carmichael looked more relieved than excited.

Daniels was grateful to her. It had been a huge responsibility for someone so young in service, but Lisa had coped with the enormous pressure and risen to the challenge of locating the targets. Everyone at MIT was aware of her contribution, not least Bright, which effectively meant she'd rise through the ranks and follow in her DCI's footsteps.

'See if you can get a quicker response, Lisa. For all we know, she may be online now.'

Carmichael was off again, entering a message into a box on the screen: *Please contact DC Lisa Carmichael urgently on this direct line.* She typed in a designated number, checked the details before confirming them.

'Now we wait!' she said.

96

The sound of the gun cocking was enough to alert her. Frances Cook had just let herself in through the front door and had her back to him.

'Frankie . . .' He said it like they were long-lost friends.

The woman froze.

'Turn around . . .' He waited. 'I said, turn around!'

Slowly she turned and found him sitting on her sofa, drinking her whisky. Her face was pale, her expression disbelieving, as if this was something that happened to other people or in dramas on the box.

He grinned arrogantly, raising his glass. 'Remember me?'

There was no sign of recognition at first – not the slightest flicker – even when he pulled down his hood to reveal his face. She was trying to make the connection – but still it wouldn't come. It angered him to think that someone who'd had such a lot to say about his life could so easily have forgotten. He felt the edges of his lips form into a wide grin. Well, she wouldn't forget again – he'd make damn sure of that.

There had been a slight delay in getting round to her, a time when he feared he might not accomplish his mission after all. But he'd shown great patience and restraint, waiting for Dotty to show, and this one had been a pushover by comparison.

'You should be more careful, Frankie. The Internet is a

danger to women who live alone. You just never know who you're dealing with. Fancy joining me for a snifter?'

Frances Cook could hardly stand, she was so terrified. He could smell her fear. Taste it, even. Funny how the colour round her lips had all but disappeared. She was the one his mother had turned to when he began to fight back, when he'd outgrown her and she was unable to control him any more. The person who'd advised his mother to put him into care, the one who'd said he was an evil child – so evil she couldn't bear to look at him.

Well, she was looking at him now and blind panic was setting in. 'Jonathan?'

He smiled. 'That wasn't so difficult now, was it, Frankie? Aren't you going to tell me how big I've grown? Tell me how lovely it is to see me after all these years?'

He waited.

'OK, suit yourself.' He could tell she was remembering his crimes in morbid detail, wondering how long she had left to live. He'd have to be quick with the filth closing in. He winked. 'Kneel down.'

97

Discarding a half-eaten sandwich, Daniels tapped a gnawed pen top impatiently on her desk, feeling stressed out. Like the rest of the squad, she was desperate for news of Frances Cook, but so far it had failed to materialize. Gormley threw an empty sandwich carton in the waste bin and drained his coffee. He too was pissed off waiting and was about to go outside for some air when a police courier arrived.

Gormley told Daniels to stay put and went to sign for the package, a delivery they had both expected earlier in the day: the results of analysis on Forster's DNA. She watched him open the document and caught his desperation before he'd said a word.

'Positive match?' She knew what his answer would be.

Gormley nodded soberly.

'Let me guess. With semen taken from Sarah Short's body?'

He nodded again and reread the document just to make sure. 'The information's been checked and double-checked independently in view of the result. There's no mistake, Kate. We've got him bang to rights.'

Daniels felt elated, yet at the same time forlorn. Awful as the news was, it meant she'd finally identified the killer who'd been eluding her for over a year. How poor Sarah had become involved in her present investigation was anyone's guess.

Daniels sensed that, to find the answer, she'd need to return to St Camillus.

She couldn't wait to get there.

Daniels remained silent, alone in her private thoughts, as Gormley drove the car. She had so many questions and wasn't really sure she'd find the answers in the church. The one thing she was sure of was that these cases were unlike anything she'd ever worked on before. Any attempt on her part to fit them neatly into one particular criminal profile was hopeless. The crime pattern was all over the place. Time lines made no sense.

Nothing made any sense.

As they passed the sign for Corbridge village, Gormley took his foot off the accelerator, slowing down to observe the speed limit. A mile further on, he pulled up outside the church. He hadn't said a word since they'd left the city. She suspected it was marital problems but didn't want to pry. She felt really selfish all of a sudden. *And guilty.* He was hurting, and yet she hadn't let up long enough to ask if he needed a break. The department was stretched to the limit and she was desperate for a result.

Oh, fuck it.

He was *her* other half as well as Julie's.

The only difference was, they didn't sleep together.

'Stay here,' she said. 'I've got something I must do. I'll only be a few minutes.'

Getting out of the car, she made her way to Sarah Short's family home. She knocked at the door gently, half hoping they weren't in. Elsie opened the door and was joined seconds later by David. Daniels looked at the floor, suddenly overcome with emotion, unable to say what she'd come to say.

David put his arm around his wife.

He spoke just three words: 'You found something?'

Daniels simply nodded.

Walking through the door of St Camillus half an hour later, Daniels felt uncomfortable for two reasons – both of them to do with death. Not only was it a reminder of the last weeks of her mother's life when she'd spent a lot of time there, praying for her to get better, but the building itself represented torment and horror of unimaginable proportions since the night she had stumbled upon Sarah and Father Simon's bodies after Forster had finished with them.

When she was alone in the small hours, Daniels had revisited the church's interior many times in her nightmares. Even now, with the altar covered in a pristine white cloth, all she could see was young Sarah's body lying there. She flinched as a priest emerged from the vestry to greet them.

'Want me to handle it?' Gormley whispered under his breath.

'No . . . I'm fine.'

'I know a good acronym for the word fine,' he joked. 'Fucked up, Insecure, Neurotic and Emotional. Any of those fit the bill?'

Daniels ignored the question. But as the priest hurried down the aisle towards them, she lost her bottle and nudged Gormley with her elbow.

'Get him out of here,' she said.

'It's his church! Mind if I ask how?'

'I don't care . . . just do it!'

She looked on as he left her side and intercepted the priest

– thwarting the man's attempt to reach her. Only once they had gone did she move up the aisle to take a seat in the front pew.

It was difficult for her to be there.

Looking up at the cross, Daniels couldn't help but think of the crazed killer she was hunting, the man who'd tainted the place forever in her eyes. She tried not to dwell on the fact that a psychopath murders someone every week in Britain, but she couldn't help herself. The fallout from that sad statistic was truly devastating: families ripped apart in a moment of insanity, left to ponder why. Like David and Elsie Short, adoring parents of an only daughter – too old to start again, even if they had wanted to – left in a miserable limbo for the rest of their days.

Daniels felt their pain as if it were her own. Each murder she'd ever worked on had eaten away a little piece of her. Most times she'd managed to carry on, to emerge from the depths of despair with her mental balance intact and a renewed determination to continue fighting crime. Her work *was* her life.

But for how much longer?

She was totally exhausted.

Gormley slipped into the pew behind her and sat there quietly, allowing her the easy quiet she craved. He was good at that. But on this occasion, he'd misread the signals. Daniels didn't have her eyes shut because she was praying. She was merely trying to find some logic in the mayhem swimming round inside her head, trying to make the connection between the double murder at St Camillus and the handiwork of the man her colleagues called *The Editor*.

Then her eyes opened wide and she swung round to face him.

'Get that priest in here,' she said.

'Make your bloody mind up!' Gormley headed off, returning seconds later with the cleric following close behind.

'I'm Father John, how can I help?'

'Could you please tell me your name?' Daniels asked.

Gormley and Father John exchanged a quizzical glance, both eyeing Daniels as if she'd gone completely mad.

'Er, sorry, Father,' Gormley said. 'Detective Chief Inspector Daniels has obviously been working too hard.'

'I'm very pleased to meet you at last, Kate.' The priest smiled and stepped forward, extending his hand. 'Welcome back to St Camillus.'

He'd been talking to David and Elsie Short.

Daniels could tell he meant well. His eyes were kind and understanding. She shook his hand. 'I'm sorry, Father, I don't wish to be intrusive, but I need your *real* name.'

'Oh, I see. Fergus O'Connor . . . my birth-name is Fergus O'Connor.'

'Thank you,' Daniels said. 'You've been a great help. Come on, Hank. We're done here.'

In less than ten minutes inside the church, Daniels had worked it out.

'Father John is a confirmation name,' she said excitedly. 'The name of a saint, nothing to do with his given name at birth.'

Gormley wasn't with her. 'And . . .?'

'I'm betting Father Simon is too. You were right, Hank.' She twisted her body in her seat to face him. 'He is killing them in order!'

The penny dropped. 'Seamus Dowd . . .'

'. . . and Father Simon are one and the same.'

'And Sarah?'

'Collateral damage: wrong time, wrong place. As simple and as pointless as that, poor kid.' Daniels took out her mobile and keyed in a number. 'Lisa, I need you to do me a favour . . .'

Gormley put his foot down, hurtling out of Corbridge at top speed. *To hell with the thirty-mile limit.*

They arrived back at the station in double-quick time and were hurrying down the corridor when a mobile phone rang. They slowed down, both reaching for their pockets. Daniels' display showed: BRIGHT CALLING. She pocketed the phone and swiped her warrant card to be admitted to the MIR.

She pushed open the door. Heads were down in the incident room, faces glum, no chatter, no laughter, nothing much of anything. It was obvious the news wasn't good. Daniels' renewed enthusiasm ebbed from her in an instant, the name Frances Cook leaving her lips almost as soon as it had come into her head.

A slight nod was all the confirmation Bright could muster.

With no time to hold his hand, Daniels went straight back to her office and shut the door. Half an hour and a few phone calls later, she had conclusive proof that Seamus Dowd had entered Ushaw College as a trainee in the eighties and was later ordained as a priest. He'd then taken the name Father Simon, a name he'd used ever since.

With Seamus Dowd and Frances Cook now dead, Daniels had no choice but to trust her Cumbrian counterpart to step up the hunt for Dorothy Smith. But time was running out and she needed to concentrate all her efforts on finding the one remaining target she had reason to believe might still be alive. Heading back to the incident room, she made a beeline for DC Brown.

'Maureen Richardson – what's the position there?' she asked.

Brown sighed. 'You're not going to like it.'

'There's not much I *do* like any more, Andy. What d'you mean?'

'There are over seventy Maureen Richardsons in our force area alone.'

'Does that include those who've since married and changed their name, or those who've moved out of the area?'

'Negative on both counts . . .' Brown was on the ball. 'Just the ones presently on the electoral roll. And I have to tell you, the possibilities are endless.'

'Any reference to Maureen Richardson on Forster's computer?'

'Not according to Lisa. I just got off the phone.'

'Everything OK at the safe house?'

Brown held up a thumb.

'Good.' Daniels took a moment. 'Well, hopefully Forster didn't get round to finding Maureen Richardson yet. Although, with Internet access freely available on mobile phones, we can't risk making that assumption. Know where Hank's disappeared to?'

'Last time I saw him, he was loitering with the Super near the coffee machine, the one in the corridor – ours is on the blink.'

She looked past him as the door opened and Gormley walked through it.

Her concern was not lost on Brown. 'Is Hank OK?'

Daniels looked embarrassed. 'Nothing he can't handle.'

She left Brown to get on with his work and headed across to speak with her favourite DS, pointing at the phone in his hand as she approached. 'Can you do that later, Hank? I need you to do something for me urgently.'

Gormley pocketed the phone. 'What's that, boss?'

'Alert the press office. If we haven't had any luck tracing Maureen Richardson by the six o'clock news, I want to go public. That bastard's not going to kill another one, not if I can help it. And while you're at it, deploy an armed response team. I've a gut feeling that Forster will make a move on his mother. He's got nothing to lose now. If I'm any judge of character, I reckon he's the type to go out with a bang, not a whimper. It's time we were one step ahead of him, not the other way round.'

98

In her peripheral vision, Daniels was conscious of faces turning in her direction, alarmed by flashing blue lights. The pavements on either side of the road appeared to be moving in both directions at the same time as a steady stream of commuters made their way home from work. She had no desire to follow suit; Gormley either, by the look of him. He sat quietly in the passenger seat, his face set in a blank stare, his thoughts a million miles away.

Despite trying to focus on her driving, all she could think of was the outcome of her televised appeal. Less than an hour ago, Daniels had faced the glare of cameras in an effort to locate Maureen Richardson in time to save her life. Her team had fully supported her plan to go public but, according to Gormley, they'd been edgy as they'd turned on the set to watch. At the end of the broadcast there had been a worrying hush in the incident room, before the phones lit up in a frenzy of activity.

MIT were in for a long night.

Daniels imagined the firearms team under cover of darkness outside Forster's parents' bungalow: crouched down, weapons at the ready, waiting for her signal. It was an image so vivid, she could almost see herself walking up the path to the front door, wondering what scene of devastation might greet her on the other side. She'd witnessed Forster's handiwork first-hand and knew it would be gruesome if he'd managed to get there before her.

The sound of a radio transmission interrupted that sobering thought:

'Foxtrot in position, as deployed, ma'am. Awaiting further instructions.'

Daniels spoke into her radio. 'Stand by Foxtrot . . . ETA ten minutes.'

The radio went dead.

Pulling off the central motorway, Daniels headed north on the airport road. As she entered Ponteland a few miles further on, she slowed to a crawl behind a long line of cars backed up at traffic lights. Sensible drivers immediately mounted the pavement to let her through.

'STOP, STOP!' Gormley yelled.

He lunged for the dashboard, killing the siren and blue flashing lights. The urgency in his voice had the desired effect. Daniels pulled up sharply, nearly standing her vehicle on its end, throwing them both forward in their seats, then back again, as the car came to a juddering halt.

'Don't tell me you spotted him?'

'No, but I spotted some other bastard.'

'This had better be good, Hank. The firearms team are waiting.'

'Well I'm buggered!' Gormley said. 'Looks like we were wrong about Maxwell. You were right to give him a second chance, after all.'

Following his point of view as he craned his neck to look out of the window, Daniels saw two familiar figures making their way along the road, so deep in conversation they were oblivious to anyone else. DS Robson was barging his way through a group of kids loitering outside the Diamond pub. Yanking open the door, he stood back, allowing the ACC to enter first. Robson began remonstrating with the youngsters, telling them all to clear off.

Daniels was disappointed to think that he might be Martin's snout. Looking back, she wondered if that was the real reason he didn't take paternity leave when he'd had the chance. Although forced to admit she'd set a lousy example of late, she demanded loyalty from her team. She was gutted to discover that one of her protégés had so little of it.

Loyalty.

Her greatest strength?

Or her Achilles heel?

Probably a bit of both, she thought. There was little doubt that the investigation into Alan Stephens' death had tested her to the full in the past few months. The case had nearly torn her apart. But would she *really* do things any differently, given the same set of circumstances? Daniels didn't think so. She'd realized that for most people there comes a time when difficult choices made life impossible.

This was hers.

'Can you believe that?' Gormley's voice interrupted her internal war. He was staring at the front door of the Diamond pub where Robson was still arguing with local youths.

'Did it occur to you that it might be entirely innocent?' she said.

'Yeah, and maybe I'm going to make Chief before I retire!' Gormley hit back.

A voice came over the radio: ironically it belonged to Max-well. 'November One to Daniels. Maureen Richardson is in safe hands. I repeat, Maureen Richardson has been located and is now in protective custody.'

'Nice one!' Gormley lifted his right hand, inviting a high five.

Daniels ignored it and got back on the radio. 'Daniels to November One. That's fantastic news, Neil. Tell the squad the drinks are on me – soon as we get back.'

'Boss?' Maxwell sounded anxious.

'Still here, November One.'

'Good luck.'

Daniels was touched. 'I hope we don't need it.'

She killed the radio, started up the Toyota, indicating her intention to pull out as Gormley began to vent his anger at Robson's deceit. The man himself glanced furtively over his shoulder, as if somehow he could feel eyes bearing down on him.

'Yeah . . . we're watching you, son,' Gormley said through gritted teeth.

Daniels leaned forwards, turned the blue lights and the siren back on, putting the fear of God into Robson as they sped off into traffic.

At the entrance to a cul-de-sac on the outskirts of Ponteland, Daniels killed the lights, turned off her engine and coasted slowly to the kerb.

She got on the radio. 'Daniels to Foxtrot . . . now in posi-tion. What can you see?'

'Lights on front and rear, ma'am. One elderly male identified a few minutes ago. He was talking to someone, I couldn't see who. He's no longer in view.'

'Did he look agitated?'

'Hard to say from this distance, but I didn't get that impression, no.'

'Anything look suspicious?'

'Negative.'

'Hold your positions. I repeat, hold your positions.' Daniels could feel the hair on the back of her neck standing to attention, her heart beating a little faster in her chest. She turned to face Gormley. 'Showtime! Give me that number.'

Gormley reached for his wallet, removed a small piece of paper and read out a telephone number as Daniels pushed the corresponding buttons on her mobile phone. Lifting it to her ear, she listened patiently for someone to pick up. Seconds later, the ringing stopped and an elderly female recited the number back to her.

'. . . double one, four, three, four.'

Daniels cleared her throat, hoping she sounded calmer than she felt.

'Is that Mrs Enid Forster?'

She didn't answer.

'Is everything in the house all right, Mrs Forster?'

Still no response.

She'd most likely watched the evening news.

Following her appeal for Maureen Richardson to come forward, Daniels had felt obliged to disclose the fact that she urgently needed to find and question Jonathan Forster, a man she was honest enough to admit could be armed and dangerous. She then issued a warning that under no circumstance should he be approached by members of the public. If that wasn't enough to scare his parents, nothing was. 'Mrs Forster, are you alone?'

Her question was met with an icy silence; confirmation that it had caused a good deal of anxiety to the old lady on the other end of the line. Then Daniels heard a heavy knock. It sounded as if the receiver had gone down on a hard surface.

Or had it been dropped?

As Daniels glanced at Gormley, her whole body tensed. 'Mrs Forster, are you still there? I need to know if just you and your husband are at home at present.'

'Who is this?'

'It's Detective Chief Inspector Daniels. We spoke at the station a few days ago. I need you to stay calm, Mrs Forster. Is your son Jonathan at home?' The line went silent again. Daniels had expected as much. The poor woman was probably apoplectic by now, terrified at the prospect of being reunited with her son. She tried again. 'Mrs Forster, this is *very* important. Please stay on the line and answer my question . . . is Jonathan there with you?'

'No, dear. I told you last time. We haven't seen him since . . . for many years.'

Daniels felt herself relax. 'OK, I'm coming to the door.'

Gormley shook his head vigorously.

Daniels raised her hand to shut off his objections. 'When I ring the bell, I'd like you to answer the door.' She paused, allowing time for the information to sink in. 'When I ring the bell, Mrs Forster, and not before, OK?'

The old lady's voice was hardly audible. 'Right-o, I understand.'

'I'm putting the phone down now and I'm coming to the door.' Daniels rang off and got back on the radio. 'Daniels to Foxtrot, did you copy that?'

'Foxtrot to Daniels . . . affirmative.'

'Daniels to Foxtrot, hold your positions. I think it's legit, I'm going in.'

Gormley leaned towards the radio, raising his voice. '*We're* going in.'

'No!' Her tone of voice was uncompromising. 'I'm not taking any risks with you, Hank. You've got family to think of, I haven't. The firearms team will cover my back. When I'm done, you can take Forster's parents to the station. That's an order, understood?'

'Oh, right! I forgot. You always stick to the rules.'

'I'm not joking, Hank!'

'Neither am I! What are you going to do, sack me? I'm following you up that path whether you like it or not, so you better let Foxtrot know, unless you want them to shoot me dead. It's your call. Anyway, I'd rather go out shouting "*Yahoo!*" at the moon than being force-fed semolina in an old people's home.'

Daniels heard a chuckle from one of the firearms team and killed the radio. She could see Gormley was in no mood to back down. They just looked at one another for a long moment, daring each other to blink first.

'Don't waste your breath, Kate.' There was no humour in his voice now. 'I'm warning you, you'll have to chain me to the fucking car.'

Daniels knew it would be a waste of time arguing. 'Come on, then. What are you waiting for?' She got back on the radio. 'Daniels to Foxtrot . . . *Two* . . . I repeat *two* officers approaching the house. Hold your positions.'

'Foxtrot to Daniels . . . affirmative.'

They got out of the car and began to walk slowly and deliberately up the road, their eyes scanning hedges and gardens as they went. Suddenly every whiff of air, every movement, every sound, took on a new and potentially dangerous significance. Though she couldn't and didn't expect to see the firearms cordon, Daniels was confident that she was already in their night-sights. They walked on up the garden path to the front door, side by side, scanning the borders on either side.

It was ominously quiet.

Daniels raised her hand to the doorbell.

Just then, the door was flung open with enough force to give them both a fright. She smiled anxiously at Gormley as Mrs Forster ushered them inside. As the door closed behind her, Daniels noticed the substantial fortifications: the control panel of a state-of-the-art electronic security alarm, a number of thick chains, supplemented by heavy-duty sliding bolts, top and bottom. Clearly the old couple feared someone.

It didn't take a genius to work out who that might be.

The bungalow was almost clinical, with little colour or warmth to recommend it as a place in which to spend much time. In the living room, pieces of religious symbolism adorned every wall, every bookcase, every available surface: Christ's crucifixion, resurrection, the Holy Virgin, doves, crosses, so many objects of righteousness it made Daniels feel uncomfortable. This was the very antithesis of Forster's depravity, but it appalled her to think that a child, any child, could have been brought up in a house like this.

Mrs Forster's weeping was non-stop, the rosary beads in her arthritic hands affording little comfort so far as Daniels could see. Gormley was doing his level best to reassure her, while Mr Forster just stood there – too terrified of his own flesh and blood to be of any use to his wife. They took no persuading to leave the house, were practically begging for police protection, anxious to get as far away as possible as quickly as they could.

When Mrs Forster crossed herself, Daniels looked at her with utter contempt, couldn't find it in her heart to give either of them any sympathy. She turned away and radioed in: 'Daniels to Foxtrot . . . Gormley's on his way out with two witnesses, I repeat, *two* witnesses. I'm staying put. Foxtrot to remain in situ until stood down.'

'Foxtrot to Daniels . . . copy that.'

Grabbing Gormley by the arm, Daniels led him into the hallway, out of earshot.

'Take my car and get them to the local nick. Tell the duty DI to make them comfortable until I get there and decide what to do with them. Get a search team down here – you know the drill. Tell them I want the whole works. Then get over to the safe house, make sure Jo's OK.'

Gormley was about to say something, when Mr and Mrs Forster suddenly appeared next to him with their coats on, ready to leave. He held an imaginary phone to his ear. Daniels nodded her understanding and watched him shepherd the couple outside. She waited for the door to shut before taking a good look around.

The first bedroom she came to smelt faintly of candle grease. It was furnished with a single bed and more religious paraphernalia, including a prayer mat on a hard wooden floor in front of some kind of holy shrine. Further down the corridor was an equally austere bedroom. Larger than the first, it too had just the basic furnishings: an old-fashioned mahogany wardrobe, two single beds with a table in between. A small reading lamp was on the bedside table, along with two framed photographs of Forster's parents and a pale blue statuette of Jesus.

Putting on a pair of rubber gloves, Daniels hooked her little finger inside a brass pull-ring on the wardrobe door and tugged. The door creaked as it came open. There were very few belongings inside: some clothes hung neatly from a brass rail; shoes lined up in perfect symmetry on a closet organizer on the floor; a couple of shoe boxes on a shelf above.

Daniels shivered. There was no heating in the room and the house gave her the creeps. Determined to leave no stone unturned, she removed one of the boxes, took off the lid and tipped the contents out on to the bed. There were some old photographs, many letters and a large brown envelope held together with a thick rubber band. She spread the items out. Turning the photographs face up, she became increasingly angry.

Jesus Christ!

Her mobile rang, startling her. She flipped it open. 'Daniels.'

Gormley was on the other end. 'You OK?'

'Yeah . . . you alone?'

'Negative . . . but you're not on speaker.'

He was still with Forster's parents.

Daniels described the stuff she found. 'And not a single snap of Forster, even as a baby. They created a monster, Hank.

It's as if they obliterated his memory, as if he never existed at all.'

'I'm pulling into the station now. Will do the necessary, then shoot off to relieve Carmichael. I'll call you from there. Any message?'

'Tell Jo . . .' Daniels hesitated. 'Doesn't matter, I'll tell her myself.'

She hung up, pocketed her phone and went back to the box. Removing the rubber band from the envelope, Daniels slid her gloved hand inside. Prayer cards – hundreds of them – spilled out through her fingers and on to the floor.

99

Inside the fortified farmhouse, the sound of tyres on gravel alerted Carmichael and Jo. The CCTV monitor had a split screen showing both front and rear doors. The right-hand screen was active, triggered by Daniels' four-by-four moving into shot. Gormley was locking the car and making his way to the back door looking straight at the camera, his features distorted by the wide-angled lens.

He waved.

Carmichael unlocked the door and locked it again as soon as he was inside. Seconds later, he joined them in the kitchen, took off his jacket and sat down. Carmichael put the kettle on and made a pot of tea. Though she looked as washed out as she felt, she seemed in no hurry to go home, despite the fact that she'd been on duty for sixteen hours straight.

'I just discovered something *really* interesting . . .' Carmichael said. 'Several jpegs in a deleted folder on Forster's computer.'

Her words and her reluctance to leave made Gormley uneasy. He loosened his tie, then tossed it on the table, glancing at Jo in the process. She looked equally concerned by this development.

'I'll take care of them later, Lisa,' Gormley said, trying to sound disinterested. 'You get off home.'

'Don't be daft!' Taking three mugs from a cupboard, Carmichael set them down on the kitchen bench and began pouring the tea. 'It's really no bother, I—'

'Just leave me the information and I'll sort it!' Gormley insisted.

It was a heavy hint that she should leave. Carmichael didn't argue, but she didn't look happy either. Glancing at the steaming mug of tea in front of her, she pushed it away and pointed to a yellow Post-it note stuck to her computer screen.

'That's the designated file name . . .' She'd clocked Gormley's agitation. 'Am I missing something here?'

'Lisa, would you mind . . .' Jo intervened, her expression apologetic as she handed Carmichael her coat. 'I really need to speak with Hank privately.'

Caught on the back foot, Carmichael put on her coat and gathered up her bag from the floor. 'Didn't see that coming,' she said. 'Well, I'll see you two lovebirds tomorrow then.'

After she'd gone, Gormley shook his head.

Jo laughed out loud. 'Oh what a tangled web,' she said.

The letters were similarly marked, all of them stamped HER MAJESTY'S PRISON. There were scores of them, but, as far as Daniels could tell, very few had actually been opened. She noticed that they had not all come from one institution and concluded that Forster must have been shipped around the country, from one prison to another, with alarming regularity during the course of his life sentence.

No surprise there, then.

She sat down on the bed to read the letters, all written in pencil on lined A4 paper. The handwriting was childish and tiny, as if a spider had walked across the pages. In letters written shortly after his imprisonment, Forster vehemently denied any wrongdoing and begged his parents to believe him, saying he'd been 'fitted up' by police. In each one he was adamant he wanted to go home. In letters written later, Daniels found that the tone had completely changed. He'd become highly agitated, slagging off his parents for rejecting him out of hand. It was clear that he hated his mother with a passion. These were the ramblings of an unhealthy mind, pages and pages of disturbed, incoherent thoughts. All of the letters were unsigned, concluding with the words: *The End*.

Back at the safe house, Gormley took his tea and sat down at the computer with Jo looking over his shoulder. He put on his specs, typed in the file name Carmichael had left stuck to the computer monitor, and set the folder to view as a slide show.

The first photographs that came up on screen were no surprise. They were images of Daniels and Jo kissing on her doorstep, matching the hard copies Forster had hidden on his balcony. It was hard to tell who was the most embarrassed but, as the slide show continued, discomfort was replaced by horror as the location then changed.

They watched in silence as the images faded and then dissolved. There were scores of photographs, all with Daniels as their subject: with Jo, with Gormley, with Bright, in different locations – including one where she was standing alone outside St Camillus' church – and, finally, either entering or leaving the family home of David and Elsie Short.

The realization hit Gormley like a sledgehammer.

'Christ! It's not *you* he's been watching, it's Kate!'

*

Daniels jerked forward as the gun nudged the small of her back. Her whole body tensed. Forster was standing right behind her, large as life, close enough to kill her with his bare hands. He spoke just four words:

'Took you long enough.'

She froze.

His words echoed in her head, confusing her, projecting her back to Jo's bedside: *Took you long enough.* Jo had used those exact words following her accident. Only this time, Daniels' reaction was very different. This time she could not afford to get emotional, not if she was going to make it out of there alive. Forster's sinister laughter brought her crashing back to reality.

'Wanna know why they're still alive?' he whispered.

Goose pimples covered Daniels' skin. She could feel his breath on her neck, even after he'd stopped speaking. She wanted to turn around, wanted to see the whites of his eyes.

Or did she?

Was blissful ignorance not a better option?

Better not to know what was coming.

Why didn't he shoot her now?

Get it over with.

Daniels swallowed hard and remained silent.

'Because I fucking chose it that way, that's why!' Forster stroked her cheek. 'Bet they were scared shitless that I'd knock on their door. You're the only one who seems to understand me, Katie.'

Daniels' radio was lying on the bed in front of her. She

remained with her back to him, not daring to move a muscle, knowing she was done for if she showed an ounce of fear.

Hearing Forster's voice again reminded her of his filthy flat, that revolting soiled armchair, the scissors he'd used for his macabre edit of *Living Faith*. She cringed as he put pressure on her shoulder, forcing her down towards the bed . . .

'Get in the car!' Gormley yelled.

Jo was hysterical, shaking so much he thought she was about to have some kind of fit. She kept repeating over and over that they were going to be too late. Forster was an animal. There was no telling what he'd do to Kate.

Gormley snapped. 'Get in the damn car!'

Daniels lunged for the radio but she was too late. Anticipating the move, Forster clubbed her with the gun, then swiped the radio across the bed, sending it crashing to the floor. Stunned from the blow to her head, she looked on helplessly as he kicked it out of reach. He grabbed her by the throat, bringing her round to face him. It was the first time she'd seen him really close up. *Or was it?* As a warm trickle of blood ran down her face a feeling of déjà vu crept over her. Something about him seemed strangely familiar. And then she realized. They had spoken in the darkness outside St Camillus church. He'd apologized for getting in her way.

He'd been watching her.

She focused on a drop of sweat snaking down his forehead. It ran along the line of his eyebrow, down over his cheek and dripped on to his coat. Her phone began to ring and she stopped struggling.

'You spoiled it for me, Katie. Why did you do that when it was all going to plan? You realize I'm going to have to punish you now?'

'I was wrong before.' Daniels glared at him. 'Your parents were right to disown you. You deserve all you get. Better still, give me the gun. I'll save us all the bother before the troops arrive.'

'Not one to squirm, are you, Katie? But don't try and kid a kidder. I heard you telling them to hang fire before your mate left – and he's not coming back.'

'I wouldn't count on it. That'll be him on the phone.'

Forster placed the tip of the gun barrel under her jaw, leaned in and licked her cheek, spreading his saliva all over her face. She wiped it off with the back of her hand and glanced along the hallway. The door was now bolted top and bottom, the chains fastened securely in their latches. A wide grin appeared on his face as desperation showed on hers.

'You know the score, don't you, Katie? There's only one way out of here . . . *for both of us.*'

Trees rushed past in the darkness as they sped towards Ponteland. Despite her seat belt, Jo had to hang on round the corners as Gormley put his foot down and got on the radio while Jo tried Daniels' mobile.

At a T-junction, Gormley turned left on to a single-track road. A short cut, he said, optimistically hoping they wouldn't meet anyone coming the other way. They hurtled through densely wooded terrain, then a couple of tricky bends. He had to use the full extent of his advanced police driving skills just to keep them on the road.

On the straight now, he glanced at Jo. 'Any luck?'

Jo shook her head. 'She's still not answering.'

Daniels had a plan: play for time, engage Forster in conversation, wait for Gormley to raise the firearms team.

'So what happens now, Jonathan?'

'My Sunday name!' Forster grinned, exposing grubby teeth, his bad breath filling the air. 'You must be *really* worried.'

'Not especially. But I hope you're not going to leave me in suspense. At least tell me how you managed to get away with it for so long.'

'Guns open doors, Katie. You should get one.'

'What? You just marched up and rang the bell?'

'Why not? Works like a charm. You should've seen poor Jenny's face when she clocked this—' Forster waved the gun in front of her eyes and took off the safety catch. 'Silly cow begged me not to shoot her. Even wanted to know why! Can you believe that?'

Crime-scene photographs of Jennifer Tait leapt into Daniels' head: a bloody scene, the woman's dead eyes, her arm extended towards the door to her kitchen, a card stuffed in her mouth. She felt physically sick as Forster rubbed the warm barrel of the gun up and down her bruised cheek, stroking her neck with his free hand, which travelled south until it reached her left breast and down between her legs.

She grabbed his hand, pushing it away.

Where the hell were the firearms team?

He pursed his lips and blew her a kiss. 'Malik even pissed himself! And in front of his grandson, too. What kind of an example is that, I ask you? Some people!' He laughed crazily, his eyes flashing. 'It felt good, teaching the boy to point and shoot. Think I'd like kids one day. Make a good role model, me.'

'You evil shit!'

'Now, now, Katie. Don't get arsy with me. Your lot had ample opportunity to stop me before I got to him. There was a security operation going on in Birmingham when I got off the train: anti-terrorist squad, the whole nine yards. It was cool. I slipped in and out without being seen. Lucky, or what? Shame they were all looking the other way.'

'You've been riding your luck for a very long time, Jonathan. One of these days, maybe even today, it'll come to an abrupt end.'

'You sound like *her* . . .' Forster glanced at his mother's photograph. 'She always said I got away with murder. And I have, quite literally. She used to complain when the courts kept letting me off.'

'They did, too, didn't they?'

'Several times.' He was gloating now, enjoying himself at her expense. 'Reckon they must've felt sorry for me.'

'It's them I feel sorry for.' Daniels meant it. 'Don't know how they sleep nights.'

Forster glanced at his weapon. The anticipation of what was going on inside his head sent Daniels' heart racing. Her hands were damp with sweat, her eyes firmly focused on his. She watched him carefully, trying to detect how far she could push him. But he looked totally in control, not a hint of anxiety in his voice, no obvious signs of distress on his face. It was unnerving, to say the least. She had to force the words out of her mouth . . .

'You're screwed, Jonathan. Do you want to spend the rest of your life—'

Forster traced her lips with his gun to silence her.

It had the desired effect.

'Oh, I've made mistakes, Katie. I admit it. Getting caught the first time was stupid. But I'm smarter these days. And now it's your turn.'

Daniels was overcome with conflicting emotions: fear for her own mortality, but also a sense of mourning for all the victims that had gone before. Any trace of sympathy she might have felt for Forster had quickly turned to rage. She willed him to stop talking, but he carried on regardless, his ramblings getting more and more egocentric. Then, suddenly, he swiped his hand out, sending his parents' photographs flying.

'Why do you hate them so much?' Daniels chanced her arm. 'I met them. They're good people, even if they *did* make mistakes.'

'You have no idea! Not the slightest idea what they're capable of!'

'You can't stand rejection, can you, Jonathan? That's your problem.'

'Yours, too, from where I'm standing.'

'You like being centre of attention, don't you?'

'Maybe . . .' He grinned. 'And when I'm finished with you, *everybody* will know my name, including her!'

'She certainly will.' Daniels locked eyes with him. 'You'll get your fifteen minutes of fame, followed by the rest of your life inside.'

'No, Katie. That's not how the story ends.'

*

'Gormley to Foxtrot. You got an eyeball on the target yet?'

'Foxtrot to Gormley. Negative. I say again, negative.'

'Fuck's sake!' Gormley was yelling now and losing concentration.

Jo's hands flew to her face. 'Watch out!'

Underestimating a sharp right-hand bend, Gormley had floored the accelerator. He now had to brake sharply, sending the Toyota into a skid. He righted the car, apologized to Jo and pushed a button on his radio:

'Gormley to Foxtrot. Is Daniels alone in the house, or not?'

'Foxtrot to Gormley. Negative, Hank. I'm sorry, but we have a situation developing here.'

'If you don't mind me asking, where did you get the guns?'

'Being banged up has its uses, Katie. I still have contacts.'

'I bet you do.'

'Nice try. I've covered my tracks well, though: a drowning, a suicide . . .' He grinned. 'Shame they couldn't stick around.'

Daniels fought to stay calm. If she ever got out of there alive, the clear-up rate at MIT looked set to improve. She wondered just how many murder victims Forster was responsible for.

Was she going to be his last?

She watched nervously as he fondled the gun before pointing it straight at her.

He pulled the trigger.

CLICK.

Her whole body juddered, her knees nearly buckling beneath her as she realized the chamber had been empty. But already he'd reloaded.

Now she knew she was in trouble . . .

*

'Foxtrot to Gormley. Unable to get a shot off at the moment.'

'Copy that, Foxtrot.' Gormley glanced at Jo in the passenger seat. She looked like a tormented soul, pained by unimaginable thoughts. He put his foot down and got back on the radio. 'What action are you taking, Foxtrot?'

'Maintaining close observational cordon. As soon as a shot is on, we shoot to kill.'

'God!' Jo began to hyperventilate.

Gormley let go of the wheel, grabbed hold of her hand and told her to take deep breaths. 'These guys are highly trained. They won't take any chances, Jo. I promise you.'

'And if they don't have a clear view?'

'They wait . . .'

'For how long?'

'Until they have no choice but to storm the place.'

Forster was enjoying the memory of his killing spree. In fact, the more he spoke about it, the more animated he became. That suited Daniels, who was trying to tease as much information out of him as she could.

So long as he was marching, he wasn't fighting.

'Did you find Dorothy Smith?'

'Oh, I found her all right – with a little help from my friends. Some idiot left a rucksack unattended, a full set of waterproofs inside. Great camouflage, Katie. Even better protection from her blood . . . And there was a lot of it, before you ask.'

Daniels tried to block him out by thinking of the last time

she and Jo had visited the Lakes. They'd been happy then, staying in a small hotel just two miles from the last sighting of Dorothy Smith.

'I take it she's dead?' Cumbria Constabulary still hadn't found her.

'As a dodo . . .'

'At least tell me where you dumped her body . . .'

His eyes had grown cold – filled with pure hatred – and his speech suddenly became rushed, manic even. 'Be patient, boy! Say "excuse me, please" when I'm speaking! Don't you dare interrupt!'

He'd flipped.

As Forster continued to relive snippets of his childhood, Daniels' concern for her safety grew. Realizing it was just a matter of time before he lost it completely, she knew better than to aggravate him any further.

His rant continued, a litany of names that meant nothing to her until she realized that his twenty-year fixation with *Living Faith* had resulted in such familiarity with his targets he'd begun referring to them by diminutives, names that any normal person would use as a term of affection.

'They always made me wait!' He spat the words through clenched teeth.

'They?'

'The God squad! Who do you think?'

'The ones featured in the—'

'Them! *Her!* That magazine was the last thing she ever gave me . . . the fucking last thing! Fucking cow! Well, I didn't want to disappoint her, now, did I? So I did what she wanted. I learned it by heart, each and every word, every face, every name, is carved in here—' He tapped the side of his head with the barrel of the gun. 'And now it's not *Living* Faith any more, is it, Katie? I'm giving it back to her, page by fucking page . . . They're all going back to Jesus!'

Daniels chanced her arm. 'If you were killing them in order, how come you went back to St Camillus?'

'I knew *you'd* be there, stupid!' He chuckled, reacting as if he'd just remembered something. 'Why were you staring at the tree? Were you thinking about Number Two?'

'Number Two?' Daniels said.

'The fucking priest. C'mon Katie, get with the programme!'

Gormley's clever observation that he was killing his victims in order jumped into Daniels' aching head. Number One must be Susan Thompson, the woman who had died of natural causes before Forster got to her. Some might say a blessing.

'Oh, I get it. Not the priest – the girl!' Forster laughed in her face. 'The one I took just for fun!'

He was talking about Sarah Short.

Forster put his head on one side. 'You sensed I was there, I know you did.'

He needed a hit now, Daniels could feel it. His eyes were all over her.

'I started without you that night, Detective. Shot my load looking straight at you.'

Was the shift from Katie to Detective significant? Daniels was sure it was. Forster was winding up for his swansong, was probably at his most dangerous . . .

As the firearms officer crept nearer to the house he could see Daniels through the window. Forster was partially hidden by the bedroom door, though his gun was clearly visible. The officer spoke calmly and softly into his radio:

'Two-eight-six to Foxtrot. Target is armed. No clear shot.'

'Two-eight-six. *You* have the eyeball. All other units maintain radio silence.'

'Tell me about Frances Cook.'

'Not very subtle, Detective. What's up? You look hot.'

'Indulge me.'

Forster grinned. 'Frankie wasn't like *you*. She was really scared. I met her once or twice when I was a kid. She didn't remember me at first, needed a little nudge from yours truly. Well, she won't forget again, will she?'

'She was a friend of your mother's, wasn't she?'

Forster didn't bite. 'When she finally realized who I was, she just stared at me, wondering how long she had left – just like you are now.'

Daniels held her nerve but knew she was running out of time. Jo had told her that he needed to dominate his victims. If he needed her terror to feed his sickness, what would the likely outcome be if she failed to comply? This was hardly a time to test a theory but she had to do something to put him off guard. Slowly, she undid the buttons on her coat. Whatever he'd expected, she was sure he hadn't expected that. His face flushed in anger as she forced a perfect smile, pulled the scarf from round her neck and teased it over her body.

It was a risky strategy, but it appeared to be working.

The hand holding the gun began to shake.

Daniels moistened her lips and inched back on the bed. He

climbed on too, never taking his eyes off her, his smile fading as she began to take control.

The Toyota screeched to a halt outside the bungalow. Gormley and Jo jumped out, just as a blue statuette crashed through the window, alerting the firearms team.

Inside the house, Forster was stunned. He didn't seem to know what was happening. He lunged forward, smashing into Daniels.

'Fucking whore!' he yelled.

They fell back on the floor in the space between the two beds. Daniels heard the 'GO, GO, GO!' command and the sound of running feet.

Outside, all hell broke loose as the firearms team rushed forward and a gunshot pierced the night air. As six officers in body armour crashed through the windows and doors, automatic weapons poised to shoot, Gormley and Jo looked on helplessly. Then they heard a shout that put the fear of God into them:

'Shots fired! Officer down!'

'Shots fired. Officer down!'

Daniels heard it too, followed by a deafening silence. And now she found herself surrounded by a thick blanket of fog. No, not fog. Lakeland mist. Definitely mist. It hung – as if suspended in mid-air – obliterating the upper slopes. The image of Jo was as clear as if she was standing right beside her. They were heading back to their hotel after a day's hiking. Jo's face was tanned and happy, her hair blowing in the warm breeze.

Daniels must've blacked out, because now it was dark

and the warm breeze had turned into a bitter chill. Jo was still there, but Gormley was with her. They were holding her hands and an ambulance was standing by.

'You're going to be OK.' Gormley's voice sounded shaky. 'It's just a graze.'

It didn't feel like just a graze. The pain in Daniels' shoulder was excruciating. She couldn't make sense of what had happened. She was sure she'd heard a gunshot before the firearms team arrived, followed by another a split second after the first armed officer entered the room. Now blue flashes lit up the night sky and someone she didn't recognize was loading her on to a stretcher, his voice calm and reassuring.

She looked up at Gormley as Jo let go of her hand. 'Forster?' she asked.

Hank slowly moved his fingers across his neck. 'You said you'd make him pay, and now you have. You kept your promise to the victims, Kate. All of them, including young Sarah. You've done her proud.'

Daniels felt herself welling up and bit down hard on her bottom lip. Gormley came to her rescue, made a bad joke and attempted a smile, unaware that a pulsating vein on the side of his forehead was giving him away. He stood back as paramedics lifted the stretcher into the ambulance and then climbed in after her, holding his hand out for Jo to do the same.

'You scared the hell out of me,' she said, almost breaking down.

Daniels managed a smile. 'I'm fine.'

Gormley cleared his throat. 'As in Fucked up, Insecure—'

'As in *fine*, Hank,' Daniels said. 'For Christ's sake, stop fretting or I really *will* start believing you're my dad.'

'What does it feel like to go from hero to zero?' he said.

'What d'you mean?' Jo asked.

'Well . . .' Gormley gestured to a second stretcher heading their way, this one carrying a body bag. 'He's the victim now. Not that we give a shit, eh? It wouldn't surprise me if Professional Standards haven't already launched an investigation.'

Daniels smiled at them both.

'That's what I love about this job,' she said.

100

Kate Daniels made a full recovery. She left the Royal Victoria Infirmary that same night, having discharged herself – against her doctor's advice. Her injury was not life threatening. She was bruised and sore, but still alive. That didn't mean she wasn't hurting like hell for the relatives of Father Simon, Sarah Short, Alan Stephens, Jennifer Tait, Jamil Malik, Dorothy Smith and Frances Cook – victims she would never forget.

There had been times in the past few months when Daniels almost lost the will to live, but her encounter with Forster had concentrated her mind. And now? Now she was able to see that life, no matter how difficult, was so much better than the alternative. Her friend and colleague, Jo Soulsby, arrived in the nick of time, just as she was leaving the hospital. They stayed close in the coming few days, recapturing the wonderful connection they had once enjoyed. For the time being, at least, it remained the camaraderie of fellow professionals. Whether it would ever be anything more was debatable.

But, where there was life, there was always a modicum of hope.

James Stephens had been able to clear up the uncertainty over a torn-up photograph found in his mother's bin. Had he known that it had formed part of the 'evidence' against her, he'd have come forward sooner. As a gesture of goodwill, Monica Stephens had pledged money from her late husband's estate to both of his sons. James intended to use his to finance a gap year before completing his education at Sheffield University. Thomas had yet to decide.

Four weeks later, Daniels returned to work to great applause from the murder squad. Detective Superintendent Phillip Bright had accepted a commendation from the Chief Constable for his team's sterling work in apprehending a serial offender who had blighted the lives of so many. ACC Martin was not available for comment. He had resigned his post with immediate effect, following sensational allegations over his personal life which very nearly eclipsed press coverage of a murder investigation involving several forces, the biggest manhunt Northumbria force had ever known. Insiders suspected that the resulting media frenzy into his best-kept secret was being fuelled either by his estranged wife, Muriel, or by someone within his own force.

Jonathan Forster looked set to join the ranks of Britain's most notorious killers, although he wasn't alive to enjoy it. Following a post-mortem examination, his body was released for burial and taken to the West Road Crematorium where a short ceremony took place. There were no mourners present.

Within a month or so of Forster's demise, Detective Sergeant Hank Gormley would apply for an order for the destruction of an item used in connection with a series of crimes; namely a computer containing sensitive information on several victims – not to mention photographic evidence proving that the late Jonathan Forster had been stalking a senior member of Northumbria Police. Inexplicably, no mobile phone or camera belonging to the said offender was ever recovered, despite extensive searches of his flat and the adjoining property. Gormley had this to say: 'It's just one of life's little mysteries. We may never know what happened to them.'

ACKNOWLEDGEMENTS

This book has been a long time coming. Any mistakes are entirely my own. I would like to acknowledge everyone who has helped make it happen.

Specifically, I owe thanks to my wonderful publishing director, Wayne Brookes, and the team at Pan Macmillan. Also, to the entire staff of Blake Friedmann, Literary, TV & Film Agency. Special thanks go to my agent, Oli Munson, who was the first to take an interest. He *got it* from day one and has worked tirelessly on my behalf since the day we met. And to my copy-editor, Anne O'Brien, for working so hard on my behalf and doing such a brilliant job on the manuscript.

For helping to promote my work and setting me on the road to publication, I'd also like to mention here Claire Malcolm and Olivia Chapman at regional writing agency New Writing North.

To my sons, Paul and Chris, also Kate and Caroline, four of the coolest kids I know: we got there in the end! To other friends and family I may have ignored during the latter stages of writing this novel, I make no apology.

But most of all to my partner, Mo, for sticking with me on this journey; for her insights, love, patience and help; for believing at times when I did not – I couldn't have done it without you.